About the author

James Warden was a teacher for forty years and retired in 2006. He now enjoys his retirement as much as he enjoyed his time in the education service and is catching up on those things which he left undone and ought to have done – in particular, his writing. He writes every morning between nine o'clock and noon, for thirty-six weeks of the year.

He is fortunate enough to be able to act in several Norwich theatres – the Maddermarket, the Sewell Barn and, with the Great Hall Players, at the Assembly House – and this experience informs his writing. His stage adaptation of Laurie Lee's *As I Walked Out One Midsummer Morning* was performed at the Sewell Barn Theatre in November 2009. His original play, *Letters from a Boy in the Trenches*, which was based on the letters of a WW1 soldier, was performed in Marchington, Staffordshire in 2015.

James is married – for the second time – and lives in Norfolk. He and his wife travel as much as possible. They have visited Italy (where they were married in 2002) several times, Canada, Bermuda, Egypt, India, the Czech Republic, New England, Poland, Slovenia, Antarctica, the Falkland Islands, Alaska, the Galapagos Islands, Australia and Switzerland. In 2018, they travelled across the USA on Route 66. They have also taken several holidays in various Mediterranean resorts – the basis for his first novel, *Three Women of a Certain Age*, which was published in July 2010, and *Bingham Goes to Cannes*, to be published in 2024.

During his years in education, he wrote about twenty play scripts for children. These included the one that formed the basis for his children's story, *The Great Gobbler and his Home Baking*

Factory at the North Pole, which he wrote in 1982 and published in December 2010.

He has three sons by his first marriage, and they inspired two of his novels – *The Vampire's Homecoming,* which was published in 2011, and *The One-eyed Dwarf,* published in 2012. With them and his first wife, he also travelled to the southern states of North America, France, Germany (West and East), Estonia and what was Czechoslovakia.

Other Writing by James Warden

The Bingham Detective Stories
Bingham's First Case (2018)
Bingham and the Runaway Wife (2019)
Bingham Seeks an Odd Couple (2020)
Bingham Pursues a Minister's Clerk (2021)
Bingham and the Traveller's Daughter
(To be published in 2022)
Bingham Along the Stuart Highway
(To be published in 2023)
Bingham Goes to Cannes
(To be published in 2024)
Bingham and the Lost Years
(To be published in 2025)
Bingham Crosses the Bar
(To be published in 2026)
Bingham's Dog Fight
(To be published in 2027)

The Haunting

Of

Thornham Staithe

by

James Warden

**Grosvenor House
Publishing Limited**

The right of James Warden to be identified as the author of this
work has been asserted in accordance with Section 78
of the Copyright, Designs and Patents Act 1988

The book cover is copyright to James Warden
Front cover design 'Backroad from Burghampton' painted by Jan Heath,
from an original photograph by Raggedness (Alamy Stock Collection)
Painting electronically produced by Snappy Snaps Photo and
Digital Specialist of Norwich
Back cover shows the author on his way to an Elgar concert

This book is published by
Grosvenor House Publishing Ltd
Link House
140 The Broadway, Tolworth, Surrey, KT6 7HT.
www.grosvenorhousepublishing.co.uk

This book is a work of fiction. Any resemblance to
people or events, past or present, is purely coincidental.

A CIP record for this book
is available from the British Library

ISBN 978-1-80381-045-4

To my youngest son,
Joseph,

with thanks for our conversation
regarding the Deliverance Ministry,
which gave me the idea for this novel.

Acknowledgements

I should like to thank Joseph Cant for reading the text of this novel and offering his advice. I should also like to thank him for several conversation in Alton, Staffordshire and many subsequent emails. These were the inspirations that led me to write the story.

I used many books as reference for the background material and should like to acknowledge the following:

Psychical Research by R C Johnson: English University Press 1955

Encyclopaedia of Ghosts and Spirits by John and Anne Spencer: Headline 2001

The Workhouse: Norman Longmate: Pimlico 2003

Ghost Hunters by Yvette Fielding and Ciaran O'Keeffe: Hodder and Stoughton 2006

Ghost Towns by Derek Acorah: Harper Element 2006

Workhouse: Simon Fowler: National Archive 2007

The English Ghost by Peter Ackroyd: Chatto and Windus 2010

The Church of England Report Into Spiritualism: Mercian Order of St George

In particular I should like to acknowledge:

Light and Liberty: Rediscovering the Power of Deliverance by Peter Mockford: Instant Apostle 2017

This book clarified many concepts regarding deliverance for me and I have borrowed heavily from the author's wisdom: any deviations, fictionalisations and misunderstandings are mine. I should also point out that the character of Neil Ilkestone is based upon an old priest I knew many years ago, and not upon Peter Mockford.

All biblical references and quotations are taken from the *Holy Bible* (King James Version) or from *The Book of Common Prayer*; and these I acknowledge.

I should also like to acknowledge the use of verses from the following hymns:

O Lord my God: English translation by Stuart K Hine
Make Me a Channel of Your Peace: attributed to St Francis of Assisi
Abide with Me: words by Henry Francis Lyte; music by William Henry Monk
Great is Thy Faithfulness: words by Thomas Chisholm: music by William Runyan

Several ghost stories have inspired my writing of this novel, in particular:

The Haunted Man and the Ghost's Bargain: Charles Dickens
Ancient Sorceries: Algernon Blackwood
Keeping His Promise: Algernon Blackwood
How Love Came to Professor Guildea: Robert Hichens
The Haunters and the Haunted: Edward Bulwer-Lytton
The Trial for Murder: Charles Collins and Charles Dickens
Was it a Dream?: Guy de Maupassant
Afterward: Edith Wharton

These are all short stories, like most ghost stories, and are readily available in anthologies.

Content

Book Three

Book Four

Characters

Gerald Henderson: a doctor
Maggie Henderson: his wife (deceased)
Lottie Henderson: his daughter
Charles Henderson: his son

Bradley Hall: friend to Charles

Edward Warburg: a composer
Myles Langstroth: a singer
Mirabelle Hurd: patron of the Saxstead Opera

James Ryder: a stranger to the town: a walker

Vernon Scuffil: a teacher and historian
Justine Sweet: partner to Vernon
Acer Sweet: Justine's son
Anthemis Sweet: Justine's daughter

Simon Pegg: landlord of the White Horse
Catriona Pegg: his wife
July Pegg: his daughter
Bruce Pegg: his son

Ned Douglas: landlord of The Swan

Reg Wilton: butcher
Myrtle Wilton: his wife

Barbara Wilton: his elder daughter
Lucy Wilton: his younger daughter

Richard Revell
Cynthia Revell: his mother
Amy Prentice: Richard's girlfriend
Revell: his father

Brian Gooch
Emma Gooch: Brian's grandmother

Carmen Quay: owner of Carmen's Quay Room
Belfast Billie: her friend
Norman Oldfield: headteacher at Thornham High School
Malcolm Francis: funeral director
Maisie Garland: leader of village dance troupe
Edith Garland: her mother and WI member
Janet Davis: owner of Meadow Farm Rescue Centre
PC Sharpe: son of former village policeman, also a police officer

Sam Witham: an orphan and loner
Ambrose Broome: grandfather of Sam Witham
Marjory Broome: grandmother of Sam Witham

Frederick Mackenzie: Anglican vicar
Jacqueline Mackenzie: his wife
Neil Ilkestone: Diocesan Deliverance Minister
Gordon Urquhart: Bishop of Norbridge
Elaine Urquhart: his wife
Father Crouch: Roman Catholic priest

Miss Amelia Pritchard: elderly villager
Mildred Ackroyd: also, elderly and her friend
Jack Dorling: a printer
Juniper Wells: his daughter

Saul Tacksman: a medium
Veronica Clud: his assistant
Esme Owen: a ghost hunter
Clifford Raine: Esme's partner

Book One

Chapter 1

Sick Visit

Gerald Henderson, one of the doctors who worked from the Thorn Valley Medical Centre, was the first to come across what was to become known as 'The Haunting of Thornham Staithe'.

He had visited an elderly patient, always addressed by her title, Miss Pritchard, the Christian name being omitted as a sign of respect by all who had dealings with her, although no one knew quite why this was so.

She lived with her friend and companion, Mildred Ackroyd, and it was she who had phoned Dr Henderson when Miss Pritchard had "one of her turns". Gerald knew she would have many more on her way out of this life but each one was special and each one was singularly frightening. Perhaps the thought that this might be one's last breath always is just that – unique and terrifying.

Gerald had spent time listening, medicating and making his patient comfortable before setting off home, where his son and daughter would be waiting with a meal his daughter, Lottie, would have prepared on her return from school. He drove along Bridge Street from the staithe, admiring as he always did the row of old terraced cottages on either side. They may have had problems with the damp that rose through their walls from the river on one side and the marsh on the other but they were attractive to the passer-by. Gerald lived out of the village and could easily have bypassed it, but never did; and so, he came to the village green on his left and The Swan on his right before driving by the lychgate of Holy Trinity church, where he had been baptised and married.

It was a wet September evening; the nights had been pulling in for nearly three months and through a dreary August. Dusk was upon the village; natural light was non-existent and the streetlamps cast a yellow glow across the road. A light rain was falling.

It was as he passed the lychgate that the two young women stepped out in front of his car. He had no time to stop, he told himself afterwards – no time, even had he only pulled out from being parked. As it was, he hit them both at no more than twenty miles an hour. One of them was thrown to the verge and the other seemed to disappear under the wheels of his car. Gerald swerved to the right, yanking his car into the centre of the road, and braked. He breathed deeply and then, his professional instincts taking over, he opened the car door and stepped into the road, wondering what he could do to help the injured.

The young woman who had vanished beneath the wheels of his car was stretched out on the ground no more than a metre or so from where he had stopped. It was only later he remembered how she was dressed: at that moment, he was concerned with the blood on her one leg and the angle at which it was twisted; he registered the thought that the leg might well be broken. He leaned over her to ascertain that she was breathing, and her eyes opened.

"Lie still," he said, "I'll call an ambulance. Your leg may be broken. We don't want to risk moving it."

He turned away and clicked open the hatch of his Volvo, pulled out one of the rugs he always carried, covered her and turned his attention to the other young woman. She had gone; it did not seem possible but she had clearly lifted herself up and walked away. Why? Had she gone back into the churchyard?

Gerald opened his nearside door, reached across to the passenger seat and felt for his phone. An ambulance! He must first call an ambulance: a stretcher would be needed: the injured woman must be lifted carefully and by two experienced people.

While he waited, he would look in the churchyard for the other young woman. She could not have gone far. He activated his hazard lights, glanced over to the Thornham Community Stores – now

4

an antique-cum-bric-a-brac shop – and saw an elderly lady watching him from the pavement.

"Keep your eyes open for an ambulance," he called out. "It'll be here in no time. I won't be long."

He collected his torch from the back of the car and entered the churchyard, which was unusually dismal in the rain and the dark. A gravelled path led down to the church. Gerald shot his beam along but saw nothing: if the young woman had stumbled through the lychgate, she must be wandering among the gravestones. The floodlit tower illuminated part of the churchyard but everywhere else was enclosed by darkness, a darkness intensified by the lights from the village. He made his way carefully, aware he was treading on the dead and embarrassed by the fact, but he had to search. The beam of his torch found nothing but gravestones including, at the far end where the fresher graves were situated, the headstone of his own wife. 'Margaret Henderson Loving Wife and Mother 1978-2016'. He would sometimes come here at night, alone, stand by his wife's grave and wonder. 'Thirty-eight years old when she died. So young. A woman in her prime.' He was doing just that – looking at her memorial and thinking about Maggie – when he heard and saw the ambulance, heard the siren-bell and saw the flashing blue lights.

His feet uncomfortable with the rain his shoes had gathered from the grass between the gravestones, feeling the tiredness of his day and the weight of what he had done upon him, Gerald made his way back to the road.

"Dr Henderson?"

"Yes."

"You rang for an ambulance, sir?"

"Yes, I'm afraid there's been an accident."

How was he going to explain what happened?

"I … there were two, young women. As you can see, I covered the one quickly with a rug and went to find the other. I thought she might be injured … I don't know why she ran off …"

"Where is the young woman you covered with the rug, sir?"

"There, behind my car. I …"

"There's no one there, sir. Just the rug."

"But ..."

Gerald looked down. It was true. His rug lay on the roadside but the young woman had disappeared. And yet the shape of her body was still apparent in the folds of the rug. It was almost as if she were still there, at least in form. He looked across at the paramedic who was on the phone.

"The police, sir. We'd better give them a call."

"Yes, of course."

Gerald was not sure why he had agreed so readily. Why did they need the police? He stooped to retrieve his rug.

"I should leave that just as it is, Dr Henderson. This is odd."

How long he stood with the paramedics in silence, Gerald was unsure. It couldn't have been more than ten minutes but seemed long into the evening. Noting the dumbfounded expression on the doctor's face, the paramedic explained briefly to the police officer what had occurred. When he had finished listening, the officer skirted round the front of Gerald's car and approached him.

"You're sure of this, sir?"

"Yes."

"You're sure you hit two young women?"

"Yes."

"There are no marks on the front of your car, Dr Henderson – no dents, not even a scratch. We'll take a closer look in daylight, but your car shows no signs of having been involved in an accident."

Gerald was silent.

"You've not been drinking, sir?"

"I'm teetotal. I've not touched a drop for two years."

"Do you object to taking a breathalyser test, sir."

"No, of course not."

He turned suddenly to the paramedics.

"I'm sorry to have brought you out on a wild goose chase. I feel bad about it. I've wasted your time and I know you're busy. I'd just like you to believe that I did hit those two young women. I can't explain what has happened but ..."

He lifted is arms in a gesture of resignation.

"We'll get back to the hospital, sir. My companion has been taking a look in the churchyard and found nothing. We'll get back."

As the ambulance pulled away, the police officer administered the breathalyser and frowned.

"It's clear, sir. Where had you come from tonight?"

Gerald told him.

"Do you feel safe to drive, sir?"

"Yes, I think so."

"You get home now, sir. We'll take one more look and be off. Someone will be round in the morning – just to check your car. You'll leave it in your driveway tonight, won't you, sir?"

He picked up the rug, which he folded and placed in the rear of Gerald's car before closing the hatch.

"You drive carefully, now, sir. You've had a shock."

He opened the car door and watched while Gerald fastened his seatbelt and fumbled in his coat pocket for the keys. He watched as the doctor drove off through the village, making for the main road and his house, which the officer had already checked was not far: a short distance out of the village, just off the road, a quiet road at this time of the evening.

*

Mildred Ackroyd looked the police officer up and down before answering, as though ascertaining for herself that he had his uniform on straight.

"Of course," she replied, eventually, as though his question as to who she was must be evident to anyone but a complete numbskull.

"We understand, ma'am, that Dr Henderson paid a visit here this evening."

"That is correct."

"Mildred, who is it?"

The voice came from somewhere in the house. Glancing over Mildred Ackroyd's shoulder, the police officer saw a figure halfway down a flight of stairs that led off the hall. He supposed this to be Miss Pritchard, who the doctor had visited.

"It's nothing, Amelia, nothing to worry about. Just a policeman."

It was reassuring to the officer that he was 'nothing to worry about' – perhaps, nothing at all as far as the woman in the doorway was concerned.

"Are you able to confirm the time Dr Henderson left, ma'am?"

Mildred Ackroyd looked him up and down again as though to assure herself that he was fit to receive such information.

"Why are you asking?"

"Routine, ma'am – just a need to confirm timings."

"Is something wrong, Mildred?"

The voice was closer now but still on the stairs.

"Not at all, Amelia. You should be resting," replied Mildred, and then turning to the police officer said, "Is there a need to be disturbing us at this time of night?"

In fact, there was not, and the police officer knew that to be the case. On their short drive out to Cookley, a scattering of houses on the backroad that led eventually to Norbridge, his fellow officer, a young woman cautious for promotion, had pointed out that they were exceeding what was required of them, since they had no reason to doubt the doctor's word and, besides, this could be confirmed by a quick telephone call to the surgery the following morning. The young man, however, feeling the need to "test the ground", had ignored her. His father had once been a village policeman and – while they were now confined to driving around in cars, watching computer screens and making telephone calls – he, personally, felt the need to "get to know the people involved". PC Sharpe was a chip off the old block.

"Sorry to be an inconvenience, ma'am," he said, "There's just a need to confirm some timings and I thought it would save a telephone call tomorrow. It's always nice to meet the people you may be speaking to."

Mildred Ackroyd caught the tone and decided it might or might not have contained an element of impertinence, but she agreed with the sentiment, having never understood why the authorities needed to remove the village police station in the first place, and her own tone mellowed.

"Dr Henderson left at about 5.30, give or take five or ten minutes either way," she answered, "Has the doctor been involved in an accident? I can assure you that he's a perfectly safe driver."

"No, ma'am – the doctor is fine. There was a small incident in the village tonight, which the doctor witnessed, and we merely needed to confirm times."

"Is the doctor all right, Mildred?"

"Yes, Amelia."

"We might telephone to be sure he has arrived home safely. It was very good of him to call."

"There'll be no need to trouble the doctor, Amelia. The young police officer assures me that he has come to no harm."

"Thank you, ma'am. Sorry to have troubled you. May we wish you good night."

*

Gerald Henderson was eating slowly through the meal his daughter had prepared and which had gone cold, much to his regret. He appreciated what Lottie did to keep the house running since the death of his wife; and appreciation was not best shown by arriving late for a meal she had taken the trouble to cook. It was a paella valenciana – a dish intended to be eaten straight from the pan otherwise the mussels went rubbery, the chicken and chorizo lost their succulence and the rice clogged.

"I'm enjoying my meal, nevertheless, Lottie," said Gerald, when his daughter pointed this out to him, "and I am very grateful."

"And very quiet, Daddy. What's wrong?"

"A long day, darling. I couldn't refuse Miss Pritchard. She's not in the best of health."

"Is it only that, Daddy?"

He was not about to lie to his daughter. They had become very close since the death of his wife and the need for each of the other was palpable. Whereas his son, Charles, had withdrawn into himself and stayed there, Lottie had opened her heart. Like her father, she had become determined to keep the home as it had always been: comfortable, tidy, welcoming – a place where they wanted to be together as a family, although as she had once said in a moment of unutterable sadness "We'll never quite be a family again, will we, Daddy, like we once were?"

She was a strange girl, quiet but determined and with her mother's beauty. Lottie was thirteen when her mother died two years before. It had been the time when her periods were starting and she managed the whole business without reference to her father. She was several months into these when the vicar's wife, Jacqueline Mackenzie, who had always been friendly with the girl, mentioned the fact to Henderson, asking whether Lottie needed any "advice". Gerald had been grateful and ashamed, and when he spoke to Lottie his acknowledgment that she was growing into womanhood brought them silently together.

Lottie was now into her GCSE year and expected to do well; everyone expected her to do well, and she did not resent the praise. Popular at school with both boys and girls, she had turned down the offer of becoming head girl much to everyone's surprise. She told her father that she did not want to be "edged into a false position", and he – a modest man himself – understood, if no one else did. He alone knew her decision had nothing to do with reticence – quite the reverse: it was driven by a desire to remain communicative with those schoolfriends she loved and appreciated.

There was no vanity in Lottie, no desire to be top cat, no wish to outshine others, although her father knew that she would. She worked hard and she was focussed; in her room at night, while she studied, her mobile phone was switched off – not for her the endless interruptions of friends calling about nothing in particular. When she needed to be alone, she was with her thoughts unfettered.

When he finished the paella, Gerald took her hands in his across the table and told her about the two young women he had run down, and Lottie listened without disturbing his account.

"You mean they were ghosts, Daddy?"

He had never grown used to her calling him 'Daddy' and now she was so grown up it seemed even more inappropriate than when she had been a child. Gerald made a mental note that they would need to talk about this at a later date.

"They were not in the least faint or ghostly figures, Lottie. I couldn't see through them as you imagine you would see through a ghost. They were as solid as you and I, and when I hit the one who was thrown into the verge I heard the impact and I saw the blood on the other's leg."

"We talk about ghosts at school sometimes."

"I'm sure you do."

"One of the girls, Barbara Wilton – she's in my year – told a story about three young women who were hitch-hiking along the Norbridge Road. One of them was to be married the following day. They were just this side of Thornton when a car came round that blind bend and ran straight into her. This was twenty years ago but, Barbara said, every now and then a motorist late at night will see a young woman run out in front of his car. She stops and looks straight into the driver's eyes, as though accusing him of killing her just before her wedding day. When he hits her, the ground seems to open and she goes under the car and he hears the thud – just like your young woman. And just like your young woman, she isn't there when he stops to look."

Listening to his daughter, Gerald was grateful that however mature she might seem, Lottie was still a child. It was a fanciful ghost story overwhelmed by its details, which were, no doubt, built upon with each telling. He smiled when she had finished her tale, a smile returned as though they both discovered something new about each other.

"Chad went to his room," she said, suddenly realising her brother had not been with them at the table listening to her father's story, "I told him to have his paella while it was still fresh."

"Quite right," replied Gerald, "I'll go and have a chat with him … It's Friday today, isn't it? I'll cook tomorrow. Something less exotic than your paella, Lottie … and we must do something together … the three of us. You're good at finding something to do. Have a scout around online."

Gerald Henderson made his way upstairs, aware that his son might be upset at having missed his ghost story. It had not been easy since Maggie died, and Charles had taken her death badly. All three of them had taken her death badly but for his son it had been a body blow akin to death.

*

Emma Gooch sat at her kitchen table, wondering what to do and who she should tell. Her hearing wasn't good and she hadn't heard what the doctor called out, but she had seen him knock down the two young women and she had seen one of them run away and she had seen the doctor open his boot and take out the tartan rug.

She hadn't wanted to hang about: it was bingo night at the Jub Club and she didn't want to miss her weekly bingo. Besides, she didn't want to get involved, not with the police, and there would be the police: the doctor had knocked two young women over and he looked as if he was going to put one of them in his boot.

Chapter 2

Music Lesson

Lottie Henderson always insisted upon cycling to her music lesson on a Saturday morning, despite her father's protests that the main Norbridge to Lowestoft road was too dangerous, but this morning, it was just as well she was emphatic: the police officers came to take a look at his car. Gerald was standing in the driveway, waving goodbye to his daughter, when the officers arrived. A glance at the bonnet and wings of the car was enough to confirm PC Sharpe's comments of the previous evening, and then one of the officers clicked open the hatch.

"Is this the rug you used to cover the young woman, Dr Henderson?" she asked.

"Yes."

"If the young woman's leg was bleeding and you covered her with this rug, there would be stains on it, wouldn't there?" she said, after examining the rug carefully.

"I imagine so."

"You see, we took a good look at the grass verge on the edge of the green this morning. There were no bloodstains and no signs that anyone had fallen there. The grass would have been crushed, wouldn't it, given the rain we've had over the last few days?"

"Yes, of course."

The young police officer folded the rug carefully and replaced it in the car.

"We also took a careful look around the churchyard where you thought the other young woman may have run. There were no signs of footmarks other than your own."

"You're suggesting I imagined running down those two young women?"

"We've received no missing person reports and there's no evidence that anyone was run down or that anyone ran from the scene of the accident you described, doctor. We could pursue this matter, but our inclination is to let it drop ... Are you on call this weekend, doctor?"

"No," replied Henderson, aware of what was in the officer's mind.

"May I suggest you take the opportunity to have a rest – take it easy?"

There was no suggestion of sarcasm in the young police officer's voice – no indication that she was patronizing him, and the doctor smiled.

"Thank you," he said, "I'll do my best."

"I'm serious, doctor. We're all very aware of how hard you and your colleagues work at the medical centre. You were driving home in the dark at the end of a busy day – a day you stretched even further by making a private visit to an elderly patient. It was raining. You were tired. Your mind was on the patients you'd seen that day and the diagnoses you still had to follow up. A tired mind is an over-wrought mind. An over-wrought mind needs to rest ..."

Gerald Henderson cut himself off from the officer's voice, amazed and realising he would never have had the nerve to say what she was saying when he'd been her age; he placed her at no more than twenty years. It wasn't just that he would not have had the temerity to speak to an older person in that manner: it was more that he would not have had the confidence to believe he had such a complete grasp of the situation.

"... If you want to speak with us again, this number will find me, or one of us, whenever the need arises," she continued, handing him a card embellished with the badge of the Norfolk Constabulary and containing several telephone numbers. He noted the name PC Sally Frost.

"I'm very much obliged, PC Frost," he replied, aware suddenly of being very old despite his age, a mere forty.

He watched the squad car drive off and treasured the smile as she waved to him from the passenger seat. A nice young woman and one who had the makings of a first-class police officer.

Gerald went back into the house, occupied with his own thoughts, wanting to join his son, Charles, for a late breakfast.

"Are you all right, Dad?"

"Yes, Charles, thanks, quite all right. What was it we were planning to do today?"

"Minsmere. You said you'd take me down to Minsmere."

"Ah yes."

"You'd forgotten, hadn't you?"

"No – not quite, and now you've reminded me, I'm looking forward to a day's birdwatching."

"Lottie's not coming, is she?"

"No. She's going round a friend's house for the day. I wonder if she packed us a lunch before she went ..."

"I can do that," snapped Charles, "I can pack us a lunch."

"Yes, of course you can. Good idea. Thank you, Charles."

While his son deliberately cleared away the breakfast remains and set about packing them a lunch, Gerald walked out into their back garden. He was thinking to himself that in some respects the police officer had been right: he was over-worked and he was tired, but he wasn't overwrought. Someone who had been married to Maggie Henderson for fifteen years had learned to cope with what was meant by being overwrought; theirs, despite what their children believed, had not been a happy marriage.

Margaret Henderson had been one of those women who demanded to be the centre of attention, wherever she was and whoever they met when out together. It was, he felt a few years into their marriage, an obsession that bordered on paranoia. In conversation with anyone, she barely uttered a sentence that did not include an 'I' or a 'me'; she was both the subject and object of her life. It had been attractive at first: such people are always at the heart of any event, the life and soul of any party, but in the intimacy of their own home it had been tiring. Gerald found, eventually, that it was impossible to hold a conversation with her that did not turn on what she had felt, thought or experienced; in short, she always ended up talking about herself.

He was unable to draw her into conversations that contained ideas he wanted to explore because there was nothing she didn't see from her own point of view. And it had continued even after they had the children: Lottie in the first year of their marriage and Charles eighteen months later. She had joined a theatre group in Norbridge, where she was well-known and well-liked, being a local girl: her family had lived in Norfolk for generations. This became the focus of her existence, a focus she thrust upon her family, particularly Gerald. He would arrive home from a long day at work to either hear her talking about the play in which she was cast or about to leave for a rehearsal, expecting him to "see to the children". He had, once, in an unguarded moment, wondered why she had wanted the children if she had so little time for them, and had immediately been assailed with demands for a divorce.

Margaret held the position of Sister in the hospital where he took up his first appointment: she a nurse of four years' experience, he a young doctor. Her beauty – which was of the Spanish-type, dark-haired, full-faced and full-blooded – and her energy took his breathe away; it was love at first sight and they were married almost immediately.

No, he wasn't fragile or overwrought: he had learned to cope with extremes of tiredness, temperament and emotion, he had learned to live within his own calm and since his wife's death the house had been more peaceful, less fraught with her demands. The children, too, had become more self-possessed now they were no longer possessed by another's obsessions. In a sense (although he could hardly admit this to himself) her death had been a relief.

No, what had happened the previous evening had happened. Call the women he had run down figments of his imagination or ghosts, if that was the way people liked to think of them, but they had not been of the frail kind – dim, imperceptible figures. He had struck solid flesh and they had thudded off his car.

Another relationship springing from love at first sight was that of Edward Warburg and Myles Langstroth – Lottie's music teachers. Strictly speaking, it was Edward who was her teacher – he being the pianist – but Myles had taken an interest in her voice – he being the singer.

They first met in the piazza at Covent Garden. Edward was a student with the Royal College of Music, hoping to be a composer but realising it would be advisable for his piano technique to be at concert level, and Myles was with the National Opera Studio.

Edward was sitting at one of the tables that reached across the piazza from the Crème de la Creperie, sipping a glass or two of Italian wine and chatting with a girl from one of his classes, when Myles arrived with a group of friends who arranged themselves in the musicians' corner and began serenading the customers with a selection of songs from Puccini. Edward failed to notice him at first but the songs took off and soon the railings above, surrounding the piazza, and the square itself were thronged with onlookers. It was Puccini: the music was everything, the words did not matter.

One of the young women began with Lauretta's plea to her father, *O mio babbino caro*, which was followed by Jack Rance promising to throw away a fortune, *Minnie, dalla mia casa*, for one kiss from the bar owner – the humour of which was not lost on the two men when they became lovers; but it was another young woman's rendering of Madame Butterfly's *One Fine Day* that caught the attention of Edward's friend and then Myles stepped forward as Rodolfo and promised to warm a frozen hand, *Che gelida manina*: it was Mimi's hand but to Edward's mind it could so easily have been his own.

Their careers had their different measures of success and they were pleased to work together as accompanist and singer at concerts across Europe and in the USA.

A concert for the BBC attracted attention to Edward's skills as a composer and he was asked to provide the background music for several costume drama productions: this not only proved lucrative but introduced him to a circle of acquaintances who could, and would, help him to get his work performed and published.

Myles continued to tour with several opera companies but it was in one of Edward's operettas, an adaptation of Algernon Blackwood's *Ancient Sorceries* that he came to the attention of a wider public.

It was first performed on Radio Three but the macabre nature of the story attracted a filmmaker, Jonathan Carpenter, who brought it to the television screen of BBC2 where it attracted a wider audience than was usual with opera. Myles took the role of Dr John Silence (written especially for him by Edward), who acted as both Prologue and Narrator, holding the tale and audience together, up to and beyond the Witch's Sabbath, with his performance.

During these years they moved from place to place, wherever was convenient for their work, but what both men really wanted was somewhere they could call home; and the chance came with the death of Myles's Aunt Flora, who left him her house in Thornham Staithe and her money.

Myles was a Norfolk man through and through and to him the county held a magic of its own: he spoke of its 'flowing landscapes', its 'endless skies', the sea 'washing against its coastline', the 'hundreds of hamlets and villages scattered among its forests', the 'call of the bittern across its marshes'.

The house was a joy – large and rambling, where they could offer weekend accommodation to their London friends – and they soon made it their own. Situated off a quiet lane and surrounded by marshes it provided the isolation two homosexual men felt they needed – although this proved not to be the case because those people who mattered in the village accepted them immediately and without reservation. Aunt Flora had been a ceramic artist (her sculptures sold nationally and many adorned neighbouring villages) and she had built a large pottery off the rear of the house. This was converted at once into a music studio and eventually became the classroom for the students they attracted.

And the permanent move to Thornham Staithe was to provide more than a home: a nearby village, Saxstead, held an annual opera festival. Run from a small concert hall built within and beyond what had once been a block of stables in the grounds of the family home of Mirabelle Hurd and her ancestors, it attracted music lovers from far and wide, from within the county and the metropolis. Saxstead Opera offered a venue for their talents and the talents of their students to be nurtured and developed locally in schools and colleges.

Lottie Henderson was one of these students, and she now cycled along Reedham Causeway ready to turn off along the little lane that led to Pottery Encore, the name Edward and Myles had given to the house of the latter's aunt.

Lottie liked both men enormously and had for the seven years she'd been their student. They didn't trouble her – as many of her friends' music teachers troubled them – by working relentlessly and tiringly from grade to grade. "We're here to develop your musicality, Sweetie – not bore you to death," Edward had said when she once enquired about grades because she wanted to know how well she was doing compared with her friends. "When you arrive at grade 8, we'll let you know, and you can storm through with the highest honours. *Then* we can begin!" He always called her 'Sweetie': Lottie wasn't sure why but loved it.

She cycled past the five-bar gate that was always open and parked her bike against the studio wall. Edward was waiting for her, dressed as always in a manner that reminded her of a photograph of her grandfather's father: collar and tie with a woollen pullover that hung down over a pair of baggy trousers and an elderly tweed jacket that seemed to be too big for his frame. He gave her the usual hug and offered her the usual humbug.

Lottie never felt ill-at-ease with Edward Warburg and found she could talk to him in a way she couldn't with her father; for one thing, Edward was interested in the way she dressed and the lessons always began with him complimenting her on her clothes, and clothes were particularly important to Lottie, a trait she inherited from her mother.

So interested was he in her as a young woman, there had been times when she'd wondered about his homosexuality. It was a silly thought, she knew, but it crossed her mind nevertheless: 'why was a homosexual man interested in women?'

Lottie put her wondering down to the odd comments she'd picked up at school where, in the playground and during lunch hours, some of the boys had laughed about 'queers' and 'poofs' and there had been comments such as 'limp in the left wrist' and 'benders and stabbers'. Her father told her that these were the remarks of young men coming to terms with their own sexuality – remarks picked up from their fathers who used them in the workplace – and were best ignored, but he did explain what they meant and why they were no longer used among decent people.

Later, when she was older and she and her friends were keen to support the annual Gay Pride march in Norbridge, Lottie – having gained confidence in their company – asked whether Edward and Myles were going. They had both laughed, loudly.

"No, Sweetie," Myles had replied, having cottoned on to Edward's pet name for her, "We've been proud since the 80s and, besides, what do you think today's queers would think if we turned up dressed in our usual manner. The gay boys and girls are somewhat more colourful these days, aren't they?"

His own style of dress was more flamboyant than Edward's and Lottie thought Myles would have fitted in well with his brightly coloured trousers, scarves and hats and his tightly tailored jackets and trousers but the good manners imbued by her upbringing prevented her saying so.

"We're content to be accepted without fuss," said Edward, "Let those who wish to parade march on and good luck to them. I think Myles and I speak through our music and that's enough for us."

On that morning – the morning following her father's 'accident' – Edward was keen to continue work on a piece he wanted her to perform "somewhere, sooner or later" he had originally said in his usual vague way that hid a clear intention.

"I think one of Mr Britten's *Burns Songs* will enhance Mr Pegg's Burns Night considerably," he confided in her that morning, "Myles has been working with one of your school friends and he thinks we might bring the two of you together."

It was the first Lottie knew of his aim when he suggested she might learn the piano accompaniment, although she had attended Burns Night at the one of Thornham Staithe's public house, The White Horse (which was run by Simon Pegg and his family), the previous January.

"While I do admire the bagpipes, Sweetie, I think we might lift the occasion with your playing and your friend's singing."

Lottie was dying to know who the friend might be and knew Edward was teasing out the information. While she played, he talked. He was often the same, almost as though he was testing her concentration.

"Benjamin composed these pieces at the Queen's request, you know. They were a present to her mother on her seventy fifth birthday. They were both huge supporters of his wonderful and beloved Aldeburgh Festival. In fact, the Queen Mother was patron. It was a handwritten letter, too. The Queen Mother, as I expect you know, was brought up in Scotland and so his choice was absolutely appropriate. It was originally composed for the tenor voice and harp but on the occasion of the Queen Mother's birthday, the harp part was played on the piano by one of her ladies-in-waiting … What a strange phrase! It makes one wonder what they were in-waiting for …"

All the while Lottie played, Edward talked; when he stopped another voice took over and Lottie knew immediately that Myles Langstroth had entered the studio quietly and listened to her playing. When she reached the fifth song in the cycle, she heard him sing:

> *Flow gently, sweet Afton, among the green braes,*
> *Flow gently, I'll sing thee a song in thy praise;*
> *My Sweetie's asleep by thy murmuring stream,*
> *Flow gently, sweet Afton, disturb not her dream.*

"That's the one, Myles. Young Bradley will present a fine rendition of *Afton Water*. We must hope Mr Pegg is pleased."

Bradley! Bradley Hall – one of her brother Chad's friends. She'd no idea he took singing lessons with Myles. He'd kept that quiet. Did her brother know? Why didn't boys ever tell you anything?

When she turned to receive Edward's comments, she found the two men with their arms round each other, well-pleased with what they proposed to do.

"And with you, Sweetie. You play divinely. I could hear the ripples on the water and the whistling of the blackbirds in your playing."

Edward accompanied Lottie to the small iron gate at the far end of their garden, the one that led into the lane that took walkers to the church.

"Enjoy your sleepover with your friend," he called after her as she disappeared through the overhanging trees.

He had his reasons for coming here: a little bridge crossed a small stream that wound its way slowly to the Thorn. He was on the bridge when he first saw the apparition.

Edward usually took an early morning walk while Myles cooked their breakfast. They always ate a good breakfast; Myles considered it set them up for the day, and it was true that they often worked through until the evening, taking only a light lunch. Edward remembered the smell of smoked haddock wafting through the house as he left and knew that Myles would be preparing kedgeree.

On his return Edward had paused on the bridge to look further along the little stream where in the spring two swans always built their nest, where both men waited with the excitement of children for the cygnets to take their first swim to the Thorn.

It was when he turned to walk back through the little gate that he saw the apparition. The man was leaning against the post holding the gate open with his left hand. When Edward met his eyes, the man indicated that the composer should pass through with a slow, sweeping wave of his right. It was almost as though he was giving Edward permission to enter his own home, and the composer felt a certain resentment at the impertinence of the gesture. It was this that overcome the fear he felt and gave him the courage to walk forward. As he neared the figure it passed from his sight but Edward could not be sure whether it strolled off through the trees of the garden or simply vanished.

When he reached their kitchen, he was shaking and the colour had gone from his face. Myles's back was towards him as he bent over the stove and Edward sat quickly at the table and lowered his head.

"Looking forward to breakfast, dear? Am so excited about our rehearsal today."

They had been invited to tour Germany and Edward arranged several German folk songs as a compliment to their hosts. Together with the successful recording of other European songs, which they had collected during their travels, both men thought their concerts would hold a wide appeal.

"What's wrong, Eddie?" asked Myles as he turned with the serving dish and saw his lover's head bowed over his plate.

"Nothing, nothing, I'm fine. Just a little faint from my walk."

"No, you're not, Eddie. I know you too well. Why do you always say 'nothing' when I know there's something? It is irritating!"

Not wishing – or, indeed, feeling strong enough – to enter into a squabble after his experience with the apparition, Edward opened his heart. Myles replaced the serving dish under the warmer, came round to the other side of the table and put his arms round his friend.

"What did this ... this creature look like, Eddie?"

Edward looked up, as though suddenly startled by the question.

"You know, it hadn't occurred to me until you asked," he replied, "but he was like someone out of a Charles Dickens' story."

"Or Sweeney Todd?"

"What do you mean?" asked Edward, remembering full well it had been that very summer when Saxstead Opera had performed Stephen Sondheim's operetta and Myles had sung Sweeney.

"You must have been daydreaming as you do. I should think both of us saw enough Victorian costumes this summer to last for a very long time. Imagination, Eddie! It plays tricks, especially with creative people. We see things others do not. You haven't it in mind to adapt one of Dickens's stories, have you?"

"No, no, I don't think so. Thanks, love. I think you're right – as always," replied Edward, giving his other half a kiss.

"Then let us not allow my kedgeree to clog!"

Both men turned to their breakfasts with a will and the matter passed from their minds and might have done so completely had another incident not occurred only a few weeks later.

On this occasion, Edward was at the piano and Myles was singing Britten's *A Birthday Hansel*; it was around this time when they decided to 'enhance Mr Pegg's Burns Night' with a contribution from Lottie and Bradley. French windows gave access onto the garden from the studio and, while Edward was playing, one of the windows opened and the man stepped in. This time he raised his right arm in a gesture of supplication. Edward's hands faltered on the keys and he rose from the piano stool.

"You see, Myles? You see him?"

"Who, Eddie?"

"There by the french windows. The man I told you I saw at our gate."

"There's no one, dear – no one at all."

"But there is. You must be able to see him," cried Edward, and clutched his friend's arm.

Myles turned and looked but saw nothing; he felt only a shiver pass through him where his friend's hand lay on his arm.

"I can feel your grip, Eddie … and when you touched me, I felt you place a noose about my neck."

Edward Warburg looked from his friend to the man who raised his hand in salute and who then walked out the way he had entered.

Chapter 3

School Bus

"Why didn't you tell me Bradley went to Myles for singing lessons?"

"Why do you think?"

Lottie and Charles were waiting for the school bus, and this was the first chance she had found to take her brother to task.

Waiting for the free bus, knowing their father could well afford the cost of a pass, was an embarrassment to them, since children two stops on, whose parents were less well-heeled, must pay.

"You tell me," replied Lottie, knowing the answer and embarrassed by her question.

"He didn't want to be called a poof, did he?"

"Or a Nancy boy?"

"Or a Nancy boy! Why ask me if you know already, Lottie."

It was not a question but a protest: his sister always seemed to need an explanation for the obvious. What he didn't realise was that Lottie wanted to talk about Bradley Hall. She liked Bradley, although he was two years younger than her and still a child; but their pairing by Edward and Myles stimulated her interest.

He was a polite boy – she knew that because he had been round to play with her brother many times over the years; but they ignored her, content with their games. Lottie also knew that Bradley got on with everybody; he valued friendship. Myles must have chosen him because his voice was yet to break, which meant … Lottie knew what it meant but was unprepared to dwell on the fact.

The bus arrived following their silence and during her wondering about Bradley Hall. The driver smiled, ignored their passes and told them to 'Hurry up'. He always said that and Charles always wondered why: they were never late.

It was in the playground that the next incident of that day occurred. Charles was leaning against the wall of the junior block, chatting to Bradley Hall, when he heard Brian Gooch sounding off about his father.

"… and Dr Henderson put this rug over the girl and stuffed her in his boot."

The comment made no sense to Charles (he'd been in his room when his dad arrived home) but it was clearly an insult and he rose to his dad's defence.

"What did you say about my father?"

"Wha'?" was Brian Gooch's response.

"You heard! You were talking about my dad."

"Was I?"

"Well?"

"Well, what?"

"What's this about my dad stuffing somebody into the boot of his car? Oh, and by the way," continued Charles, looking purposefully at the boys who were listening to Brian Gooch, "our car doesn't have a boot."

"So what?"

"So, what are you talking about?"

"My granny said."

"How does she know anything?"

"She was there on the other side of the road and Dr Henderson said something but she wasn't sure what 'cos she's deaf."

Charles was flummoxed by now, not so much by the other boy's prevarication but more by the fact that he knew nothing himself. He was angry and het up. He lunged out and caught Brian Gooch a blow on the jaw. Brian responded and soon they were involved in a tussle, typical of a boys' fight where neither intended to hurt the other but wanted to make his feelings felt. A ring of their contemporaries gathered round, cheering them on, and soon the teacher on playground duty intervened.

"Come on, come on," he called, "what are a couple of nice lads like you doing fighting each other?"

He did not want to know; he merely wanted to prevent any consequences and get on with his lessons that morning.

Charles said nothing: it was his fault and he knew it. Brian scowled, angrier at the teacher than his attacker.

"Well?" insisted the teacher who felt obliged to have an explanation.

"Nothing, sir," said Charles.

"Nothing?" repeated the teacher, relieved.

"No, sir."

He turned to Brian Gooch.

"And you, Brian – what have you to say?"

"Nothing, sir."

"Nothing?"

"No, sir."

"Then I suggest we shake hands and call it a day, don't you?"

"Yes, sir" replied both boys at the same time, relieved and amazed at their solidarity.

"Did you get into a fight with Brian Gooch, today?" asked Lottie, when she met her brother on the way to the bus.

"No."

"Yes, you did."

"Don't tell Dad."

"You know I won't, Chad … Oh, and I might be going round Barbara's, and Dad's going to cook, anyway. So, I'll get the later bus."

Charles nodded and made for the layby where the school buses waited.

Lottie was not 'going round Barbara's': they were friendly but not having-tea-at-each-other's-houses friendly. She was going to the village corner shop – in reality, a small Co-operative superstore – hoping to bump into Bradley Hall. She knew he always dropped into the shop for a chocolate bar or whatever took his fancy on the way home. She was right and he blushed with embarrassment when Lottie spoke to him on the way out.

She was two school years ahead of Bradley and scared the life out of him. He was at the age when he was beginning to be aware of the sexual differences between girls and boys – not in a technical sense (he'd known that for many years) but an emotional one. He felt, whenever a girl approached him, that he was now obliged to behave in a certain way, a way he could not define clearly in his mind. Lottie Henderson possessed something that was attractive, demanding and overwhelming; just being seen talking to her made him feel awkward.

"Myles told me he's teaching you to sing one of Britten's Burns songs," she said with a smile, flicking back her hair in the way Bradley found disturbing.

"Yes, we've … eh, practised a few of them."

He wanted to move away, to seek the shelter and security of the green, to sit on one of the seats and enjoy his chocolate bar; he didn't want to be seen talking to this amazingly attractive girl who, in so many ways, was like a woman.

"Edward has been working with me on *Afton Water*. From what they said, I think he wants me to accompany you at Mr Pegg's next Burns' Night."

The very thought was shocking to Bradley; the idea that this beautiful girl would be sitting close and playing *for* him was almost unbearable.

"Myles never said. I thought it was just a song. I don't mind."

There you go, he thought, what a banal thing to say – 'I don't mind'. It sounded so ungracious. He was delighted and should have said so.

A crowd was gathering on the forecourt of the shop, a crowd that only added to Bradley's discomfort.

"I'm looking forward to it," said Lottie, "have you ever been to a Burns' Night?"

"No."

He was drying up; he only managed a word in response, and all this lovely girl was doing was being friendly.

"I've never been," he added, "but I'm looking forward to it, now."

"Perhaps we'll get a chance to practice together."

It wasn't a question. Was she proposing that they …? No. Myles and Edward could be relied on to … to make the arrangements, to get them together.

"They'll let us know when we're ready," he added.

"Yes. I'll see you at Pottery Encore."

Bradley laughed: it was funny name. Lottie laughed with him. It would never be the same again when he went round to play with Charles. Bradley knew that to be true.

"Cradle-snatching are we, Lottie?" enquired Barbara Wilton, when Lottie arrived at the bus stop, and her friends joined in the laughter.

Lottie was not sure how to respond.

"Where are you going?" she asked, lamely, knowing that Barbara lived in the village, her father being the butcher, Reg Wilton, whose family had owned the butchery 'since time immemorial', as Barbara's grandfather said once.

"Beccles," replied Barbara, a trifle put out by Lottie's calm response; she expected a denial, "Is it true what they're saying about your dad? Did he run someone over?"

"No," said Lottie.

"Brian Gooch said …"

"Brian Gooch!"

Lottie said no more: contempt can be conveyed in an exclamation, she felt. At least, now, she had discovered why Chad fought with Brian Gooch. Brian Gooch – a bigger gossip than his grandmother.

At home, Charles and his father – who was cooking their meal that night as Lottie said – had come to an understanding. Not being a secretive boy, Charles made a clean breast of the fight to his dad. He also pointed out that his dad 'never told him anything. It was always Lottie', and Gerald Henderson, knowing this to be true, apologised.

"The fact that you were in your room last night has nothing to do with it, I know," said Gerald, as reassuringly as he could, "if you'd known about the ... accident, what the boy said wouldn't have come as a surprise. I'm sorry. You're right – I talk with Lottie a great deal, and place too much on her shoulders. It's just that she's the woman about the house and ... girls talk more, don't they?"

Charles acknowledged that to be true: he was quiet, he loved the peace and calm of his room. It wasn't just his dad's fault that Lottie loaned her ear more readily; but he had been jealous and he had been upset.

In his room, the smell of roasting potatoes wafting up the stairs, Charles calmed down and his mind turned back to the day. A boy in his class called Sam Whitham had shared a story with him during the lunch hour.

Sam often sat alone and Charles, feeling angry with himself over the fight, joined him. Sam Whitham was a loner – the kind of boy who teachers are aware is an isolate. He was not disliked by anybody but had no close friends. He was a boy who hid his loneliness in books, a boy who – in the quiet of his room – really wanted to do something big, something amazing that would establish his credibility forever among his peers. He never talked much about himself or his family, he never offered opinions in class; but it was generally known that his father was dead and that his mother had disappeared, but where no one knew. He lived with his grandparents, Ambrose and Marjory Broome, who ran a business in the village; they lived in the old water mill, a legacy from Ambrose's ancestors. Sam's mother was Marjory Broome's daughter.

Brian Gooch's story had percolated among the pupils by now and Sam was ready to talk if anyone wanted to listen, and Charles, it seemed, did. After they settled to their packed lunches, Sam talked.

"My dad was a soldier," he said, "he was killed in Afghanistan. He was esteemed – that's what my granny says – by the other soldiers. When he was in the hospital before he died, he saw a ghost. It was late at night, sometime between midnight and one o'clock in the morning, and all the patients were in bed and all the lights in the ward were out except the one where the duty nurse sat at her desk."

Charles, listening at first only out of politeness, became aware that the story he was hearing, spoken as it was by someone his own age, was being told in a language Sam had learned. Charles was certain – although he couldn't explain this to himself – that the manner of the telling was that of an adult.

"My dad woke feeling a weight on his legs. He tried to sit up and when he did the man in the bed opposite called out 'Hey, Sam' – my dad had the same name as me – 'there's somebody sitting on your legs'. My dad looked at the bottom of his bed and saw someone get up from it. This person walked round and stood over my dad and my dad told me that even he was frightened – and my dad was never frightened of anything!"

Charles, listening intently now, realised the story had taken a turn: the words, the feelings, were Sam Whitham's.

"'Who are you? What do you want?' my dad called out; and the figure leaned over my dad and said: 'I am the man you buried last year', and dad could see he was a soldier. He was in uniform, and my dad remembered that he had been the one who laid out the corpse. 'What do you want?' he asked again, and the ghost said that he was to write a letter to his wife who was in Scotland. The ghost then said that if my dad did as he asked, he would never bother my dad again. Then he walked away and stood by the far wall of the hospital ward. When he came back, he leaned over my dad for a second time and whispered in his ear what he was to write."

"What was that?" asked Charles.

"My dad would never say: it was a secret between him and the dead soldier."

"Did he write the letter?"

"Yes."

"And the ghost kept its promise?"

"As far as we know. My dad died soon afterwards. My granny and grandad learned all this in one of his letters," replied Sam.

Chapter 4

Family Butcher

Reg Wilton's family was full-blooded as properly befitted the wife and offspring of the village butcher. 'Full-blooded, firm-muscled and rarin' to go' was a favourite phrase of his when his kin gathered; and gather they did 'every Sunday, high day and holiday' with their mountain bikes. They cycled many miles each weekend; it was easy cycling in flat Norfolk but they made up for this whenever a holiday came around and they took to the hills of Wales, the Peak District and Scotland – anywhere the gradient offered a challenge to the muscles of the arms, legs and just about every other part of the body.

His wife, Myrtle, was a local girl. She had been his choice because of her thighs, and his daughters, Barbara and Lucy, took after their mother. Both girls, even at fifteen and eleven, glowed with muscle, muscle of the staunch type, 'big and firm' as Reg was proud to say of his women.

Myrtle's understanding of how they came to be married was slightly different. She had eyed Reg in the playground of the village school when she was seven and decided there and then that he was to be hers; for Myrtle it had been love at first sight and love ever since. When they left school nine years later, she had pursued him wherever he chose to spend his free time and had Reg wedded and bedded – in that order – before he was out of his teens. It was a happy marriage and lacked only one thing to make it complete – a son; but Myrtle was working on that concern, although wondering, eleven years after Lucy's birth, why it was taking so long.

Above the door of his shop, which stood on the corner of Ditchingham Road and Butcher's Lane, the sign built into the marbling made it clear to the public at large that his business had been **Est. 1836.** He was keen to say that other butchers might 'come and go' – such as the one down the road who had tried to tempt villagers by providing meat 'marinaded ready for the barbecue or oven' – but 'the Wiltons go on forever'. Reg was a hard worker who had strengthened the family business in Thornham Staithe and taken his meat out to surrounding villages.

Nothing was too much trouble for Reg as far as his butchery was concerned, but he put himself and family before anyone. 'First look after yourself, and then you're better placed to look after others' was his motto.

At one time, he had killed his own meat and the slaughterhouse still ran off the back of the shop, although it was now used as a store, where several times a week Reg slid aside the large doors to receive the carcases ready for butchering. Reg always undertook this part of the business because he needed to examine the corpses, but Myrtle and the girls 'earned their livelihood' working in the shop; and Reg not only involved them in the butchering but also took them out to watch their 'future prosperity' grazing in the neighbouring fields and insisted that the girls accompany him to the local abattoir on several occasions. 'Abattoir' was not a word Reg used and had pointed out to Barbara, once she had learned it in one of her French lessons, that it was 'a word soft people used because they didn't like to face the truth of the joint on their plate'.

It was after one of their Sunday biking marathons when the family sat together in the evening in the rooms above the family business – steaming from their endeavours and the late lunch, a traditional beef roast, Myrtle had served – that Barbara mentioned for the second or third time the story of 'Dr Henderson's Ghosts'. It had become quite a favourite with her and she enjoyed embellishing the incident with additional details regarding the amount of blood involved 'with the one who was crushed under the car' and how 'the other of them ran screaming into the churchyard'.

Reg had no time for such nonsense and pointed out that ghosts did not bleed or scream but the girls only laughed and felt urged on to enjoy the telling even more. Myrtle, too, gave no credence to the existence of ghosts and sided with her husband in pouring scorn on any belief in life after death.

But Myrtle was uncomfortable because of an incident that had occurred the previous Monday in the shop. She would not allow herself to believe that it was anything but tiredness and imagination, but nevertheless Barbara's tale unsettled her again.

She had been alone in the shop at the time – Reg was seeing to a delivery – but the shop had been full of customers, so full that a queue built itself along Ditchingham Road almost as far as the old chapel. Myrtle was feeling hot under the collar of her blouse because the corner presented a tight turn for traffic choosing to enter or leave the village by that road – although why they should choose that route was a mystery to Myrtle. She knew her customers well – they were all regulars: the holiday boat people chose to buy their meat from the Co-op – and she passed the usual time of day with each of them.

It was on one of the rare occasions she had a chance to look up from wrapping their orders that she noticed the man. He wasn't a regular; in fact, she'd never seen him in the village. He had a hard stare, an uncomfortable stare. Myrtle, had she believed in evil, would have used the word to describe the way the man looked at her – evil and angry. He was a short man, well below the height of the others in the queue, and so tended to look up at her. She had to blink several times to convince herself that he was watching her and moving closer as the queue grew shorter; and then, just as she was about to serve him, he disappeared. More exactly, he simply wasn't where he'd stood; Mildred Ackroyd had been standing behind him and was now waiting to be served.

"Where did he go?" asked Myrtle, irked that a customer should have left their shop.

"Where did who go?" said Mildred in her usual snappish manner.

"The man who was in front of you."

Mildred Ackroyd's eyebrows rose several inches, almost reaching her hairline – not that she had much of one left – and her lips pursed before she answered, as though she might be talking to a fool.

"One of the ladies who live in Farthing Court was in front of me, dear. You've just served her. Not a man in sight."

Farthing Court was where the well-heeled elderly in the village retired when they gave up their homes, something Mildred was determined Miss Pritchard would never do. Her pronunciation of the name, as well as her use of the term 'dear' held a distinct note of disapproval.

"But ..."

"No buts, dear, and I'll take two pork chops – lean pork chops – when you are ready."

Myrtle had remained uneasy all morning but refrained from mentioning the man to Reg; uneasy though those eyes had made her feel, she couldn't bring herself to talk about them to her husband and so she drove the memory from her mind rather than dwell on it alone.

But Barbara's joy in telling her tale had stimulated the recollection. Perhaps, therefore, it was destiny – or just unfortunate – that Reg was looking through the family's photo albums that evening: the ones he called 'ancestral albums', those that went back to the early days of photography. Moving away from her daughter and snuggling down on the sofa with her husband, Myrtle saw the man again, the one with the evil eyes who had been in the shop in front of Mildred Ackroyd.

"Who's that man?" she asked, her voice so unnaturally high that Reg looked at her questioningly.

"My ... let's think ...uh, great-great-great-great-grandfather – or is it just three 'greats'. I can't remember but he's the one who started the business 'Wilton's Butchers'."

"Not him," urged Myrtle, "The one he's talking to!"

The original Wilton butcher was leaning back, looking exceptionally comfortable, on a wooden chair, his head turned slightly from the photographer. He was wearing a panama hat and a lightweight suit that looked as though it might have been white: it was hard to tell because the photograph was black and white, but he looked very smart. His collar was starched stiff and he wore a tie that hung down over his chest; his trousers had turn-ups and one leg, the left one, was crossed over the other, the ankle resting on the knee. His feet were shod in laced-up leather boots. Prosperity was clear in every line of his being.

Beside him on a bench sat the man Myrtle was sure she had seen in the shop: the photographer had captured his face, particularly those eyes. He, too, wore a suit but it was of a heavy cloth and looked as though it had survived – or nearly survived – many summers and winters. Although the day – judging by the ancestor's mode of dress – was clearly one in summer, the man had a scarf round his neck and fingerless gloves on his hands. His hat was the trilby type, narrow-brimmed and well-worn.

"I don't know," replied Reg, "Someone my ancestor knew, I suppose. They seem deep in conversation."

"Where was the photograph taken?"

"In a garden by the looks of it. There's a lawn and a hedge, and there's several people in the background. Looks like a get-together of some kind. Why d'you ask?"

"Nothing," replied Myrtle, not wishing to raise … the dead? But she was sure it was the same man – she could tell by the eyes – and she knew she'd seen the garden, or one very like it, somewhere before.

*

They retired early as always so that the girls would be fresh for school in the morning and Reg and Myrtle could plough the nightly furrow they hoped would lead to their son; but her mind wasn't on the job and long after Reg was snoring his way into the morrow she lay awake thinking of the man with the green, evil eyes. Yes, they had been green. She remembered now: unusual eyes – not many people had green eyes.

She glanced across at Reg to be sure he was fast asleep and slipped her legs over the edge of the bed. Myrtle needed the toilet but didn't want to wake Reg in case he wanted to start all over again: she wasn't in the mood.

The landing was dark. She didn't want to put on a light: it might wake Reg and he'd wonder what she was doing, and so Myrtle made her way to the toilet by feeling her way along the walls. Once she'd manoeuvred herself on the seat, Myrtle realised she didn't want the toilet at all; she knew that wasn't the reason she'd been called from her bed, and Myrtle was frightened. Firm-muscled and 'as strong as an ox' (as her dad would say) and yet she was frightened. Nothing much had ever frightened Myrtle – not bullies in the playground, not her own children's illnesses, when Reg had been near to tears and her mother thought them 'at death's door'. No, Myrtle Wilton nee Taylor was not one to be phased by much; her feet were firmly on the ground.

She settled her nightdress and stepped out onto the landing. Her eyes were getting used to the dim light now, and she could see. The bottom of the stairs was in darkness, shadowed only by the moon coming in from the skylight they'd fitted when one of the children, Lucy, slipped down the stairs one night on her way to be comforted after a nightmare.

Myrtle made her way carefully down the stairs, holding tightly to the banisters: she didn't want to fall, she didn't want to be doing that, not for anything. He'd be waiting for her in the shop where she'd seen him that morning – the man with the green eyes – and she didn't want him mounting the stairs and going up to the bedrooms for her girls. A poker in her hand would be a good thing; people always said to have a poker in your hand if you heard burglars. Not that this man was a burglar. He was something worse than a thief. There was a coatrack at the bottom of the stairs. Reg kept a walking stick there and Myrtle reached out for it. As she did, an arm slipped into her own and Myrtle realised the man must have followed her down the stairs, which meant he'd been up there with them. The thought made her sick.

The man's grip was firm, determined rather than brutal. He steered her, unexpectedly, towards the back door. Myrtle wanted to look at her captor – and captor he was because there was no way she could pull from him – but couldn't bring herself to do so, couldn't bring herself to look into those hard, green eyes. She saw his hand reach out and open the back door, turning the key first, twisting the knob and easing the door open. His hand was old and reminded her of the bark of a tree. It was like her grandad's hand.

He was still to the side and slightly behind her when they walked out into the garden. Their garden was small and neighboured that of the old chapel, now owned as a home by a couple from London. A gate linked the two – a gate that was usually locked but which no one had troubled to replace with a fence. The man opened it and they walked through into the grounds of the old chapel, and there was the lawn and the hedge, just as in the photograph.

Myrtle knew what she was going to see when that happened: a bench and beside it a chair. On the chair would sit Reg's ancestor, the original Wilton butcher, and beside him, on the bench would be the man in the old, worn suit. Only that wasn't what happened. The man's grip on her arm relaxed, he walked towards the bench and sat facing the chair. On the chair sat Reg, looking much like his ancestor, his eyes fixed on the other man, the look on his face not one of a conversational nature but one of utter terror.

When Reg found her a few hours later, Myrtle was still rooted to the spot, staring at an empty bench and chair in their neighbour's garden, with the dew of the night clinging to her clothes.

Chapter 5

The Walker

On the Friday evening Dr Gerald Henderson knocked down the two young women, a rambler arrived in Thornham Staithe. James Ryder was walking the Wherryman's Way and had arrived from the direction of Great Yarmouth. He was enjoying a meal and a few pints in The Swan, where he had booked a room, when the accident occurred by the lychgate of Holy Trinity.

James remained blissfully unaware of the misadventure on the High Street as the drink – together with the pan roasted chicken supreme, braised leg and pearl barley stew and fondant potato followed by blackberry mousse, apple sorbet and honeycomb – drove him into a doze after his long walk.

At his feet, equally exhausted, equally well fed (James always saw to his friend before settling down to his own meal) and equally enjoying the comfort of the public house, lay his black Labrador, Roland.

Both were well into their night's sleep when the landlord, Ned Douglas, tapped Ryder gently on the shoulder.

"We're closing, Mr Ryder. It's after eleven."

"I'm sorry," Ryder muttered as he and Roland stirred.

"It's closing time, Mr Ryder. Your room's been ready for a while."

"Ah, yes, thank you," responded Ryder.

He wasn't the first, and was unlikely to be the last, who would drop off in front of the fire in that little side room: the soft chairs and their proximity to the flames made sleep inevitable on a full stomach. James Ryder yawned and shook himself, suddenly awake, as night closed in. Roland at his heels, he mounted the stairs, passing the last locals as they leaned on the bar, giving him the sideways glance that all locals give to strangers. In a sense, he supposed, they had that right: as regulars it could be said they owned the pub.

The room was pleasant enough and en-suite. Aside from the bed, there was a small table he might use as a desk together with a hardbacked chair, an easy chair on one side of the bed and a side table on the other. Next to the bed there was a rug and room to undress, whereas in many of the places he'd experienced there was barely space to swing the proverbial cat.

The window over-looked the village green with its war memorial and the church with its lychgate. While Roland settled himself at the end of the bed, leaving Ryder just enough room to stretch his legs, Ryder looked out at the damp autumn night. The road was clear, now: Gerald Henderson, his ghosts, the paramedics and the police were nowhere to be seen. The pavements glistened, the first leaves to fall wet with mist.

He unpacked his rucksack, placing the contents on the table, spreading open the OS Broads map with his guide and notebooks, and undressed slowly, folding his trousers over the back of the easy chair with his shirt on top. His walking boots he stood under the desk, his thick socks he spread on the side table; his waterproof coat he hung on the hook in the door, his underwear he stuffed into a polythene bag inside the rucksack and Ryder was soon in his pyjamas ready for sleep. These little details of placement he was to remember vividly later for at that moment there was a hard tap on the door.

Ryder always brought pyjamas with him on a long walk because he disliked sleeping in the clothes, even the underclothes, he would wear during the day, but now felt decidedly ridiculous as he walked across the room to open the door. He'd heard the locals leave and the landlord lock the front and back doors. He wondered who could be knocking.

It wasn't the landlord, as Ryder expected, nor anyone he'd seen at the bar: a stranger, then, to Ryder - a shortish man wearing a long riding coat that reached well below his knees and a wide-brimmed, waterproof hat. It was an expensive coat and something about the fit across the stranger's shoulders told Ryder that it had been acquired by the man rather than bought by him; the coat had been intended for, and perhaps originally worn by, a taller, broader man In his right hand, the stranger held a half-finished bottle of whisky and in his left, two glasses.

"The landlord sent them up," he said, "He thought you might appreciate a nightcap."

The riding coat was damp with the mist of the evening – not wet, just damp, and Ryder supposed the man had come in off the street. But why, and why with a bottle of the landlord's whisky?

The stranger walked passed Ryder, placed the two glasses and the bottle on the desk table between Ryder's map and notebooks, easing them aside, and poured two generous measures, one of which he held out to Ryder before settling himself in the easy chair with the other. Ryder, taken aback though he was, felt pleased the man wasn't dripping on his papers.

"You've walked the Way?" the man asked.

"Yes," replied Ryder.

"Then we are fellow travellers on life's road. Richard Gabriel is my name and you are a Ryder?"

"James."

"Yes. You will stay here."

There was something peremptory in the man's tone, something that almost amounted to a command.

"I beg your pardon."

"It has been a long walk for you."

In fact, the day had been a short and pleasant one. Ryder had walked only from the Ferry House, where he'd stayed the night.

It was the previous day that had been somewhat tedious: the long stretch by Breydon Water with the tide out and the mudflats heavy on the eye and then Reedham marshes, huge stretches of reed-lined dykes broken only by clumps of alder and poplar trees, isolated and bare of human life. Experienced walker though he was, Ryder had been glad of his map and compass on that first day of his journey. The dykes would appear suddenly, treacherous to the unready traveller, and Ryder had been reminded of a comment he'd once heard that this part of Norfolk was "fit only for boats".

On that morning, he'd crossed on the ferry and walked to Thornham Staithe. It was true he had felt hemmed-in between the River Thorn and Hardgrave Flood, an area of shallow lagoons and reedbeds all but impassable, but his enforced detour through farmland and a country road had brought him to the White Horse in the early evening where a pint, if not a bed, had awaited from the amiable host, Simon Pegg.

Ryder looked across at his guest – the unwelcome guest who had stirred these memories – and he waited, refusing to be intimidated by the stranger's intrusion and taking the opportunity to take stock of the man.

Richard Gabriel's face was a brown, muddy colour; it was an ill-nourished face and dark shadows underlined the bright eyes. Ryder noticed that the lids never seemed to move, as though their owner was unable to blink or simply determined to watch Ryder intently. It was clear to Ryder that he was being weighed up by a man who thought he knew something about him. Eventually, he felt obliged to ask, as though the questions were forced from him.

"Who are you? Why have you come to me?"

"You have no idea, have you?"

"I know we have never met before. I have a memory for faces."

"Do you? How far does your memory go back?"

Ryder, who had been standing by the open door, closed it and moved slowly to his desk table, where he sat heavily on the hardbacked chair. He was frightened. He knew that to be the case: his hand shook so much he had to place the whisky glass on the table where the contents continued to shudder in the glass. He steadied himself and looked again into Richard Gabriel's eyes; there was pain there and years of mental anguish.

Ryder was an engineer by profession and had worked in many places with many people. He wondered who he might have upset or disadvantaged to such an extent that the person would have suffered as this man had suffered. He cast his thoughts back over the years but his conscience was clear: engineers tended to make life better for others, rather than worse.

He took a long pull at the whisky and emptied the glass, noticing as he did that the other man had not so much as raised his to the lips. It was very strange: uncomfortable and unsettling. Richard Gabriel offered nothing; he seemed to be there only to prompt Ryder's thoughts, but the latter was disconcerted enough to want to rid his bedroom of the man as quickly as possible.

"Perhaps we could go down to the bar, do you think? We might continue our discussion there."

"I think not," replied the other man.

"Then perhaps you would tell me what I can do for you?"

"You sat awhile in the churchyard when you arrived, did you not?"

Ryder had spent time on the bench at the smaller church, All Saints, when he'd come off Hardgrave Common. He remembered a peaceful spot and the sound of children's voices from a nearby grassy playground but he'd met no one. He was as sure of the fact as he was certain he'd not been watched.

"You did not look round the graveyard."

It wasn't a question: the tone was an accusative rather than a questioning one.

"No."

"Perhaps you should."

"I don't understand. I'm tired and wish to sleep. If we are fellow travellers, perhaps we could continue this conversation over breakfast, tomorrow morning."

Richard Gabriel smiled as though the very idea of breakfast was amusing.

"I think not."

He stood as he spoke, walked towards Ryder, placed his glass beside the bottle on the desktop and looked down at him. His look was indiscernible; it could have been one of contempt, but Ryder concluded it was one of acceptance, an acceptance of the fact that the world was as it was and could not be changed through the efforts of mankind.

"We shall meet again, James Ryder. Now that I know you, we shall meet again, if not in this world …"

With that comment left unfinished, Richard Gabriel walked out of the bedroom, brushing against Ryder as he did so. Ryder followed quickly, as much to lock the door as with any other intention but he did open it and look along the corridor from which the other bedrooms bore off. There was no one in sight. The night lights were sensor driven and would have come on to show the way if anyone had passed along but the corridor was in darkness.

*

From a night riven by waking dreams, a slumber tossed and turned, James Ryder woke ragged, wretched, tired and not a little frightened. He wasn't a man nervous by nature; he'd travelled the world and found himself in parlous situations, but the calm assurance of the stranger had convinced him they would meet again and Ryder was not enamoured of the fact. Not to put it mildly, he was terrified but could not understand why.

When he went for his trousers and shirt, he found them both creased where Richard Gabriel had leaned against them on the easy chair. The whisky bottle was on the desktop, where the stranger had placed it, pushing aside Ryder's notebooks and map; his own empty glass was where he put it down and beside it, the stranger's full one.

When the landlord brought his breakfast – a full English: Ryder was one for getting his money's worth – he asked Ned Douglas about the other guests.

"There's just the old couple, Mr Ryder. It's never a busy time, September, but we do get elderly people about now, once the kids have gone back to school. But they're not up yet. It's home from home here at The Swan. It's a sentimental journey for them. I believe they had their first home here in Thornham. They come every year. Never take breakfast with us. They like to go down to

Carmen Quay's at the staithe. You'll have to visit Carmen before you walk on. She's a character. You wouldn't want to miss her. Johnny Depp went to Carmen's place for her fish cakes last summer. Kept him waiting an hour-and-a-half, they said, she was so flummoxed, but he never batted an eyelid and left a tip so big her eyes popped out of their sockets ..."

"The other walker," cut in Ryder, glad of a pause in his host's story, "the one you sent up to my room with the whisky – which is his room?"

"There's no one else here, Mr Ryder," replied Ned Douglas, "If you found a bottle of whisky in your room, you're a lucky man."

"Is there a chance it was one of the staff?"

"Only the wife and I live in. If she paid you a visit during the night with a bottle of whisky, I might have a few words to say ..."

"No, no, I didn't mean anything ..."

"Just a jest, Mr Ryder," replied Ned Douglas, sensing that Ryder was upset, "You say you found a bottle of whisky in your room?"

Ryder couldn't bear to go into the story but had to ask one last question.

"I heard you lock the doors last night. There's no other way that anybody could have got in, is there?"

"None at all. It's a nice enough village. We don't get a lot of crime here – the occasional litter bin knocked over is about the height of our crime wave, if you see what I mean, but we keep the premises secure. I'd know if anyone got in. I can't explain why there was a bottle of whisky in your room, Mr Ryder."

"I'll pay for the bottle," replied Ryder, eager to end the conversation, "I drank a glass last night."

"It sounds as though you might have had more than one, Mr Ryder," replied Ned Douglas, laughing, "Enjoy your breakfast before it gets cold."

Back in his room, Ryder realised by the dog's expression that he had forgotten to feed Roland. While the Labrador ate – a matter of seconds – Ryder examined the bottle and glasses again.

"Someone was here, my son," he said to Roland, "There was more than one spirit in this room last night."

And then his second post-breakfast realisation came to him: Roland hadn't barked. Dogs always bark at ghosts: anything supernatural has their hair standing on end, their ears pricked, their tails upright.

"But you didn't even emit a low growl, did you, Rollie? What the hell's going on?"

By the time Ryder was in the street, ready for whatever the day might bring, he had booked another two nights at The Swan. He was still frightened but also angry. He hadn't imagined what happened the previous night! He wasn't yet certifiable! If someone or something was playing games with him, Ryder would teach them a lesson they'd never forget.

Calmer, out on the High Street, Ryder crossed to the village green, planning his day: All Saints churchyard, Carmen's Quay Shop, the village library (if there still was one), anywhere that might lead him to a Gabriel. But first, Roland must have his morning walk: he'd waited long enough. It was Saturday, of course; there were children about doing nothing in particular – chatting, idling. Isn't that what the weekend was for? He hadn't planned to walk far that day: back to the Yare and then stay the night at Surland St Mary – the pub there had a room for him. He'd phone ahead and postpone his visit.

With these thoughts running through his mind and with Roland sniffing on the loose, Ryder arrived at a narrow lane that led from Holy Trinity churchyard. A girl passed him on a bicycle and smiled as he stood aside for her; the girl was Lottie Henderson, on her way from her music lesson to a friend's house where she planned to sleepover. He wasn't to perceive it at that moment but Lottie and he were going to come to know each other well and in circumstances far more terrifying and conclusive than his ghostly visit had been.

The walk took the man and his dog past Pottery Encore and so to a small, country road that led down to the Thorn. There was a picnic spot by the riverside, complete with brick ranges on which the holiday boaters could barbecue when they moored up for the night. It was a short distance from the village, which was reached across the water meadows: a peaceful spot with a parish council noticeboard and information leaflets kept dry in a plastic case. Ryder hung around for a long time. He'd never kicked the habit of smoking and what better place to enjoy a pipe than on one of the benches, watching the river sparkle in the bright morning light. It was one of those autumn days, early in the season, with a chill in the air, a chill that freshened rather than nipped.

Roland wandered back and forth seeking for any scraps the boaters might have dropped and left, but always the dog returned to Ryder before setting off in another direction. It was when he looked up at one of these returns that Ryder noticed the boy. The boy had been eyeing the dog and was clearly keen to stroke him.

"Go on, son. He likes a bit of fuss."

The boy caressed the dog's head and chest carefully, kneeling on the damp grass, until Ryder told him to take a seat. Roland closed in, at ease with the boy, and nestled his head between the boy's legs.

"What's his name?"

"Roland, but I call him Rollie. What's yours?"

"Sam. Sam Whitham."

"Do you live in the village?"

"Yes. I live with my grandparents at the watermill."

Ryder looked the boy up and down. He'd never married and never had children by default, and so knew little about them. This one he judged to be about thirteen; he was on the edge of puberty, and Ryder remembered what a difficult time that was for a lad. For those first five or so years into your teens you never knew what was expected of you by anyone – parents or girls. At that age, Ryder had sought the companionship of his mates, but this lad looked to be a loner. You could always tell. Once his mates got caught up with girlfriends, Ryder has been a loner. It was his education and his work that saved him from isolation: you always found friends at work.

"It must be an interesting place to live," he replied, rather lamely he thought.

"It isn't a working mill but it was once. There's been a mill here on the Thorn since 1086. This one was built in the nineteenth century. It's a weatherboarded building but it's on the original site at the head of navigation. It'd be great if it did work."

Ryder laughed and could see, immediately, that he'd embarrassed the boy.

"I'm not laughing at you, son. God forbid that I should! What you said interested me, that's all. I'm an engineer. I've worked all over the world."

"All over the world!"

"Yes," replied Ryder, laughing at the boy's admiration.

"I'd love to do that."

"You sound like an historian, to me."

"It's my subject but I'm good at physics and mathematics, too."

"And you think they're subjects that would be useful to an engineer, do you?"

"Wouldn't they?"

"Oh yes. You're spot on. You're a bright lad, aren't you?"

"I don't know."

"Take it from me – you are!"

Ryder was curious about Sam Whitham living with his grandparents. Where were the lad's parents? Did he have any parents? The boy hadn't stopped stroking Roland's ears, neck and head since he arrived. Ryder decided it was time to move on.

"I'd better carry-on giving Rollie his walk," he said, "I can get back to the village across the water meadows, can't I?"

"That's where the mill is. Can I come with you?"

"Why not! I'd like to see your mill."

And so it was that the two of them, friends at first meeting, made their way along the side of the Thorn. They crossed the meadow where the river had its widening at the staithe and came to the little bridge and the boatyard.

"We can go through here," said Sam, as Ryder started to walk along the track behind the King's Head pub.

"It says private," replied Ryder.

"That's because they don't like you going through the boatyard but it's always been a public-right-of-way and it cuts off having to walk up past the pub and down the High Street."

Ryder smiled: he heard the boy's grandfather talking. They had almost reached the small gate that led to the staithe itself and the free 24-hour Broads Authority moorings when a large man, sullen of face, stopped them.

"You're trespassing," he said.

Ryder had met the type before, many times: the know-all who would have been a bully at school, the kind of person who was only too eager to assert their rights because it seemed to give them dominion over others. He was inclined to ignore the man, but Sam Whitham spoke out.

"It's a public right-of-way."

"Who says?"

"I do, and the law does."

The man's eyes flickered towards Ryder, and the engineer knew that had he not been there Sam would have received a clip round the ear or perhaps a punch in the mouth. The man stood aside.

"Don't let it happen again … or else."

"Or else what?" replied Sam.

The man's eyes flared: he wasn't used to a kid mouthing back. He looked at Ryder again, as though weighing up the odds.

"I'll be looking out for you," he said.

Once they had reached the staithe, Ryder asked:

"Who was that?"

"Richard Revell's dad."

"Who's Richard Revell?" asked Ryder, knowing the answer full well.

"The school bully."

"Has he bullied you?"

"No. I keep away from him."

Ryder wondered whether to give the boy some advice – he'd been troubled by bullies himself – but decided against it; after all, he wasn't his father, and it wasn't his business to do so.

They cleared the staithe and Sam took Ryder to admire the waterwheel from the steps that led to the mill itself. He could see that the wheel had been motionless for decades. After the recent rains, the Thorn was full and its waters gushed over the lower paddles, which remained obstinate; he could see it was what an engineer would term an undershot wheel, the wheel being set into the flow of the mill race. He remembered hearing from someone or other that an overshot wheel was more efficient. Ryder pencilled a reminder into his cerebral notebook to find the reason.

From where they stood, he also noticed a small bridge that crossed the point where the Thorn flowed into the small marina; the bridge was barred off at each end.

"Is the bridge unsafe?" he asked Sam.

"No, it's the posh people. When they built those houses along Quay Lane, they put in that little garden there on the other side of the bridge. The posh people didn't want people crossing the bridge into the garden."

"The garden's private is it?"

"No. You can get into it from the road but not over the bridge from the staithe."

Ryder smiled: it was the way of the world – money talking. He judged that none of the "posh" houses, each of which had its own mooring, could be worth less than £600,000, probably more. He wasn't a socialist by any means but did feel that the people of Thornham Staithe should be able to walk over their own bridge.

Marjory Broome, as he later came to know her, was waiting for Sam when they crossed the road to the mill itself. She chided him for being "nearly late for his dinner" in a friendly enough, if bossy, manner, but made no move to welcome the boy with a hug or a kiss. Sam smiled. He seemed at ease with his grandmother.

"Go and wash your hands. Your grandfather will be here in a minute."

"This is Mr Ryder," said Sam, "He let me stroke Rollie."

"You make sure you wash your hands properly then."

"I'd love to have a dog like Rollie."

"Messy things – and a lot of work. Isn't that right, Mr Ryder?"

"But great company," replied Ryder, "You're never alone with a dog."

"I'm sure," replied Marjory Broome, in a tone that suggested she was unconvinced and might argue the point if pushed.

"Mr Ryder is an engineer. He thinks the mill wheel might be able to turn again."

Unused to the enthusiasm of children, Ryder was taken aback by the boy's claim and was about to modify it when a harsh voice boomed from the vicinity of Carmen's Quay Shop, which was a few yards up the road.

"Oh, he does, does he? Perhaps Mr Ryder would like to buy the mill then!"

The speaker – or, rather, boomer – was a foxy-faced man, his physical appearance at odds with his wife who was on the plump side, jolly of face if not entirely of nature. Ryder judged this to be Sam's grandfather.

"It's a millstone round our necks," said the boomer, "Look at that woodwork – costs a fortune to upkeep. If you want it, I'm sure we can arrive at a fair price. It's been in the family for years. My father's father and his father's father before him were millers here – but that's a few years back – not to say a century or so. Ambrose Broome. I run the general store but this is where we live."

"Who have you left in charge of the store, Ambrose?" asked his wife, her mind clearly on matters other than selling their home.

"Richard Revell."

"Him? Can you trust him?"

"We've got cameras. He knows I can keep my eye on him. Wouldn't trust him otherwise. Not a Revell. They'd pilfer and barter anything they could lay hands on. Still, at least the lad's prepared to do a bit of work on a Saturday morning," replied Ambrose, casting a none-too-friendly look at his grandson.

"Leave the lad alone, Ambrose. He works hard at his schoolwork and his recorder. He needs a break at the weekends. Go and wash your hands, Sam. Your dinner's ready."

"Goodbye, Mr Ryder," said the boy, as he nipped inside.

"Goodbye, son."

"Schoolwork! Whenever did schoolwork buy the bread, let alone butter it."

"It's what his mother would have wanted," replied Marjory.

Ambrose Broome's reply was a mere grunt and he followed his grandson into the mill.

"Sam's mother was your daughter, then?" said Ryder, when he and Marjory stood alone on the narrow pavement that crossed the road bridge.

"Yes. It was a tragedy, the boy losing both parents – his dad in Afghanistan and then his mother with cancer, but we do our best. You'll have to excuse me now, Mr Ryder. They'll be wanting their dinner."

"All Saints Church – is it further along this road?"

"Yes, you can't miss it. Go right at the junction just before you get to the White Horse and then right again down a little alleyway just passed the carpenter's shop. I must go now."

"Of course. Thanks for your help, Mrs Broome. My regards to Sam."

So, saying, as he watched Marjory Broome disappear into the watermill, James Ryder set off for the churchyard of All Saints to look for Gabriels.

Chapter 6

At the White Horse

It wasn't usual for the parish council to venture to the White Horse after their meetings but on this particular occasion it seemed right: it was Jack Dorling's birthday and a celebration seemed in order. There was nothing Jack Dorling enjoyed more than a chat.

He ran the printshop in the village, one that dated back to the previous century with machinery to testify to the fact. A village wit had once suggested that **J DORLING AND SON – PRINTERS** should be declared a World Heritage Site, an idea that pleased Jack but never reached the ears of the powers-that-be. Jack, in fact, did not have a son – he was the great-grandson of the original J Dorling – and had only one child, a daughter. He was a generous man and provided printing services to village people at more-or-less cost price, making his living further afield by dint of his reputation for excellence and value-for-money.

Simon Pegg, the landlord of the public house, had often suggested that the council made use of his upstairs' rooms – free of charge, of course, but on the assumption that the beverages they consumed during the meeting might swell his coffers slightly and mellow the proceedings; but his offer had been regularly deferred on the grounds that the town hall had always been their venue and always would be.

Simon was a family man and ran his pub in the same spirit; it was the only family pub in the village and hosted appropriate events throughout the year: their Autumn Beer Festival being the next one. He and his wife, Catriona, had bought the business twelve years previously and there were people in Thornham who still treasured their pint glasses from 2006. Both their children, July and Bruce, had been born in the village and photographs of them adorned the walls of the White Horse. July had been expected in June and was to be named after the month; when she arrived a trifle late, Catriona saw no reason to change her mind and, anyway, July was a distinctive name: not one you'd forget in a hurry. Bruce had been named after two people: Robert the Bruce, who Catriona (a Scot as her name suggests) admired and the American singer, Bruce Springsteen, of whom Simon was a fan.

Among those who walked into his pub with Jack Dorling on that evening were Reg Wilton, Ambrose Broome, Edward Warburg and Myles Langstroth. There had been several absentees from that night's meeting (it being a wet and cold one, following a wet and cold week), including the vicar of Holy Trinity, Frederick Mackenzie, who had been called to the bedside of an elderly communicant.

Simon was pleased to see them: the White Horse, too, was experiencing the adverse effects of the weather.

"You've got no ghosts here, have you, Simon?" asked Reg Wilton, indicating what had been the main topic of conversation at the parish council..

"We've a Ghost Ship," replied Simon with a laugh.

"That'll have to do then," said Reg, eager to pass on his thoughts about the hauntings and wanting everyone settled, "Jack, Edward, Myles, Ambrose – what will yours be? Can I get you one, Simon?"

"That's thoughtful, Reg. What's this about ghosts?"

"You haven't heard?"

Simon had, of course, his children being at school, but you didn't get people talking and drinking by cutting off their flow of conversation. Besides, Simon was a thespian and thespians enjoy listening to anyone: it gives them ideas for portraying a character. His children belonged to the village dance troupe, Maisie Garland's Dancing Feet, and he had plans for a show, provided he could persuade the right people to support his idea to replace the annual pantomime with a musical version of *A Christmas Carol*.

"Go on, Reg," he said.

"Well, it started with Dr Henderson, didn't it?"

"Is that right?" replied Simon, moving along the bar as he pulled the various pints.

"Barbara and Lucy were full of it – Dr Henderson ran down two young women on the High Street but when he came to look for them, they weren't there …"

"Or one ran off," cut in Ambrose Broome, "and he shoved the other in the boot of his Volvo."

"You can take your pick, Simon," said Edward Warburg, with a laugh, "depending upon whether or not you have faith in our good Dr Henderson."

"The first place one would want to find oneself should one fall foul of an injury would be in the care of our Dr Henderson," chipped in Myles Langstroth, by way of supporting his friend.

"I wouldn't care to find myself in hospital," said Jack Dorling, "My old mother hated the places – 'the scourge of our age,' she said, 'much as the workhouse was for a previous generation'."

"Who's been telling these tales?" asked Simon, eager to keep the conversation on track.

"Brian Gooch was the one talking about it in school," replied Reg, "He's supposed to have heard it from his granny."

"Reliable source of information," smiled Jack.

"Now then, Jack – let's show a bit of respect for our elders," chastened Ambrose.

"Did your Sam have anything to say about these ghosts, Ambrose?" asked Jack.

"He don't say much. He's got his nose in a book all the time."

"He's a nice lad," snapped Jack, "You'll be proud of him one day … and so would your daughter if she were alive to see it, and his dad, killed defending his country. Sam's got a lot to bear."

"I know that!"

"Yes – well bear it in mind," replied Jack, uneasy he'd said too much in too hasty a manner.

"He's certainly a fine boy," added Edward, in support of Sam's champion. "I've come across him at school. He has a musical ear and plays a fine treble recorder. Works hard at his craft and always listens to advice ... Speaking of musical matters, Simon, I am trusting we will be ready with a truly enchanting song for your Burns' Night."

"Bradley Hall and Dr Henderson's daughter," added Myles, "We picture them together with Robbie's *Afton Water*. We will need to have your piano tuned, Simon ..."

The beers pulled and with Edward and Myles closing in on Simon,, the rest of the group moved towards 'Snug Corner', a small area to the left of the door, where Simon had retained a soft, leather sofa and chairs in front of a log fire; it was unusual in a modern pub to find somewhere cosy but was one of the qualities that made the White Horse special.

On the farther side of the fire, comfortably ensconced at the old table under the dart board, sat a man none of them recognised. He nodded agreeably to them as they sat down but appeared to be engrossed with his own thoughts. He was dressed in a long overcoat that looked a little outdated – which he had opened at the front to reveal a waistcoat with a chain and watch that disappeared into its pocket – but which he had not removed despite the warmth of the early fire.

Ambrose, nettled at Jack Dorling's rebuke over Sam, asked him about his daughter.

"Has Jane settled down, Jack? Given you a bit of trouble in her time, hasn't she?"

"Juniper's more than made up for that, thank you, Ambrose," Jack replied, cautiously.

"Still having them tattoos done, is she?"

"I'm not sure she has a lot of space left for more, Ambrose," replied Jack, refusing to rise to the other's bait and appearing to agree with his criticism rather than be put out by him.

Jane Dorling was known throughout the village as a 'wild card'. Her mother had died while she was young, leaving Jack to raise his daughter on his own. He'd been at a loss as to how he should handle her when she reached her teenage years, which she did when she was about eleven. At thirteen, she was leading her own life, spending much of her time in Norbridge with people Jack did not know and would not have liked if he did. It was at that stage she changed her name: Jane Dorling became Juniper Wells. He wasn't sure why she'd chosen to be so called but knew the berries of the plant contained a powerful oil that was beneficial in small quantities but dangerous in large amounts; those facts and the spiky nature of the trees themselves seemed to sum up his daughter. 'Wells', she told him, 'were the source of all life'. But – and for Jack Dorling it was a huge 'but' – Juniper had a heart of gold alongside a deep and devious knowledge of computers and all things computing. Had she been a boy, Juniper would have been branded a 'nerd', but nobody dare do that to her: nobody had the nerve. It was she who had brought **J DORLING AND SON – PRINTERS** into the twenty-first century and saved the firm from extinction.

"You were saying your wife had a strange experience, Reg," Jack continued, keen to change the course of the conversation.

"Ah, the bugger with the green eyes," replied Reg, "Followed her down the stairs he did, took her out into the neighbours garden and left her there."

"Upstairs was he, Reg?" said Ambrose, a laugh in the question, "Can't say I'd fancy having a ghost in my bedroom. You never know what they might see."

The comment, intended as ribald, did not produce the reaction he'd wanted: Jack had been celibate, due to circumstances, since his wife died and Reg had been trying so hard for so long, he'd lost heart.

"Are you gentlemen from the parish council?"

It was the stranger who spoke: the man in the long waistcoat sitting at the table under the dartboard. By now, Edward and Myles had walked round to the other three and Simon stood in the entrance to the bar, having lifted the counter clear.

"Yes, that is so," answered Edward, "and you are?"

"Kent is my name. I couldn't help overhearing your conversations when you arrived and this gentleman's reference to a ghost. Always fascinating, isn't it – the other world and where we

go when we get there. Do you hold your council meetings here
often – in the public house, I mean?"

"Not often enough!" replied Simon.

Kent smiled.

"It used to be the customary practice," he said, "Many
organisations met in the local public house, where the fate
of so many was decided and where so much ended across its
counter. Are you a member of the vestry – parish council, I mean
– landlord?"

"Oh no," replied Simon, hastily, "My family and I are new to
the village."

"I thought so," replied Kent, "If you gentlemen will excuse
me."

The stranger rose immediately and passed out between them to
the front door.

"Well, what do you make of that?" asked Ambrose, when they
saw him pass by the window.

"I don't know," replied Jack, "but he made my blood run cold."

"Another one of the village ghosts, perhaps?" suggested
Simon.

"Village ghosts! I'll give them village, bloody ghosts if I catch
one of them, I can tell you."

"You may not recognise one when you see it, Reg Wilton,"
called a voice.

The men looked towards the door, which hadn't shut with its
usual warm thud. Juniper Wells smiled at them, an all-embracing
smile.

"I think I'd know a ghost if I saw one," insisted Reg.

"Mary Boyne didn't."

"Who might Mary Boyne be?"

"The wife of the man who disappeared without trace when the
stranger called on him. It was Mrs Boyne who met the man in the
garden when he called at their house. It was Mrs Boyne who told
the man that he would find Mr Boyne in the library. She told him
where to go, only she didn't 'know till long, long afterward' that
the man was dead."

"Poppycock! You've read that in a book, haven't you?" said Reg.

"Edith Wharton – an American writer. It's one of her short stories – *Afterward*, it's called. You should read more, Reg Wilton."

"And you should get out more is what I say," was the butcher's response.

Chapter 7

History in the Making

"Fancy you saying that!" said Jack Dorling, as he and his daughter walked home.

"Scare them, did I, Dad?"

"As though you cared."

"I don't care – not about them, but I do care about you. It won't hurt them to be upset for a bit – too smug, by far, you local businessmen."

"You said nothing about our gentleman in Victorian costume, Eddie? I thought it might add a little zest to Reggie's rather mundane account."

"It didn't frighten you?"

"Lovely Marj escaping the marriage bed for the cool of the garden? No, dear, no!"

"You've forgotten the noose about your neck – the noose I placed there?"

"It sent the shivers down my spine at the time, Eddie, but these … *peculiarities* are best placed in a neat, little pigeon-hole at the back of one's mind with the door firmly locked."

Ambrose Broome stayed on at the pub after the others left, chatting to Simon Pegg about one of the understandings he had with the landlord. The White Horse owned the land on which the local bowls club had their green and keeping the grass looking like the baize of a snooker table was one of the side-lines of Ambrose's general store business; autumn was here with winter settling in and before he committed time and effort to preparing the green for the winter, Ambrose needed to know their understanding would continue into the following season: scarification and thatch control to remove organic matter needed to be completed before the green was aerated and Ambrose always followed these procedures with regular drag brushing to disperse the dew and raise prostrate stems for the mower blades before moving on to top dressing. To be fair on the man, his interest extended beyond the financial: he was passionate about the quality of the green.

Pleased with himself following their conversation, Ambrose sank another couple of pints before strolling the short distance to the mill. He was far from drunk but Marjory didn't like the smell of beer on his breath when he kissed her goodnight and so Ambrose decided to spend a few minutes on the staithe.

He was standing on the road bridge, leaning over the rail, watching the water rush beneath him when he saw the child. He thought at first that it was Sam, while knowing full well that Marjory would have had the boy in bed long ago – reading under the covers, no doubt, but in bed and out of the way. He felt bad about his daughter's child. It wasn't that he disliked the boy, but they weren't 'the same sort'. He knew he was in the wrong, and feelings of guilt came over him when he saw the child.

"Sam! Sam what are you a-doing there? Sam!"

The child turned and Ambrose saw at once that it was not Sam. He would have been shocked to see the boy looking as this child did: its eyes were dark hollows and it looked as though it hadn't had a square meal for months.

Ambrose thought for a moment that it must be a gypsy child, so wild and reckless was its appearance. It was the look of the thing, of course, that made him think in that way: the corduroy and the hard, blue serge of its clothes and the shaved head. Hair had begun to grow on its head but it had been shaved – and roughly – and dyed purple in places.

Ambrose, though thoughtless regarding his grandson, was not an unkind man. He moved away from the road bridge and made his way down the steps that led to the edge of the staithe. The child was watching him carefully, as though noting his every move.

"Who are you? Where have you come from?"

The child didn't speak but returned a ghastly smile, a smile that sent palpitations to Ambrose's heart. It was a smile of torment: that was the only way the shopkeeper could explain it to himself. As he got closer, the child walked towards him. He seemed to be holding out a tray or a server of some kind. It was a huge dish – far too large and heavy for the child to be able to carry, and yet that was just what he was doing. It was laden with food – chicken, soups, cheeses, sweets – and it was drawing Ambrose back in the way flashbacks do in films.

He became frightened as the child neared him: frightened of what this apparition meant, frightened of its impending touch. Although the smile was ghastly, the expression in the eyes was one that beseeched.

As the child offered the server and Ambrose reached to receive it, the dish vanished. He couldn't have touched that server, couldn't have put the chicken wings or legs to his mouth. It was a relief it had gone.

As it did, the child turned and walked – no, limped. The child limped to the foot bridge: the bridge the posh people in the new houses on the north of the staithe had had cordoned off.

This seemed to make no difference to the child who walked onto the bridge as though the wooden bar no longer existed – and it didn't; the broken bridge was in good repair. The child made its way to the centre, turned and faced Ambrose, and then looked down into the river.

It had rained endlessly for weeks and the Thorn was swollen and high. When the mill was built, the river had been diverted from its original course to accommodate the needs of the waterwheel; but when in flood it would return to its natural flow and now poured through the archway that supported the road bridge above.

It was dark under the willow trees that drained the bank of the staithe, one of which grew from a small islet in the centre of the river, just where the flow was at its most fierce and where mallards would shake their feathers dry in summer. Only the moon was reflected from the waters that now rushed under the footbridge where the child stood watching.

"Careful! You don't want to fall in there!"

The child smiled back and waited. Ambrose, fearful for the child's safety, hurried along the staithe-side and clambered up onto the little bridge. When the child saw the shopkeeper, it turned and ran. There was no garden on the other side, now – just moorings, a yard where stood a hay wagon and a few warehouses where the posh houses once stood.

As Ambrose reached the centre of the bridge, the child, in full flight, turned once more, smiled and disappeared under the wagon. Ambrose stopped; he watched, through the slats of the now broken footway, the river flowing hurriedly beneath him, turned to make his way back and saw the bridge once more barred. Panic overtook him; attempting to make sense of what had happened and fearful for his life, he hurried forward, caught his leg in the jagged teeth of the broken slats and was tipped over the side-rail into the river.

Where he caught his head was uncertain – it may have been on the bridge or one of the mooring posts – but the rent in his skull was clear to all. He was alive but unconscious when he entered the water and the Thorn filled his lungs in no time.

Watching these tragic proceedings was a man known as Frank. He watched from an arched passageway across the road, just a few yards along from Carmen's Quay Shop. The passageway, which led to the rear of a house backing onto the marsh, was closed at night by two black doors and it was in front of these that the man stood. He was dressed smartly in what used to be described as a suit of the English colonial style; white and slightly creased, and very unsuitable for a British autumn. He had spent some time in the house on whose pavement he now stood, as its owner was to discover. Pleased with what he thought of as 'the proceedings' on the bridge having gone satisfactorily, he allowed himself a little smile and walked off towards the village green.

*

One of the parish councillors who did not repair to the White Horse following the meeting was Vernon Scuffil, village historian and teacher at the local high school. Vernon wasn't averse to a drink but he was averse to boring company and an hour or two with his fellow councillors had been enough for one day. He might have considered sharing a drink with Jack Dorling on his own or with the two musicians but a melee of conviviality was not to his taste.

Vernon was the owner of the house with the doored passageway, a house he bought when he had returned, reluctantly, to Thornham Staithe. It wasn't that Vernon was unhappy in his work; in fact, he was a popular teacher, a circumstance due to the way his pupils responded to his manic delivery of any historical subject. He was an enthusiast; but he could – and should, in Vernon's view – have been so much more: a professorship had once loomed large on Vernon's horizon but had been snatched by another when what he considered his seminal work, *Practical Results of the Workhouse System as adopted in the Parish of Burghamton 1833-34*, had failed to attract the right calibre of academic attention.

Upon his return, Vernon had taken up with an old school friend who by then was divorced with two children and they had formed a partnership, mutually agreeable to both. They lived separate lives but in the same house, and provided each other with physical, intellectual, emotional, social and cultural sustenance; it was a marriage of sorts – one both were adamant they did not want formalised in church – but a marriage that respected each other's right to a private life.

Justine Sweet was an eco-warrior; in fact, Justine was *the* warrior for any currently fashionable cause, which meant days spent in London on various protests. She was grateful, at these times, that Vernon was there for the children. She was also very active in Thornham, secretary of both the Horticultural Society and the Gardeners' Club, their own garden being a testament to her skill, wisdom and endeavours.

Vernon never touched so much as a weed in the garden and Justine never so much as entered his study, which was situated in a room a previous owner had had built on the back of the house as a granny flat. He was puzzled, therefore, when he returned from the parish council meeting on that night to find several of his books had been moved: not by much, not enough for him to be sure they had been moved but enough to unsettle Vernon.

While he was puzzling over who might have done this to him, never for the moment considering it might have been Justine or one of the children, he thought he saw a movement in the garden. It was a long garden, which ended where the marshes began, and the lower end, beyond the duck pond, was gated off to keep the chickens from the crops during the day. Sharing this part of her domain with the chickens were Justine's beehives, four colonies all settling down for the winter, some forty thousand bees at this time of the year but topping three hundred thousand come the summer.

The gate was open, something Justine never let happen, and someone was standing beyond it, next to the chicken run. Vernon was sure of the fact. There was an anger in Vernon, which often expressed itself in verbal assaults on those who did not appreciate his former academic excellence or who engaged him in small talk when his mind was otherwise engaged. That anger was expressed now on the fact that someone had the audacity to be in his and Justine's garden at ten o'clock at night. He grabbed a torch, without looking, from where he always kept it beside the turntable of his stereo system and stormed into the garden.

"Excuse me! May I be of assistance?" he bellowed in the loud trumpeting voice that emerged from his exceptionally large head, a voice as overbearing as its owner and which seemed to resonate in every cavity available: chest, pharynx and nose.

He stormed across the lawn and found the gate shut, although he could have sworn it was open when he turned to reach for his torch. He flashed the light around, disturbing the chickens, lighting the darker corners of this part of the garden where he knew rats hung out and a fox might be seen on some nights. The willow dripped gently, the stinging nettles hung with the day's rain, the earth was soggy under his feet, a pile of twigs and branches ready for bonfire night were caught in the beam and cast spider-legged shadows; but nothing moved, nothing at all.

Vernon poked around for a while and then returned to his study. Something was wrong. His books had been moved again, disturbingly slightly but moved. He wasn't imagining things! And there was someone in the room; someone who had it in for him. He had company. Someone had entered his study for a second time that night and touched – moved – his books. And then a voice whispered in his ear:

"Remember the ready back-slaps, the stunning clout over the ear, the blow with the open palm on alternate cheeks?"

He didn't remember (how could he?) but Vernon knew.

Chapter 8

Bless this House

Myrtle Wilton was adamant: she was going to get the Reverend Mackenzie to bless their house. It didn't matter what Reg had to say or whether the neighbours thought them daft; she knew that the man with the green eyes had a hand in Ambrose Broome's death.

She'd spoken with Marjory Broome that very morning. Marjory hadn't heard anything until the commotion started and then she'd rushed out to find the paramedics on the staithe. Someone must have phoned the police and ambulance and Marjory was sure she'd seen a man on Bridge Street in old-fashioned clothes. This was enough for Myrtle, who had never recovered from her experience in the garden with the stranger.

That 'very morning' was several days after Ambrose's death, and Myrtle hurried to the vicarage, dashing up the narrow alleyway between Jack Dorling's printshop and the new apartments that had replaced the old police station. The vicarage opened on to a grassy path that lead down, past the house of Lin, who owned the fish and chip shop called Lin's Plaice, to the water meadows, a favourite haunt of dog walkers.

The vicar, the Reverend Frederick Mackenzie, was out but his wife, Jacqueline, wasn't and she welcomed Myrtle with a smile of reassurance.

"Come in, Myrtle. Fred won't be long and, in the meantime, we can have a little chat."

It was Jacqueline's role to calm parishioners down before her husband was constrained to listen to their concerns. Jacqueline not only loved her husband, but she also cared for him; and was aware that if they had their way parishioners would be quite ready to run him off his feet. Jacqueline felt it her business to see they didn't 'have their way'.

Myrtle Wilton wasn't exactly a parishioner, in the sense that she rarely graced the parish church, but she did live in the parish of Holy Trinity and Frederick Mackenzie was, as Cure of Souls, responsible for her spiritual welfare. Besides, Myrtle was a prominent figure at autumn and spring fairs, where she organised stalls in aid of church funds; along with her husband, Reg, she was also very active in the organisation of the Harvest Supper, 'a tradition that went back centuries' and in which WILTON BUTCHERS EST. 1836 had always been involved, both as a means of supporting the church and the business.

Myrtle poured out her story to Jacqueline, who listened patiently over a cup of tea and a few chocolate brownies. When Myrtle finished, Jacqueline rose.

"You go home, now, Myrtle, and I will see that Fred calls on you and your husband before the day's out. You know Fred – he'll put your mind at rest."

This wasn't what Myrtle wanted; she wanted to speak with the vicar himself. But Jacqueline was equally determined that her husband should enjoy his lunch and guided Myrtle to the door and on her way.

Frederick Mackenzie, in the meantime, had spent most of the morning with Miss Pritchard and Mildred Ackroyd.

Miss Pritchard had woken during the night. This wasn't unusual because she often needed the toilet; in which case, being unsteady on her feet, she always rang the bell for Mildred, who slept in the next room with her door open, as arranged. But she felt no sensation of needing the toilet, and lay wondering as to what had disturbed her sleep. It was only after several minutes, and as her eyes acclimatised to the dark of the room, that she had the feeling someone was sitting on her bed. Peering around the corner of her duvet, which she held close to her nose, Amelia saw an old woman watching her. She knew immediately that this was not Mildred:

Mildred, as her companion, had always shown Amelia the greatest respect – no nonsense, but always polite – and would never have dreamt of imposing herself in that way. The old woman said nothing but simply looked down upon Amelia with a look of disdain. In her, Amelia detected a note of triumph.

Amelia Pritchard was not of a nervous disposition. She had been seventeen when war broke out in 1939 and immediately joined the WAAFs where she served as a Flight Officer and was later awarded the Croix de Guerre in acknowledgement of her services to the French Resistance; but the look in the woman's eyes terrified her to such an extent that she dare not stretch for the bell that would summon Mildred lest the old woman's hand reached out to prevent her intention. None of the terrors she experienced during the war years had steeled her for this experience.

How long they watched each other she could not recall, but eventually the old woman stood and, with one backward look that left her determination in no doubt, went from the room, passing out through the open door and, "presumably, down the stairs", as Amelia said afterwards when she regained her composure and summoned Mildred, who in her turn summoned Frederick Mackenzie the following morning.

Miss Pritchard had protested but Mildred brooked no opposition. Never had she seen her friend in such a state as she made clear to the vicar on the phone.

"I am not, as you know, vicar, a religious person," said Amelia, "With no disrespect to you, I must say that the horrors I witnessed and saw reported during the war cast grave doubts about the existence of a benevolent god. But I have no doubt that this woman – this spectre – was not of this world … What are those lines from Macbeth – the ones he speaks when Banquo appears?"

"*Avaunt and quit my sight! Let the earth hide thee. Thy bones are marrowless, thy blood is cold. Thou hast no speculation in those eyes, which thou dost glare with*!" said Mildred, pleased with the speed of her recall.

"Yes, they're the ones, Mildred. Thank you. But this woman did have speculation in her eyes. This creature was evil, Vicar, while at the same time wretched. There were moments as we watched each other that both she and I yearned to speak, and I knew what she was wanting to say… Do you believe in telepathy, Vicar?"

"I believe there are some grounds for such a belief," Frederick replied, "We all experience something of the kind from time to time, even on a domestic level – especially on a domestic level: my wife and I know what each other are thinking or about to say without the other having to open their mouth."

Mildred Ackroyd laughed; widowed now, but a long time married, she understood Frederick precisely.

"It's similar with Mildred and me," said Amelia, "but that's easily explained, isn't it – familiarity?"

"Yes, of course … Did this woman remind you of an event – something you'd experienced, been told or read about?" asked Frederick.

"Why do you ask, Vicar?" replied Amelia with a hesitation in her voice that suggested he had touched a nerve.

"Some years ago, one of my parishioners (I'll call her Penny) was watching her daughter being taught to turn somersaults by a family friend. Her daughter was only two or three at the time and so Penny was concerned about the child hurting her neck. She didn't say anything because she didn't want to hurt the feelings of their friend. However, that night, when Penny was in that drowsy state just before going to sleep, a picture of her daughter with a broken neck flashed into Penny's mind. The next morning, as they sat over breakfast, her daughter said to Penny 'My neck isn't broken, is it, Mummy?'"

"You're saying that what was on the mother's mind was apprehended by her daughter?" asked Mildred.

"Yes."

"Did you have anything on your mind, Amelia – something that might have been stirred by this woman?"

"I might have done, Mildred."

"Did she have something on her mind that triggered a memory in yours?" asked Frederick.

Amelia Pritchard looked at him, a mixture of admiration and awe in her eyes. She hesitated only for a moment and then spoke as though he was taking her confession, a novel experience for an Anglican priest.

"She spoke – I mean *thought* – of heartless acts of cruelty, oppression and neglect towards the sick and the dying, whereby it was usual for them to be left to suffer and die alone in the darkness of the night ... and of the matron driving furiously through the streets, vomiting in her drunkenness over the side of the cart."

After a long silence, in which neither he nor Mildred Ackroyd felt able to exchange even a glance, Frederick said:

"And you knew of this?"

"Yes – but how, I am unsure. I have never worked in hospitals or hospices or been responsible for the suffering and the dying."

"No," said Frederick, kindly and softly.

The three of them sat together for another hour, sharing general topics of conversation and a coffee with one of Mildred's fruit scones. When Frederick left, he felt that a temporary composure had returned to the house but set off to walk home through the village from Cookley with an uneasy mind.

Frederick sat in his church, Holy Trinity, in a state of thoughtfulness. He had been home and listened as Jacqueline recounted Myrtle Wilton's request. He now wanted to settle his mind. He had some experience, through his work, of what people called the 'supernatural' and knew what bedevilled the imagination of both women: puzzlement, consternation, and fear accompanied by a 'knowing' that superseded all rational thought. A strange sense of urgency would be pervading them both, telling them that what they had experienced was important but beyond their understanding.

Accounts of the failings of his own kind had once brought him into contact with one who had passed on. He had been sitting in this very church, recalling what he had read about a priest who pilloried sinners, homing in on their sins rather than their chances of redemption before God. The priest in question had been called upon to intervene in the case of a woman 'delivered of an illegitimate child', as the phrase went in 1845. He had spoken to her about her 'adultery and false oaths' and the woman, Elizabeth Beeston by name, had been alarmed, denying she was a 'common prostitute', although acknowledging she had four children by different fathers, a fact testified to by the absence of a father's name on any of their birth certificates. The woman had applied for parish relief and been subjected to 'sniggers and knowing winks' rather than the kindness needed.

Frederick's thoughts about this had been strong enough to send 'alarm signals to his adrenaline glands' and set his brain in 'search mode' (he knew the terms but this brought no comfort). His heart thumped faster, nervous excitement welled in his stomach and, when he turned in the pew, he was not surprised to see the woman, who he knew without having to be told was Elizabeth Beeston, sitting behind him. The sense of knowing had been indisputable.

She had said nothing; her look had been enough – one of contempt for his calling and his cloth, for the whole edifice on which he had built his life and raised his family.

He turned, now, half-expecting to see her there once again – but no, the church was empty. Frederick rose and walked down the aisle towards the font, where all Christian life begins. The present is always with us, and he had a job to do, a worry to put at rest. It was evening – another wet, dreary evening of that autumn – and he made his way to the Wilton's.

In the churchyard he met Vernon Scuffil hurrying through with his wife's two children, Acer and Anthemis, eager to get home. A strange man, Scuffil – one who seemed to lack the natural graces of human interaction; but Frederick spoke, nonetheless. After all, both children, when younger, had attended his Junior Church. Both liked him – Frederick knew that to be so – even if, at fourteen and thirteen, they had drifted away.

"Good evening, Vernon, Anthemis, Acer. I expect you're looking forward to your half-term break next week?"

"Hmm? Yes! Naturally – why not? Is that all? No more to say, then? We may as well be on our way!"

With that battery, leaving the children no chance to speak, he scatted from the churchyard through the gate that led onto the village green and was gone from sight, leaving Frederick to wonder why the man seemed to dislike him so much. Wondering but not too bothered: life goes on and God was in his heaven – 'sufficient unto the day ... thereof'.

Myrtle Wilton was waiting by the front door of the butcher's shop.

"Oh, Fred, I knew you'd come. Thank you so much. I've been so worried since poor Ambrose was killed."

Frederick was known as Fred throughout the parish and beyond, and not only by those who attended his services regularly. Only Amelia Pritchard ever addressed him by his formal title, and that was to be expected in much the same way as everyone addressed her as 'Miss'.

"Ambrose fell from the broken bridge, Myrtle. We have no reason to suppose he was killed."

"Then what was he doing on there? He was lured. I know it, just as I was lured into our neighbour's garden by that man. You will bless our house, won't you, Rector? I can't have him here."

Frederick smiled at Myrtle's adoption of his title – not that he was a rector but it indicated her seriousness. He knew the butchery well; although a vegetarian himself, he accepted his wife's taste for meat and respected that their eldest child was a dairy farmer in Perthshire: tolerance was one hallmark of a Christian and Fred possessed this quality in what his wife described as 'oodles'.

He knew he shouldn't be undertaking this 'Deliverance'. At one time, maybe, but such events were now supposed to be handed to the Deliverance Ministry Team. Frederick had decided to skip the formalities: good as the team was, Myrtle needed someone she knew.

"Would you like to assist me, Myrtle?"

"May I?"

"I think it would be a good idea."

"Can Reg and the girls join in – they're in the sitting room."

"Why not? Go and fetch them."

In religion, theatre was everything; there was great comfort in ritual and ceremony. How many times had he taken funerals for people who did not know him or him them? And yet he had brought solace to their grief.

With the family, he sat first in the kitchen and listened – listening was at the centre of his ministry. By this time, Myrtle's own fears had infiltrated the family. Despite Reg's masculine objections, his daughters, Barbara and Lucy, explained how for many weeks they had felt several 'presences' throughout the house. These included seeing figures walk through doors, feeling someone in the room and on several occasions physically being touched by something while in bed.

Frederick asked a few questions around any tensions in the household, any stories attached to the house, anything traumatic that they knew about, how old it was, what it was built on, whether anyone outside the house had experienced anything, whether anyone else had tried to 'get rid' of the 'presences'. They didn't recall any noises being reported and there was no single specific place in the house where the incidents took place.

Leaning forward across the table to convey an air of companionship and a sharing of confidences, Frederick explained a little about Deliverance. He then suggested that they should tour the house – the rooms where they lived, the shop and the neighbour's garden. Leading steadily in a small, tight group, Frederick said some prayers, inviting the family to join where they could and certainly on each of the 'amens'.

Their circuit complete, the Wilton family found themselves back at the beginning, in the kitchen.

"If you would be so kind, Myrtle – a clean glass bowl and some salt would be useful."

By now, their priest had their trust. The bowl was duly filled with warm water and the salt absorbed. He took out his *Book of Common Prayer* and read, blessing the salted water before leading the family once again on a tour of their home.

In each room and passageway, he said a Prayer of Deliverance and splashed the walls, floors and doors before going outside the house where he splashed the brickwork, before finally entering the neighbour's garden where he sprayed the seat on which the man with green eyes had sat, covering what may have been there in the past.

"Oh, Rector, I don't know how to thank you," said Myrtle, as he took his goodbyes at the door of the shop.

"There's no need to thank me, Myrtle. You know where I live and I'm available 24/7, as they say. But you'll not need me. Your house is blessed and at peace, and your family safe."

"Oh, Rector, I know that now. Our home feels better already. There'll be no more evil doings going on here, I'm sure."

Later, both had reason to remember their words on that day and to wish dearly they had been true.

Book Two

Chapter 1

Please to Remember

Burghamton, a nearby parish to Thornham and only a few miles from the town, was the strangest of hamlets: strange because it always seemed to be inaccessible – except, that is, on Bonfire Night, when it hosted the neighbouring villages, and in the summer, when it created its renowned Sculpture Trail.

Driving or cycling to Burghamton, visitors usually missed the village and could never understand why this was so: the signposts were clear enough and there were many of them on the approach roads – all single track but passable – and yet it was almost invariably the case that people found themselves in adjacent places seeking to turn back; and when they did, facing the same problem.

Walkers fared no better: several official footpaths and numerous farm tracks led to Burghamton, but few seemed to arrive. Even experienced ramblers, armed with map and compass, were confused, ending up in one of the neighbouring settlements and having to ask the way. The response from locals was always the same "Yew, doan wanna gew there" – a phrase that somehow seemed to carry a warning.

The hamlet itself, if one did manage to find it, seemed a place out of time. The lack of bustle and noise helped to create this sensation but it was also the spirit of the dwellings and of the people that most impressed: the attitude of both seemed to say, 'We'll be found if we want to be'. In Burghamton, a visitor tread carefully, as though an unseen sentinel had whispered in their ear 'make no sound here, lest we be woken'. It was not a place to disturb, not a place that welcomed intrusion: walking its byways, one stepped back into another time.

Nevertheless, on the two occasions in the year when Burghamton did want you it opened its portals widely, and the fifth of November was one such.

Most people arrived by car and found ample spaces to park. Barbara and Lucy Wilton arrived with their parents and parked in the field by the small Saxon church; Charlie Henderson came with Bradley Hall's parents (Lottie had decided to stay at home with her father who was working late that night) and parked next to the village hall; Vernon Scuffil and Justine Sweet brought her children, Acer and Anthemis, and found a space in one of the many farmyards that bordered the hamlet.

A few walked, of course: some because their parents were loath to drive, others for reasons of their own.

One of these was Sam Whitham, urged reluctantly by Marjory Broome to "go and enjoy yourself but be careful". Sam often walked the byroads of Thornham and assured his grandmother that he could "find my way blindfold", which was near enough true. Once across the Norbridge-Lowestoft Road, he made his way along the tracks of farmers who knew him well, through small woods where he'd found the burst shells and glistening brown seeds of the horse-chestnut earlier in the season and past the mere by the house of the same name.

Another walker was Richard Revell, son of the boatyard worker who Sam had annoyed, and boyfriend of Amy Prentice, a girl of fifteen described by teachers and neighbours as "too old for her age". Amy certainly thought of herself as grown up and a woman, but was nowhere near as mature as Lottie Henderson, who she despised as a freak. Richard and Amy had decided a walk might give them a chance for "a snog and a bit of a feel" in one of the barns they'd pass on the way there and back, "on the understanding I'm not going the whole way", as Amy put it.

Richard Revell was looking forward to the bonfire and fireworks for reasons other than a chance to get to know Amy better. It was one of those nights of the year, like Halloween and the Victorian

Evening in Thornham, when he could make "a bloody nuisance of himself" (his dad's words) without getting caught. If he were lucky, he could rope in a few other kids as well; they might get nabbed and take the blame, but hard luck – you've got to look after yourself.

The bonfire, a huge one, was always erected on a long stretch of land well to the fore of what had once been the parish workhouse and adjacent, safely adjacent, to Church Farm. No one was sure when Bonfire Night at Burghamton had begun but it was now a tradition; when the moment came each year, it was as if by instinct the villagers knew and were ready with their produce and preserves. From September onwards, the locals brought all their inflammable rubbish and stuffed it on and between the bones of the wooden skeleton erected by the farmer. There was no charge for attending the bonfire but sufficient profits were made by the various stalls – hotdogs, beer and cider, waffle, baked potato, burger, flapjack, conserves and preserves, candy floss, toffee apple, hog roast and so on – to make the few inhabitants of Burghamton feel it worth the intrusion.

It always seemed to be a dark night and a cold one; if the wind wasn't blowing, frost was on the ground and there was inevitably a nip in the air. Well-wrapped up in heavy coats, scarfs, gloves and mufflers the crowd gathered between the fire and the stalls that lined what might be called the main street and curved round in a lanterned arc to the village hall, where the toilets were opened and waiting. For the children, their torches (as well as the sparklers, rockets, roman candles, volcanoes, fountains, Catherine wheels, poppers, snappers and snakes, smoke bombs, bangers, peonies, spiders, horsetails and barrages) were a fascination in themselves as they gathered – the young ones cuddled close to their parents, the older seeking each other out – in the warmth and blaze of the fire and under the sparkling brilliance of the night sky.

For Richard Revell, his torch was of cardinal importance, and for him the two fireworks that offered the greatest promise of excitement were the banger and the jumping jack – particularly the latter. The few houses that lined the village street, and the sideroads from it, offered letter boxes that were irresistible: if the owners were out – as was usually the case on this night – he could scare the life out of the dogs and cats as he popped one or the other of his treasures into the house. There was the chance of setting fire to something but this had never happened: it was the frantic barking and screeching that gave him the most awesome thrill.

Tonight, he had rounded up a couple of weaklings – Brian Gooch and Bradley Hall: kids who didn't want a smack in the mouth if they refused to come with him – and he'd roped in Acer Sweet, the weird woman's kid, and Charlie Henderson. He didn't know why the doctor's kid had come – they weren't mates – but he'd be a good one to get into trouble if the shit hit the fan.

Charlie did know why he'd gone with Revell: he'd seen Bradley dragged off and felt responsible for his friend. Charlie didn't think Bradley was easily led but knew a singer didn't need a punch in the mouth. There was a group of them now and Revell was leading them away from the crowd, into the dark beyond the glow of the fire, towards the old workhouse; the building, having been used at different times to rear pigs and then turkeys, was now being converted into a row of terraced houses, mews, flats and apartments. Richard thought it might offer new targets and new commotions.

The gang of boys was tense with excitement. Unsure what Revell intended, except that it would be "a bit of fun", they dodged stealthily towards the sprawl of a building; torches seeking the ground, they stumbled and fell until the building reared from the darkness, seemingly miles from those watching the fire and the fireworks. Regularly the sky was lit with a barrage of light, exploding into the blackness, and this only added to their sense of awe, their feeling of separation from those they knew and had known all their lives. They were alone in the dark night; it was an adventure.

One boy had not joined them and that was Sam Whitham. Seeing Charlie Henderson drawn off by Revell, Sam had followed, fearful for the reputation of the boy who had sometimes sat beside him at playtimes, the boy who had listened to the tale of his dad's ghost. But as he moved in pursuit, a hand grabbed him and Sam, turning to struggle against what was a forceful grasp, found himself looking up at the face of James Ryder.

"Mr Ryder?"

"Don't follow them, son. They're up to no good. You don't want to get involved."

"But my friend …"

"Your friend has made his choice. It doesn't have to involve you. Say hello to Rollie."

Sam wasn't sure afterwards why he hadn't objected to Ryder's suggestion, why he hadn't insisted on following Charlie, but at that moment his attention was taken by the dog whose tail was wagging and whose head was pushing forward into Sam's crotch. Sam couldn't resist the temptation and he knelt to stroke the Labrador.

"Stay with him, son. I won't be long," said the walker, and strode off into the distance.

Ryder had returned to Thornham the previous week, curious about his night-time visitor, Richard Gabriel, and more than curious about the gravestone he had found in the small church of All Saints: *Elizabeth Gabriel 1822 – 1864 Loving Mother RIP*. It seemed more than obvious that the woman buried beneath the very simple stone was Richard Gabriel's mother but who she was, why his attention had been drawn to her and how they might be related remained a mystery Ryder was determined to solve. He had a fortnight's holiday due to him and decided to spend the time in Thornham, where his landlord, Ned Douglas at The Swan, recommended the Burghamton Bonfire.

He had seen the Revell boy make off with the other children and recognised the name as that of the man who had accosted them by the staithe. Revell, the school bully, didn't seem a good companion for Sam Whitham and Ryder stepped in. When he returned it was with a couple of cheeseburgers, a beer for himself, a Pepsi for Sam and a hotdog for Rollie. The boy was saved, the night was theirs and they turned to watch the display.

Lured by the promise of excitement, especially excitement on the edge of the permissible is one thing: bringing it to fruition, quite another.

The gang had watched Revell shove the first jumping jack through the first letter box and had retreated into the darkness, torches covered, waiting, laughing, tight with fear; they'd watched as the houseowner had thrown open his door angrily and cursed them into the night. They'd laughed when Revell had pitched his first banger into the enclosed garden of the second house; they'd laughed when the cat screeched and leapt up on to the wall; they hadn't laughed when Revell tossed his second jumping jack onto the wall next to the cat.

It seemed even less funny when he turned and asked who was going to throw the third firework into the fun of the night. Revell instinctively knew that they all had to be involved, all culpable when the reckoning came. Bradley Hall backed down aided by Charlie Henderson, Acer Sweet drew away; Brian Gooch was centre stage, drawn in by the reluctance of the others to cross that line in the sand drawn by society, the line that told them what was and what was not acceptable fun, legitimate only in that they might get away with it once. Richard Revell had crossed that line and they had watched and felt bound to laugh; it was another thing to cross the line themselves.

Brian Gooch, almost wetting himself with fear and the impending shame of what he was to do, approached their third house, which was at the far end of a mews. It was the one house showing a light and the one chosen by Revell as most likely to bring the most fun. He lit the blue touch paper and retired, leaving Brian holding the firework. What might have happened then – whether Brian would have had the courage to pop the banger through the letter box or whether it would have exploded in his hand – was not to be known: at that moment, the houseowners, clothed for the cold, opened the door and stepped outside. Brian dropped the firework and it discharged in a melee of blue and yellow flame at the man's feet. He roared, gave chase and the boys ran, dispersed into the darkness, heading for the safety of their parents on the far side of the fire.

All but Richard Revell. Revell wasn't to be cowed. He was used to angry grownups. He'd known one all his life, and his father was handy with his fists into the bargain. His gang dispersed, Revell decided to have one more go – at least one more – for the sake of his street cred. At school on Monday, he'd make the others squirm remembering their cowardice, remembering they'd run away when he stayed to fight. It'd make him look good in Amy's eyes. He'd seen teachers off; he'd see this bloke off.

He waited in the darkness close to a curve in the wall, wondering where to strike next, when he noticed a gate further along. The gate was partly open, as though by way of invitation, and he thought he might see what was going on, if anything, on the other side. Perhaps the open gate should have been a warning – people living in posh houses like those in the converted workhouse weren't usually careless about what their money had brought them; but Revell wasn't disturbed. Not one to resist temptation, he pushed open the gate and stepped inside the garden beyond. In an enclosed space, the half-dozen bangers and jumping jacks he had left would make a right old din. If there was a cat or dog in the house, so much the better. He'd check that first, before he lit the fireworks. If only he had a rocket.

What happened next, Richard Revell never comprehended. The second he got inside, the first firework, which he held ready, and the box of matches were snatched from his hand and his coat pulled from his back. He turned to expostulate – no one had the right to treat him that way – and a bucket of cold water was slung over him; a night on the edge of freezing suddenly became a real threat. He was pushed to the ground, kicked, punched and thrown bodily out of the garden, the gate slamming-to behind him.

Squirming up from the wet grass, he turned to protest and saw a man watching him, a man whose face was quite impassive. He was standing in front of the gate he had closed and Revell knew at once, mainly by way he was dressed – the crushed top hat, the ill-fitting coat – that the man was not of this world: at least, not of this time. Richard Revell staggered to his feet and ran into the night.

Sam Witham left the Burghamton Bonfire as soon as the last firework exploded in the sky. Mr Ryder had asked him who he'd come with and how he was getting home and Sam had been instinctively worried. It wasn't that he didn't trust Mr Ryder. He liked him. He'd been nothing but kind and Sam felt he was genuinely interested in the old watermill. He was an engineer and Sam looked up to him as a man of the world. He wasn't sure what that phrase meant but he'd read it somewhere and it seemed to fit Mr Ryder.

No, it wasn't that he had doubts about Mr Ryder but he and his friends had been warned so often about *strangers*. Don't talk to *strangers*, don't trust anyone you don't know and beware of people you might know who offer you lifts in their cars. Don't put yourself in a position where you could be abused. *Beware of Strangers!*

He had made his excuses and thought Mr Ryder understood. He was sure Mr Ryder understood. He had smiled and told Sam to enjoy the rest of the evening. He had seemed worried when Sam told him he walked to the bonfire but he didn't press him to accept a lift home to Thornham.

And so, Sam began to walk back along the paths he had come.

He couldn't be seen like this. Fuck! He'd be a laughingstock. Dripping wet, freezing, fucking cold. His coat had been nicked. He felt a right, bloody idiot. Even swearing didn't liven him up.

Richard Revell was on the trail home, worried sick about what his father would do if he caught him without his coat, hoping his mother would be the one to meet him at the door. She never hit him; she never did anything; she was quiet as a mouse; but she was all right. It was a lonely trail on your own, stumbling along farm tracks, although the moon was bright and you could see your way.

He'd passed White Heath Farm – the place that had the barn where he and Amy Prentice had stopped off for a second time on the way to the bonfire – when he suddenly thought of her. How was she getting home? Never mind – she'd bum a lift off someone. He needed to get home before his dad got back from the pub and before he froze to death. Richard Revell wasn't one to think of other people: his needs were always uppermost in his mind.

He'd been a "blood nuisance" (a phrase he loved) all his life. There wasn't a class he hadn't disrupted, a teacher he hadn't got the better of, a school that hadn't excluded him. One of the older staff at his last school had said he'd "make his way through life spawning another generation of Richard Revells to plague the world". The boy himself hadn't heard the remark but would have been proud if he'd been lucky enough to be earwigging at the staffroom door, something he'd done in the past to the amusement of his mates.

He was passing through the woods that ran alongside the river when he saw the man standing in his path. It was the man in the funny gear who'd tipped the bucket of water over him. How the fuck had he got here? Richard Revell told himself he didn't lack courage – he could use his fists if he wanted – but he wasn't partial to ghosts. 'Partial to ghosts'! Where had he heard that phrase? One of his English teachers – yeah, that one: the sexy bitch he'd have liked to have stuffed.

It was gloomy under the trees, despite the moon. When he looked up again, the man had vanished. Perhaps he'd imagined it? He was so cold he could barely think. Once out of the woods, the track was clear to the road, close to the river but straight on to the road once he'd passed Mere House.

As you approached Mere House, standing alone by the side of a field was a door set into a wall. Nothing else: just the door and the piece of flint-faced wall. At one time, it must have been part of a farm labourer's cottage. Bit by bit the locals had taken away the flints and stones they wanted and left the door in the wall. The local kids used to play there, running in and out of the door. It was an old door, heavy and gnarled, but the knocker was still in place and it had been fun when he was young. No one ever asked why the locals had left the door; perhaps it tickled their sense of fun to have a door standing but leading nowhere?

Tonight, the door was open – half open – and Richard Revell paused in his tracks. He'd had enough of half-open doors. He was alone. He'd never been here alone before: he'd always had a mate or a tart with him. But now he was alone, abso-bloody-lutely alone. He stopped in his tracks and crouched under a horse chestnut tree, hiding himself amongst the pile of withered leaves, fungi and broken branches at its roots. He took hold of the trunk and waited, clutching for dear life. He had to admit it: he was afraid. Not the fear he felt with his dad: this was different. He shivered, and not only with the cold.

How long he knelt in the safety of the tree, Richard Revell wasn't sure, but eventually, inevitably he knew, he left what had been a hiding place and began to move in a crouch-like manner towards the door. Hr groped his way, fearful of standing in case he was seen. He was unable to explain this terror, this dread of being seen but it was there, deep within him. Cold, distressed, seeking a reassurance he could not understand, he stumbled and groped his way along the edge of the ploughed field, clutching at the blackthorn hedge, until the door rose before him, and he knocked. Knock-knock! Who's there? The door opened and he was pulled inside by the man he'd met by the bonfire.

"Remember me? No? I am William Quire. You will remember me."

Once more, Richard Revell was soaked in water, thrown to the ground, punched and kicked.

And then, struggling from the ground, he arrived back on the outside of the door. Once more, he knocked. Knock-knock! Who's there? Once more, he was yanked inside as soon as he crossed the threshold. Before him stood another man, dressed in rough, blue serge.

"Remember me? You will remember," and he held out a knife, not a knife Richard Revell had ever seen but one he seemed to know. He reached for it as though by right and the man retreated, back into the ground. Still, by the side of the door, holding it open in welcome, stood the man who had called himself William Quire.

Yet again, Richard Revell found himself knocking on the door. Knock-knock! Who's there? Yet again, he was tugged across the threshold. Before him reared the walls of what seemed to be a prison, and he was there, smashing glass, tearing at the wooden frames, laughing, while all around lay white-faced men and women, shivering in the cold blasts of winter air, pinning him against the destruction with their eyes.

"Remember us? Remember us? You will remember."

He didn't. He climbed down from the sill on which he'd strutted, while tearing out the windows. And the man, William Quire, watched him.

Again, he was knock-knock-knocking. Who's there? Again, he was across the threshold. This time he was the man!

"Where is she?"

It was his voice, one he hardly recognised. And what was he saying? Who was 'she'?

"Upstairs. She is upstairs," replied the man who was William Quire.

"I'm going to sleep with her."

"You'll do no such thing."

"I gave her threepence to sleep with her, and sleep with her I will."

"Remember me?"

It was a young woman, ill-dressed in little more than a slip despite the cold of the winter's night – because wherever Revell was that night, winter had arrived – hugging a child to her breast.

"Remember me? You will," and she retreated into the darkness beyond.

How long into that night and the early hours of the following day his interrogation continued, Richard Revell never knew. He was among ruffians singing obscene songs, cursing, swearing, bragging of some begging they'd done; he was kicking down another door, long ago, demanding entry into he knew not where; he was tearing clothes he'd been given, clothes he neither liked nor recognised; he was ripping apart bedding; he was turning bodies from their beds and searching their pockets ... and so the night went on. Knock-knock! Who's there? Punched and kicked and soaked, with mocking laughter all around him, echoing down time itself.

At last, he came to be wandering among gravestones, nothing but gravestones. Exhausted, he tried to rest on one but it vanished beneath him. He could hear his heart beating and felt his knees crumble. He staggered from the place with the noise of voices in his head but could understand nothing. Shaking to his bones with the fear and the cold, he eventually collapsed somewhere along the farm track, near to death and scared witless.

Chapter 2

Sons and Daughters

Alone, Sam Witham had been witness to that night – not to Richard Revell's torment but to the man on the road and to Revell himself from whom the younger boy had hidden. Revell had passed him on the track shortly after Sam saw the strange man, the one with the crushed top hat and the ill-fitting clothes and what looked like a walking stick or a cudgel in his right hand.

Sam then took another trail back to Thornham and sat wondering in his bedroom at the watermill what he should do. He couldn't say anything to his grandmother: she was still too distressed at the death of his grandfather. Should he talk to Ryder? He thought he might when morning came.

Gerald Henderson was the first to know. Called early from his bed next morning, he drove straight to the Revell's house where the father had insisted (against PC Sharpe's advice, urging that the boy should go straight to hospital) his son was to be taken home. It had been Cynthia Revell who reported Richard was missing, instigating the long search that followed.

Gerald Henderson brooked no arguments from Revell and called an ambulance immediately; with the boy's mother, he followed the ambulance to the Norfolk and Norbridge.

In her father's absence – not an unusual occurrence – Lottie saw to it that she and Charlie had breakfast and left to catch the school bus. She noticed her brother was quiet but said nothing: he'd reminded her several times that he "didn't need mothering".

Gossip buzzed in the playground: children who lived near the Revells had seen the police cars and the ambulance and heard their mothers' speculations. It was in the playground that Amy Prentice first heard the news: she may have been Richard's 'girlfriend' but no one, not even his parents, took that seriously.

Lottie Henderson was the first to comfort her; although in the same school year, the girls were not friends. Their destinies were poles apart and even at their age both girls, with the realistic wisdom of women, knew it. Bewildered looks passed between them as Amy talked and Lottie consoled.

"He left me at the bonfire. We were supposed to be going home together but he left me. Bab's dad took me home. Why did he go off like that?"

Barbara 'Babs' Wilton with her sister, Lucy, were among those who chipped in their concerns and worries. It was a time for worry; worries can be enjoyed when they are other people's and there was an element of this in the crowd that gathered around Amy.

"He was found in the road," said Lucy.

"How do you know that?" asked Amy.

"I don't know. My mum said."

"How did she know?"

"I don't know. She just did."

It was tittle-tattle, nothing more, and did nothing to comfort the girl.

One of those in the circle gathered around her was Anthemis Sweet, a girl who shared her mother's sharp intelligence and Vernon Scuffil's thirst for knowledge. Anthemis had already obliged her brother, Acer, to explain where he had "run off to" when they were at the bonfire; hearing the story of Richard Revell being found in the road, she began to wonder what was going on.

"Has your brother said anything?" she asked Lottie.

"Why would he?"

"He was one of those who went off with Revell."

"Don't call him that!" cried Amy.

"That's his name, isn't it?"

"His name's Richard."

Amy was right, of course, but everyone referred to him as 'Revell' for the same reason that his father was called only by his surname in a village, where everyone knew everyone else: nobody liked either of them, both instilled fears.

"Where did you go – this gang of yours?" asked Vernon of his stepson.

"It wasn't a gang," insisted Acer, but, nevertheless, he came out with the whole story.

"I'll speak with you, later, Acer," said his mother, Justine, when the boy had completed his confession, "In the meantime, you're telling us that once you'd all run off, you never saw this boy again? Be sure now."

"Never."

"Where did this story of him being found in the road come from – hmm?" asked Vernon.

"I don't know. It wasn't me!"

"No one said it was, Acer," said Anthemis, "It was most likely one of the women who live near the Revells and saw him brought home in the police car or taken away in the ambulance. Lucy Wilton said her mother was told that he was soaking wet and freezing cold when he was found."

"Do you think he fell in the mere?"

"It's not funny, Acer."

"No, it's not. Anthemis is right," snapped Justine, embarrassed by her son.

"Is it ringing bells with you, Vernon?" asked his stepdaughter who had always used his Christian name.

"It might be," replied Scuffil looked hard at the girl with respect in his eyes.

When her father arrived home that evening, Lottie, having squeezed the truth from her brother, was eager to have a word. She had never felt easy since the night he ran down the two young women at the lychgate. She simply knew her father had not been mistaken; that being so, the two young women had to be something supernatural. Call them ghosts if you must. What, then, had impelled Richard Revell to go back to Thornham alone, along a lonely road when he clearly intended to have Amy Prentice with him? Was something going on in and near Thornham that was unnatural – what she'd heard described as paranormal?

"We do not know, Lottie. The young man had been dowsed many times in water. He suffered hypothermia for many hours. He wasn't coherent. His mother has sat with him all day, and he raves. He talks of things that make no sense at all and, particularly, of a man who assaults him – a man he met on the road. I don't think you need to worry, dear, but let's have you home early as the nights draw in further."

"Why you, dad? Why was it you who ran those women down?"

"I've no idea, Lottie."

"What have you got in common with Richard Revell?"

"Apart from our common humanity, you mean?"

"I didn't mean to sound snobbish."

"You didn't. It's a natural enough question. One difference is that Richard has been left terrified. If the term 'horror-stricken' means anything at all, it describes the expression in that young man's eyes when, occasionally, they do open and he does talk."

Richard Revell was not destined to talk much more; on the very night of the day he was found, the young man, the bully, the scourge of younger children in the village, passed from this life, his mother at his bedside. His death certificate read 'hypothermia' as being the cause but those who were with him at the end, especially his grief-stricken mother, knew he had died from another cause: terror.

Another tear-stained face looked at herself in the mirror that night as she prepared herself for a bedtime without sleep; and as she watched her wretchedness in the glass another face looked out at her. Richard Revell might be dead but somewhere he was alive and well and watching his former girlfriend.

Chapter 3

Priest and Publican

Frederick Mackenzie did not hesitate to visit the Revells when the news of their son's death reached him the following morning. They were not a church-going family – far from it; the boy had attended the Junior Church but soon left without explanation. The priest had not followed it up; 'you can take a horse to water but …' seemed reason enough.

But that morning the boy's mother was glad of the comfort he offered and as he listened, he learned; in his ravings Richard Revell had talked of punches and kicks, soakings and knives, a door opening and closing, a man in a crushed hat, smashed glass and shattered window frames, white-faced women cursing him, a tart holding a baby, torn beds, stolen clothes, obscene songs and boastful beggars.

"Your boy was disturbed, Cynthia. He would not have known what he was saying. You mustn't dwell on these things. You have grief enough without them."

Words of comfort rather than a desire for the truth governed what Frederick said. He sat quietly for a long time, while the mother's grief was shared, spilled out into his ear. But Frederick was disturbed, knowing what he knew of the village, historically and recently. He remembered sitting in his church prior to blessing the Wilton's house; he recalled Marjory Bloom believing she had seen a man on Bridge Street following her husband's death; he was reminded of Elizabeth Beeston.

Leaving Cynthia Revell, once she was calmer and "more herself", and assuring her that he would "see to the arrangements",

Frederick made his way to the White Horse on a mission of an easier nature.

For several years, priest and publican had come together before Christmas time to organize a carol service at 'The Horse', as the place was called in the village. A certain humour, shared by both men, lay behind this idea – that God's word should find its voice in a public house – and the humour had been part of the success of the occasion, one enjoyed by all and attracting, among others who did not normally frequent the pub, the Thorn Valley Singers.

It was easily arranged over a pint or two of Adnams's Ghost Ship, the two men enjoying each other's company in the snug area by the fire, and their conversation, lubricated by the beer, drifted into the topics of the day. July Pegg, Simon's cherished daughter, had come home full of excitement over what had been said at school the previous day.

"The children seem to think that the boy was drowned."

"It would be good to dispel that rumour, Simon. It can only cause Mrs Revell further grief – unnecessary grief because it's untrue."

"But he was found soaked to the skin?"

"Yes, I'm afraid so."

"It wasn't a wet night – no sign of rain. Just freezing cold. It's always cold on Bonfire Night and Remembrance Sunday. Have you noticed?"

Frederick had noticed: watching Cubs and Brownies, Guides and Scouts standing ready with their flags and banners, he'd wondered whether God would want them waiting in the cold, but their faces were always cheerful even if they looked frozen, and it gave him the chance to talk to them directly from the pulpit. Not that he ever talked to children from the pulpit: he always walked and talked among them; one reason for the success of his ministry.

He decided to confide in Simon Pegg, who he admired as a family man, a power in the community and an important figure in the life of his village – a caring man, one who took the trouble to be involved. Moreover, publicans were privy to a huge amount of gossip and chatter denied to most other people, especially priests. He shared his thoughts, carefully.

"You talk as though you think the village might be haunted, Fred."

"It's a thought."

"You're serious."

"Yes."

Simon didn't like to ask what the church's view was on ghosts and spirits: he rather thought it would be discouraging. The faithful found peace with God when they passed on; Simon couldn't think the church wanted them wandering around in the netherworld. As for the others, he wasn't sure.

"Have you come across anything, Simon?"

"A great deal and nothing, really," replied the landlord, and related to Frederick what had been said in the pub following the parish council meeting in September.

"This man Kent. What makes you say he was 'odd'?"

"The way he was dressed, mainly – waistcoats with watch and chain aren't common these days – and the way we all felt after he left. Even Jack Dorling said the bloke made his blood run cold, and you know what a placid man Jack is."

"And this 'afterwards'?"

"Ah, that was a story Juniper Wells was talking about – just fiction."

"What did you make of Dr Henderson's experience?"

"Tired, overworked. He's a good doctor. I bet he gets home exhausted most nights."

"I imagine that applies to you as well, Simon. How many women have you knocked down on the way home?"

Simon Pegg laughed and looked at his watch, suddenly. He was relaxed in the clergyman's company and had forgotten the time; they had been talking for over an hour.

"Am I keeping you?"

"No, no."

"But I am, and you've a pub to run. It's been nice talking with you but you've lines to clear and meals to serve."

It was true: not the beer lines – Simon had cleared those earlier – but today was Sunday and the usual roasts brought in a large crowd. Several roast meats accompanied by the appropriate sauce or stuffing and the vegetarian alternative – all served with roasted potatoes and parsnips, carrots, broccoli and cauliflower cheese, fine green beans and a Yorkshire pudding – took time, love and a toll on the staff.

And Simon liked to be in there, hands on, with an eye to his favourite desserts: apple crumble with custard, New York cheesecake with fresh berries or chocolate fudge cake, both with pouring cream.

Simon had a sweet tooth and, also, an eye for business. He and Catriona had made a success of the White Horse, and choosing appropriate events was his metier. His talk with Fred Mackenzie was on his mind as he served his guests that lunchtime and when the last meals had been cleared and the pub was emptying he made a phone call.

A fellow landlord who ran a pub in Norbridge had experimented with what he called Psychic Suppers; these involved two sessions with a local medium and a three-course meal, all at £29.95. Catriona had attended one and was quite taken with the outcome: an elderly aunt whose funeral she'd missed (due to her being in labour with Bruce) had got in touch and wished her well. At least, that was what the medium, Saul Tacksman, had said and he certainly described her aunt to a tee. Simon estimated that counting the drinks people would buy to accompany the meal he would pull in at least £40 a head.

Simon was a people-person and wanted a face-to-face word with the medium, rather than relying on a phone call, and so it was arranged that they would meet at the White Horse the following Wednesday.

Saul Tacksman didn't immediately appeal to Simon. He arrived looking the worse for wear and sweating profusely. He wore an open overcoat over an old tweed jacket over a shabby pullover; these he pulled off as soon as they were seated, dropping them over a neighbouring chair and sitting in his shirt sleeves. Once seated and offered a drink he chose green grenadine topped up with soda water; the resulting syrup looked like something one might find in decaying vegetables and the cherry Simon insisted on adding did not add to the look of the drink. His hair was all over the place, as though it hadn't seen a comb for weeks, and his eyes were drawn and bloodshot.

Saul Tacksman did apologise, however, explaining that he had "undertaken" – a carefully chosen word, Simon thought – two seances in the past twenty-four hours and that they were a drain on his psychic energies. Simon – somewhat dubious about the credibility of the whole business and wanting to laugh – said he understood perfectly; the previous evening, Catriona had been quite forceful in telling him to "take it seriously".

"So, you would provide a séance in the pub, would you?" asked Simon, "I'm thinking about how we might arrange the tables to get enough people in to make it worthwhile – make it worth your time, I mean," he added, hastily, "and still get enough people round to make the séance possible."

"I don't think you understand, Mr Pegg," replied the medium., "What I shall be holding here are called readings, not seances. I had better explain.

The word séance comes from the French 'sitting'. A group of people will sit, usually around a circular table, palms down with the tips of their little fingers touching on either side to form a chain of energy. A lighted candle is placed in the centre of the table – the flickering of the flame will indicate the movement of the spirits. Everyone closes their eyes and empties their minds, while the medium recites a prayer of invocation and protection. You see, it is impossible to predict what sort of spirits will come to the group: some may be harmful. Once contact is made with the spirit world, anyone can talk to them or ask questions of them."

Saul Tacksman was so deadly serious that it took away Simon's scepticism. He had not expected the man to be in such earnest; suddenly, what had appealed as rather a jolly evening took on a different tone.

"You understand," continued Saul Tacksman, "that this will not be possible with the numbers you envisage. I shall undertake two readings in your restaurant, one after the main course and the other at the end of the evening, after your staff have served coffee and everyone is settled. Only I shall be in direct contact with the spirit world; they will speak to me and I shall pass their concerns on to the people they wish to contact. Not everyone will be contacted – make people understand that fact. I have no control over which spirits will want to be heard."

At home that night, Simon relayed what had been agreed to his wife, Catriona.

"I told you he was good. You ought to know, Simon, that some of the readings can be distressing. He was contacted by the mother of three sisters who were sitting next to me at the last one and these women were in tears – in fact, he asked if he should stop. He felt he had misjudged the situation and that the mother's spirit was imparting information the women couldn't handle. The father had been an unpleasant man in life, but this had never been acknowledged by the sisters or the mother. She was now telling them she had known all along that their father was unfaithful to her. They had no idea how they were going to handle that news when they met him again. It was very upsetting."

Simon Pegg, listening to his wife, wondered what he might have set in motion.

His concerns were shared by Frederick Mackenzie, sitting in his study, having spoken with Simon on the telephone earlier. He'd approached Simon for information and to share thoughts; he never envisaged the landlord moving into the realms of spiritualism. The Church had instigated an investigation into just that subject as far back as 1939. Several eminent people had been involved, including the Bishop of Bath and Wells and the Dean of St Paul's.

Frederick had a copy. It read like a traditional Anglican document: its intention being to offend no one. The assertion that:

> ... *the accounts sometimes given of the mediatorial work of Christ frequently fall very far below the full teaching of the Christian gospel, seeming to depend rather upon some power of working a miracle of materialisation* ...

seemed nicely countered by:

Nevertheless, it is clearly true that the recognition of the nearness of our friends who have died, and of their progress in the spiritual life and of their continuing concern for us, cannot do otherwise, for those who have experienced it, than add an immediacy and richness to their belief in the Communion of Saints

Was the report condemning the practice, supporting it or simply seeing both sides? Frederick felt he had no doubt of the answer to that question but this knowledge didn't offer him immediate assistance.

He read on:

There seems to be no reason at all why the Church should regard this vital and personal enrichment of her central doctrines with disfavour, so long as it does not distract Christians from their fundamental gladness that they may come, when they will, into the presence of their Lord and master, Jesus Christ Himself, or weaken their sense that their fellowship is fellowship with Him.

The tone now seemed to be categorically in favour of keeping an open mind and, moreover, encouraging such activities as Simon Pegg was proposing – and yet, Frederick had come across the activities of mediums who were anything but spiritual in their outlook, men and women who sought to grow rich in their control of people struck down by grief:

It is strongly urged that if we do not accept the evidence for modern psychical happenings, we should not ... accept the Gospel records either. It is certainly true that there are quite clear parallels between the miraculous events recorded in the Gospel and modern phenomena attested by Spiritualists. And if we assert that the latter must be doubted because they have not yet proved capable of scientific statement and verification, we must add that the miracles, and the Resurrection itself, are not capable of such verification either.

And here, again, was a clear statement that these hauntings – if that is what they were – could not be simply written off as nonsense, unless one was to do the same for what might also be called the 'paranormal' events in the Bible. And the writers of this document were priests, men of high intellectual calibre who had every reason to cast strong doubt on those who claimed to be in touch with the spirit world and the motives of those who claimed to have seen these apparitions.

Frederick stood and walked to the window of his study that overlooked their back garden. It led down across a field where a local farmer kept sheep in the summer months and, eventually, to the water meadows where cows grazed and where local gypsies brought mares to foal. In his own garden, at the very bottom, were his beehives – not his, exactly: they belonged to Jack Dorling's daughter, Juniper Wells, who owned and cared for them and shared her honey for the use of the land.

He did not believe because of '*demonstrable scientific evidence*', as the report went on to point out; his beliefs were based on faith. His grounds for his faith were not mystical – not for him the Road to Damascus – but, more simply, on his apprehension of the ethical and spiritual values contained in the Gospels. He did not accept the Gospels because they recorded wonders but because they rang true to his deepest powers of spiritual apprehension.

His mind clearer, he went back to the report and read further:

... it is not legitimate, and it is unquestionably dangerous, to allow an interest in Spiritualism, at a low level of spiritual value, to replace that deeper religion which rests fundamentally upon the right relation of the soul to God Himself

The view has been held, with some degree of Church authority, that psychic phenomena are real but proceed from evil spirits.

His mind was made up; he was at peace with himself and his God. He would attend Simon's Psychic Supper; he had a duty to attend; it now only remained to persuade his wife, Jacqueline, that this was a good idea and to hope she would agree.

Chapter 4

Psychic Supper

Jacqueline Mackenzie did agree and, furthermore, persuaded him that he ought to begin keeping an account of the events in which he was involved. Jacqueline was a great diary-keeper; every moment of her day noted, if not in a diary then on a planner.

Whereas her husband had come to his faith quietly and thoughtfully, Jacqueline had arrived suddenly as a Born-Again Christian, one of those people often referred to as a Happy-Clappy, usually, if not always, by atheists. Like many converts, she was enthusiastic and eager to lead others to the Truth as she saw it. Frederick had calmed her down, pointing out many times that "people are caught, not taught". She did not agree with him, explaining that "a person broken by Jesus, stays broken"; she used the term 'broken' as meaning broken to the faith.

It was not a term Frederick liked but he accepted his wife's sincerity. She in turn extended an understanding towards his needs as a priest, an understanding that marked much of their married life.

Edward Warburg and Myles Langstroth approached the Psychic Supper in quite a different, although shared, frame of mind. Neither man had particularly strong religious views; in Edward's case, the Church was something he admired and appreciated; in Myles's, something he tolerated. Edward had been brought up in the faith: a village without a church was something he could not imagine. Myles, although born in a Norfolk village, had skipped what was then called Sunday School as often as possible.

For both men – the composer and the singer – the Church offered an outlet for their creativity and their artistry. For both men, this was quite good enough.

Carmen, who ran the Quay Café, was Spanish by descent and a Roman Catholic by birth: she attended St John's, a small church on Edmund's Lane. Her friend, Belfast Billy, was, as his name suggested, from Northern Ireland and had been raised as a Protestant, although he had nothing whatever against Catholics in general and huge admiration for one in particular.

Mildred Ackroyd had been a convinced atheist all her life, considering what the Church had to offer was nothing more than "paganism in fancy dress". Her prime concern, approaching the occasion, was that she had been obliged by her friend, Amelia Pritchard, to attend at all. Miss Pritchard's "you may learn something" was countered by Mildred's "it's nothing more than hocus-pocus, Amelia".

Cynthia Revell had come under threat: Revell didn't want her to go. She'd waited until he left for the pub, hoping he'd return so plastered that he wouldn't notice she'd been out at all. On the way, she had met Marjory Broome and the two women, one elderly and the other barely out of her youth (at least, in years), entered the White Horse together.

Propping up the bar, they met Juniper Wells, two pints in hand, one being for her father, Jack, who was sitting talking to Gerald Henderson. Juniper nodded a smile and passed on, and Simon Pegg, aware that neither woman was familiar with the pub, approached them with his usual welcoming smile and wondering what they would like to drink.

The White Horse was heaving with customers; Simon could not have been more pleased. He was a good boss and, therefore, kept a loyal staff. They mixed and mingled with the customers, taking orders for further drinks and ensuring that lone people were not left alone and without conversation. Mildred Ackroyd, for one, appreciated the thoughtfulness.

Among the villagers, his backside to the fire in the snug area, was James Ryder. He'd been keeping an eye on Thornham and heard of the event. Keen to know more of the Gabriels and possibly to hear from his guest of that first evening in the village back in September, Richard Gabriel, he decided to attend. The bonfire night had taught him nothing; perhaps the Psychic Supper would prove to be different.

One by one, group by group, those looking forward to the evening were guided to their seats in the restaurant until the bar area emptied and was still. It was at that moment, Saul Tacksman arrived with his partner, who always took notes of his Readings for those visited.

Gerald Henderson – ordering quietly a bottle of Valpolicella for his table (he wanted to treat Jack Dorling and his daughter) – caught sight of the medium, pacing back and forth, downing a glass of the green liquid he drank while arranging the session with Simon. Tacksman looked quickly away when their eyes met and, curious as to why, the doctor introduced himself. The medium was already perspiring furiously and, when Gerald removed his hand from the shake, which he'd insisted upon, his palm was ringing wet. The medium's eyes were glazed and shining. It was almost as though the man was exuding moisture from every pore in his body. Gerald was reminded of the stories he'd read of Victorian seances, where a green substance called ectoplasm was often said to discharge from the medium.

When the doctor left for his meal, Tacksman collapsed at the bar and the barmaid slid another of the green drinks across the counter without his asking; his partner, Veronica Clud, accepted a glass of sparkling water, explaining that she needed a clear head to take notes of the Readings. In her company, Tacksman relaxed, his head bowed, looking up only to acknowledge Simon, who had come to see how his guest was feeling.

The landlord was excited. He had not expected such an enthusiastic take-up of his idea, but the book had been filled within twenty-four hours and he saw the chance to maximise on the interest by organising the same event, perhaps monthly. Simon was aware that people's fascination with spiritualism sprang from anything but religious motives, as Fred Mackenzie had taken the trouble to explain during their telephone conversation, when the landlord outlined what he planned. It was more often, the vicar felt, an interest in the bizarre, the appeal of the unorthodox, which stimulated their curiosity. He'd also heard that it could be dangerous: unbalancing the mentally fragile and, for some, reaching dead relatives became an obsession. But not at the White Horse! A light touch was what was needed: a delicate finger on the pulse and a sense of humour.

Back in the restaurant, Simon watched as his customers, most of whom were also friends, enjoyed their starters and main courses.

Mildred Ackroyd had chosen to sit with Gerald Henderson and Jack Dorling, together with his daughter, Juniper Wells, who she found fascinating. Mildred had dispatched, and approved, his chilled pea and chervil soup with crème fraiche, and was tucking into the roasted salmon and artichokes as though wartime rationing had just come to an end.

Simon was over the moon. It would soon be time. His customers were well fed and watered: full stomachs brought satisfaction and alcohol oiled the works. He rubbed his hands and cruised through to the bar to fetch Saul Tacksman.

When the medium entered the dining room, the atmosphere changed from one of enjoyable feasting to one of serious intent. Tacksman leaned forward, his body hanging from his waist as though what he carried in his mind was heavy indeed and weighed him forward. When he spoke, it was with a voice that sounded reassuring and reasonable.

"The spirit world is on a different frequency to ours. As a medium, I have been able to tap into this frequency. I can slow the frequency down. This is not something I have learned, but something I have been given and so I can hear the spirits more clearly. If any of you suffer from a loss of hearing, you will know that the slower someone speaks, the easier it is to understand what they say. It's like that with the spirits; they have learned to slow down their frequency – their sound waves – so that they can communicate.

Let me be clear and say that I cannot control who comes through. Not everyone here tonight will receive a message. Those who have recently passed may not have learned how to slow the sound waves ..."

Cynthia Revell looked across her table at Marjory Broome, her eyes tearful. She'd come to the pub tonight desperate to hear from her son. Whether he observed her sadness or whether he intended to offer some hope, anyway, Saul Tacksman continued:

"Some spirits make their presence felt in other ways: by a remembered smell, by a touch as they pass by ..."

At the thought of being touched, Myles cast a glum glance towards Edward, who raised one eyebrow in acknowledgment rather than disturb the others at their table by answering his friend. They had joined Fred and Jacqueline Mackenzie and had been joined by Ryder and another man who nobody seemed to know and who had introduced himself as John Thomkins when he asked if he might sit with them.

"Some spirits offer only odd phrases. I seldom make sense of what they say. This is where you who knew them in life can be helpful. Try to piece together what is said ... Someone is coming through. There's a rush. He's eager to get to the front. Pushing his way. Ambrose! Does that name mean anything to anyone? The lady over there at the corner table. I have this for you. Does Ambrose ... I think it's Ambrose ... Arthur ... is it Arthur ...?

"Ambrose – no, Ambrose, my Ambrose," cried Marjory Broome.

"He says you're not to worry," continued the medium, "He say he's all right but it wasn't an accident ...Do you know what this means?"

"Yes, yes! I knew it! I said he would never have gone onto that bridge ..."

"Your husband enjoyed a drink, didn't he?"

"Yes! He'd been here at the White Horse but he never came home drunk ..."

"He says he wasn't drunk ... There's a child ... Is there a child?"

"Sam, but Sam was in bed. I know ..."

"No. This child is a girl. He says ... I can see a bridge. It's a small bridge and it's broken. No, no it's not broken. Ambrose is on the bridge. The child, the girl, is running ahead of him. He's following her ..."

"I knew, I knew. I don't understand. Ambrose wouldn't chase a child, let alone a girl."

"He's not chasing her. She's calling him. Calling him – does that make sense?"

"No, no, nothing makes sense. Is he all right?"

Marjory Broome was in tears; sorrow and grief fell from her eyes. Cynthis Revell put both her arms around the older woman's shoulders.

"He is all right," continued Saul Tacksman, "He says not to worry. He's going now and I'm going over there ..."

The medium pointed towards the far end of the room where the priest's group sat.

"You, sir, the gentleman in the tweed jacket ..."

John Thomkins stood and looked around the room.

"Me?" he asked.

"Yes, you're coming through very strongly ... no, it can't be ... you ...there's a basement somewhere. Are you in a basement? Does that mean anything?"

"It might."

"It helps if you just answer yes or no ... it's dark and there's a stone floor, beds and sheets and there are shirts grey with dirt ... I've never experienced a Reading in this way before. It's very clear ... There's a crowd of people and you're waiting ... waiting for ... I can't see it ..."

"A ticket?" suggested John Thomkins.

"Yes, there's a man and he's waiting for a ticket ... it's a miserable place ... it's sad ... there are nurses – nurses in black caps and ... Some of these people are sick and the nurses ..."

"Do nothing?"

"There's an old woman ... she must be over sixty ... don't go near that bed ... there's a man on the bed and he's swarming with vermin ... distress and misery ... I'm sorry. You must excuse me for a moment."

Veronica Clud, obviously bewildered, her face showing clearly that nothing like this had ever happened before, looked up from her notes at the medium and rushed after him as he hurried from the room. John Thomkins followed, leaving Simon wondering how on Earth he might salvage his first Psychic Supper.

"The desserts!" he said, quickly, "Serve the desserts!" and followed Saul Tacksman.

In the bar, the medium was hunched over the counter, another green drink in his grasp. Beside him stood John Thomkins.

"You did well," he said to the medium, "Very well."

"You cannot channel yourself through me, whoever you are. I will not allow it. You cannot penetrate me unless I give permission."

"You misjudged the situation."

"I pulled away in time."

"I spoke through you. They needed to know."

"We needed them to know," said another voice.

The man who spoke emerged from the snug, where he had been sitting comfortably ensconced at the old table under the dart board – the man who had introduced himself as 'Kent', when the parish council gathered by the pub fire following their meeting. He greeted Simon with a knowing smile and turned to the medium.

"You have served us well, Mr Tacksman, and we are grateful. But you are exhausted now and ..."

"You possessed me?"

"We spoke through you."

"No. I will not allow that to happen. I have the resources to come back into my own body."

"You never left it, Mr Tacksman. You are tired – rest now. We wish you a good evening."

With a curt inclination of his head, Kent motioned to the other man, apparently his friend, and they walked from the White Horse and out into the night, leaving Simon more nonplussed than ever.

"Are you all right, love?" asked Veronica, moving to Tacksman and placing a firm, fat arm round his shoulders to comfort him.

"It takes a while to recover. I'm all right."

"Several days, sometimes," said Veronica to Simon, "He loses his appetite and has trouble sleeping."

"Not at my Readings, Mr Pegg. I didn't expect this. This doesn't usually happen. This was very negative – the energy, I mean. I must go back and … and comfort your people."

"If you feel up to it," replied Simon, not really meaning what he said, just hoping to salvage the evening.

In the restaurant, the desserts had been served and Simon was quick to offer "coffee on the house", by way of an apology, and conversation – disturbed but excited – filled the room.

Myles tackled Frederick on the subject of religion and spiritualism, more by way of provocation than out of any interest, but the vicar seized his opportunity.

"There is among many Christians a hesitancy to have anything to do with it," said Frederick, glancing at his wife, in case she was about to offer an opinion, "but we must face the fact that if spiritualism does have so strong an appeal it is, at least in part, because the Church has not proclaimed its faith with sufficient conviction. Spiritualism claims to be making accessible a reality that the Church has proclaimed but of which it seems only to offer a shadow."

"I take your point, Fred," replied Edward, feeling sorry to hear the priest on the defensive, "but I am more given to the belief that spiritualism has to do with the here and now rather than the afterlife."

"That is so, Fred," joined in Myles, supporting his friend and feeling slightly sorry he had raised the issue, "Modern psychology has revealed a wide range of powers in our subconscious minds. I feel spiritualism has its basis in us – in powers we possess but fail to understand rather than in anything spiritual."

"You are saying that what Mr Tacksman claims to see and hear comes from him rather than any incarnate spirits?" asked Jacqueline.

"Yes, I suppose I am," replied Myles, taken aback at the being challenged on a subject to which he'd given little thought.

"I must disagree," argued Jacqueline, "I cannot explain what happened here tonight but that man who sat at our table was not human – not in the way you and I are human – and he was leading Mr Tacksman, and not the other way around. John Thomkins was here with a purpose. I don't know what his purpose was but it was devilish."

Listening to this exchange of views, James Ryder subdued the urge to contribute his own experience with Richard Gabriel to the conversation, but it was relevant. He knew it was relevant and that sooner or later he must speak or act.

Back in the restaurant, shaken but determined, Saul Tacksman sought to calm his guests and retrieve his evening.

"I'll be honest with you," he began, "I am not clear about what happened earlier this evening," stressing 'earlier' as though it referred to another time and place. "I am clairvoyant but not in the way things occurred this evening. With Readings, I hear; I do not see. Tonight, twice, I saw – the bridge and then the basement. The psychic energies are strong here, and I would like to open myself to those spirits who want to come through … again, with your permission."

Saul Tacksman didn't wait for an answer; he didn't want one.

"Let us close our eyes and open our minds … and wait. If the spirits want to come through, they will … The gentleman over there. Yes, you sir. You're Irish. Am I right?"

"You wouldn't be far wrong," replied Belfast Billy, with a chuckle and a nod to his table companions, Cynthia Revell and Marjory Broome, and a wink to his partner, Carmen Quay, "it's not often I'm mistaken for an Englishman."

Laughter around the room; Saul Tacksman, deadly serious.

"You have a strong auric field, sir."

"Would that be good for mushrooms?" whispered Billy to Carmen who gave him a hard shove with her elbow.

"There's a lady linking in here. In her nineties. A strong lady … She was muddled towards the end … She says you should have more of her things ... You did everything you could ... William – is that a brother?"

"It was my father's name."

"South Africa. I'm getting South Africa."

Carmen looked up at Billy, her hand reached for his arm.

"And Lillian, is it? Or is it Lorna?"

"Lorna was my sister – is my sister."

"Mum sends her love ... Your wife got on well with her, didn't she, but she likes your new companion ... There's healing for your back and that left knee ..."

Billy's face had lost its look of blithe humour. His back had troubled him for years and the knee he'd pulled on a long walk, and it now troubled him to even get up the stairs.

"Some of her china should have been yours. Royal Worcester. Duck egg blue. Be careful with it, she says ... There's been a break-up in the family. But she's proud of you and knows you're proud of her ... She's going now but you should get the smell of flowers ..."

Saul Tacksman looked away, as though pulled, and moved his attention across the room.

"I'm over there now. The lady in the floral dress ..."

Billy was in tears, Carmen's arm around him. How in God's name did this man know his father had deserted the family – gone off to South Africa? And the row with his sister? It was all over years ago.

And so, the evening wore on, bringing comfort to some, distress to others. When it ended, Veronica handed out the notes she had made and Saul moved among his guests, listening and talking, trying to reassure where he could.

Cynthia Revell was among the latter; in tears she poured out her story and her sorrow.

"Do you remember I said earlier that the spirits have learned to slow down their frequency – their sound waves – so that they can communicate?"

Cynthia nodded.

"Those who recently passed, like your son, may not have learned how to do it yet. Give your son time. He will come through to comfort you."

"You will be coming back?"

"I hope so. You must ask Mr Pegg. But remember, some spirits are not in this world all the time, but just return now and again to see loved ones or to visit places that were important to them in life."

"Do you do private readings?" asked Marjory Broome.

"I do, if that is what you want, but I cannot guarantee your loved ones will come through. I cannot make them. It is what they want."

"Yes, yes, I understand."

"Your Ambrose was very keen to reach us. I think what he was trying to say was a warning. I think we need to listen to him. He was trying to help."

Saul Tacksman was not the only troubled person who left the White Horse later that evening, braving the cold wind of the November night, knowing he needed a word with someone.

In James Ryder's case, on the way to his room at The Swan, he paused at the staithe to look at the bridge across the marina and to feel the autumn leaves rustle beneath his feet; but his mind was on what Jacqueline Mackenzie has said and Ryder knew he must speak with the vicar, sooner rather than later.

Chapter 5

Beyond Care

Amelia Pritchard had *not* been keen on her companion, Mildred Ackroyd, going to the Psychic Supper that evening; she had felt, quite simply, that it was the right thing to do – both for her and for Mildred. There was a considerable difference between what one *wanted* to do and what one *ought* to do; it was simply a question of expectation.

Standing under their porch – she always thought of it as *their* porch, as distinct from *her* porch or just *the* porch – she had waved Mildred goodbye and watched her friend walk stubbornly along the road from their little hamlet of Cookley to the White Horse, a distance of, perhaps, a mile or so. 'Stubbornly' because Mildred could quite easily have called a taxi. It was a dark road at the best of times and the night was cold, not frosty but chilly, an unpleasant chill, one she thought rather spiteful; but then, it was the end of November, and one must expect the weather to deteriorate with the season.

Once Mildred had disappeared from view, Amelia sat down to listen to some of Mr Britten's seascapes. It was a long time since she had talked with Edward or Myles and she missed their conversation; perhaps one evening during the winter she and Mildred would invite them round. They were delightful people and such an asset to the village.

It was always cosy in their little parlour and Amelia was soon dozing, sitting in her armchair close to the fire, but still listening to the sound of the sea as it broke on the Suffolk shore, blown in by an easterly wind. *"What harbour shelters peace, away from tidal waves, away from storms? What harbour can embrace terrors and tragedies?"* The words of the opera came as her mind wandered back to the years of her youth. She had found peace and a safe harbour at Thornham.

The village had been attractive because her family owned farming land nearby, land and a few cottages that had once been the homes of labourers. It was in Thornham she met Mildred, who was secretary at Cookley Independent School and whose husband had been kind enough to undertake a number of small jobs about the house; another bonus had been the fact that Mildred was involved with Saxstead Opera. When Mildred's husband passed on – a comforting phrase – it seemed natural for the two women to make a home together. They talked endlessly but never pointlessly – Mildred was such a cultured woman; her mind was always active – and Amelia saw her final years as ones of contentment.

It was in this state of mind she thought she heard the knock on the door. Strange because no one ever called this late in the evening. Amelia struggled from her armchair – it was a struggle because her arthritis was getting no better – and made her way across *their* parlour to the door, which she opened without a thought for her safety. There was no one in the porch. It was not a relief: it was a worry. Amelia was sure she heard a knock. Knock – knock-knocking! Who's there? No one. It couldn't be children – not his far out of the village, and the Cookley boarders would be in their dormitories, by now.

Amelia sighed. Going out to check something so trivial seemed a million and more miles from her work in the WAAF during the War: almost not worth the bother. But she bothered; her generation always bothered. Perhaps it was their curse; perhaps a more relaxed attitude would have served them better. But then, they would never have defeated Nazi Germany. She stepped outside, leaving the door open behind her because she had no key – not on her person: they always kept the spare one on a hook by the door.

It was cold, and she had forgotten her coat – no, not forgotten. She had not expected to be out so late. Amelia walked round *their* home to the back where the garden overlooked the fields her family had once owned and the orchard, which still belonged to her. It was then she saw the figure cross the orchard, go along the rear of *their* garden and walk into *their* house by the side door, and so to the drawing room.

The thought appalled her; it was beyond endurance. Who was this woman that she had the temerity to treat their home as if she owned it? It was the old woman who she had seen sitting on her bed; Amelia had no doubt. Not daunted – indeed, angry – she followed. The figure took up its position opposite the settee in the bow window. She watched Amelia enter the room. Amelia felt she was expected to sit on the couch and listen. For a moment or so the two women watched each other; both seemed keen for the other to make the first move.

When Amelia said nothing but gazed at the woman as she once gazed at the enemy, the figure moved away, passing out through the garden door. Amelia sighed with relief and doubted herself. She wasn't afraid, was she? Why had the woman come again and why, then, had she vanished? Her determination had been tempered by reluctance. Amelia was sure this was so. But she was driven. Amelia was sure of that, also.

She went suddenly cold and remembered she had left the front door open. Looking outside, she felt the coming frost in the air.

"Who are you?" she cried, her voice unexpectedly hoarse, "I think I know why you've come. I saw what you wanted me to see last time. It's been on my mind over many years but ... I don't feel responsible. How can I? The Vicar was very astute, wasn't he? 'Did she have something on her mind that triggered a memory in yours?' he said. That was his question to me, and he knew ... An awful thing about growing old is that one remembers what one might have done better; one lingers on regrets rather than successes. I'm sure that is so. But it was a regret in the family. I remember my grandparents talking about it when I was a child ..."

Amelia shivered; she really was cold now and she was rambling, her mind going back generations, even before her time. She shut the door and went back to her chair by the fire. It was warmer there, but Mr Britten's music had lost its charm.

Now, near her time, she seemed more strongly connected to her family's past than she had ever been in a life spent very much in the present. Amelia hadn't been one to dwell on regrets – hers or those of others.

There was determination in the air and Amelia felt it gathering around her: the woman had grown bold again and was determined to communicate. By the warmth of the fire, she felt safe but the rest of their house – *their house* – unexpectedly became alien. On the stairs she heard footsteps and they were coming down to her. With the footsteps there was another sound, a faint sound as though something, someone, was being dragged. And then, a thump; and all was still and the silence was unbearable.

When Amelia gathered herself together, sufficiently to be able to move, she became aware that the woman was standing behind her armchair. Without looking up – she didn't want to see the face – she said:

"You've come to keep a promise, haven't you?"

"Honor Sheen," said a voice.

"Yes, I know. I have read the account. Sixty-six years old – Mildred's age – much younger than me. She dragged herself across the floor, didn't she, and collapsed? 'A serious bowel condition' was what was written on the death certificate."

"It was neglect," replied the voice, quite impassively as though its time had come.

"Yes. 'Unfit to have the management of the sick'. I have read the report of the inquest."

"She complained of feeling ill ..."

"I know! I know!"

Amelia felt a hand upon her shoulder. It tightened for a moment and then the grip was relaxed: the ghost's business was finished.

When Mildred Ackroyd arrived home from the Psychic Supper, she found her friend sitting by the fire; she had been dead only a short time, her body still warm, the expression on her face one of ineffable sorrow. Mr Britten's *Sea Interludes* were still playing.

Mildred supposed her friend had the CD on continuous play. It was *Moonlight*, an unsettling blend of motion and stasis: nothing at rest. Mildred turned off the player.

"Amelia was old, of course," she said to Dr Henderson, when he arrived, "but she wasn't ready for death – not yet. I know. What will you write on the death certificate?"

Gerald Henderson did not reply. His own world had been shaken that evening: twice in just a few months might not be a coincidence.

"I'll have a word with Fred," he said, by way of avoiding the question and by way of offering a hand.

He wasn't sure what to write, but 'old age' seemed the safest bet: there had been nothing wrong with Miss Pritchard's heart.

Chapter 6

The Man at the 'Séance'

Gerald Henderson spoke with Frederick Mackenzie on his way home, but he didn't tell him everything. He wasn't ready to share too much of his personal life yet – at least, not until he had spoken with his children – Lottie, in particular: he didn't know how Charles would take it.

*

Frederick Mackenzie had proved his usual helpful self: he had been to comfort Mildred Ackroyd and had phoned the undertakers, a well-established firm in the village. Malcolm Francis, who owned the enterprise had been seeing to the last needs of Thornham residents since 1934: he was now eighty-four but bespoke funerals with kindness and compassion were the order of the day, each day and every day.

Frederick now sat at the desk in his study hoping to complete his regular article for the church magazine, a monthly publication that carried articles by every organisation in the village and advertisements by most of its tradespeople. His page was always headed 'Ministerial Musings'; it had a softer ring than 'Reflections' or 'Meditations', terms used by his predecessors in the post.

It was now the end of November and he knew he must address the subject of Christmas for the December issue. Jack Dorling had nodded a few hints in his direction already, Christmas being a particularly busy time for printers. It shouldn't be a problem: after all, Christmas was a joyful time. But it could also be very stressful. What he always felt obliged to do was make – no, encourage – people to 'look beyond our immediate annoyances'. He wasn't sure about the last word: it suggested 'displeasure', 'pique', 'irritation'. No – perhaps, 'considerations' would be a better choice: 'look beyond our immediate considerations'.

Can we change our mindset in relation to Christmas? Can we see beyond the shopping, the parties and the decorations, and think about why we have this festival? One thing is certain – it's not really about Santa and reindeer, or expensive presents or even families, but rather about an event that has both amazed and puzzled people for over 2000 years. When Jesus was born in Bethlehem, he did not come to start a commercial festival. Rather, he came to bridge the gap between people who are imperfect and God who loves us so much.

Yes, that was the way: straight from the shoulder. Frederick was well-liked but that wasn't enough: he had a ministry to pursue, he was responsible for the Cure of Souls.

But his mind was not really on his article; it was on what he'd been told by Gerald Henderson and the stranger, James Ryder. The former had been to see him the previous evening, directly after the Psychic Supper, which was followed so tragically by the death of Amelia Pritchard, and the latter that very morning. Jacqueline had tried to ward Mr Ryder off but he'd been persistent and what he'd had to tell Frederick, along with the doctor's comments and what he, himself, knew already, did anything but fix his 'mindset' (an unpleasant word: he'd change it later) on the Christmas musing.

Both had been concerned about the man who had sat at Frederick's table: the man who called himself Thomkins. Gerald had enquired about him, as though they'd met sometime previously; James Ryder had queried Jacqueline's comments about the man being 'evil' and then came out with that extraordinary story about a midnight visit by another man called Richard Gabriel.

Men like those expressing disquiet (there he was, using emollient language again!) about what was happening in the village was cause alone for worry, but Frederick knew he'd been sitting quietly on other considerations. There had been the Blessing of the Wilton's house along with what Myrtle had told him; there had been Marjory Broome's belief she had seen a stranger in the village on the night Ambrose died; there had been his own experience with Elizabeth Beeston; Cynthia Revell's revelations concerning her son's ravings; his talk with Simon Pegg in the White Horse only a few weeks ago; and there had been that business earlier, when Gerald Henderson had claimed to have run down two young women who then disappeared.

Quite a catalogue of what the popular press would call 'hauntings' and what intelligent people would laugh off. Frederick did not want to look a fool – not simply from personal vanity but more importantly because he needed to be respected as a priest. The respect wasn't just personal: it was respect for his calling. But he must act; he knew he must act. But how?

*

Gerald Henderson sat with his daughter and son at their kitchen table; he had decided that more harm would be done by excluding Charles from the confession than by being open with him. He had cooked the meal that evening – a straight-forward chilli con carne served on a bed of rice; it was a dish he'd often knocked-up when he arrived home to find a note from Maggie saying she'd left for the theatre.

It was a dish the children had always enjoyed and they now sat together, stomachs full, contented in the warmth of their kitchen, Lottie and Charles drinking squash, while he sipped a cup of scalding tea. It was a cold night and the children had arrived with their fingers nipped. It was good to be home with the doors shut against the night.

It was a prime moment but Gerald still hesitated. It would be so easy to draw the wrong conclusions from what had happened and yet he felt, in view of what had occurred in the village, that the children ought to be warned. And yet, he wasn't sure what he was warning them against.

He thought he'd recognised the man who called himself Thomkins. He was fairly certain it was the same person who had called at the medical centre not long before Maggie died, but only fairly certain: he'd given the man but a passing glance at the time. The vicar didn't seem to know him, even though he was sitting at the same table during the supper; he also seemed reluctant to talk about the man, and yet, surely, he must have found out something – they'd sat together all evening until the disturbance, the ruckus that occurred when the medium left in a hurry.

Maggie was a part-time nurse at the centre and sometimes covered the reception desk if one of the regular women was off sick. It so happened that she was doing just that on the day Thomkins decided to register with the practice. They had struck up a friendship when she discovered he was a photographer: Maggie being Maggie loved having her photograph taken. She thought it might lead to bigger roles and even paid work in films.

Gerald had seen no harm in the idea. His wife had been an energetic and creative woman and it would give her an outlet. And so, on that fateful day she had gone off with Thomkins to be photographed at different places around the village: the church, the mill, the staithe, the marina, the country lanes, the picnic site, the river …

It was at the side of the river they found her dead. Day became evening and evening, night. When her mother failed to come home, Lottie rang the surgery and Gerald rang the police. It was the local officer, Sharpe, who found her, soaked to the skin in the grass on the banks of the Thorn, a mile or so from the village. The postmortem had been inconclusive; yes, she'd swallowed water but she had not drowned; there were no signs of violence on her body but several veins had burst in her head.

The gossiping had started, of course. What was a married woman doing there with a stranger, especially a stranger who took photographs? Gerald had ignored the sly looks, the knowing smirks, the mutterings: he had no reason not to trust his wife.

The details had been kept from the children: Lottie and Charles had always believed their mother had met with an accident by the river. They knew nothing of Thomkins, who had reappeared in the village.

"What's wrong, Daddy?"

"Nothing Lottie."

"You've been very quiet."

"The end of a long day."

Gerald knew by the way his daughter looked at him that she realised he was keeping something important from her. Women are always so perceptive about such matters and didn't like 'being kept in the dark'. That was one of the phrases both his mother and Maggie used. But what could he tell his son and daughter – that on the day she died their mother had been with a virtual stranger and that man was now back in the village?

But the man had to be a threat. He must have been with Maggie when she died, however she died, and yet made no attempt to bring her back to the village or fetch help. Was he a threat to Lottie, as well?

Gerald Henderson, carefully, painstakingly, began gathering his thoughts. 'When your mummy had her accident, she was having her photograph taken by a man she'd got to know. We didn't see him after … after – was that the right word?... but he's now come back to the village and …' He was already going round in circles, and then he remembered the two young women, and his mind cleared. He accepted what terrified him. Gerald placed his cup carefully on the table. 'By the horns – take the bull by the horns!'

"Do you believe in ghosts?" he asked.

Chapter 7

The Medium Speaks Out

Four angry men and another about to become one: Gerald's talk with his children had not gone well, and so he was angry with himself; Frederick, still uncertain as to how he might proceed, likewise; Saul Tacksman was more terrified than angry, but in such circumstances tempers flare; James Ryder was frustrated with the lack of progress in his search for Gabriels, a search that had now taken on a greater urgency and was about to rouse the ire of Vernon Scuffil.

Gerald's talk with his children had not gone well. The ghosts – or the possibility of ghosts – was not the problem; the problem lay in his resurrection of the memory of their mother's death, one that Lottie felt she had come to accept through caring for her father, one that Charles had stuffed securely in a locker to which his father had now handed him the key.

"When did you see this man, Daddy?"

"On the morning he came to fetch your mother. It was only briefly. They went off in a hurry – something to do with the morning light."

"And you're sure it was the same man?"

"Eh yes – certain enough, now I've thought about it."

"But you didn't get a chance to speak to him?"

"No. I couldn't believe what I was seeing at first, and then matters moved quickly, as I said. Thomkins followed Mr Tacksman from the room and was gone before I had a chance to speak with him."

"Are you going to phone the police?"

It was the first time Charles had spoken, and the light in which he saw Thomkins was clear.

"Your mum wasn't murdered, Charlie. There's no need to think that way."

"You don't know that! He must have been the last person to see Mummy alive!"

Gerald heaved a huge sigh of regret. Dull by the horns? He should simply have told them to be careful of strangers; but they were both too intelligent not to have asked why the sudden interest.

He had never believed in ghosts; the very idea was ridiculous, but in the light of his experience with the two women it seemed the most likely explanation. He had this fear that Thomkins was a malign force: Maggie had been chosen and Thomkins had been responsible for her death. It wasn't murder in the usual sense of that word – it wasn't the kind of case the police would be able to investigate – but Gerald was now convinced his wife had been killed. And then his own reflections overcame him, his thoughts that life had been calmer, more peaceful since she left them.

It proved to be a long evening in which the three of them talked round in circles, angry with each other, angry with themselves at being angry, in a vain attempt to find resolution. At the end, Charles had taken himself off to bed, where Gerald later heard him crying, and Lottie had busied herself with some ironing that could easily have waited until the weekend. Gerald sat up all night, waiting for them to settle, waiting until he saw their eyes close.

Frederick Mackenzie, too, had a sleepless night. Sitting at his desk, unable to complete his article, unable to see a way forward, he had left the vicarage by the side door – the one that led directly through the wall to the churchyard – and had prayed.

"Lord, I am alone in this unknown wilderness. I know my parish, I know my people but this other world I do not know, this world of returning spirits. Am I to believe, Lord, that they are forever present, watching us daily and have access to our lives and our souls? How am I to approach these ... these visitors, the dead and the long dead? It is held to be true, I believe, that the attitudes to truth and goodness taken up in this life persist in the next – and yet ... I need to understand what is happening before I am able to ... able to intervene ..."

Many times, he had come to know that simply talking to God was enough to enable him to see the way ahead and it was that simple word 'intervene' that did the trick on this occasion. Jesus had intervened, *was* intervening when people let him into their lives, between His Father and mankind; and he, Fred Mackenzie, was a priest of the Church and through his faith he too had the power to intervene – not just comfort, as he had with Myrtle Wilton, but intervene.

"Thank you, Lord. I knew you would answer me. In the name of your Son, Jesus Christ and the Holy Spirit. Amen."

His resolution strong, Frederick left Holy Trinity and crossed the churchyard home, where he sought and found Jacqueline, eager to talk; Jacqueline was always a good listener. He didn't know where he would be without her love.

"Spiritualism lacks the high standards of Christianity, Fred. Our faith rests upon God through Jesus Christ. When have you ever heard a medium speak of God? Has anyone's prayer life been strengthened by their spiritualist experiences? Has anyone through attending one of these seances ever been brought closer to God? Do men like Saul Tacksman have any sense of God the Father, God the Son and God the Holy Ghost? No!

I know you have a duty to *intervene* – but you are taking to a road that leads only to Hell if you are not fully armed. Pray before you venture against these spirits. I do not doubt that these ... *apparitions* are real. I also do not doubt that they are evil. They seek to enter our world and, therefore, our souls through people like Saul Tacksman. Saul Tacksman is not a priest ..."

Frederick listened and while he appreciated his wife's opinions, he could not agree with her wholeheartedly. If there were evil spirits, then it was quite likely there were also good spirits. It was a question, he felt, of what held them to this world. When she finished, he said, deliberately quietly:

"A life grounded in the love of God, darling – as yours is, as mine is – has, I hope, nothing to fear from evil influences of any kind. Prayer and worship are our business."

"I know, I know and I know you sought God's help tonight; but for me, for the children, for all our sakes, please be careful. I'm frightened."

Had Jacqueline been with Simon Pegg in the bar of the White Horse the following morning she might well have felt she had met a fellow believer. Saul Tacksman phoned the landlord demanding an immediate meeting. Saul, too, was frightened.

"Those men – the one who penetrated my auric field, Thomkins, and the one who met him in the bar – are malign influences. He, Thomkins, channelled his vision through me. He entered and made me see what he wanted me to know. I am clairvoyant. I can see the other side but not in the manner of last night. I was in that basement and Thomkins placed me there. Do you understand?"

Simon shook his head; gone was his idea of quiet evenings calling up the relatives of those at his suppers.

"Thomkins himself is a full manifestation."

Tacksman clenched and unclenched his hands, turn round, bowed his head and stared at the carpet. His right hand still clenched, he whirled on Simon.

"Ghosts, Mr Pegg. How do you imagine them?"

"I don't understand what you mean."

"Would you expect to see through them?"

Simon smiled, but only just, at the double meaning held in the question.

"Yes," he replied, taking Tacksman's actual meaning.

"They are transparent, aren't they – faint? The Grey Lady and so on?"

"Yes."

"But these ghosts are not. These ghosts are flesh – not flesh as you and I know it but, at least, substantial. And did you notice anything else about them?"

"Go on," replied the landlord, wondering whether to call a doctor or the police.

"They spoke. They not only spoke; they interacted with us. Your classic ghost goes through a set routine. They appear, they walk across the room, they pass through a wall where there was once a door – you know the general pattern?"

"Yes."

"But these didn't, did they?"

"You're not telling me that Mr Thomkins and Mr Kent are ghosts?"

"For want of a better word – yes!"

Saul paused as though wondering whether it was worth explaining, but he had come because he was frightened and that fear needed purging.

"Do you mind if I ask for a drink?"

"Of course, of course, I should have thought," replied Simon, pouring Saul his usual green mixture or grenadine and soda water and taking a whisky for himself.

"As a medium, I am used to the spirits of the departed speaking through me, I am used to them guiding my vision to what they want me to see. I am even used to them entering my body – *when I permit them to do so* – when they are desperate to express their personality, *but – and this is a huge but –* I make my own decisions as to when I channel a spirit. Last night, I didn't. Thomkins controlled me, which is why I ran from the room ..."

Simon had thought the Psychic Supper salvaged and he'd pencilled in plans for the next; perhaps the New Year when the Christmas festivities were done and dusted. Not one to be discouraged from pursuing a possible business opportunity, he began a suggestion.

"Do you think they will return if we ... if we ..."

"Ghosts are not my business, Mr Pegg. I am a medium, not a ghost hunter."

"Ghost hunter?"

"Or parapsychologist. There are people who take an interest in these things. A parapsychologist would tell you that I was in what he would call 'a dissociated state' last night, that what you witnessed was simply another aspect of my own personality coming through, that my brain was coming up with information based on things I was already thinking about …"

"And that Mr Thomkins and Mr Kent were just real people/"

"Yes. Bystanders. Two decent men eager to help. But I know differently."

Saul Tacksman seemed to have calmed down; sharing his knowledge and his concerns with Simon had proved beneficial. The landlord's hopes rose.

"What can we do to prevent this happening again?" he asked, adding, "The Readings you gave were well received. It would be a pity not to have another."

"As I say, I know little more than the average man or woman about ghosts but I can tell you this – anger is what keeps those two men here. I could feel it in both. You need to get rid of them or they will return. They used me as a physical medium."

With a lessening of the tension, Simon didn't pursue any interest he might have had in what a 'physical medium' might be. Saul seemed calmer; he didn't want to rouse him. Simon smiled: here was hope.

"You need a ghost hunter – I believe that's what they call themselves these days."

"A ghost hunter?" he said for the second time that morning.

Simon smiled as he asked the question. Here was happiness: the answer to his problem and a laugh or two with Catriona tonight. There might even be a chance to make an event of the hunt – a Ghost Hunt Supper; perhaps, first a tour of haunted places in the village, finishing for a meal at the White Horse?

"Do you know of one?"

"Yes. There's a couple: Clifford Raine and Esme Owen. I'll give you their number."

Saul Tacksman sounded relieved.

James Ryder had decided to seek the help of Vernon Scuffil. A conversation with the vicar, Fred Mackenzie, after the supper, had brought the village historian's name to the engineer's attention.

He now made his way down Bridge Street to the arched passageway closed by the two black doors. He'd heard Vernon was a teacher and waited a day; this was Saturday morning and he hoped to find Vernon at home.

Vernon had just finished breakfast. He and Justine were planning their day with her children, Acer and Anthemis, when Ryder knocked on the front door. This was unusual: anyone who knew the couple always made their way through a collection of plants and bric-a-brac that Justine kept in the archway and were always for sale: villagers would take what they wanted and drop the money into an honesty box.

Vernon frowned: weekends were precious. He looked at Justine and her expression suggested she thought he should be the one to answer. Vernon opened the door and frowned again; he remained silent, watching Ryder as though the engineer was a specimen of some kind. Used to gamesmanship among men, Ryder returned the stare, and received Vernon's trumpeting noise; his resonance chambers were working well that morning.

"Hmmm!"

"Mr Scuffil."

It wasn't a question and Ryder hadn't intended it as such.

"Hmmm!"

The sound seemed longer the second time, more pronounced despite the lack of vowels. As the visitor, Ryder capitulated.

"My name's James Ryder and I'd appreciate your help in finding someone, an Elizabeth Gabriel, who lived and died in this village a long time ago. I understand that you're the village historian."

"Hmmm!"

It wasn't often Vernon managed three trumpeting sounds before a conversation had started and he was pleased with himself. His large, cavernous head was clear; his nose quivered in the morning cold.

"Is there any chance you could return at a more respectable hour? Say coffee time? If you haven't had breakfast, Carmen does a full fry-up at her Quay Café."

Having trumpeted triumphantly, he closed the door and returned to his breakfast.

Ryder wasn't a man to be put out easily, if at all; besides, he had little regard for teachers. To him they were simply part of the pampered public services. He had enjoyed a good breakfast at the Swan but decided to call on Carmen Quay, who he met briefly at the Psychic Supper.

Her cafe was a treasure, a small one; if it held eight people at one time that was all it held. The story that Johnny Depp had once sat for an hour-and-a half waiting for one of her fabled fish cakes had been confirmed by Ned Douglas on one of Ryder's previous visits. A table for two by the window was already taken by cyclists, a married couple; one to Ryder's left was occupied by an old man and a young girl, obviously locals, and they looked up with a smile; a third table placed against a central buttress might have held four people at a pinch provided no one else was sitting down at the same time; the fourth table, up against the service counter, was nestled under a bookshelf that looked ready to fall. Ryder sat down, admiring the multitude of paintings and photographs by local artists that adorned the walls. On various shelves and on the windowsill were displays of ceramics, mainly jugs and flowerpots, also for sale.

Carmen bustled from the cooking area, which reminded Ryder more of a galley than a kitchen. She beamed him a genuine smile. Her voice was high-pitched and in a state of constant excitement; her sentences turned up at their endings.

"I saw you at the supper. I saw you with Fred and his wife and the stranger who upset Mr Tacksman …"

She rattled on for quite a time, giving Ryder the chance to take in her particular form of beauty. Carmen could have simply been a name chosen by her parents because it sounded exotic, but this wasn't the case: Carmen had Spanish blood. When she stopped talking to take his order, he asked her where she came from.

"I'm glad you asked. Many people don't like to. It's a small town called Guaro del Mar …"

"On the Costa del Sol?"

"You know it?"

"I've travelled a great deal for my work. I'm an engineer. I've been to your hometown – lovely place. How long have you lived here?"

"Ooh, a long time."

"Glad to leave the Costa?"

"Yes – but it's nice. Not what people think ..."

They talked on and Ryder began to wonder if Carmen ever got round to serving meals; but her company was good. She was a pleasant lady, and the talk came round to her partner, Belfast Billy.

"Billy was in tears. How in the name of all that's holy did the man know his father had deserted the family – gone off to South Africa? And the row with his sister? It was all over years ago ..."

"Your friend is OK now?" suggested Ryder, guessing the couple had talked about the issue for hours.

"Yes, he's here. We have a little garden by the staithe. He's tidying it up ready for the lunches ..."

Eventually, she took his order and Ryder, not liking to say he'd already had breakfast, found himself eating a second one: not a full fry-up but an eggs benedict served properly on an English muffin.

Full to the brim, he again sought Vernon Scuffil who appeared to be in a better frame of mind than previously.

"Gabriel – hmm! Related, are you?"

Ryder hesitated to give his reason for seeking Elizabeth Gabriel's history: Scuffil wasn't the kind of man you took into your confidence. He could see the raised eyebrows, the smirk, the bewildered look and hear the loud trumpeting of disbelief.

Bearing in mind Vernon's own experiences, Ryder's decision was unfortunate, delaying as it did any chance the two men might have had to join forces in a common cause.

"Yes, possibly, a long time ago."

"Ancestry – hm! Fascinating subject. Time consuming. Have you tried the websites?"

"Yes, but ..."

"Only adds to the confusion. I know. Too many Williams, too many Walters, too many Georges ... and so on. And then people interfering – setting up their own little, wretched family trees and sharing them as though they were useful or even accurate Hmmm!"

"You obviously have a great deal of experience in these matters?"

"Do I? What makes you think that – hmmm?"

There seemed to be no answer other than that the man was an historian, and Ryder supposed he might have explored the odd family tree or two. Impatient with Scuffil's rudeness he said so.

"Oh, you do, do you? What makes you say so?"

"Look, Mr Scuffil, I appear to have chosen a bad moment to ask for your help."

"Really?"

"Perhaps I could return at a more convenient time."

"You think so?"

"I'll make my way out."

"I thought you wanted my help," called the historian as Ryder passed through the gate from Scuffil's study and along the path that led to the arched passageway, meeting Justine on the way.

"Was Vernon of any help?" asked Justine Sweet, who met him on the path, as he ducked under the crab apple tree.

"He seems preoccupied."

"You mean rude. He's always like that but doesn't mean it. It's his nature. He's been in his study since you left, earlier. Come on."

A smile on her face, Justine led Ryder back to Vernon's study. Before he or she could say a word, the teacher-historian blew a loud blast from somewhere deep inside him: a herd of elephants would have recognised the sound.

"Ah, you've decided to come back! Gabriel – yes! Unfortunate woman. Admitted nine times to the workhouse between 1839 and 1844. On her first visit she arrived with her husband and five children. A year later, April 1840, pregnant and deserted, she entered the house again with her children. Her daughter was born and died, and she lost a son before she was discharged in September 1841. She was back again a week later and stayed until March 1842. This went on – discharged, readmitted, discharged, readmitted – until October the same year when a son, Richard, was duly born. She claimed the father was the workhouse master, but that was never proven. In May 1843, the entire family was discharged but readmitted the same day. They were then discharged in July and readmitted in August. The family spent the winter as indoor paupers and were discharged in April 1844. A month later, the younger children were readmitted, abandoned at the gate. In July, Elizabeth and the older children were readmitted. Two days later they discharged themselves. After that, Mrs Gabriel and her family vanished from the parish, but it's likely that the children spent most of their upbringing in other workhouses. Helpful?"

Vernon had not paused for breath and his voice had reverberated around the small study; he was clearly delighted to be thundering down information he believed Ryder would fail to remember.

"Yes, thank you. So, in 1864, when Elizabeth was buried in the churchyard at All Saints, Richard would have been a man of twenty-two?"

"Obviously."

"Do you happen to know the name of the workhouse master?"

"Happen – hmm?" asked Vernon, indicating that knowledge didn't just happen, "Yes – Ryder, like yours. Henry Ryder. Lots of Henrys in those days."

Chapter 8

Guests at a Funeral

Frederick Mackenzie was good with funerals, as one might expect of a man whose feet were firmly on the ground in his parish. Nevertheless, after his initial efforts to help, Mildred had taken charge, feeling it was the least she could do for her old friend, and the first people she approached were Edward Warburg and Myles Langstroth.

"I've come to ask a favour," she said, accepting a seat from Edward and a mild coffee from Myles, "One piece of music of which Amelia was tremendously fond was Elgar's *Salut d'Amour*. I was hoping, Edward, that you would be kind enough to play this for her at the funeral. I will, of course, see that the piano in All Saints is tuned beforehand."

For a moment or two neither man spoke, but she was used to this kind of response: both men were not only musicians but dreamers, and already they were visualising the setting and listening to the music as it would appear and sound in the church.

"We will see to the piano, Mildred. There's no need to trouble yourself," replied

Myles, "Certainly, the acoustics there are preferable to those in Holy Trinity …"

"… although we would be honoured to perform anywhere for Amelia," continued Edward, glancing at his friend, a note of disapproval in his tone, "Why was this piece so important to her?"

"She would never say but whenever we heard it – especially if it took us by surprise – her eyes would fill with tears …"

"A lover," said Myles.

"I think there was someone, once. She was a very affectionate person."

"Perhaps during the war years," said Edward, musingly, "It's certainly very romantic. Elgar wrote it for his fiancée. He gave it to her as an engagement present. She was very fluent in German and Elgar called the piece, *Liebesgruss*. It was the publishers who changed the title – perhaps fortunately! I believe it was originally written for piano and violin but there have been many arrangements since – one for a quintet if I remember correctly."

Mildred Ackroyd smiled to herself. She knew both men from their work with her at Saxstead Opera over many years. They were the only people in the village who had ever felt comfortable using Miss Pritchard's Christian name.

"Mildred," continued Edward, stressing and holding her name, "will you leave the arrangement – and the arrangements – in my hands. I feel that this is an opportunity for our young musicians. Can you hear the score, Myles – piano with a string quartet? There are so many talented young people! We must include them!"

"Amelia would love the idea," replied Mildred, "You're thinking of those you teach in the schools and your own pupils – those who have played at the Saxstead?"

"Yes! Oh, Mildred, it's so wonderful to have someone share our enthusiasm," said Myles.

"You bring me to my second request," said Mildred, "It's for you, Myles."

"Really!"

All in a word! Mildred was striking gold for her friend.

"Yes. Two years ago, we performed Britten's *A Midsummer Night's Dream* at Saxstead. Do you remember?"

"Do I remember? You're teasing me, Mildred!"

"You sang the part of Oberon."

Myles smiled. Saxstead wasn't Glyndebourne, but that was the whole point of their annual festival; neither he nor Edward wanted Saxstead to become fashionable 'We don't want the snob audiences from London or, indeed, our own county set'. They wanted a festival where those attending could walk to the venue and enjoy a beer in the local pub at the interval.

"Amelia loved Oberon's aria '*I know a bank where the wild thyme blows ...*'.

"Eddie and I first saw it performed at Covent Garden in 2005. Oberon was sung by a countertenor on that occasion, as Benjamin intended."

"But previously arranged for Peter to sing, I believe," said Edward.

"Not at all – you know very well he wrote the part for Alfred Deller. Peter sang the part of Flute in the original production at Aldeburgh."

"Yes, yes, Myles – of that, I am *fully* aware. Nevertheless, I have always felt ..."

"Feelings have nothing to do with authenticity, Eddie. You will insist that Benjamin originally intended the part for his friend but there is no provenance for such an idea."

"Having arranged it for your voice, dear, I do claim some *ownership* to the belief that the origin of the idea for the aria was inspired by the tenor voice."

"It was written specifically for the countertenor voice."

"Nevertheless, Oberon's music never requires the countertenor to sing at the top of the alto range ..."

Mildred could see that both men were exercising their relationship; whether for her benefit or because it was something they enjoyed and indulged often she was unsure, but when she caught Myles's eye he laughed.

"Married couples, Mildred! Not that Eddie and I are, but you know what I mean!"

"And you also know you can leave these two contributions for Miss Pritchard's funeral safely in our hands," said Edward.

She did and knew, also, that Frederick Mackenzie would welcome both offerings.

He welcomed, too, the choice of All Saints for the service. It was the smaller of the two churches which came under his jurisdiction in the parish and was cosier than Holy Trinity. He didn't expect very many people at the funeral and it would be nice to fill the church; no doubt many of the Saxstead Opera people would come but Amelia Pritchard was not well-known in the village – not these days, he thought.

On the morning of the service, Frederick arrived early. There was always peace and quiet in a church; it was somewhere you could ease your mind and prepare it for the day ahead. Making his way across the churchyard he saw a figure standing at the open grave, where soon Amelia Pritchard would find her endless rest. He approached quietly, not wanting to disturb what might be a close friend or even a long-lost relative in their moments of final reflection.

The figure turned as he closed in. It was an old woman and she bestowed on Frederick a smile of utter contentment.

"Are you the priest who will lay this lady to rest?"

"Yes."

"Have you been in the parish long?"

"For a number of years."

"And so, you know its people well?"

"I like to think so."

"What will you have to say about Amelia Pritchard? 'She was a good friend and staunch supporter of the cultural life of the village – loved by all who knew her – kind, honourable – awarded the highest honour the French could bestow for her courage and bravery during the dreadful years of World War 2 – a women with an open heart – affectionate to a fault …?' Do you want me to go on?"

"I think not," replied Frederick, shocked that the woman had touched upon some of the very things he intended to say, "I find your tone dis …respectful."

He had hesitated to say 'disgraceful' and regretted not doing so. Who this woman was he had no idea but she had clearly come to make herself a nuisance.

"How well did *you* know Miss Pritchard?" he asked, determined to keep the occasion friendly but wishing by emphasising the pronoun to express his displeasure.

"My memories go back a long, long way and the Pritchard family are among the less happy among them. They are buried here, are they not, in this little country churchyard, a family who exploited their position for personal gain with no regard for those they injured, neglected and killed?"

"You do not speak of the Miss Pritchard I knew."

"No! You knew only the lies we all feel happier acknowledging. It spares us the need to think, to judge the dead among the living. 'Don't speak ill of the dead' – you will no doubt be familiar with that phrase, Vicar?"

"I think it a wise one."

"Walk among these tombstones with me now and read what is written. How much of it is true? How many of these kind, honourable people were malicious, dishonest, liars, rogues and hypocrites? How many 'good' husbands deceived their wives? How many 'loving' wives were shrews? How many 'devoted' sons cared not a damn for their parents? How many 'loving' daughters took only what they wanted, giving nothing in return?"

Frederick had sometimes wondered as much himself; but the thought was not a charitable one and best shelved.

"If we cannot right these wrongs in life, I see no worth in pursuing them after death," he replied.

"No, you cannot! I would expect as much from a priest! But in the life that hangs heavily beyond death we have time to think and grieve. Besides, *I have promises to keep*," replied the woman, adding with a chuckle, *"and miles to go before I sleep, miles to go before I sleep."*

It was only as she turned and walked away that Frederick knew the woman; but where had she heard those lines from one of his favourite poets?

"*I am the resurrection and the life, saith the Lord: he that believeth in me, thought we were dead, yet shall he live...*", intoned Frederick, now on familiar ground, now bringing comfort to the bereaved, going before Amelia Pritchard's cortege as it entered the little church.

Myles Langstroth's fine tenor voice accompanied the coffin down the aisle; Edward Warburg, watching with confidence from where he sat with his quintet, smiled to himself and then to his musicians.

"I know a place where the wild thyme blows,
Where oxlips and the nodding violet grows,
Quite over-canopied with luscious woodbine,
And with sweet musk-roses and with eglantine ..."

Myles, standing at the receiving end of the nave, smiled when his song was finished, pleased with himself.

And then came the psalm they all loved, which Frederick thought sounded well sung as a hymn:

"The Lord's my shepherd, I'll not want
He makes me down to lie
In pastures green; He leadeth me
The quiet waters by.

My soul he doth restore again,
And me to walk doth make ..."

Frederick had a good voice and he led the congregation along paths that even those who no longer attended church seemed to remember from a time in their pasts. He knew some of those he now faced from where he stood beside the coffin, where his hand rested.

"... So, also is the resurrection of the dead: it is sown in corruption; it is raised in incorruption ..."

He liked Paul's words to the Christians at Corinth; they had always brought comfort and, as importantly, understanding.

He searched among the faces he knew, those who had also known Amelia Pritchard: Gerald Henderson, PC Sharpe, Simon and Catriona Pegg, Marjory Broome with Myrtle Wilton, Jack Dorling, Vernon Scuffil and Justine Sweet, Carmen Quay and her partner Billy. His own wife, Jacqueline, looked up at him from the front pew and smiled, a smile to bring him confidence.

Apart from them, the villagers, sat Mirabelle Hurd and members and supporters of Saxstead Opera, the singers and musicians.

"*O death, where is thy sting? O grave, where is thy victory?*"

Had Amelia Pritchard in those last few moments of her life known the sting of death? Frederick remembered the time he had been called to her side. 'I have no doubt that this woman – this spectre – was not of this world'. They were her very words, and he had seen into her soul. No, such a power was the Lord's only! He had read her thoughts. 'Did she have something on her mind that triggered a memory in yours?' he had asked.

He looked up towards the back of the church, preparing for his sermon.

"We come here today to say farewell to our friend, Amelia Pritchard, a lady loved and admired throughout the village and beyond ..."

The woman was there, in one of the rear pews, watching him. Her eyes never flinched but Frederick's did as his gaze wandered across the faces in the church. Scattered among the congregation were other faces, faces he did not know but whose names came to him as they watched his hesitation by the coffin: the man who had lured Myrtle Wilton to her neighbour's garden – Lansmore; the man Marjory Broome had spoken to Myrtle about, the man who had been standing in the street the night Ambrose fell from the bridge – Frank; Elizabeth Beeston – his own nemesis; Richard Gabriel who had appeared to James Ryder; the man Cynthia Revell had spoken about after she had listened to her son's ravings – Quire; Kent – the man at the White Horse; and Thomkins, who sat by him during the psychic supper.

All there among the congregation – the dead dispersed among the living; and there were others he did not know and whose names would not come to him but who he recognised for what they were – a curse among the living, and he, Frederick Mackenzie, the Cure of Souls.

His sermon finished, if not completed as he would have wished, Frederick turned to Edward. The young musicians were waiting, their instruments tuned, their futures before them. He recognised Lottie Henderson at the piano and several of the other children he knew from his visits to the local schools. 'Always welcome at morning assembly, Vicar'. There was the cello player and the two violinists and the boy with the viola. Edward Warburg was a talented musician, a gift to the village.

And the beautiful, romantic strains of *Salut d'Amour* filled the church with the love Elgar had felt when he composed the tune.

And when the performance was completed, Frederick said:

"Let us pray.
Lord, have mercy upon us ..."
And the congregation responded:
"Christ, have mercy upon us"

If only they had known then what they were saying, what their prayer meant in the face of God. If only ...

Chapter 9

The Ghost Hunters

Taking Saul Tacksman's advice, Simon Pegg contacted the ghost hunters. As he said to Catriona 'it would do no harm and could only be good for the pub'. Landlords are, by their trade, the least sceptical of people – at least in public – and Simon was adept at agreeing with everyone, but it was his enthusiasm that let him down when he spoke with Clifford Raine and Esme Owen.

Clifford Raine had been fascinated by the supernatural all his life – a childhood interest in the macabre became an adulthood obsession – but it wasn't until he met Esme Owen that the obsession became a way of life: Esme was a genuine psychic. Together, they wrote books and led investigations; their house was crammed full of the equipment they used in their work: notebooks and pens, torches with spare batteries, recorders with spare discs, digital cameras, video camcorders with tripods, a night vision system, spotlights, headsets, a Geiger counter, an EMF, infra-red thermal scanners, air ion counters …

"*Ghost walks* are not in our repertoire, Mr Pegg," Esme's voice told him on the phone and the emphasis her Welsh accent put on *ghost walks* and her selection of the word *repertoire* were sufficiently cutting to put the landlord firmly in his place.

Simon built a mental picture of Esme, just listening to her voice: she was strikingly beautiful with natural blonde hair, cut severely and not one strand of it out of place. He imagined her eyes as large and piercing, eyes that looked through her listeners with a touch of arrogance in the gaze.

He didn't pursue his request but apologised and drove home that evening, leaving his trusted regular staff in charge of the White Horse, to seek Catriona's advice. It is said that behind every landlord is a forceful landlady and this was certainly true of Catriona.

"You need to convince these people that you are serious," she said, once they had retired for the night.

It was the first chance Simon had of speaking with his wife. Arriving home, he'd found his daughter, July, standing on a chair with Edith Garland fussing around her, while Catriona looked on admiringly and his son, Bruce, sat glumly waiting his turn. Edith was Maisie Garland's mother and a very active member of the WI. It was coming up to pantomime time; Maisie organised the annual event with her Dancing Feet troupe and her mother bulldozed her organisation into producing the costumes.

Simon supposed it wasn't the moment to put forward the idea of replacing the pantomime with a musical or mentioning ghost hunters; but his moment had arrived as he and Catriona waited to fall asleep.

"Why not involve Fred? Having a vicar taking an interest will show you are genuinely concerned ... and Dr Henderson! He was at the psychic supper. He saw what happened and there's that story going round about the young women he's supposed to have run down ..."

Catriona talked on until she fell asleep, but the seed had been sown in her first four words. Fred was the man! And he'd know others who had experienced these ... ghosts ... Was that the word to use? They'd talked together at the Horse a few months back and there'd been that business when the parish council turned up for a drink after their meeting in September ... Tomorrow morning, he'd start afresh.

Frederick Mackenzie only hesitated for a moment. Although he couldn't bring himself to admit a belief in ghosts, enough out-of-the-ordinary events had occurred to warrant an investigation by people who might know what they were doing. Moreover, there was James Ryder, who had come to him with that fantastic story;

and there was what he'd talked about with Simon; and there was the unaccountable incident at the psychic supper. Only a fool or someone not wishing to appear a fool turn their back on evidence. Evidence – was that the word? He'd get in touch with James Ryder.

James Ryder was more than willing to meet the ghost hunters and felt that Vernon Scuffil, willingly or not, should be invited along. Scuffil was an awkward character but his knowledge of the village's history would prove useful. He would lay aside some work he had in hand and go along to Thornham as soon as a meeting could be arranged; and he'd pay Scuffil a visit.

It was fortunate for Ryder that Justine was gathering up windfalls from the crab apple tree on the path that led down to her garden when he arrived; but for her, Scuffil would have undoubtably snorted a refusal.

"Come on, Vernon," she said, "You've had a few frights yourself."

"Hmmm!"

"Vernon eventually told me he'd seen someone in the garden last September when he got home from a parish council meeting. More than that, he is sure his study is haunted. Someone's in there and they keep moving his books and other items around – only slightly but enough to annoy Vernon. Come on Vernon, tell James!"

Ryder had not expected the teacher-historian to look embarrassed: he somehow felt that the man considered himself above such an emotion, but he was wrong. Vernon blushed to his roots and trumpeted loudly.

"Aaah – I'mmm – Hmmm! There's a presence in my study. I can't express the feeling any other way. And I think it's the person I saw in Justine's garden that evening. While I was running after him – or her – or it, it got into my study. I left the door open. Why shouldn't I – hmmm? My study. Every so often I become aware that I'm being watched. I've never seen anything – just what it does – moving my things. And sometimes it speaks – I'm not imagining this, Ryder! I'm not doolally! The only peace I get is when I go out or am in the house with Justine and the children. It's interfering with my work. I enjoy my peace and quiet ... I eh ... that's it! Hmmm!"

"So, go along and meet these ghost hunters as James suggests," said Justine in the practical manner of women, "If nothing else, it will put your mind at rest."

Vernon looked tenderly at his partner. In the look, little more than a glance, the walker realised what he was missing as a bachelor: someone who cared for him, another point of view. It was the look that drove Vernon to be walking to the White Horse, where Simon had put aside a back room that evening for their meeting with Esme Owen and Clifford Raine.

Esme's partner had nothing of the psychic or mystic about him; his face suggested he might be the man who had come to fix the boiler; if any face can be described as 'ordinary' that would be a face like Clifford Raine's. He was a big, burly man with what, one day, would be a double or treble chin. He stood quietly watching the others before he took the seat offered. He presented a reassurance that contrasted with Esme's faraway, almost haughty, manner. But between the two, Ryder observed the same intensity of connection he had witnessed in the glance that passed between Vernon and Justine; it was a look of intellectual intimacy.

Despite Simon's offer, neither ghost hunter accepted an alcoholic drink, preferring coffee. The little group gathered around two heavy tables Simon had placed together, assuming (although he couldn't think why) the hunters would not want others close. Esme and Clifford listened without a murmur, while the events of the past few months were placed before them.

"Before we proceed, I think you should understand the nature of the work Esme and I are involved in," said Clifford, who spoke without looking at his partner, suggesting that this was their method of operating, "We are ghost hunters, although we prefer the term paranormal investigators. Ghost hunters are people who look for evidence of ghosts; they are not people who, necessarily, believe that ghosts exist. We approach every investigation with an open mind. When we talk of ghosts, we mean the visual appearance of a dead person – nothing else. Do you understand?"

Those around the tables nodded, relief and disappointment in their faces. Neither hunter continued immediately but merely allowed their gaze to move across the faces of the others as though waiting for a question. None came. Vernon narrowly avoided a snort; Gerald Henderson was almost asleep after a long day at work; Simon wondered what the future held for him and the White Horse; only James Ryder looked puzzled

Eventually, it was Esme who spoke.

"We have listened carefully to what you have said. We feel it warrants an investigation, and so we need to explain a little more about ghosts; there are several types ... Save your cynicism, Mr Scuffil! It was you who invited us here: we did not ask to come!"

Esme paused to cast Vernon a not unfriendly glance and he – reared to have good manners – apologised, noting, at the same time, that she had read his thoughts as she had read those of her partner.

"I will confine myself to describing the ones your accounts suggest. The first type is what we refer to as a *presence*. No ghost is seen but is felt – sometimes a sense that someone is there – or known by smell or sound or ... touch. Your ghost has touched you, hasn't it, Vernon?"

Vernon looked at the others, his face pale, and nodded, his eyes on Esme.

"The second type is the *poltergeist*. The ghost itself may not be seen as a figure, but its appearance is in no doubt. Poltergeists have been called haunted people as distinct from haunted places. There is substantial evidence that this phenomena springs from the living."

Esme looked around the table as though expecting a question. There were none but Fred and Gerald exchanged looks, remembering Richard Revell.

"We come, then, to our third type: the *interactive ghost*. These have a purpose and can speak or communicate in other ways with the living. There is intelligence at work here; they think, plan and carry out intentions."

"The fourth type is the *timeslip ghost*. This is where the living find themselves in another time and place. It may be that they feel themselves to be there or simply glimpse an earlier event; this feeling may be brief or last for an extended time."

Esme looked around the table and could see her listeners were exhausted. She looked at her partner. He smiled.

"There are others, naturally, but these seem to be the ones most likely to be calling for our attention in Thornham and we propose to begin with you, Vernon. Your visitor falls into at least three of our categories. During tonight and tomorrow we must prepare; the following day we call for you all."

"One moment," said James Ryder, the only one who seemed able to speak, "I have a question."

"You are wondering why your dog did not bark when Richard Gabriel came to your room with the whisky and the glasses?"

"Yes," replied the engineer, hoping to keep the surprise from his voice: he wasn't used to having his thoughts read.

"There are people with psychic abilities who are totally unaware of the fact. You are one of them, James. I knew it the moment we were introduced. You are what we call a 'physical medium' – and that makes you dangerous. People like you aid the forces of the spirit world. You focus them and bring them forth. Rollie did not bark because he detected your presence in Gabriel."

"I'd never heard of the ... man!"

"You had no need. He had heard of you. Why did you come to Thornham? How did you happen to be there that night? Once we have the answer to those questions, Richard Gabriel's purpose will be clear. There's no point in jumping to conclusions: we wait and watch for the moment. And James, when you come, bring Rollie."

*

When Fred, Gerald, Simon and James with Rollie answered the call, it was very apparent that Esme and her partner had been busy. She met them on the pathway and drew the four into the main house.

"Vernon and Justine are in the garden helping Clifford. We can talk freely here. We will not be overheard."

Fred wasn't sure whether this comment referred to the couple or the presence, but he assumed the latter. Esme looked at him, a puzzled flicker across her brows.

"The first thing we did was to get to know the house and the family. It's homely. It's inviting. Justine is lovely – very forthcoming and delighted we have come. We chatted with them over a cup of coffee and perceived no obvious signs of tension."

"That would have been important, would it – signs of tension?" asked Fred.

"Of course – many phenomena referred to as paranormal or psychic are nothing of the kind. They spring from the living, not the dead. Justine and her family are natural, warm people ... I know what you're thinking, Fred. Perhaps Vernon is an exception?"

Fred smiled and made a note to guard his thoughts, if that was possible from this woman.

"We'll come to that later, but first I must make you understand the nature of what we face here ... Neither Justine nor the children have experienced this presence. It seems to limit itself to the garden and Vernon's study. Its focus is Vernon. Fortunately for him, his partner is a down-to-earth person, not given to wasteful fears."

"You consider fear to be *wasteful*?" asked Gerald, who had confided to Fred that he found Esme's manner "irritating".

Esme frowned with her usual flicker of the eyebrows but ignored the question.

"Our usual method in these investigations is, firstly, to familiarise ourselves with the house and the people, as I have said. We then conduct interviews – usually everyone concerned but that seemed unnecessary in this case, and so I interviewed only Vernon."

Fred wondered how much she obtained from a man both reclusive and rude.

"Vernon's family goes back a long way in Thornham and several of his ancestors have been teachers of one kind or another. Vernon knew this and was ashamed, which explains his silence. He knew because he had researched much of the town's history ... You understand that what I am about to share with you is confidential?"

Esme waited until all four had acknowledged her request and then withdrew a slip of paper from a folder waiting on the kitchen table.

"This is an account of something that happened in 1843. I want you to read and understand its implications. Vernon eventually gave me this of his own free will. It is taken from a government document called *Pauper Children, their Education and Training* published in 1858. It is an attempt to right wrongs that had gone unpunished and provide a blueprint for the future. The account is from one of the children."

Esme handed the paper to Fred, indicating that the others were to crowd round him. The clergyman looked up to see that they were in place and proceeded to read the account:

No slave ever underwent such discipline as those boys under the heavy masterful hand of James Scuffil. The ready backslap in the face, the stunning clout over the ear, the strong blow with the open palm on alternate cheeks, which knocked our senses into confusion, were so frequent that it is a marvel we ever recovered them again. Whatever might be the nature of our offence, or merely because his irritable mood required vent, our poor heads were cuffed, and slapped, and pounded, until we lay speechless and streaming with blood ... If, while ... he was reading to us, he addressed a question to some boy, the slightest error in reply would either be followed by a stinging blow from the ruler or a thwack with his blackthorn. If a series of errors were discovered in our lessons, then a vindictive scourging of the offender followed, until he was exhausted, or our lacerated bodies could bear no more.

No one spoke for how long no one was sure; James sat with clenched fists, Fred and Gerald looked thoughtful as though their knowledge of the world left them in no doubt that the account was true; Simon turned away, tears in his eyes. This ghost thing had seemed a bit of a joke; after all, no one takes ghosts seriously, do they? His thoughts were a muddle; his ghost walks an abomination of an idea.

Eventually, Esme broke the uncomfortable silence.

"You comprehend, don't you, that this changes everything. Our annoying *presence* becomes a vengeful *interactive*. He is intelligent: he thinks, he plans, he has intentions."

"This is the one Marjory Broome swears she saw on Bridge Street the night her husband was killed," said Fred.

"It would seem so."

"One of those I saw in church at Miss Pritchard's funeral. He was dressed smartly in what used to be described as a suit of the English colonial style, and his name is Frank."

"How do you know?" asked James.

"As I told you at our meeting two days ago, I saw these … *figures* in church at the funeral. Their names came to me as I spoke by Amelia's coffin. I don't know, of course, that he is the one but I feel it to be the case. How many deaths are down to these … these ghosts?"

"We have never come across an investigation such as this one," said Esme, "I was puzzled when you mentioned the apparitions you saw in church, Fred, but no longer. We must act – and now. We will call Clifford and he will tell you what we have prepared."

Clifford's bulk in the small kitchen offered a false reassurance as he explained what he had been doing.

"We have placed lock-off cameras in what we call the 'hot spots' – those places this figure or presence has been seen or felt. After our walk around with Vernon and Justine we have set up EMF meters in the study, the garden, the area beyond the lower gate where Vernon first saw this man, under the archway and along the path …"

"EMF meters?" asked Fred.

"Electromagnetic field meters," replied Clifford, "They help us to identify any EM source that does not have a plausible explanation. I spent most of yesterday locating any natural source such as a kettle, computers and so on – any wiring into any appliance creates such a field."

"I see," replied Fred, clearly not doing so and receiving an understanding smile from Esme.

"Ghosts are an energy source," she said, "and can disrupt our electromagnetic field."

James cast a sympathetic eye towards Fred, finding himself, once again, in the world of hocus-pocus; a look both ghost hunters ignored.

"And your 'lock-off' cameras lock-on if they detect movement?" he asked.

"Or a source of heat," replied Clifford, "We also have thermometers placed at certain places. A change in temperature may indicate a presence."

"What do you want us to do exactly," continued James, eager to pin down their purpose.

"Be here as witnesses to what may happen."

Simon's thought that he could not leave his pub for an unknown period was left unspoken but read by Esme, who said:

"Come and go as you please, Simon – as your work dictates. We may be here for many days. Some investigations have spanned weeks."

This was not what any of them had expected; truth to tell, none of them knew what they had expected. The strange occurrence at the White Horse and the conversations that followed suggested that these people might locate the ghost or ghosts; how they might do this remained a mystery. Searching in the dark without a torch was the thought that came to Fred as they waited; it seemed that the ghosts held the initiative, whereas he had, perhaps, hoped that Esme and Clifford might lead the way. It was also peculiar to be waiting in broad daylight for a presence that the precautions suggested might not be visible and yet the figures he had seen in church were solid enough.

Before morning became afternoon, both Simon and Gerald had excused themselves and Justine had come and gone, taking her children to school, shopping, cooking and then fetching them home.

It was one of the wettest Decembers in living memory. Mornings opened with an overnight frost still hard on ponds and water bowls and a sodden mist clung to all it could drape. A few, brief hours later, as darkness closed in the late afternoon, the mist was back and the damp cold with it.

The watchers moved about during the day from Vernon's study to the kitchen, where Justine fed them, down to the lower garden, where Vernon had first seen the figure and then along the path under the crab apple tree to the archway closed by the two black doors. During this time, Esme and Clifford barely exchanged a word and yet their existence was felt everywhere.

The first day passed into another; on the second, Simon and Gerald called in when their work freed them; on the third, James Ryder was called away by a firm consulting his engineering expertise, and the absence of Rollie cast a shadow into the winter's gloom; the company of the black Labrador with its unquestioning loyalty to Ryder had been a comfort to them all.

It was as another cold evening approached on the third day that the investigation moved rapidly forward. Darkness had fallen sufficiently for Clifford to turn the spotlights on to the back garden, lighting the lawn and the little terrace that fronted Vernon's study as well as casting a beam through the open gateway to the lower garden. Simon had left some time before, since the White Horse was already serving evening meals and Gerald, having called in briefly, had left to be with his children and enjoy another of Lottie's dinners.

Justine was upstairs with the children, earlier than usual but nervously wanting them out of the way "just in case"; Fred was standing by the kitchen door talking with Esme and claiming some warmth from the stove; Vernon was alone, as he had been for most of the three days, half-standing on the path, half-crouching under the apple tree; Clifford was on the back lawn by the children's trampoline, adjusting one of the lamps.

The figure Fred had called Frank emerged from the study. Only Clifford saw him and watched as he appeared from the door, seemingly invisible within the study but a solid figure outside. With deliberate steps, Frank walked to the gate that closed off the path from the garden and lawn and stood quietly watching Vernon. When the teacher looked up, their eyes met across almost two centuries. Each knew the other; each knew the other's purpose.

Vernon had been even quieter than usual since the investigation began, but had determined, now the truth was out in the open, to confront his tormentor in whatever way suggested itself when the time came. The time had now arrived.

"What is it you want from me – hmmm! In the business of giving me a good hiding, are you – as though for one moment that will right the wrongs of the past – of my ancestors and yours."

It wasn't a question but a challenge and delivered as only Vernon's elephantine trumpeting could deliver it. The figure stood unmoved, small-framed but filling the gateway with a blackthorn in hand.

Esme and Fred moved down the path, positioning themselves across it and to Vernon's rear; in the garden beyond there was no sign of Clifford.

"*For I, the Lord thy God am a jealous God, visiting the iniquity of the fathers upon the children of the third and fourth generation of them that hate me,*" said Frank, anger repressed in his voice.

"And you see yourself as the hand of God, do you – hmmm? God with blackthorn in hand – come to mete out the same violence – once imposed on others – once denounced by the likes of you – now furthered by the likes of you. Hmmm?"

It was strange, almost comic, how Vernon's short burst of phrase reverberated in the narrow space between house and path. His large head tossed and waved, brushing back the branches of the crab apple tree.

"We heard it loud and clear enough, when we had our catechism and our Bible beaten into us."

"And it has held you here, down the generations, seeking a vengeance you can never satisfy instead of releasing you to the peace beyond the grave, has it?"

Esme moved forward as she spoke almost but not quite between the ghost and its intended victim. The blackthorn jerked in Frank's hand.

"Answer me! I'm calling you," she continued.

"I will smash your glasses and strike you to the path on which you stand. I will beat your prostrate form until there is no strength left in me to beat it more – do you remember, Scuffil? Do you remember the beating I gave your forebear?"

"I read of it and cannot blame you ..."

"Cannot blame me! It was a scratch on the table, and he announced his intention to flog us one by one!"

Vernon adjusted his own glasses, pushing them further along his hawk nose. Frank still did not move from the gateway.

Frederick Mackenzie, as a priest, held back. Should he intervene or wait? So much of his training and, to be fair, his experience, told him to wait. Nothing was to be gained for man or God by anticipating, was it? But Fred was a priest of the new order – intervene and change!

"There is only one Lawgiver and Judge," he called, "the one who is able to save and destroy. But you – who are you to judge your neighbour?"

Esme looked back at him, unused to religious intercession but relieved; she had found an ally.

"James – a prophet of the new religion! What care the likes of us for him! We who were brought up in the religion of hard knocks!"

"Then cast your mind to the old religion," said Fred, now in his element, *"The fathers shall not be put to death for the children, neither shall the children be put to death for the fathers; every man shall be put to death for his own sin."*

A smile crossed the face of the ghost, similar to the smile that crosses that of a man who has met his equal in any contest. He held his ground.

Esme felt there was delight in the smile. She had challenged spirits before but only when necessity demanded. She was glad of the priest's support but, while he focussed on the one ghost to the exclusion of all else, she was aware of other energies at work in the garden.

Somewhere beyond the ghost, these spirits were showing themselves to another in the grounds. She felt, rather than saw or heard, lights and noises. There were hotspots, as Clifford forecast, where something stood and waited and watched. And there was malice, an evil intent and they – whatever *they* were – moved forward. But where? She heard a cracking sound, almost like the branch of a tree breaking off.

"Step forward!" she commanded.

Vernon cast a glance, very briefly, behind him. Fred kept his eyes on Frank. From behind the ghost came a grunting and Esme knew that these spirits she felt were grounded. Somehow, they were those of people who had never overcome the way they left this life. Now, she needed Clifford and those willing to make a circle to send them onward. Sometimes, when spirits receive the chance to move on, they are unsure how to react. If only she had Clifford's help, she might envisage a pathway of light, a path that would lead these lost souls home.

As she wondered how to reach Clifford, Esme heard footsteps. Neither Fred nor Vernon was aware of this new occurrence; neither turned and yet the footsteps were clear and coming along the street. She turned to look at the black doors that secured the arched passage.

And then they all heard the banging – fists thumping on the black doors – and Fred and Vernon turned, taking their eyes off the ghost.

"Grandmama, grandmama!"

It was a child's voice, a young child judging by the tone – no more than ten or eleven – and the voice was exhausted and terrified.

"Grandmama, Grandmama!"

Fred turned, ran quickly to the doors and drew one open. Into the passage stumbled a girl. Her feet were bare and her face blackened by soot. She had on a thin dress of blue serge that was stained in places as though she had fallen on wet soil, and her legs were covered with smears of earth and grass. It didn't take too much imagination to realise she had come a long way to be knocking at her grandmother's door.

She was breathing heavily; what breath she could seize from the night air came in rasps. Her eyes scoured those who watched her: dark pits of fear and yearning. She looked wildly around, rushed at the closed door of the kitchen and repeated her banging.

"Grandmama, grandmama, they took her clothes off and beat her! Let me in! Let me in! Until the blood came – and the other they stripped her chemise from her and laid her bosom bare ... stripped their upper bodies naked to allow him to scourge them with birch rods on their bare shoulders and waists. In my fear, I broke only a jug, and they said I would be birched in the morning. Grandmama, grandmama!"

From the kitchen, drawn from their beds by the banging, Acer and Anthemis watched terrified, held close by their mother. Bang! Bang! The girl's fist thudded at the door. Tears welled from her and those who watched.

Fred and Vernon, unsure what was happening, could only wait, while Esme moved towards the child and reached for her shoulders. As she did, the thin gown slipped and the green and yellow welts of an old flogging could be seen across her back. On Esme's touch the girl turned and looked up at her.

"Who are you?" asked the ghost hunter, "Give me your name."

"Susan Farmer. This is my grandmama's house."

"Take my hand. There is a way from here."

Susan cast out a sound that might have been a heartless laugh, a cry for help or a blend of both, and then she ran, past Esme and Fred, pushing aside Vernon, into the lower garden, where silence had replaced the din of breaking branches. When the three of them turned to watch her flight, they realised that Frank was no longer barring the way. They followed. Arriving beyond the gate, they found Clifford face down on the grass.

Esme ran to her partner. With a huge effort of will rather than strength she turned him over and cradled him across her arm. Clifford's head fell back.

"He's dead! There's no life in my Clifford. What in the name of Heaven is happening?"

*

It was several days before Esme's question came anywhere near to an answer: days of a post-mortem, many prayers, some research and a meditation.

Fred was the one who prayed and who felt, in the answer he received, that they should come together after the post-mortem. Sitting in his study, he invited each one to speak.

Esme was the first, quiet and resigned. With Christmas but two weeks away, she knew the festive season would no longer bring her cheer ever again; but the Welsh psychic was made of stern stuff and her meditations had brough the answer she sought.

"Vernon was a distraction; it was Clifford they were after. The ghost, Frank, blocked the pathway and the girl drew our attention away from what was happening beyond the little gate. But why Clifford?"

Vernon coughed and leaned forward, his bumptious persona quelled.

"What the child, Susan Farmer, had to say was a fact I had discovered in my research; on-line ancestry told me the rest. Clifford is a local man. At one time, an ancestor of his was the porter at the local workhouse – Myles Raine was a sadistic man. His case, which the Poor Law Commissioners refused to pass on to the courts, was fully reported in *The Times*. I'm sorry."

"What for?" asked Esme.

"In the sense that it was my haunting brought you here."

"But what killed him?"

"Gerald?" said Fred, quietly.

The priest and the doctor had spoken earlier; both had made statements to the police and knew an investigation was pending.

"At the post-mortem … I'm sorry, Esme, but you will be told this later and it might be better coming from me … It looked as though he had been whipped to death. His back from the shoulder to the waist was covered in green and yellow lash marks ..."

"But ..."

"Let me finish. Many years ago, a friend of mine established a practice as a hypnotist in Harley Street. He told me of a case concerning one of his patients – a woman. She came to him with similar marks on her buttocks and lower back. After only a few sessions, relief brought out the truth. Her husband was a man who could not begin sex until he had been whipped – I know, we laugh at such practices between consenting adults now, as though they are a joke. But it wasn't a joke for her; she was the one he wanted to whip him and it was a torment for her. So much so that she visited the guilt back on herself. In your line of work, you are very aware of the power of the mind ..."

"You are saying that Clifford's flagellation was self-imposed?"

"Yes. How these creatures brought it about, we can only guess at this time."

Simon had said nothing during these revelations; he now turned to Fred.

"It looks as though these ghosts are waging a campaign against the village."

"Yes," replied Fred, "Let us pray."

Book Three

Chapter 1

The Butcher's Shop

Christmas had arrived and the village was in good spirits: their Victorian Evening at the beginning of December, when the Christmas lights were always switched on, had been a genuine success.

The shopkeepers who promoted the event could not have been more pleased; the undertaker, Martin Francis, a portly, kindly man known for his sensitivity and discretion, had persuaded a significant number of the villagers to invest early in their own demise, offering mulled wine and hot mince pies as an inducement; Simon Pegg at the White Horse collaborated with the churches of the village and the Thorn Valley Singers to provide an evening of Christmas carols, as always; Marjory Broome, now in charge of the general store, ran out of Christmas wreaths; tables were full at The Swan, where you could sit and eat without venturing out into the cold night to watch Father Christmas listening to the children's wishes as he strolled through the Christmas Market, held every year on the village green; elderly villagers sat on the terrace of The Terrace, watching the youngsters and remembering their own childhoods.

Throughout this festive excitement, the Thornham Players continued to rehearse their annual pantomime, which always took place early in the New Year. The actors had already reached the stage when rehearsals might usefully move from the small warehouse on the Cookley Road retail estate (where Maisie Garland's Dancing Feet troupe always met each week) and take place on the small stage in the church hall of St John's, the Roman Catholic church on Edmund's Lane attended by Carmen Quay.

This move never failed to signal a greater sense of urgency, amounting almost to impending doom, in the ladies of the WI led by Maisie's mother, Edith. July Pegg was no longer the only girl standing on a chair while their mothers and the costume makers fussed around them; Bruce Pegg no longer the only boy wondering how he'd managed to allow himself to become involved in what seemed a female-dominated crusade. Children became quite simply part of the props department, whizzed hither and thither across the village to be fitted with hats by one person and cloaks by another.

It was no surprise to Reg Wilton, therefore, when a lady called Ruby Land arrived at his shop commissioned by Edith Garland to "fit Barbara out with her costume".

"We won't be long, Mr Wilton. I'll bring her back looking like a queen."

Reg's view of his older daughter was summed up by his favourite expression, 'full-blooded, firm-muscled and rarin' to go', and he didn't quite see her as a queen, a species he thought of as frail, weak-wristed, overly delicate and fussy about what they eat, whereas his girls "ate what was put in front of them on the table".

He was busy at the time; the centrepiece of many a family's Christmas dinner hung from a hook in his cold store or lay stuffed on a shelf and the shop was heaving with people.

"Can you call her for me?" insisted Ruby Land when Reg seemed to hesitate.

Reg saw her as one of those women who were never happy unless they were bossing somebody about and Ruby's next request convinced him of the fact.

"I must get her fitted, see. I've lots to do to this morning."

Reg had lots to do and was surprised the woman didn't realise the fact since she was standing in *his* shop holding up *his* customers. He looked her up and down, wondering where Myrtle had got to: she'd left for her hair appointment what seemed ages ago.

"She's probably in her room," he replied, "I can't leave the shop now."

Ruby seemed to relent.

"I can come back, I suppose, but ..."

She left the offer hanging in the air and Reg, a kindly man at heart, realised that the woman was giving up her time for the sake of the children; besides, he knew, despite her complaints about rehearsals, that Barbara was looking forward to the pantomime.

"You're fitting her in when you can find the time, I suppose?"

"Yes – I've come a long way this morning."

He knew that the Thornham Staithe WI reached far and wide for its membership and was upset at himself.

"Of course," he said, "You'll find her in her room, I expect. If you go round by the side door – it's off the garden there on your right – and call up the stairs, she'll hear you."

The woman disappeared towards the old chapel and that was the last Reg thought about her until his wife arrived home rather later than expected because she'd "taken the opportunity to pick up a few things in Beccles". Reg commented on how nice her hair looked (he'd been married long enough to know what was expected of him at such moments) and Myrtle went off to assure herself in the mirror that it was true.

They didn't usually take a break for lunch – not at this time of the year when the shop was so busy – and so it wasn't until early afternoon, when Myrtle thought the girls might be hungry, that she enquired as to where she might find Barbara.

"Why should I know?" responded Lucy, "She went off with the lady to get her costume for the pantomime."

"What lady was this?"

"The one who called for her."

"Did you see her?"

"No, Why should I?"

Reg, an extremely busy morning behind him, was no more help.

"I'll give Edith a ring," said Myrtle, "She'll know."

Edith didn't and many phone calls later Barbara's absence remained a mystery.

"Well, she can't have gone far," insisted Reg.

"No one seems to have heard of this Ruby Land. Don't you see?"

"See what?" replied Reg, taking refuge in his masculine stubbornness.

"I'm phoning the police," said Myrtle.

"There's no need to bother them. She'll be back in her own good time. You know Barbara."

Myrtle did know her daughter, knew how inconsiderate she was when it came to doing what she wanted but, nevertheless, made her phone call.

"And so, you've not seen her since she went out with this Mrs Land?" asked the constable, not for the first time, "You have phoned round her friends?" he continued, having investigated many disappearances of teenage girls that turned out to be anything but.

It hadn't occurred to anyone that Barbara might simply have dropped off at a friend's house when her costume fitting finished.

"I never thought of that," replied Myrtle, feeling foolish, "I was so worried about this woman no one seems to have heard of."

"Perhaps it might be a good idea?" suggested the constable, "In the meantime, perhaps you could give me a description of this Mrs Land?"

"You saw her, Reg," said Myrtle.

Reg had seen her but barely noticed what the woman looked like.

"She was wearing a hat, I think – yes, that's right. It was a strange hat – not one you see about much nowadays. It had a wide brim and a round top like them gypsy women used to wear when they came round selling pegs."

"Was she short, tall? What was her face like? Anything you can remember might help?" suggested the constable, sure now that nothing much was amiss but that he might as well round off his on-duty time that day with this family who would, no doubt, have much to say to their daughter when she did turn up, hungry and wanting her tea.

Lucy, also feeling her sister would arrive home that evening and now enjoying the attention, chipped in.

"She had a shrill voice," she said, "I heard her when she called up the stairs."

"But you didn't see her?" asked the constable, "What did your sister say when she went off with Mrs Land? Did she seem too know her?"

"She just said she hoped to come back with her costume."

"Nothing else?"

"Try to think, Lucy," urged Myrtle, "Which of the WI ladies have been working on your costumes?"

"Mrs Garland did mine."

"We've already phoned Edith," said Myrtle, I don't like to trouble her again. She said she'd never heard of this Ruby Land."

"But she might be one of those women who help out with the costumes," suggested Reg, "They're not all in the WI."

"No, you're right there, Reg, they're not."

"But Mrs Garland would know who was helping with the costumes, wouldn't she?" suggested Lucy, helpfully if not reassuringly.

"What was your sister wearing when she left?" asked the constable, "It might help if we have to look for her."

"She had that big, floppy coat on – you know the one she loves so much – the faux fur one."

"What print was it?"

"Leopard skin – oh and her Doc Marten boots."

The two items – ones that, apparently, his daughter couldn't live without – had set Reg back a bob or two and he remembered them well. He couldn't make out why she needed to wear such expensive items with torn jeans, but he had learned to live with women. To be honest, Reg wasn't too worried. He knew what was upsetting Myrtle and sending her off phoning everybody: it was that funny business way back in September when she'd sleepwalked herself into the garden, and then that nonsense at Simon Pegg's Psychic Supper. Psychic Supper!

"What did you say, Reg?"

"Nothing, nothing! I was just thinking."

"Well try not to think out loud then!"

"Look, Mrs Wilton, I'll be off now and make out my report," said the constable, feeling that a family row wasn't to his taste.

They were upset – he could see that was the case, but things would turn out all right when the girl came home.

Evening came and Barbara still had not returned. Self-centred as her mother knew her to be, it was unlike the girl not to have arrived home at least for dinner, one they had eaten in silence: in fact, Myrtle had barely touched a morsel and had looked on askance at her husband and Lucy tucking into their meal.

"I'm going out," she said, "I can't stand this any longer. I'm going to look for her and if I find her at Lin's Plaice, I'll give her a piece of my mind in front of her friends or not!"

"Where're you going to look. It's raining out there and cold. There's no point in you just wandering round."

Myrtle didn't answer but left the table to fetch her coat, and Reg followed, knowing it would be the wisest move to make. As they went out by the side door, Lucy called after them: she didn't want to be left in the house alone.

They made their way, huddled together against the wet and cold, along the High Street. But for the interminable drizzle and the worry associated with their quest, it might have been a pleasant walk. The Christmas strings of light enhanced the road and each house they passed offered a tribute to the season: winged angels in flight, wreaths on doors, candles in their holly-bedecked holders, brightly lit elves in front gardens, Father Christmases on rooftops, babies in mangers, wise men astride camels on windowsills, shepherds herding their sheep and the house next to the antique-cum-bric-a-brac shops offered all and sundry. On the village green, the traditional Nordmann was resplendent with multi-coloured lights and the surrounding beech trees cast a kindly, yellow glow across the grass. Beyond the war memorial, Myrtle saw the cross on the tower of Holy Trinity illuminated for all to see, encouraging the villagers to worship, as many would be, drawn to the Blessing of the Crib, in two days' time.

"I don't know where to go from here, Reg," said Myrtle, suddenly, and she felt Lucy clutch her arm.

The hundreds of miles of cycling on their mountain bikes across the hills of the Peak District, Wales and Scotland or even the discreet inclines of Norfolk suddenly seemed not only a distant memory but one not to be repeated.

"Well, we can ask at Lin's. He'll know if she's ... if Barbara's been there with a friend, but I don't think ..."

"It doesn't seem – or does it?"

"I don't know. How can I? It's not like her."

"Let's go round by Market Place."

They passed the house off the green where two dogs and one cat always sat in the window when the sun was on the sill (but not at this time of year when it was decorated with a full Nativity set) and the hairdressing salon and came to the lights of the vicarage.

It was tempting to knock at the door. Fred always answered. But no, not tonight. Tomorrow, maybe. Tonight, the need was to keep on the move, to keep looking.

They came to the back of the old surgery – now converted as two houses and a narrow passageway took them towards Lin's Plaice – the best fish and chip shop for miles around. People drove from Norbridge for Lin's fish and chips. Barbara loved them. Had she dropped off at a friend's? It was the only possible explanation but ...

The narrow passage took them passed the printer's workshop: **J DORLING AND SON – PRINTERS.** Reg thought back to that night at the White Horse, after the parish council meeting when he'd shared a pint with Jack Dorling on his birthday and that daughter of his, Juniper Wells as she called herself, arrived. 'Village ghosts!' he'd said, 'I'll give them village, bloody ghosts if I catch one of them, I can tell you'.

And she'd said, in that knowing way of hers, 'You may not recognise one when you see it, Reg Wilton. Not know 'til afterward'.

Chapter 2

Sam Whitham Speaks Out

Sam Whitham's conscience had been in turmoil since the night of the Burghamton bonfire. He had seen the figure with the crushed top hat and the ill-fitting coat ahead of him on the road and hidden. What else was he to do, meeting a stranger at that time of night? Whilst hidden, he had seen Richard Revell dash past, and had then taken another path home. It wasn't until he was at the school the next day that he heard the other boy had been found collapsed on one of the tracks and still later that he had died in hospital.

Mr Ryder was the only one he felt able to confide in and he'd missed his visit to Thornham just before Christmas. Sam wasn't sure what he might have told Mr Ryder. Did the stranger have anything to do with Richard Revell's death? How could he be sure what he had seen was relevant?

Besides, Sam felt guilty that he had sought another way home on that night. If he had followed the other boy, could he have saved him? Someone said that Revell had died of hypothermia after laying sodden wet by the mere on a freezing cold night. In his heart, Sam Whitham knew that he could have prevented that death; but was he to blame?

It was on Boxing Day, after a very lonely Christmas Day with his grandmother, Marjory Broome, that he finally broke. He was surprised how closely his grandmother listened and even more surprised how sympathetic she was towards his predicament. No, he wasn't to blame; yes, he did the sensible thing in finding another way home; and yes, he should tell someone. If he couldn't speak with Mr Ryder, would he like to talk with the vicar?

Sam wasn't sure, although he knew the vicar was a nice man. He might try and find Mr Ryder; the landlord at the Swan might have his number because Mr Ryder always stayed at the Swan when he came to the village. His grandmother agreed and said the pub was sure to be open on Boxing Day because that was the day when people went for long walks and always arrived at the pub for lunch.

And so it was that the boy, one described as an 'isolate' by his teachers, stood looking at the door of the Swan, wondering whether or not he should go inside. It was only a short step into the bar, through a narrow space made difficult by a double door. It was just too early for lunches to be served and only a few men sat at the bar, but all turned their eyes on Sam.

"What you want, boy?" asked one, with a wink at his fellow drinkers.

"I'm looking for Mr Douglas," replied Sam, surprised at the ease he felt.

"Are you now? And what would you be wanting with Ned – Mr Douglas to you."

"That's what I said – Mr Douglas."

The group of men exchanged glances. Sam didn't realise it but they were acknowledging a boy with spirit.

"I reckon he's too busy to speak with you, don't you?"

"Why don't you order a pint while you wait?" suggested a second man, again with a wink at his companions, and the group burst out laughing.

"I'll pop round the bar and pull you one if you like," said a third, and the laughter re-doubled.

"You ain't told us yet what you want with Mr Douglas?"

Sam looked at the men. They were smiling, and he realised they were teasing him and bore him no malice. He wasn't sure why they were teasing him but he was to remember the moment and cherish it.

"You looking for a job, are yer? I can see you behind the bar but you'd need a stool to stand on."

More laughter and Sam smiled. He felt more at ease among these men than he did among his schoolfriends. He was puzzled.

"Well, speak up, boy! What you want with Mr Douglas?"

It was the first man who repeated his question, stressing the *Mr* Douglas..

"I'm not rightly sure that's got anything to do with you," replied Sam, emboldened and taken aback by his own cheek.

More laughter, much louder than the previous rounds.

"Is that right now? You reckon that's none of my business?"

Even more laughter

"You reckon a young feller like you should be in a public house, do you?" asked the second man.

"I reckon we'd be within our rights to call the police – get that PC Sharpe here double quick," suggested the third man.

"Or that Sally Frost," suggested the second man, "I'd rather clap eyes on her. She's a bit of all right."

The laughter was now continuous and Sam felt it embraced him. He remembered the name 'Sally Frost'; he recalled her coming to the school to talk to them. She was a very attractive young police officer and he knew what the men meant when they called her 'a bit of all right'. He felt they'd taken him into their confidence.

How far the ribaldry might have continued along those lines he was not to find out because as the laughter soared Ned Douglas came in from behind the bar. He summed the situation up immediately and smiled at the boy.

"Ignore them, son. What can a I get you?"

"He'd like a pint of Ghost Ship, Ned."

The laughter revived.

"And I'd lose my licence, John. What can a I do for you, son?"

When Sam explained that he needed to contact Ryder, the landlord frowned. He was a big man with a mane of thick, wavy, yellow hair and a beard to match. He reminded Sam of a Viking. The frown made him look menacing, and this puzzled the boy.

"I don't know as I can rightly give you his number, son. What do you want with Mr Ryder?"

Sam wasn't given to lying but, at the same time, he couldn't explain why he wanted to speak with the walker.

"He's interested in the watermill and I thought he might like to see it."

"What now – at Christmas."

"I thought he might be on holiday."

"He might be, but not here. It's not the time of year for long distance walking, is it?"

The laughter resumed around the bar, and the doors – back and front – began to swing open as the Boxing Day walkers came for their lunch.

"I'll tell you what I'll do, son – you're Sam Whitham, aren't you?"

"Yes."

Those propping up the bar looked at each other. They hadn't known it when they were teasing him but this was the boy who had lost his grandfather back in September.

"I'll tell you what I'll do, Sam," repeated Ned Douglas, "I'll give Mr Ryder a ring when I've finished here and he can get in touch with you. Will that be all right?"

"Thank you," replied Sam.

When the boy hesitated to leave, Ned Douglas said, reassuringly:

"I promise. As soon as we've finished doing the lunches … Would you like a glass of lemonade?"

"I should think on a day like this, Ned, the boy 'ud do better with a hot drink," suggested the first man, who the landlord had called John, "How about a rum toddy?"

The laughter took any doubt out of the situation. These men were on his side, and Sam, downing the lemonade in one, left the Swan, a smile on his face, the men's talk ringing in his ears.

"He'll be a right boozer when he's older, Ned. He'll be propping up your bar every night of the week!"

Outside, on a chill but pleasant midday, Sam wondered what to do. He didn't want to go home: the watermill was even lonelier now his grandfather was dead. Sam and his grandmother had spent

Christmas Day wondering what to do with each other. Should he see the vicar? Rev Mackenzie was a nice man but … but how could he just knock on his door?

Sam wandered onto the village green and sat on the seat by the war memorial. It was cold and a bit wet but he didn't mind. He needed to think. It was as he sat lost in doubt that he heard the voice.

"Hello, Sam."

Looking up, he saw Charlie Henderson standing by him just as he sometimes did in the playground at lunchtime when Sam sat alone eating his packed lunch. With Charlie was his sister. Sam knew her; she was one of those beauties who was beyond his kind of person. Sam wasn't sure how he knew that to be true, but the very sight of Lottie Henderson created a gap in his world.

"Hello, Sam," she said, "We've just got back from a long walk."

"On the Warren Hills," added Charlie.

Sam knew the Warren Hills, a place home to scores of rabbits: but they weren't hills – just a stretch of meadows that went up across the Norbridge Road to Heckingham Hall. Sam knew all about the hall and Heckingham Green. Mr Scuffil told them about it in history. The Green was common land but was only to be used for cattle – no sheep or geese were allowed to graze there; and cattle could only be graze from the 19th May to the following 1st March; this was to let the grazing recover with spring growth.

"We're going to the Swan for lunch," said Charlie, breaking into Sam's reverie.

"I'll let Mr Douglas know we've arrived. Why don't you have a chat with Sam?"

Sam had not been aware of the man who stood behind the children but looked up when he spoke and recognised Dr Henderson.

"We didn't know how long we would be, Sam," continued the doctor, "it's a long walk – two hours or so."

This was true. In summer, Sam had sometimes spent a whole day exploring the Hills.

Lottie, her boots caked with mud, sat down beside the boy and leaned towards him. Charlie joined her. Suddenly, he felt enveloped in warmth. It was the girl's breath he felt, as she talked.

"Where are you going?"

"I've been to see Mr Douglas. I wanted to talk to Mr Ryder and he stays at the Swan. He has a dog – a black Labrador called Rollie."

Lottie remembered cycling along the lane from Pottery Encore after one of her music lessons with Edward and Myles, and a walker with such a dog standing back for her to pass into the churchyard. She said so.

"Mr Ryder is a nice man," replied Sam, "He would step aside for ... for a lady."

Lottie laughed and it was as though the boy's whole world lit up. He blushed but he didn't mind.

"What did you want to talk to Mr Ryder about?" asked Lottie

Was it that women were always nosey or was it that he felt able to confide in them just as he'd been able to confide in his grandmother only yesterday? He looked at Charlie Henderson.

"Do you remember the night of the Burghamton Bonfire, Charlie?" he asked.

Charlie and his sister exchanged glances; it was Charlie's turn to blush.

"Mr Ryder was there," continued Sam, "He stopped me going with you all. He said Revell was up to no good. He bought me a cheeseburger and a Pepsi and a hotdog for Rollie. I wanted to come with you, Charlie, but he stopped me."

"And very sensible, too," said Lottie, giving her brother an admonitory look.

"It's all right, Sam," said Charlie, "We didn't know what we were doing."

It was as though another weight had been lifted from Sam's shoulders, a weight he never realised he bore until he spoke – the weight of guilt at not having gone with Charlie Henderson on that night, at not having supported his only friend.

"I went home by myself – Mr Ryder offered me a lift but I didn't like to ... and I saw Revell ..."

The whole story poured forth, the one he had shared, at last, with his grandmother and wanted to share with James Ryder. Lottie and her brother listened without interrupting. It didn't take long – he'd only seen a strange man ahead on the road and the school bully run past; it was the guilt that had taken the time.

"And there's no need to feel that way," said Lottie when Sam finished.

"We'd have all done the same, Sam," said Charlie, "It was the right thing to do."

"Why don't you do what your grandmother said – speak to Fred if you can't find Mr Ryder?"

They probably hadn't spoken for more than ten or fifteen minutes but it seemed as though they'd known each other for a lifetime when Gerald Henderson came for his children.

"We can't entice you to join us, can we?" asked the doctor, "I'm sure Mr Douglas can rustle up another plate."

Lottie and Charlie looked at Sam, eager to share what he'd said with their father and wanting to be friendly.

"My grandmother would be upset, I think," replied Sam, both reluctant and relieved that he couldn't join them, "She will have a dinner for me when I get back."

"Of course, she will!" replied Gerald, "I understand. Perhaps you could come round and play with Charles some time. That would be good."

It would be good. Sam knew that was true as he watched the Henderson family cross to the Swan and then made his way through the churchyard to the picnic site where he had first met James Ryder and Rollie before heading home across the water meadows for his dinner, light of foot and lighter of heart.

It was late afternoon when the phone rang at the watermill. Sam was in his room, full of turkey flan with leeks and cheese: his grandmother knew what to do with leftovers and there were plenty of those this year. His grandmother may not have been cuddly but she could cook. 'Waste not, want not' was her motto.

He was engrossed in a book called *The Wherryman's Way* – one his grandfather had bought him for his eleventh birthday – and his mind was full of black sails, staithes, coal, timber, abandoned windmills, long-forgotten ferries and the ghosts of wherrymen when he heard his grandmother call him from the bottom of the winding stairs that led to his room.

"It's the phone, Sam! Mr Ryder wants to talk to you."

He didn't – Mr Ryder wanted to listen – but grownups like his grandmother always supposed it was the adults who did the talking and the children who listened.

"Hello Sam. Ned Douglas gave me your grandmother's number. What can I do for you, son?"

It seemed to Sam, as he listened to that voice with its unwavering offer, that all his troubles were over and he spilled out his heart for a second time that day.

When he finished, and James Ryder had listened without interrupting, the walker spoke.

"I'm in Wales, at the moment, Sam. There's been a bit of trouble with a bridge in the Brecon Beacons. When I get back, I'll come to Thornham and see you, and so don't worry. In the meantime, go and see the Rev Mackenzie. He's a nice man. He will listen to you and he will help you understand. None of this is your fault – not with Revell or anybody else. There's a lot going on and we're going to have to come together. I'll get over as soon as I can."

Sam replaced the receiver, relieved; it seemed all roads led to the church.

Chapter 3

Consternation at the Vicarage

Frederick Mackenzie listened attentively and gave Sam the same assurances the boy had already received twice before that day: he should not blame himself. He walked the boy home and offered a few words of advice to the grandmother, Marjory Broome, promising Sam that he would do something.

Walking back to the vicarage, he wondered what that 'something' might be. Even now he could scarcely bring himself to believe what his senses told him must be true.

The police investigation was ongoing and unpleasant despite PC Sharpe's comforting, local presence amongst those officers who neither knew the village nor were likely to believe what Gerald Henderson had told them. Foul play by person or persons unknown seemed to be the general consensus.

Frederick's phone call to Gordon Urquhart, the Bishop of Norbridge, had brought the advice that "remaining quiet and prayerful was the best way forward at this time". Frederick had prayed, prayed and spoken endlessly with his wife, Jacqueline, whose attitude was that action needed to be taken; although she was a little short on ideas as to how this might be effected.

On top of this, he now contended with Barbara Wilton's disappearance. He had hesitated to say he thought she would turn up later in the day because he didn't believe she would do so. Instead, he phoned the police and advised them that a girl had gone missing. He then accompanied Myrtle home and waited with her. He was there when the police arrived.

That had all been before Christmas. It was true that the annual services did much to draw the tragedy from the village and for precious moments distract his own mind from the task ahead; and it was a task and Frederick saw himself as central to its resolution. Who could he call upon for help? When he asked Jacqueline, she consulted her diary.

"You recall what I had to say on the night of the Psychic Supper, do you?" she asked.

"You disagreed with Myles and Edward when they suggested that these hauntings had more to do with what modern psychology had taught us about the power of the mind than with the afterlife or with anything spiritual?"

"Yes. The *man* Thomkins was devilish and with a purpose. We need to focus on that, Fred, and not be drawn aside. I like Myles and Edward but I do not think they will be of much help."

"And James Ryder. What do you think of him?"

"From what you told me the ghost hunters had to say, I worry about him. Is he a channel for these hauntings?"

"James wasn't here when Ambrose fell from the bridge or Myrtle had her visitor."

"But he was on the other occasions and he was at the Psychic Supper, the night when Amelia Prichard died, and he was with you during that terrible business at Vernon Scuffil's!"

As she spoke, Jacqueline flicked backwards and forwards through her diary. Frederick smiled. He wasn't organised in quite that way and disagreed with his wife about James Ryder; but he did admire her thoroughness. She must have gone through her diary, recapping the events and noting the details as she did.

"James wasn't with us on that final night at Vernon's," said Fred, quietly, "He'd been called away by a firm as a consultant."

"But he had been there during the day!" insisted Jacqueline, consulting her diary frantically.

"He'd been called away during the day. I remember because we all missed Rollie."

"Mm!"

Frederick liked his wife's 'mms': they were an acknowledgement she had been wrong and he watched as she amended her diary entry.

In addition to her thoroughness, he admired her instincts. He remembered what she said to him the night following the Psychic Supper, when he'd returned from praying in the church, 'I know you have a duty to intervene ... but these apparitions ... are evil. They seek to enter our world and, therefore, our souls'. She was right but so was he: a life grounded in the love of God has nothing to fear from evil influences of any kind.

But her fears had held him back, and now Barbara Wilton had disappeared; and Frederick knew his reluctance to accept the obvious was to blame. He recalled Amelia Pritchard's look of admiration when he asked: 'Did she have something on her mind that triggered a memory in yours?' He'd known then, if only he had been ready to admit the fact.

"Have you thought of inviting Esme?"

"Esme thought of inviting herself. She's ready when ... when I've put a plan together – and if I don't, she will."

"You will invite Gerald Henderson.."

It wasn't a question and Frederick answered only with a smile

"And Vernon?"

That was a question because Jacqueline was aware of her husband's doubts regarding Vernon Scuffil: a loose cannon, a rude man, not a team player, a putter-up of backs.

"You will need him, Fred. His historical knowledge will be invaluable. It must have occurred to you that these ghosts are haunting the people as much as the place."

Yes, it had occurred to Frederick; despite Simon Pegg's comments about 'a campaign against the village' it was clear that these ghosts were obsessed with people – and not indiscriminately. Jacqueline was right. Vernon's presence was essential.

He was rather taken with the idea of involving the landlord of the White Horse. Simon would be a good ally, and yet, he had children. Had he any right to put further children at risk because at risk they would be. These were vengeful spirits.

He was for seeking further, knowledgeable aid. If they were to hunt these spirits down and remove them from the world, it would be a grim venture. The Bishop of Norbridge, Robert Urquhart, had been reluctant to involve the Diocesan Deliverance Team. Frederick had a natural aversion to teams, anyway, and had agreed. But there was a man, one he'd met several times but who was now retired and living somewhere on the south coast.

The Rev Neil Ilkestone had been the Deliverance Minister when Frederick first came to the diocese. He had liked and trusted the man. It was in the days when individuals rather than teams took responsibility for outcomes, the days of a more confident world when leaders led.

*

They sat in Frederick's study and talked: each keen to state their case and their concerns, each keen to rid themselves of what haunted them.

From the moment they arrived and made themselves comfortable, it was Esme Owen who took the lead. She had insisted, when Frederick discussed his views on the phone, that everyone who had been haunted should be invited to the meeting. Frederick agreed with the exception of Myrtle Wilton, who he felt had enough worries of her own.

"We will use Christian names from here in," said Esme, before each one spoke. "That is how it must be. Trust is everything between us."

Only James Ryder was absent, having phoned his apologies from the Brecon Beacons. Nothing new came from their sharing except Gerald's story of his wife's death. Jacqueline sat making notes in her diary, and when they had all spoken, Esme asked her to sum up, keeping her comments to the number of deaths and hauntings.

"We have had four deaths – Ambrose, Richard Revell, Amelia and Clifford – all in strange circumstances, and one disappearance, Barbara Wilton.

Gerald has experienced two hauntings, his own with the two young women, and his wife's, with Thomkins the photographer. Vernon has experienced several, by the man Fred tells us is called Frank. Fred, at least two by Elizabeth Beeston. James, two by the man who called himself Gabriel. Myrtle, by a man called Lansmore and the disappearance of her daughter with a woman calling herself Ruby Land."

"Thank you," said Esme, "You will know from what I had to say previously that these ghosts are grounded spirits. They are earthbound, unable to move on to whatever realms our spirits inhabit after our deaths.

There are many reasons why this should happen. Sometimes, spirits do not realise they have passed on: they may have died suddenly, perhaps through an accident; others are afraid because in this life they have been wicked and they cling on here, fearing they will be held accountable in the afterlife; others have suffered or witnessed some injustice in their lives and stay to see justice done … Yes, Vernon, you are right in your thoughts: these are the ones we face."

Vernon neither trumpeted nor snorted. A resounding hmmm! may have reverberated throughout his cranium but it went unheard.

"It is our task to help them move on, to help them cross over, to find the light."

"And you think this can be achieved?" asked Gerald, doubt rampant in every syllable.

"You may have realised from the manner in which I addressed Vernon's ghost that I have psychic powers. I am able to act as a medium. These are not powers I call upon, unless the need is great. With Clifford, I was a ghost hunter – nothing more. You are aware we approached our work with an open mind, always a sceptical one, and in a spirit of scientific investigation. Yes?"

Esme waited until they had all answered, her eyes demanding one from each of them.

"Good," she said, her thoughts far away, "Now, it will be different. We must help them leave this earth. You will remember, I told the child there was a way from here? Yes?"

The others merely nodded, feeling perhaps that words were not wanted.

"I need to envisage a pathway of light, a path that will lead these lost souls home, and I must have your help. Do you understand?" asked Esme, pausing as a teacher waiting for a child to grasp a new concept. No one spoke. "We will approach these ghosts one by one and lead them from this world."

"You're proposing a séance, aren't you?" said Jacqueline, speaking for only the second time since the meeting began.

Frederick thought it typical of his wife that her question was a challenge to contradict her. Esme never faltered.

"Exactly."

"No."

"There is no other way."

"The church is not happy with this meddling. We are very much against such things as Ouija boards and spiritualism. They are dangerous! Interaction with the spirit world is at best the province of the priesthood and, even then, is approached through prayer and meditation. There is always the *very strong probability* of attracting evil entities."

Frederick had never heard his wife raise her voice before. She was terrified – something he had not realised – and he would have reached for her hand had he not known she would snatch it from him.

"The evil is already here, Jacqueline, if you wish to use that word. I prefer *lost souls*."

"From what Fred has told us, hmm!" said Vernon, "The church has rather drawn back – has it not? – hmmm! We can, naturally, approach this prayerfully – whatever that may mean – or we can simply get on with it. I'm a sceptic. Ouija boards, seances, channellings mediums, readings – need I go on, hmmm! – are nonsense to me – always have been, but then, so was what happened in Justine's garden. Esme offers us a way forward and I suggest we take it. Hmmm?"

The final Hmmm, posed as a challenge, was worthy of whatever elephant may have been part of Vernon's ancestral DNA

"I understand your fears, Jacqueline," said Esme, soothingly, "but I have no option but to proceed. If you and Fred are unable ..."

"My husband must speak for himself."

"You may count me in, Esme," said Frederick, very quietly.

"Thank you."

"And me," said Gerald, "I stand with no one on in this matter. As a scientist, I share neither Jacqueline's spiritual concerns nor Vernon's scepticism. I have an open mind. I cannot explain what has happened and, by the same reasoning, I cannot dismiss it."

"Thank you," said Esme, "Let us be clear. Once we commit ourselves to this task, there will be no room for doubt."

"You said 'one by one'. Hmm! Where do you plan to start?"

"With the living," replied Esme, "if it wasn't for what happened there and if it wasn't for the children, I would say Justine's garden. You see, what I must have is a feel for the energies of the place ..."

"It is the people, not the place, these creatures haunt," said Jacqueline.

"You are right, Jacqueline, but it is at a place this séance must be conducted. Once I have a feel for these energies, I will be able to sense any spirits who have stayed behind after their bodies left this earth. It will then be the purpose of our séance to remove their fear or hatred of the light before leading them to their pathway."

Esme paused and looked around, judging whether her class understood.

"Our visitors have a purpose – revenge – and one we know of is drawn to his mother's grave. Richard Gabriel goaded James to the churchyard of All Saints, where Elizabeth is buried. This is the same churchyard where Fred met the strange woman before Amelia Pritchard's funeral."

"You are planning to hold this séance in the churchyard?" asked Frederick.

"It must be so, once James is with us. Now, I will explain what a séance involves and what I shall require from each of you."

Fred listened, his mind on his constraints as a priest. He certainly shouldn't be taking part in a séance in a churchyard without permission from a higher authority, and his 'higher authority' was Robert Urquhart, Bishop of Norbridge, who had already made clear his views. And yet ...?

Chapter 4

Silence at the Printers

Jack Dorling was alone in his workshop. This was not unusual: it was the place where he felt most at home. He liked the old machines, although he knew they should go to make room for modern technology; but they still had their uses. There was the Stanhope from 1842, a favourite of his grandfather, and the Reliance from the 1890s, the machine that had fascinated him as a boy when he had stood looking up, awed by its height. His father would stand him on the beams when he was very young and let him pretend to turn the handle. It was a giant of a machine, standing seven feet high and built in Germany of iron and wood. You could always rely on German technology.

Next to it stood what his father called the 'jobbing press', and Jack still used it on occasions for billheads, business cards, letterheads, flyers and envelopes. He could set it up in fifteen minutes and run off over a thousand copies in an hour. Juniper always laughed at him but it sometimes took her that long to run them off digitally. He had used it recently for the missing person posters Reg Wilton wanted; there was one in every shop and on every noticeboard, billboard and lamppost throughout Thornham and the surrounding villages.

But they had failed to turn up any information regarding Reg's daughter, Barbara, still missing and, Jack feared, likely to remain so. He remembered Reg talking about a man with green eyes who had taken his wife downstairs and left her in the neighbour's garden. But it was supposed to be a woman who had come for the girl, and not a man. Made no sense at all.

His chat with Reg had been one of the conversations at the White Horse back in October, when he'd had a go at Ambrose Broome over the man's dislike of his grandson, Sam Whitham. And then, Ambrose had gone and got himself killed, falling off that old bridge, one they should have repaired or taken down long ago. It had once been the way to the warehouses where they stored the grain before, and the flour after, milling; but the bridge led nowhere now and was best removed before it did any more harm. That was the night they'd met that strange bloke who called himself 'Kent', the one who seemed to know all about what he called vestry meetings, a kind of parish council meeting, which he said they held in the local.

He hadn't seen Kent since but he'd heard of him. Someone said he turned up at the Psychic Supper when the medium, Saul Tacksman, had caused Marjory Broome so much distress by saying that Ambrose's death hadn't been an accident. Terrible night that was: Marjory in tears and the medium rushing out of the room looking distraught, anything but in charge of himself or the spirits.

Spirits! There'd been a lot of talk about spirits and ghosts in the village. Everyone was on edge. The whole business was best left alone. When we die, we die and that's it. What happens afterwards nobody knows and, anyway, it's the Lord's business. The church always taught that if you led a good life it would be enough. Not that many of us manage to do that – at least, not all of the time. You just hoped God was merciful when you met Him.

Juniper had been there that night, coming across the bar with a pint in each hand, deliberately to embarrass him in front of Dr Henderson; but he hadn't really minded. She was wild and a bit of a ... well, he wouldn't use that word about his daughter but he'd heard the village gossip was that she'd had a few boyfriends too many. But she had a good heart; she wasn't the kind of daughter who'd stick you in an old folks' home rather than take the trouble to look after you when the time came.

He hadn't seen Juniper in the last few days but she was calling in tomorrow or maybe tonight – she wasn't sure; a local writer had written a play for one of the Norbridge theatre groups to perform and wanted it published as a proper book. The writer had dropped the data-stick off that morning and Juniper was the one to set it up.

Loneliness was one of the reasons he was in the workshop. It was sad being in the house on your own. He thought he would have got used to it by now – his wife had passed on when Juniper was very young – but you never did get used to being alone. Sometimes Juniper would stay over, cook him a meal and they'd talk. But not often enough, and the workshop was a good friend. It housed many of his memories.

He sniffed and looked around his domain. His main desk, now sporting a modern computer, was opposite the front door of the premises, while a smaller desk, where he kept his local bills, some still spiked, was to the left of the door. On a buttress wall to the right of the door, pinned to a noticeboard, was a photograph of his father, a photograph from a newspaper, one that he'd always intended to frame and never quite got round to doing so. It was a photograph commemorating his father's work for the local Lions over sixty years. Other newspaper cuttings, whose dates went back decades, were pinned around it.

Jack stepped up into the main workshop, leaning for a moment on the German printing press to secure his balance. In the near right corner were stacked boxes of ink cartridges, all spaced and shelved by one of his staff, a young man with a family who lived in the village and who Jack had taken on when the boy left school. Jack was never sure which cartridges were where but the young man could place his hand on the right ones immediately.

Next to these and spreading itself almost along the entire length of the wall was a large chest of drawers, those on the lowest, third, tier being the largest. What these drawers contained no one, not even Jack, was sure but it was certain that the contents went back as far as the nineteenth century: each one a museum piece. An antique dealer – one of those from London who scour East Anglia looking for local people muggins enough to part with a valuable heirloom for next to nothing – had once offered to take the chest off Jack's hands, "to make a little bit more space, you know, guv" but Jack had shown him the door.

On the wall above this chest were several printing trays holding old, used metal letterpress in mixed fonts and a large, wooden clock with Roman numerals and a small pendulum that could be seen swinging back and forth in a small window at the clock's base, while scattered along the chest's surface were ink rollers, typographic print blotters, piles of paper, several old composing sticks and a stack of galleys.

Most of the remaining walls were festooned with posters printed in bright colours advertising events ranging from the **Norbridge Gay Pride March** to *Wine-tasting at the Thorn Valley Vineyard.* There were also several menus promoting events at the village hostelries, among them the **White Horse Psychic Supper.**

Jack made his way to a three-legged stool, which was situated in front of a job case and sat down. It was his favourite spot in the workshop. He remembered his father sitting there bent over the narrow drawers that held the movable type, the capital letters located in the upper drawer or case, as it was called. The case was a beautiful example of the cabinet maker's art, each of its dozen or so drawers equipped with brass nameplates and handles. His father would be bent over the sloping work surface and Jack would sit on another stool one of the old workmen put in place for him and watch speechless.

He looked about him. There were filing cabinets everywhere, propped against tables or under them; several fire extinguishers, placed strategically, held necessary by the health and safety executive, deemed by Jack to be unnecessary and an encumbrance to free movement about the workshop; cans of oil-based ink; three portable typewriters often loaned to drama groups in the city; a huge white paper roll pushed into one corner; old print number pegs crammed into long unused print trays; several untidy stacks of old books with bookmarks in different directions on different pages; a selection of new books, printed for people who lived as far afield as Cromer on the north Norfolk coast, neatly arranged in a pristine bookcase on the far wall.

Home! Jack knew that was so for him but wondered whether Juniper saw it in the same light and would carry on its traditions when he departed this life. He looked up at the new printing machines, all linked to various computers, including the one on his desk, and smiled.

It was while he was lost in these reflections that he thought he heard the front door open. It wasn't unusual: people often dropped in for an ink cartridge or a ream or so of copy paper, but during shop hours, not at night. Besides, Jack thought he'd pushed the door to when he arrived. But there was a presence, certainly a presence in the workshop. He felt his heart skip a beat but was reluctant to leave the stool. He wanted to be transfixed; movement seemed dangerous.

"Dorling?"

The speaker was the man who called himself 'Kent', the man who had introduced himself that night at the White Horse, the man dressed in the long overcoat that looked a little outdated, which opened at the front to reveal a waistcoat with a chain and watch that disappeared into its pocket. He was standing on the step that led up to the workshop.

"*Mr* Dorling, yes," replied Jack, irked that a stranger should address him with discourtesy.

"Dorling will do," replied Kent, "One Dorling along the line of many."

"What do you want? Can I get you anything?" said Jack, eager to keep the conversation on business lines.

"That large chest – the one with the many drawers – have you ever wondered what it contains? Open the top drawer on the far left."

The unease with which he viewed the stranger was slowly being replaced with anger. Jack was an easy-going boss but he was boss in his own workshop.

"I don't know who you are but ..."

"You soon will. Let me open the drawer for you."

Kent didn't move but the next moment Jack saw the very drawer the man had mentioned jerk open; he smiled at the fear he smelled in Jack, and Jack knew.

"Take a look inside, Dorling."

Kent stood between him and the front door and Jack felt the man would have him before he could reach the back one. The urge to run was, nevertheless, overwhelming. He approached the drawer and found it contained a number of very old books.

"Do you know what they are?"

"No."

"They're the poor books. One of your ancestors – another Jack Dorling – printed them but they were kept at the shop, the one most recently owned by Ambrose Broome, whose family worked the mill. It was a nice arrangement."

"I don't understand."

"You will. Scuffil could have told you. *Practical Results of the Workhouse System as adopted in the Parish of Burghamton 1833-34*. Do you remember his thesis? You printed it for him."

"I remember but …"

"But back to the business of the evening. Your ancestor, Dorling, was one of the guardians, wasn't he?"

"I have no idea."

"You should. We should always learn the lessons of history. Leaving it too late is dangerous. You know how history repeats itself. Dorling was the guardian but the poor books were kept on the counter of the village shop. Very convenient. Dorling's answer to anyone applying for relief on the parish was always the same, 'apply at the shop', where they were always informed of the decisions of the vestry, which met at the public house … You remember?"

"I remember you telling us that evening in the White Horse."

"We like to keep people informed."

"We?"

"You'll see. Pleasant surroundings, the pub. Pleasant surroundings to decide the fate of those thrown on the parish. Dealt with at the vestry according to their docility in the shop, where prices were up to 40 percent above those anywhere else. I believe Dorling shared the profits, did he not?"

"How would I know?"

"You should know. It's your civic duty to know. J Dorling and Son grew fat on the shared profits of the shop. A nice arrangement, as I said. Educated men, you printers. It was Dorling or his wife who kept the parish books, wasn't it?"

"I believe so," replied Jack, irritated beyond measure by the man's mocking tone, aware that violence was in the air: constrained anger often hid vengeful wrath. He remembered from somewhere back in his childhood when his great-grandfather, who always insisted on a game of draughts when Jack was old enough to play, would talk of their "important forebears", and along the line, among the boasting, there had been mention of 'parish books'.

"You are remembering?"

"Yes."

"Open the neighbouring drawer. Now!"

Jack, his hands reluctant and shaking, did as he was told, wondering how this man knew where to look in drawers that had not been opened by him in years. Only Vernon Scuffil had shown any interest when writing his thesis.

"What do you see?"

"Lists of names against dates," replied Jack as he flicked carefully through the dusty pages.

"And the headings on the pages?""

"One says 'Low Women'."

"Low Women! Who might they be – the poor, the destitute, those whose husbands had lost their jobs?"

"I have no idea."

"But you should. Turn on. What do you see above the longest list?"

Jack turned a few more pages and came across 'Hilly Jittimites'.

"No Biblical implications, Dorling," said Kent, with a smile that could only have emerged from cruelty or a very dark humour, "Just an ignorant woman's spelling of 'Illegitimates' – the girls who came for help bearing the children of men they barely knew, or those children, some babies, dumped at the door of the parish. But perhaps we should excuse the spelling? After all, many educated people today are no better than the uneducated wives of your ancestors were in the nineteenth century. Make your way to the next drawer – no, not that one – the third along the second tier."

Jack obeyed, wondering how he might outwit this stranger who clearly knew more about his ancestors than he did and who Jack knew full well intended him no good.

"They are account books," he said.

"Read – any page. Take your pick."

"'For sparrows 2s. 6d'."

"The paupers were paid fourpence a dozen for shooting sparrows, Dorling, and remarkably their bag always came to just 2 shillings and sixpence. How many times does that entry occur? Never mind – it was regular enough to secure a 'nice little earner' – I think that's the modern expression – on the parish. One more and then we will get down to the business of the evening."

Despite the fear he felt, Jack could not help smiling at the next entry, which occurred as a regular item week after week: 'For tolling the church bell 1s.'

"These guardians, Dorling, were making a nice profit on the parish while treating the people in their care with a degree of contempt beyond belief, were they not?"

"It's a long time ago. I can take no blame for the behaviour of my ancestors."

"Oh, but you can – the iniquity of the fathers. Remember? Now, the business of the evening!"

Jack suddenly became aware of what that phrase meant when the first metal letter struck him in the face. He looked, caught Kent smiling and was struck again. Kent's smile deepened. Still, Jack was unsure what was happening until he was struck again and again; each time the letter caught him on the face.

"D – upper case, of course, O, R, L …"

It was Kent's voice, seemingly far away, and then three more letters struck Jack and he felt the blood running down his cheeks and along his lips. He looked up at the wall above the long chest of drawers and saw the letters flying out from the printing trays that held the old, metal letters.

"Castellar! We must have the font right for Dorling and Son, must we not, Dorling?"

The tone was mocking again but this time with no lightness of tone: cruelty was in every syllable. Jack recalled the font used for the firm's name above the front door. How long, he wondered, had this man planned his revenge.

A drawer opened from his father's job case, slammed shut and another opened.

"We are short of an 'S' and an 'N' among the letters on the wall. We must have things hunky-dory for a DORLING, must we not."

It wasn't a question but a challenge and Jack, still bewildered by the speed of Kent's actions, still not understanding what really was happening and feeling the blood now trickling down his neck, staggered back to his father's stool.

Kent had not moved from the step that barred the way to the front door.

A galley rose from the stack on the chest of drawers and spun, frisbee-like, across the room and then another and another and another. They flew rapidly over Jack's head, twisted round and flew back to their resting place. Had the frames struck Jack as the letters had done, he knew by their sheer weight that they would have taken his head with them.

"Think of the orphans, Dorling, and the paupers begging for bread at the door of the parish and ask yourself whether your line should survive, whether your ancestors should be remembered by a clock."

The clock, the one with the small pendulum, struck nine; the front casing snapped open and the hands spun from the face and left the numerals forever. Immediately, the body of the clock followed: glass smashed against a filing cabinet; wood splintered on the concrete of the floor. Awarded to a J Dorling in 1901 in recognition of services to … Jack couldn't remember; he wound the clock each week but had forgotten its purpose.

As he sought for an explanation as to what was happening and planned to run for the back door, hoping this devil of a man was not fast on his feet, the posters behind him ripped, one by one; gay pride was dashed, wine tasting at Thorn Valley Vineyard spat out, the Psychic Supper at the White Horse scattered in the dust.

Piles of paper rose from the antique chest, dividing in mid-air and spinning themselves across the workshop; the typographic print balls flew at Jack's head, pounding him dizzy and knocking him to the floor. He struggled to his feet, grasping one of them by its wooden handle, resting the dog-skin against his other palm, although what the intended to do with such a weapon he was unsure.

Still, Kent had not moved. The man's eyes were almost blank of expression; the hate he was feeling showed only in the tautness of his body and the deathly set of the lines on his face – the lips pursed, the crow's feet etched deeply. As Jack watched, waiting his moment to run, he realised the man's energies were focussed on the destruction around him.

One of the old typewriters began rattling its keys against the rubber roller. Even in the extremity of the danger he knew he faced, Jack couldn't stop himself wondering what the machine might be typing had paper been inserted. 'Once a printer, always a …' he thought to himself, and as he did the first ink composing stick, rising from the chest, dug into him. His nose split and as the other sticks followed their leader, he felt the skin fall loose from his nostrils. Blood was in his eyes now, streaking from the broken nose and running into his mouth.

Jack wasn't an old man and nor was he a weak or nervous one; it was simply that the destruction of his workshop had started so quickly he'd had no time to gather his senses. His thinking was slow and methodical by habit; he was a man who progressed in his endeavours step by step, and events had overtaken him.

Still, Kent had not moved.

Jack staggered from the floor for a second time, just as the first filing cabinet toppled over, spilling its contents across the shop floor. The second followed.

Jack made a dash towards Kent as the Stanhope reared up on what amounted to its back legs; squat, chubby, austere, iron-clad it appeared as a knight in armour. Supporting its massive weight only for seconds, the printing press lurched sideways and crashed to the ground. The sheer weight of the machine was daunting. What kind of power, Jack asked himself as he skirted aside and rushed at Kent, had been harnessed to move it?

*

Seeing the light on in the printer's workshop, Vernon Scuffil decided to call in on Jack Dorling when he left the vicarage that night. Jack probably had several copies of his thesis in hand together with the research notes that accompanied it, which Vernon had had printed separately in book form, expecting his work to be admired across academic circles far and wide; if not, now seemed the moment for reprints.

He knocked on the front door but there was no answer and so Vernon pushed it open and called Jack's name. Still no answer, but familiar as locals were with Jack's friendship, Vernon did not hesitate to step up into the workshop.

The untidy stacks of old books with bookmarks in different directions on different pages were slung hither and thither; the pristine case of new books had toppled forward on the floor, their contents beneath it; the huge, white paper roll had curled and twisted itself around every piece of furniture or equipment; fire extinguishers had rolled across the floor and lay on their sides; Jack was lying on the frame of the Reliance, his face against the platen which had been windlassed down using the long handle Jack had loved as a boy and was known to printers as the Devil's Tail.

Chapter 5

A Song at Dawning

The following morning, Myles Langstroth was busy preparing breakfast as usual, while Edward took his walk. The singer enjoyed their early mornings together, first their unhurried rising followed by the quiet of the house as he cooked and then their sharing of the food. It was always a substantial meal, the first of the day and in many respects their favourite. Myles prided himself on always surprising Edward and this morning decided to use a cauliflower they had purchased (but hadn't needed for their supper the night before, when at the last minute they decided to eat at The Swan) at the farm shop on the small retail estate at the far end of the village.

In their early days at Pottery Encore, the walk to the farm shop had been their way of testing the reaction of the inhabitants of Thornham Staithe to the presence of two homosexual men living among them; and it had been the welcome they received that kept them loyal to the local shops, where they soon became well-known and respected figures. Neither of them was a publicly demonstrative man, both preferring to show their feelings through their music, but their closeness was obvious to all, and even in the blokeish atmosphere of the village's third pub, The King's Head, their standing together at the public bar did not send others, leaning there, slipping away as had happened many times during their years in London.

Myles had cooked the cauliflower until it was just firm and placed it to the side in a gratin dish and was melting the butter in the rinsed-out saucepan ready to stir in the flour and milk to make his sauce, creamy and smooth, before adding the Cheddar cheese, when he felt the arms around him.

At first, he thought it was Edward back early, and was annoyed because he did like to have the table perfectly set and the food at that timely point, when it is best enjoyed before his friend returned. The arms tightened into a hug, pinning his arms against his sides, and he felt the pain in his ribs. Edward never squeezed him that way, never enough to hurt. Myles tried to turn but the grip only tightened further, holding him in place at the stove, and he was unable to move to see who had invaded their home. Bending his arms at the elbow he managed, using his hands as best he could, to slide the pan from the hob to prevent it burning the sauce (without wondering why it seemed important to do so) and struggled against his attacker.

He was by no means a weak man: singing professionally had strengthened not only his chest but also his arm muscles. Besides, during those years in London Myles had learned to stand up for himself. He breathed in to expand his chest against the arms that held him and flexed his shoulder and arm muscles; then released the tension quickly to create a gap between him and his assailant, a gap just big enough to allow him to turn.

He struggled round to face his attacker and saw no one. There was, quite simply, nothing. The wall on the far side of the kitchen was visible: he saw their cookery books, bread bin and toaster as he stared ahead, and yet he was being manhandled by someone or something. His immediate feeling of horror was replaced – strangely, he thought – by one of curiosity, curiosity filled with a sense of loathing, witnessed by the sickness that rose in his throat to his mouth.

What he did realize was that this invisible creature meant him harm. It was breathing. He could feel the warmth of its exhaled air against his face. It smelt dank: the backstage smell of old costumes. It was excited. It was angry but exulted. It had chosen its moment.

Myles brought his arms up between himself and the creature, struggling against the coarseness of a thick woollen coat with a wide collar, and felt for its throat. He gripped the throat, a human throat he realised, and squeezed, pressing his fingers into the Adam's apple. A man, then? A groan followed by a choke rose from the creature and it pulled back its head; but its grip remained unyielding. Myles turned aside his head and breathed in rather than share the air this thing breathed out.

His assailant, now no longer holding Myles's arms against him chose to tighten his grip on the singer's waist and with a strength Myles could scarcely believe, lifted him from the ground. The creature stumbled forward on heavy feet (Myles heard the shuffle of leather boots on the kitchen floor) carrying his victim with him, step by step into their hallway. Myles now felt his body held firm and close against the man, but his arms were free and with one hand he struck frantically against the head, grasping the coat collar with the other. It was a man; he was sure it was a man. The hair was coarse and long and the face bearded roughly. Myles felt a hat, which his beating threw to the ground.

They were at the foot of the stairs when Myles felt the grip loosen and he fell to the floor. It was a moment's relief to know he was free, but only that of a moment because his assailant held the advantage; while he watched Myles sprawled in the hall, the singer had no idea where the thing stood and where he might strike next. Myles struggled to his feet, knowing he should have retained his hold on the coat. All he could hear was the breathing, heavy and painful, but he knew there was rage. It was palpable in the hallway between them.

He waited. The creature was as exhausted as himself. It was a terrible and tense time, waiting to be attacked. Myles realized his only option was to render his attacker unconscious but that could only be achieved once it made its move. He imagined it watching him, aware of the weakness of his position. Why couldn't he see what it was? In the turmoil of his fear and his thoughts, Myles recalled his words to Edward in the studio, back in September, 'There's no one, dear – no one at all'. 'But there is,' Edward had replied, 'You must be able to see him'. And his friend had clutched his arm.

As Myles groped for an answer, he heard voices, all seemingly from his opponent:

'It's time that boy was getting his own living'.

'He is at work, sir. He gets up at quarter to five every morning and goes around with the milkman for sixpence a week.'

'Well, can't he earn more than that?'

'Well, sir, the milkman says he's a very willing boy and always punctual, but he's so little – he's only eight – he doesn't think he can pay him more than sixpence yet.'

'He can earn more, we think, and feel disinclined to continue the out-relief '."

To understand them as the ravings of a madman was the only sense that Myles could place upon the words as the voice faltered between what he took for the man's own voice and that of another – the boy's mother? And he had no time to think further back, to dig deep into memories: the man was on him as soon as the last words had spilled angrily from his mouth. Myles was pushed back against the stairs and the man's knee was on his chest, crushing him down. His oppressor rested for a moment and Myles heard him panting, and then he was struck violently in the face, a blow so forceful it knocked him unconscious.

When he woke, Myles realized that he had been carried to his own bedroom. He and Edward always slept apart; both were restless during the night and, aside from their times of intimacy, preferred sleeping alone. Sometimes at night one or the other would wake and go quietly to the music studio where they might compose or, simply, feel the music and words that had driven them from sleep.

He looked around him but the man was nowhere to be seen. He looked up. It was an old house and tie-bars, which stretched across some of the rooms, held the walls together. Slung over the one that crossed his room below the high ceiling, Myles saw a noose. He became aware that his hands were behind his back and tied. He remembered a shiver passing through him when Edward had placed his hand on his arm.

The noose was a souvenir. Myles had sung the part of Captain Vere in Britten's opera, *Billy Budd*, many times and kept the hangman's rope with which Billy had been executed, brought from his cell at four o'clock one morning and hanged before the assembled crew.

"Vere, as an old man, acknowledged he could have saved Billy but failed to do so," said Myles's captor.

The voice was calm, relaxed, relieved, all anger spent, as though, at last after so long, justice was to be done.

*

Edward started from his reverie.

It had been a pleasant walk so far, longer than usual but Myles told him not to hurry and the composer was much occupied with his thoughts. He walked to the picnic spot by the edge of the Thorn and sat for a while, a melody resisting his attempts to capture and orchestrate it.

After a while, he crossed the little footbridge and so onto the water meadows right by the riverside. Boats belonging to the yards on the far bank were moored, some waiting for their winter overhaul, others gleaming with new paint. They always looked so clean, the whites pure, the blues the colour of a summer sky.

It was early morning and he decided to sit on one of the benches along the path. No one was about when he heard Myles's voice:

"Eddie".

No one else ever called him by that pet name; no one else knew his pet name. Edward stood and turned. From where he sat, their home was very visible, just beyond the water meadow and the higher meadow where sheep safely grazed in summer, he could see its red pantile roof and white walls. He had a sudden sense that something was wrong; a feeling of panic invaded the peace of his morning

"Eddie."

There it was again. It couldn't be his imagination. Myles was calling him and the voice sounded frightened. Edward didn't know whether to hurry back the way he had come or cut across the meadows; the lower one was wet at this time of year – boggy in places but it would be the quickest way. He scurried back to the gate that led from the picnic site and then made his way along the small stream that ran down to the Thorn, passing under the little bridge near their back gate, the bridge where he had come across the apparition that had appeared a second time in their music studio, the ghost Myles had not been able to see.

As he neared the far end of the first meadow, just as he was approaching the gate that kept the sheep safely grazing, at a low point where their house disappeared behind a rough hedgerow, he saw the figure of his friend and lover. It was unbearable to watch but loyalty went beyond the urge not to witness.

Myles was standing on a chair, his hands tied behind his back, and he was crying. He was pleading with someone Edward could not see because whoever it was stood just outside the range of sight allowed by the vision. Myles's face was so clear, so very pale, the cheeks stained with tears and there was a noose about his neck.

"I can feel your grip, Eddie ... and when you touched me, I felt you place a noose about my neck."

Myles's head was thrown slightly back. The eyes were wide open, fixed on someone in front of him. His legs were shaking and the chair rocked. It was the spindle-back chair, the one Myles kept in his bedroom and always sat on to tie his shoelaces in the morning.

And then the image vanished, and Edward rushed on through the kissing gate, up and across the field until he reached the stile that led into the churchyard. A different man, now, from the one who had sat so peacefully by the riverside only minutes before, he reached their back gate, skirted the house and hurried in through the kitchen door.

There, by the stove, was the saucepan containing the milk, a bag of plain flour, butter, a packet of Cheddar cheese and some Parmesan, a grater, nutmeg, the cauliflower in the gratin dish. All objects amounting to nothing but observed in a flash as though they held some clue as to what was happening.

Edward part-fell, part-stumbled up the stairs, tripping and falling as he went from step to step. He knocked on his friend's bedroom door – it was a habit: they never imposed on each other's privacy – and when there was no answer, he pushed open the door, fearing what he would see; and there was Myles, the chair kicked away, his head jerked forward by the knot of the noose at the back of his head, strangled to death by hanging.

Chapter 6

Séance in a Churchyard

Jacqueline Mackenzie hurried through the churchyard of Holy Trinity and so along the little lane that led to Pottery Encore. A phone call, intended for Frederick, summoned her to Edward Warburg's side. She wasn't used to displays of abject emotion by men: both her father and her husband were men who contained their feelings; and so, just for an initial moment, she hesitated as she heard sobs racketing from the kitchen of the musicians – but only for a moment.

Edward was at the kitchen table, his head in his heads, tears pouring through his fingers. Jacqueline went to him and put her arms about his shoulders.

"Have you phoned the police?" she asked.

"Yes. I can't touch him. Myles is hanging there, his face blue, and I cannot help my friend down."

"It's best that way. The police will need to …"

Jacqueline hesitated. The police will need to do what, she wondered. It wasn't a crime scene – not in the ordinary sense of the word. Myles must have hanged himself, but suicide isn't a crime, not anymore. It was decriminalised so that those who failed in the attempt would not be prosecuted. She was sure that was so; she and Fred had talked about suicide on occasions, usually when a parishioner had committed the act.

She didn't like to pursue the subject with Edward. She thought it best just to listen to his sobbing and keep hugging him. He didn't stop; the tears abated but the sobbing became dry and relentless.

Jacqueline was a small woman and found it difficult to embrace the musician fully: her right arm seemed forever partway across his shoulders. When Edward did cease sobbing it was suddenly. He turned to Jacqueline as though his mind had just taken in what she'd said.

"It wasn't suicide. Myles would never do such a thing. He was murdered."

"I don't understand."

"We never told anybody. It seemed so … so revealing … I don't know why I said that. We've always been private people. How could we talk about a ghost Myles had never even seen? We lived, publicly at least, through our music. That is how the people of Thornham know us."

Edward's face held a desperate appeal.

"We should have said, shouldn't we? Where's Fred?"

"He's in the churchyard at All Saints. Let me get you a cup of tea, Edward, and then you must tell me all about this ghost," replied Jacqueline with a weak smile, "The police will be here soon."

*

Esme had insisted that the séance group should set out early. The spot they had chosen for their ritual was not visible from the footpath that skirted the church or the children's playground that neighboured it and the church itself was unlikely to be visited by many in the course of the day but they all agreed that early was best and so arrived severally before dawn broke. They all knew of Jack Dorling's death; Frederick had been called out immediately by Vernon, and Gerald had been the one to sign the certificate. None wanted to be in that churchyard on that morning, none except Esme whose quiet, cold determination insisted they came and did their part. Whatever the cause of his death, she said, retreating on their part would not help him now any more than it would help her Clifford.

It was a cold day in late December and a red sky breaking with the dawn promising sleet if not snow. All six were wrapped warmly against the weather.

It was not the first séance Esme had held in the open but it was the bleakest. The previous evening, as Jack Dorling was attacked in his workshop, she had explained what she needed from each of those gathered. They assembled now in the circle she desired without a word, gloved hands touching gloved hands. She was overjoyed that James Ryder had turned up, having phoned through to her in the early hours that the Welsh hills would have to wait their turn. "Besides," he had said, laughing, "Snow has already started falling and there's little I can do now." It was always easier holding seances when at least one other of those assembled was also a psychic and James, however unwittingly, was one. Rollie was nowhere to be seen,

"Tucked up on my bed at The Swan", said James, bringing a cheerful note to a ritual most of them feared.

"Ease the circle back, slowly," said Esme, "We want it as nearly perfect as possible. And if you could spread your feet, standing at ease with the toes of your shoes or boots touching your neighbours."

Esme stood opposite James with Vernon and Frederick to her right and Gerald and Justine to her left. Vernon's wife had insisted on accompanying him, whether Esme liked it or not; but as it happened, the medium preferred an even number in the circle. Moreover, she liked Justine, seeing her as independent-spirited and a calming influence on her husband, who had, initially, called off the idea once he'd found Jack Dorling in the wreckage of his workshop.

"We must be calm, now – quite peaceful. Relax completely. Shake the strain from your shoulders gently. Let your arms hang loose. Ease backward on your hips. A slight shiver of the knees. Let the tension go from those muscles. Circle your heads nicely. Let them sit comfortably on your shoulders. Close your eyes ..."

Her voice, with its beautiful Welsh lilt, was soft and reassuring. She spoke thus for several minutes until she was sure everyone was on the point of sleep.

"Now, let your minds go blank – just darkness, and slowly in the darkness a scramble of light. Let the light settle and become a point, a focus. Hold it there carefully and open yourself to it. Feel it now, a path of light. Draw it in. Let it infuse your head … your chest. Let it flow out through your right arm into the hand of the friend next to you. Good, good. And now you will feel your left arm filling with the light from your friend on that side … Eyes still closed. Nothing to fear."

Esme took a deep breath and spoke. Both Vernon and James were, by nature, sceptics and hearing a voice asking if any spirits were present would under normal circumstance have produced a trumpeting from Vernon and given James a reason to move on. Both men remained silent, however, taken in by the Welsh medium's sincerity: she had so recently lost her partner and it didn't seem possible she was anything but wholehearted.

Almost immediately, it was Justine who sensed a presence and she knew – and it was frightening to know – that it was the man, Frank – the one who had plagued her husband. She said nothing, compliant with the instructions Vernon had given her when she insisted on accompanying him, instructions drilled into the party at the vicarage the previous evening. Esme was to do the talking.

Fred felt something touch his arm. It was a gentle touch but a careless one; the touch, he thought of an old woman. A grip meant to be reassuring that was anything but; it squeezed his shoulder carefully as thought searching for a break.

"Remain calm," said Esme, her voice softer than ever, "There is nothing to fear. And keep your eyes closed. Do not engage. Say when I ask, your voice low, if you have felt a contact."

She asked each name and Fred and Justine answered. She breathed in deeply, feeling the pathway of light that linked each member of her circle, trying as quietly as she knew how to visualise it. One of the grounded spirits, she knew, was standing within the circle; the one – the old woman – who actually touched the priest. She was compliant; her work here was done. Of the other, Esme was unsure.

"You came to avenge an injustice – did you?" she asked.

"I came to keep a promise to a friend."

"And now it is time to find peace at last. Do you feel the light? Can you sense its power? We will hold it for you as long as we are able but the choice is yours."

"I am ready," replied the old woman, "but I see no path."

"You will. Close your eyes ..."

"We are not finished. We cannot be complete until all is done."

It was the voice of the other one – the one who stood outside the circle – Frank – and the voice was angry and directed, not at Esme but at the old woman.

"Your name," said Esme, "Give me your name."

"I am Honor's friend."

"Bertha Long," said Vernon, forgetting he was not to address the spirits except through Esme, but knowing Honor Sheen's story.

"Yes, a good woman among the bad and very bad, so bad as to be evil."

Vernon knew the voice intimately – he'd heard it often enough, whispering in his ear – but Fred also recognised the speaker as Frank, the one he'd challenged in Justine's garden.

"Let her go," urged Esme, "She is ready."

"But we are not."

It was a third voice, that of Richard Gabriel. He, like Frank, was outside the circle, approaching it, his voice on the move and loud.

"And you are?"

"Ask Ryder."

James did not speak, knowing the circle to be already weakened by the confrontation with Frank.

"You are Richard Gabriel," said Esme, "James told us of you. Come – join the pathway."

"I seek no pathway from here."

"Then leave us for those who do."

"That cannot be. None leaves until our mission is completed. So many decades it has taken to bring us together and now we are one," replied Richard Gabriel, now close, so close that James felt him breathing down his neck.

"Ryder."

"Stay calm everyone. As I have said, they cannot possess us without permission."

But these were, also, the words of Saul Tacksman who had been possessed, much to his annoyance, much to his fear; and Esme knew.

"Bertha Long, Honor's friend, we are with you and for you. Do you want to cross over?"

"Oh yes, oh yes. I have been here so long."

The circle of friends shuddered. The sun should be rising; it had to be rising but the Earth remained cold and forlorn. They seemed to have been standing in the graveyard so long that the wintry rawness they'd felt was now intensified. Toes and fingers were frozen, faces nipped; and yet they must stand, silently waiting for Esme to complete her task. Outside the circle, the two spirits moved round, restless and intent of thwarting Esme's intentions.

Esme had never been possessed. It was a question of whether she felt the spirit was trustworthy and not whether she felt sorry for it. The pathway of light could be accessed through her and Honor's friend could, now she was willing, pass over. The cold of the winter's day was weakening the circle. She knew that was so and must act swiftly – if she was to act at all. The doubt was there, deep within her, not so much a fear as a regret. She hadn't wanted this gift and, as a child, had turned her back against it, an effort that made her grandmother – a woman of the Welsh hills – smile. 'A gift or a curse, Esme, it is yours, like it or not'.

She knew that once she gave permission, she would lose control and, more importantly, be unaware of what was happening to her and the spirit of the grounded one; only afterwards would she know whether her sacrifice had been successful. There would be that terrible time of coldness when her own spirit left her body and she felt dislocated. That was the only word she could find that came anywhere near describing such a feeling: dislocated, displaced, disengaged. Only a short time, usually, but terrifying.

"We must keep the circle safe," she said, eventually, "safe, intact. It must not be broken. I can feel the pathway of light passing though us. It has weakened but it is there. We must not falter – not now. Remain calm, remain focussed. Let nothing distract any of you – James, Fred, Justine, Vernon, Gerald."

Apart from herself, the doctor was the only one who had remained absolutely untouched; he had given out no sense of being aware of the spirits around them or within the circle. Esme was relieved; before, when she'd been obliged to commit herself in this way, she had been grateful for a doctor.

"I am with the light, now, Honor's friend. Relax and enter. You are safe within the circle. There is a way."

They all felt the trembling, all six shivered in the cold and with the loss that ran through the circle, through their linked arms and their feet, feet now without feeling. Their whole body juddered with the strain and each wept, so emotional was the feeling that here good was being achieved but at a price none might have chosen to pay had they known.

Over and above the feelings of relief and release and the joy they brought was the sensation that someone – perhaps many – had walked over their graves; and then the weight was lifted from their shoulders and they opened their eyes and saw the dawn, feeling that good had taken the day. A nice feeling but accompanied by the unnatural racing of their pulses as hearts beat faster.

They shivered uncontrollably. Never had any one of them felt such cold or such loss of energy. The circle broke and they wrapped their arms about themselves and each other. Whatever spirits had been conjured had gone.

Esme looked about her and fell, and Gerald was quick to her side.

"Only Honor's friend has passed over," she said, "Look – there and there!"

She pointed to the arched gateway, the entrance to the pathway of the church. The other two, Frank and Richard Gabriel, stood watching and conversing, their eyes on the six who knelt around the medium who now leaned heavily against Gerald Henderson.

"My legs!" cried Esme, "I cannot feel them. And my arms – they are gone!

"Are you in lots of pain?"

"Yes."

None of the others had known quite what to expect and Esme, clearly a tough woman, was in agony.

"It was quiet at first," she said, suddenly as though understanding for the first time, "I did feel disconnected but not troubled until I felt the aggression. It was very powerful. I cannot stand. My mind is wandering. It seems not to be here."

"We must get you somewhere warm," said Gerald, "as quickly as possible, and then to hospital."

Chapter 7

A Village Chorus

Simon Pegg was always at work by seven o'clock, a fact not known and, therefore, not appreciated by his customers; but it was the way of the landlord – someone had to be at the pub to receive the early deliveries; and the churchyard of All Saints was only two alleyways and a short stretch of road away from the White Horse; and so the party were soon ensconced around the log fire James Ryder lit in a hurry at Simon's request, enjoying hot toddies or coffees with warm, buttered toast prepared by Simon.

Esme lay on the leather sofa, where Gerald placed her on arrival, her knees tucked up almost under her chin; exhaustion was in every curve of her body and when the breakfasts arrived, prepared hurriedly by Simon's chef who lived above the pub, she waved hers aside with an apology.

Breakfasts were not normally served at the White Horse, the pub having no tourist accommodation; Simon had roused his chef especially for his uninvited guests and was a little put out until Fred explained the reason for their early morning call at which the landlord's eyes lit up. He had never shelved completely the idea of further psychic events and had faith in his own ability to persuade those who might be interested, which included both Saul Tacksman and Esme Owen, to see things his way.

Simon had not witnessed the lashing of Clifford Raine, had yet to learn of Jack Dorling's death, let alone that of Myles Langstroth; his personal experiences of the hauntings were limited to those on the night of his Psychic Supper and the incidents Fred related to him. Like the rest of the village, his knowledge was piecemeal and, more importantly, unbelievable; people need to make sense of the world around them and the unexplained is tucked safely away somewhere at the back of the mind; the impossible is cast aside and ignored.

But rumour spreads like the proverbial wildfire and two deaths in the village occurring in a single night had to be explained if only for the benefit of the gossips; and the local media were on the story, avid for an event to spice up the evening news and the daily papers. Despite all PC Sharpe could do to divert attention from the village, the journalists took a direct road to the doors of all and sundry.

One of Gerald's colleagues at the Thorn Medical Centre was called in to certify the death of Myles – Gerald having taken Esme first to the Norfolk and Norbridge Hospital and then home, promising the medium that someone would bring her car later in the day – but he learned of it soon enough and hastened to talk with his daughter. As her father anticipated, Lottie was devastated by the news and asked after Edward, wanting to see and comfort him. Gerald was amazed that his daughter – still a child as far as he was concerned despite her taking on the mother's role in the house – had the courage to face grief but gave her permission and phoned the school to explain she would be late that day.

Edward, too, was amazed to see her but pleased that she cared enough to want to be with him. The composer was quiet, very quiet, perhaps for Lottie's sake, perhaps because his grief had been cried out for the moment and the real shock was yet to come. She stayed with him until he made it plain that he "would be fine" and she "ought to go to school". He was a very traditional man in so many ways, careful to protect children from the vicissitudes of life; besides, grief was coming on again and he wanted to be alone or as alone as the police were able to leave him.

Lottie, anyway, was grateful to be away: she hadn't realised (how could she know?) how devastating it was to share the torment of another's loss. And she thought of Bradley Hall, the singer

Myles and Edward had planned to pair her with for the Burns' Night Supper. She must find and tell Bradley before the gossips.

Bradley took the news in his stride; with no experience of death and dying, he could only relate to what he knew and that was confined mostly to books, where death happened to others, others we might love and admire but not really know. But he was pleased Lottie had taken the trouble to find and tell him; her concern meant a lot.

Lucy Wilton heard the news at school from Brian Gooch, whose grandmother knew everything, and found a friend and an ear in Amy Prentice, who was only too pleased to talk about her boyfriend, Richard Revell, who "everyone seemed to have forgot had died only last month on bonfire night". They made a sad pair walking home together and Lucy returned to an even sadder home, a place where the talk was always of her sister, Barbara, who had vanished so mysteriously and (Lucy thought privately) would never be seen again. Her mother and father barely spoke these days, each consumed by their own grief, each blaming the other, mutely, for Barbara's disappearance.

Amy returned to her bedroom and her dressing table where each night the dead face of her boyfriend grinned at her from the mirror. She had tried talking to his mother, Cynthia, but she hadn't really wanted to know, strapped into her own grief, just an arm's length away from her husband's ready hand.

Those at the séance avoided the media; they knew too much and journalists had a way of wriggling out information, however piecemeal, and that word typified the general response in the papers and on the television. Two of them, anyway, had decided upon courses of action that they would not wish to share: James Ryder and Frederick Mackenzie.

Fred had decided to telephone the bishop for a second, or was it a third, time. Jacqueline would know from her diary. This time, he decided it would be to state his intentions rather than seek an opinion. Neil Ilkestone, once Diocesan Deliverance Minister had already come to mind and Fred had determined to find him.

James had been less than impressed with the séance. He did not doubt the hauntings – he had enough personal experience to be sure they were genuine and were happening – but what really occurred in the churchyard. Had Bertha Long, Honor Sheen's friend, really found the pathway of light promised by Esme Owen? He did not doubt the medium's honesty but there was no evidence that anything at all had taken place. Besides, Esme had talked of tackling the ghosts – or grounded spirits, as she called them one by one, as the only possible choice; and look at the state of her after one séance: exhausted, debilitated. No, there had to be another way and James decided it was time to play his hand.

He ambled down to the staithe in the late afternoon, partly to smoke his pipe and look at the water, partly in the hope he might meet Sam Whitham and find out how he felt so many months after his grandfather's death, which had occurred on the very bridge the boy must see every morning and every evening, come what may.

It was as he left the Swan and was passing the small Co-operative supermarket that he bumped into Lottie Henderson on her way to the school bus. They had met only once and briefly, last September, when he was walking the Wherryman's Way, decided to stay in the village and had strolled to the picnic site where he'd met Sam. He remembered standing aside to let her pass on her bike; she remembered him doing so; they smiled at each other.

"Hello," he said, taking the pipe from his mouth.

"Hello," she replied, smiling at him doing so: smoking was one of those habits her generation thought odd, especially in public and especially as neither of her parents had ever indulged in private.

It's a simple fact that some people know, like and trust each other immediately. James saw the grief in her; Lottie saw the understanding in him. Without passing a word, they both sat on one of the memorial seats that lined the village green and Lottie poured out her heart. James didn't say anything; he didn't have to do so: it was enough, more than enough, that he listened. She began by recalling where they met, the lane that led to Pottery Encore, and finished by talking about "those lovely men, Edward and Myles". It was a simple bond, made instantly.

Eventually, Lottie walked to her bus and Ryder went along Bridge Street to the staithe, where he hoped to meet Sam, but somehow both knew they would see each other again.

Look Anglia, the local television news programme, secured an interview with Juniper Wells and she was featured talking to one of the programmes regular presenters, Stewart Burch, a man adept at pinning politicians to his questions while being gentle with those suffering distress of any kind.

He hadn't visited Thornham personally but one of the reporters had and produced a short film, which preceded the interview. The film had drawn together the views of many inhabitants, each possessing a small amount of knowledge; but the purpose of the report had been to highlight the death of Myles Langstroth. Myles and Edward were not merely local celebrities: they had performed around the world and their living in Thornham added an additional frisson of interest to the programme.

Stewart was, therefore, taken aback when decency obliged him to commiserate with Juniper over the death of her father and she responded by saying:

"My father wasn't killed by a burglar as the film suggested. He was killed by a ghost."

"I'm sorry."

"A vengeful spirit, if you must."

"A vengeful spirit?"

"The report concentrated on Myles Langstroth, didn't it? Perhaps naturally since Dad was nowhere near as famous. But if you'd seen his workshop, you wouldn't have any doubts that the wreckage was the result of poltergeist activity."

Stewart almost heard himself repeating his interviewee's words for a second time but managed to hold back 'poltergeist activity?' and attempt to take control of the conversation.

"Perhaps you could describe what you saw to the viewers?"

Juniper did so without missing a detail. Stewart, still eager to hold the interview to the tragedy of both deaths, asked:

"Had your father spoken to you of any concerns he might have?"

"Not Dad. You know what that generation is like when it comes to talking about anything that might make them sound silly. They clam up. Dad was reserved, anyway. He never shared feelings he might have about anything emotional. There was a lot of talk about ghosts at a parish council meeting back in September ..."

Stewart smiled but only to himself, thinking that the conversation might have livened up the usual parish council proceedings. Juniper continued:

"... and then they met a man in the White Horse, a man who called himself Kent, who one or two of them thought might be a ghost."

"Why did you suppose they thought that?"

Juniper, primed by the question went on to talk about Gerald Henderson's women, the village gossip concerning the strange death of Richard Revell and the events she had witnessed at the Psychic Supper.

It was a longer interview than Stewart had intended but he ignored the voice in his earpiece and encouraged Juniper to talk on. The interview was the most intently watched for many months – nobody felt the need to go into the kitchen and make a cup of tea – and opened the floodgates for the national press and television companies to begin their investigation into what became headlined as **THE HAUNTING OF THORNHAM STAITHE**.

Chapter 8

A Call from the Bishop

Frederick Mackenzie's intention to place his decision before Robert Urquhart, the Bishop of Norbridge, was forestalled by the man himself when at eight o'clock that evening the vicar lifted the receiver to hear his superior's voice. Fred smiled to himself – in the midst of life we are in death, in the midst of tragedy there is humour – since he had supposed that the bishop, a naturally cautious man, might have slept on the decision, and Fred had braced himself for a call the following morning.

"You saw Stewart's interview this evening, did you, Fred?"

It always fascinated Fred that people like Robert Urquhart, a toff if ever there was one, always referred to public figures, especially local public figures, as though they were old friends: perhaps they were, he thought. Another layer in the class structure of the country: church and state together in friendship.

"Yes, my lord," he replied, reluctant to help the bishop out of his difficulty.

"May I ask what you thought of it?"

"You mean do I consider Juniper Wells to be sincere?"

"Ye-es."

He didn't, of course: he wanted Fred to say he considered further action necessary, that remaining quiet and prayerful had, perhaps – there was usually a 'perhaps' – had not proved to be the best way forward at this time.

"Did you ever contact Neil?"

"I was waiting for the right moment, my lord."

He had almost said he had remained quiet and prayerful, as advised, but sarcasm wasn't one of Fred's tools of life.

"I think now is the moment, Fred, but tread carefully. Neil is a good man and was an excellent priest but ... but he had very definite views on ... how shall I express this? He had very definite views on Heaven and Hell. You've read the Church's report on spiritualism, I believe?"

"Yes, my lord."

"Well, Neil was one of those who opposed its publication. He thought it soft on the spiritualists and dangerous. You understand me, do you, Fred?"

"Yes, my lord."

And Fred understood only too well. A timider man would have suggested that they used the Deliverance Ministry Team before approaching Neil Ilkestone but Fred was far from timid and had already put through a phone call to the one-time Deliverance Minister, anyway.

"He approved of what you've done, did he?" asked Jacqueline, who had entered his study when she heard him on the phone to the bishop and was standing by her husband's side, a habit that irritated Fred but about which he remained silent.

"I didn't tell him. Juniper's allegations provoked the call, as you will imagine, and the Church must be seen to be doing something, whether or not it believes in ghosts."

"It's time."

"Yes."

He didn't add that while his wife's attitude had always been that action should be taken, she'd been a little short on ideas. He appreciated a quiet marriage – at least, as quiet as possible when living with someone who held strong views about almost everything. He also knew that she was frightened for him. Jacqueline had always believed in the evil nature of these ghosts and had known her husband must be involved but did not want him to be. It was a classic situation in their marriage: do something but don't do it – whatever 'it' might have been.

"I always agreed with what Neil said, Fred, but he seems a far throw from our gospel of love, doesn't he?" she said, probably knowing what was in her husband's mind.

"He's our man. I just hope he gets back to me soon. He's an old man, now, and he's not been well. I just hope he's up to what must be done."

"The bishop suggested him – he approved?"

Fred heard, again, the worry in her question: get involved but not too involved. He decided not to reply.

"Answer me, Fred!"

"Yes, Robert suggested it was time to consult Neil."

"Good."

Robert Urquhart had, in fact, been considering the possibility since Frederick's first call. As Fred supposed, the bishop was reluctant to have the diocese involved in ghost hunting and, provoked into discussing his worries with his wife, Elaine, had confessed as much.

Elaine – another woman with strong views on just about everything – had disagreed. Elaine Urquhart was a devotee of documentaries – the BBC in particular, but ITV also produced some interesting ones, in her view. Once a presenter of one of these programmes found favour with Elaine, the person was elevated to the status of a minor deity and his (it was usually a man) views on more or less every aspect of life had as much importance for Elaine as the Oracle of Delphi had for the Greeks. Among those at the top of her list was Brian Blessed, as famous for his mountain climbing as for his acting, and she recalled an interview he gave in 2000 about his experience when climbing Everest in 1993.

"Brian said that his grandfather had appeared to him on that occasion and told him he would climb the mountain one day but now, he must go back down. Brian said he would and turned away, but when he looked back the old man was still sitting where he had been when they spoke. 'He wasn't in my mind,' Brian said, 'He was as tangible as you are'.

Robert wasn't sure whether Elaine was referring to him or the interviewer, so assured was her statement.

"He went on to say that he thought the lines were very well connected between the living and the dead – oh and added he would be keeping an eye on his daughter from wherever he ended up. I think, Robert, that if Brian has given his blessing to a belief in ghosts, the church has little to fear in doing the same."

"Yes, of course, dear," replied the bishop, almost relieved at having his mind made up for him.

Chapter 9

James Ryder Plays His Hand

James Ryder returned Esme's car to her as promised; he was more than pleased to do so. He'd taken a fancy to Esme: not sexually driven – after all, she'd been with a long-term partner when they met – but taken to her as a person. He admired her independent spirit, her intelligence, her willingness despite the tragedy of her loss, to pick herself up, dust herself down and tackle her grounded spirits; and he felt sorry for her, sorry that she was pitting every quality she had against an enemy he felt she did not comprehend.

When he arrived and saw her, his admiration was deepened. The strain of the séance in the churchyard, of her attempt to find a pathway of light for Bertha Long, showed in every line of her body. Esme was a young woman – he guessed somewhere in her thirties – and looked older than his mother when he entered the house to her call. The medium was lying on the settee, exhaustion clear in every muscle.

"Have you eaten?"

He wasn't sure why he'd asked the question; it just seemed to James that food was fundamental to good health and he'd been to countries, lived in conditions, where the native people had little to eat and drink, a little often garnered at great effort.

Esme laughed. It was a good sound and James felt relieved.

"I haven't felt able to move from my couch," she replied.

"Let me see what I can do."

There were eggs in the fridge and bread in the bin and soon Esme was enjoying, however slowly and with difficulty, her first meal since she'd arrived home.

"Rescues are always tiring. Sometimes I sleep for days afterwards. As Clifford and I told you, we are – *were* – ghost hunters. I have these abilities but I am loath to use them unless I feel I must. I wouldn't work as a medium in the way Saul Tacksman does, for example. He must be drained every time."

"You think he's genuine?"

"I don't know," replied Esme, looking James up and down sceptically, "I understand that stage magicians can work in the same way with an audience but then magicians are frauds themselves, aren't they? I've seen strange and impressive results from Readings, but yes, I imagine some of them are as fraudulent as the stage magician."

"You spoke of tackling these grounded spirits one by one, Esme. It will kill you."

"I see no other way. Do you?"

James was not prepared to disclose the thoughts that had kept him awake since the séance. He'd travelled widely and come across cultures where ghosts were not considered a laughing matter but creatures that induced real fear. Often the spirits of ancestors they were seen as returning to create havoc in the world. If they could be induced to leave then all was well and good; if they could not, then other measures had to be taken. James had already decided what he must do.

"Is there anything I can get you?" he asked.

"No, thank you. Clifford and I always kept the fridge and cupboards well-stocked. Don't worry about me. You avoided my question."

"Yes. You don't need to be worried any further. You need to rest."

"Clifford always said I looked like a ghost after a Rescue. I'll be back in Thornham in a few days."

They sat quietly for a time, each content to be in the company of another person after the ordeal they had been through. The knowledge that they had shared a terrible experience was bond enough, without conversation. The scrambled eggs brought colour back to Esme's cheeks. The eyes Simon Pegg imagined as 'large and piercing that looked through her listeners with a touch of arrogance in the gaze' had regained their shine, but tiredness still showed in the recline of her body when she lay back on the settee and her voice when she spoke.

"Clifford and I were what people call 'soul mates'," Esme said eventually, "We took a liking to each other from the moment we met. Do you believe in the soul, James?"

James rarely thought about such matters. He'd thought of the soul, when he thought about it at all, as the part of a person that lived on after the death of the body. But he could not visualise any place where a spirit might reside.

"I've never really thought about it," he replied, "I cannot imagine where my soul might end up!"

"The idea that the body and soul separate on death is a medieval one, part of our Christian tradition, but in many cultures the soul is the person. When these believers talk about the soul, they are referring to their living selves. Even in our faith, there is the belief that the soul is not a part of a person but the whole person, that in death we have a spiritual body. Other cultures – the Greeks for one – did believe that the body and soul were separate. For them, the soul was the living on, after death, of a person's actions or teachings during their lifetime. There was no suggestion that the soul went to any particular place."

James had known people he would describe as 'soulless', but this simply meant they had no warmth, no natural empathy for others; some, in fact, bore a natural antipathy to other people, usually of a neglectful kind but sometimes actually hostile. He said so and they talked for a while until he saw that Esme was tiring again, almost asleep, and he rose to leave.

"Be careful, James. Whatever you plan to do, have someone with you. You shouldn't be facing these creatures at all and certainly not alone," she said.

"Don't worry. I'll not be alone."

*

This was true; he planned to take Rollie with him. Not that Rollie had behaved in a doglike manner when Richard Gabriel first appeared at the Swan: there were no raised hackles, no shaking in fear, no scurrying for the nearest door, but Rollie was always good company and a sure guard against human intervention and it was people James Ryder had reason to fear most that night.

James Ryder urged by Richard Gabriel to 'look round the graveyard' of All Saints Church at Thornham had done just that; furthermore, he had taken the trouble, with the initially reluctant help of Vernon Scuffil, to research the Gabriel family.

Elizabeth Gabriel had vanished from the parish of Thornham Staithe in July 1844 but the historian had no doubt that her children spent most of their upbringing in other workhouses. Elizabeth passed away in 1864 and Richard seemed to have given his mother a decent burial in the churchyard. Was a pauper's child doing well for himself was the question asked by Ryder. It turned out that Richard had become a farrier and moved to the nearby market town of Bungley where he lived and worked for the rest of his life to be buried, when his time came, in the small graveyard of the Bungley church that bore the same name as that of his mother's burial place, All Saints.

James Ryder had visited the church and seen Richard Gabriel's grave *Richard Gabriel: A Farrier in this Town: 1842 – 1901*. It was of no significance but Vernon had pointed out that the year of his death had also been that of Queen Victoria's, finishing the revelation with a triumphant elephant impression. James had noticed that Richard Gabriel's headstone was inscribed with the same font as that of his mother's.

He bore the man no malice but he couldn't remain haunted for the rest of his life and Gabriel's attitude – the aggression Esme experienced at the séance and the manner in which he conversed with Frank at the entrance to the pathway of the church as the two ghosts stood watching the collapsed medium – suggested they had further plans.

'These have a purpose and are able to speak or communicate in other ways with the living. There is intelligence at work here; they think, plan and carry out intentions.' Esme's words came back to Ryder as he set out with Rollie for the churchyard of All Saints, Bungley that night. He needed the dark for what he intended to accomplish and the evening was pitch black by five o'clock. He had a long, grim task ahead but couldn't set out until most folks had retired for the night; he had no hope of returning in time for a drink at the Swan.

He packed a pick, a shovel and a screwdriver, although he doubted he would need the latter, together with a shielded lantern he had found – fortunately, since it would serve him better than a torch – that afternoon in the antique-cum-bric-a-brac shop on Thornham High Street. He also packed a long holdall, one he had inherited from his father and always used to carry his clothes on trips abroad.

The drive was a short one, mainly along cross-country roads, which Ryder had chosen deliberately. The moon was in its last quarter; Ryder would have preferred to wait for the rising of the new moon but was anxious to see his business done. Rollie sat on the back seat of the car not quite sure what was happening. Somehow, it didn't seem a walk was planned: wrong time of day and his master was tense, but Rollie was just happy to be with him. Ryder entered the town, after a necessary but short run along the main road that ran southwest to Bury St Edmunds, drove past the Green Dragon public house (where the landlord brewed his own beer) and the Fischer Theatre, dropped to the left before making a sharp right along a narrow street to All Saints Church.

The iron gate of the church was chain-locked but the place was surrounded only by a low wall and Ryder, having parked his car conveniently close to the entrance and looked carefully about him, dropped his tools over. He then lifted Rollie to the top of the wall and the Labrador scrambled along and down onto the grass of the graveyard and watched his master take another quick look both ways along the street before joining him.

They gained a narrow track that led off the main pathway of the church and so to the Saxon tower, where they passed under the arch of a flying buttress and into the older part of the graveyard. Passing the tower, Ryder smiled when he noticed a small sign warning potential thieves to **Beware Forensic Smartwater**; but Ryder wasn't after lead from the roof. His purpose was far more sacrilegious; he was after a body from its grave – the body of Richard Gabriel, dead for over one hundred years and, by now, no more than a skeleton. He wasn't looking forward to the task; he wasn't approaching it in anything but a respectful manner. It was, quite simply, something that must be done.

On one of his trips abroad as an engineer he had come across a village plagued by a particularly malevolent ghost and the people's solution – having tried all manner of persuasions – was to exhume the skeleton, cover the bones with salt and burn them. The villagers had undertaken the task with great respect and in the dead of night so as not to distress the man's relatives more than needs must. Once the bones had been thoroughly salted, they had been burned like logs on an open fire. Standing in the graveyard, Ryder remembered how quickly they disappeared and he remembered the smell as they did so. The ghost was never seen from that night on.

Following his reconnaissance trip, he had no difficulty locating Gabriel's grave. It lay by a slightly higher wall on the far side of the churchyard about twenty yards from the church. There were no shadows. Nothing stirred as he placed his tools, together with the holdall, carefully within reach of the grave; Ryder would need to be able to reach them once he was several feet down, since he had no intention of raising the coffin and he would need to pack the bones, since burning them on site would be impossible.

He gave Rollie a quiet nod and set to work with the pick and shovel, first cutting away the turf and then loosening the soil above the coffin, pausing occasionally to look about him. On the far side of the wall but at a safe distance on a downward slope he could see lights in the houses, lights that gradually extinguished one by one.

He knew the soil type in this part of Suffolk was predominantly clay and was expecting to earn his success that night but, as it turned out, the earth was surprisingly friable and he made good progress; before midnight, and with frequent pauses to check that no one was passing by, he was down four feet into the grave, watched by Rollie whose expression showed he was becoming more and more puzzled as time wore on. Ryder was a strong man. His work obliged him to spend much time in the open air and so he was also fit; nevertheless, a break seemed in order and he climbed from the grave before giving Rollie and himself a drink and Rollie a chew.

It was a cold night – no sign of frost but with a distinct chill in the air – and Ryder was pleased it was so. His hair was already dripping sweat and his shirt clung to his back. He shivered and gave Rollie a wink. It wouldn't do to pause for long.

He took a further reccy around the churchyard, troubled that someone might hear his digging and pay him a visit. Had towns like Bungley still possessed a village bobby, Ryder's mission would have been impossible but, fortunately for him, governments some years before had decided local policing was unnecessary.

He returned to the graveside, continued his task and came, in the early hours, to the coffin. He didn't feel good about what he was doing but with a grim smile began to loosen the earth around the decayed wood; as he had supposed, the screwdriver was unnecessary. The sweat was pouring from him, despite the coldness of the late December night, as he eased aside the coffin lid.

Richard Gabriel lay before him, a skeleton, yellow and grey in the light of the fading moon. He must reach in and remove those bones, one by one, placing them in the holdall as respectfully as possible. The enormity of what he was about to do came home to him, not for the first time since he'd made the decision. He'd thought his purpose through, he was sure he was right, and yet Ryder knew he was defiling a grave. Perhaps it would be possible to return the ashes once the burning was completed?

He looked up, wanting to share his thoughts with Rollie; however unspoken those words might be, it was always good to share them with a friend, and he and Rollie had been close friends for so long. Except when he went abroad, Rollie accompanied him everywhere. Ryder stood up, rested his hands on the sides of the grave and looked around for his dog.

Rollie was on his feet, his tail wagging, looking at something beyond the headstone. Ryder followed his friend's gaze and saw straight into the eyes of Richard Gabriel. The apparition that had haunted him on and off for months was watching the engineer with a discreet smile on its face. Rollie, seeing both his master in the grave and his master's ghost watching him, turned his head from the one to the other. 'Rollie did not bark because he detected your presence in Gabriel. You are what we call a physical medium.' Esme Owen's words came back to Ryder.

He hauled himself out of the grave swiftly, lifting his weight on his hands. He knew he needed to face this creature, as he had – however unaware he might have been of its purpose – that night in his room at the Swan. Ryder was bent double for a moment as he turned from the graveside before regaining his feet, and then he was up and facing Gabriel. In that moment, the ghost had stepped forward, picked up the shovel and now gripped it on the handle's end. Ryder realised with horror, and too late, what the creature intended to do; he saw its intentions so clearly a second before the shovel was swung, extended to its full length in Gabriel's hands, and crashed into the back of the engineer's head. Ryder was unconscious as he toppled into the open grave.

Gabriel did not waste a glance on his enemy's body but turned on the dog. This time he drove the blade-end down, intending to drive it into the animal's side. Rollie bayed (he'd never barked in his life) and leapt backwards, puzzled that this person who possessed his master's scent seemed eager to harm him. It wasn't a game: his attacker's eyes and manner told him so. He twisted to the side and moved to circle his enemy. He wasn't a fighting dog; he'd never had to be. By nature, Labradors are gentle, family-orientated animals. Occasionally, another dog might have menaced him but his size was always an advantage and he'd suffered only minor bites. Gabriel turned with Rollie and jabbed at the dog with the shovel, at his face, at his huge chest. Rollie backed off. His master was nowhere to be seen and he couldn't leave without him, but the man was coming at him again and again. Rollie dived under the blade, eager to reach the grave's edge, but his enemy was on him;

this strange creature meant him harm. The thrusts of the blade would soon drive home, cutting into his flesh, cracking his bones. He must go – not far, but far enough to avoid the blade, to avoid the killing, to avoid his death. Rollie dodged past Gabriel and made for the way they had come. Along the track and around the tower and there was the wall and he was over and gone.

Gabriel shrugged his shoulders. He wasn't to chase a dog through the town; there would be another chance, if needed. He turned to his grave and began to fill it in, shovelling back the earth.

Chapter 10

Vernon Scuffil's Visitor

Vernon Scuffil had never been so tormented and even Justine seemed unable to help him. His visitor, the presence that had haunted him since the night Ambrose Broome fell from the bridge, seemed to enter a period of quiescence after the death of Clifford Raine but this had lasted only a short time, and when it returned did so with a vengeance: it never left him for a moment. Not one moment's peace did the presence give him.

Vernon may have been a loose cannon, a rude man, a putter-up of backs, a man whose voice was as overbearing as his manner, but he was also a man who valued his privacy and the quietness his relationship with Justine had given him. The presence had invaded and destroyed both.

The moving around of the items in his study was annoying enough; pens, pencils, books, maps and a dozen other things could never be found where he knew he'd placed them. He'd returned many times since September to find them shifted; now they were being moved while he was actually using them. He never quite saw this happen. It was still subtle, making him wonder at first whether he was mistaken; but no, he was not dreaming. Vernon always placed whatever he was using at a distinct and deliberate angle on his desk. His notebooks were always to his right; his pens and pencils sat close to the computer, tucked tightly to its side; his reference books were always placed to his left, just beyond any maps he might need and at an angle of forty-five degrees; his rulers were always, but always, on the window sill, propped against the letter rack; if he had coffee with him, the cup was just beyond the point where he might knock and spill it, next to the lamp his mother always kept at her bedside when she'd been alive. Now, everything was being moved and moved frequently.

This interference would have been annoying enough had he seen it happening but he never did; items were always moved while his attention was elsewhere. He'd be making a note in his book, ready perhaps for a lesson he was to teach, and his reference material inched away; he'd reach for a ruler and it was no longer where he'd placed it; he'd be engrossed in reading a map, move to make a note in his book and find the page turned; he'd go to pick up a pen or pencil, always without looking because he knew where it was set, and the writing implement had gone – not far, and that made this constant intrusion even more irritating.

He often recalled the night he had first become aware of this intruder. He remembered grabbing his torch, without looking, from where he always kept it beside the turntable of his stereo system and storming into the garden. Nothing, except the dripping willow, the stinging nettles hanging under weight of the day's rain, the earth soggy under his feet, a pile of twigs and branches ready for bonfire night caught in the beam of his torch and then returning to his study to find someone in the room, an invisible someone, someone who had it in for him.

All that had been bad enough, but the situation now was infinitely worse. The creature's first whisper in his ear has stirred memories from his research; not good memories – memories his family would have best left forgotten. *'Remember the ready back-slaps, the stunning clout over the ear, the blow with the open palm on alternate cheeks?'* The voice had come back to him many times, always with the same refrain; but more recently with other, disturbing accusations.

"Are you the schoolmaster?"

"Yes."

"What do you teach the children?"

"Nothing."

"How then are they employed?"

"They do nothing."

"What then do you do?"

"I keep them quiet."

The first of those conversations had taken place as he sat wondering how he might best introduce the subject of the Saxon Shore to his pupils; not an engaging subject unless the children had travelled, had been and seen the sites; the guilt of every conscientious teacher began with not making their subject interesting.

When the voice questioned him, Vernon's answers had not been his, even though he gave them. Guilt and memory: what a devastating combination; the answers he had given came from his research and a long time past; the guilt of the memory of his ancestor, also a teacher in Thornham – or thereabouts. He didn't always respond, sometimes he was able to shut out the voice, but it still whispered, still left its mark on his mind.

"Boys under fourteen could be beaten, but only by the schoolmaster ... with a rod or other instrument approved by the guardians."

The voice was always that of the man, Frank; always quiet, always insistent, always a hissing whisper in his ear, always just as he settled to work or his mind had, at last, engaged itself on a productive line of planning. It was as though the creature knew what he was thinking, as though it could read his very thoughts, unspoken as they were.

He remembered every occasion the beast spoke to him with such clarity; the clarity was awful. He had been standing by his bookcase when the presence shared the thought:

"A schoolmaster has no difficulty in aweing an unhappy pupil, who probably has not a friend in the world."

And leaning against the door of his study watching Justine among her cabbages when the voice whispered:

"The schoolmaster was in the habit of tying up with a handkerchief the jaws of boys whom he thought deserved punishment, to prevent their screams being heard."

And attempting the finishing touches to a lesson plan when the voice reminded him:

"The master said he could not keep the boys in order though he had broken several sticks on them."

All this Vernon contained within himself. He was not a man to confide in others unnecessarily; he had no desire to hurt Justine or her children, Anthemis and Acer. The pain of his schoolmaster ancestor was his pain, and not theirs; the knowledge his, as the result of his research into that seminal work that had proved anything but and lost him the professorship.

It was not his intention to inflict his suffering on his family, but then the creature had taken that dreadful step, a step so dreadful that Vernon's mind had begun to disintegrate. While previously it had tortured him only in his study, Frank had now moved into the house with him, the only place where he had been able to find peace and quiet.

It happened insidiously at first: the ghost's presence was always insidious. Vernon had been sitting at the dinner table. Justine was a good, if basic, cook and that evening they were enjoying a stew with green dumplings, a recipe from her own cookbook, *Recipes from Four Norfolk Villages*, one she had edited along with three other women from Thornham and the surrounding villages, and published with the help of Jack Dorling and his daughter, Juniper Wells. Vernon had been savouring a mouthful of beef and carrot when the voice spoke directly into his ear:

"One day I saw a little boy with red eyes whose heart seemed bursting. He'd been roped."

How Vernon had controlled himself he was unsure. Looking around the table, it was clear to him that neither Justine nor the children had heard the voice. Vernon shifted his chair as though to shove the intruder aside and hurried on with his meal, eager to finish it and leave the table as quickly as possible. Justine had given him a look – since he was a man normally fastidious about table manners – but said nothing.

Later that evening, as they sat watching University Challenge, Vernon felt the presence nudge him and whisper in his left ear:

"It was common practice for the younger boys to be beaten with a thick hair rope, made specially on purpose. It had two knots at the end and a loop for the hand."

Vernon had been sitting, his right arm about Anthemis on the sofa and it took his entire strength of personality not to scream; even so, the girl looked up at him and frowned, sensing through the sudden tension in his arm that he was disturbed.

"What's wrong?" Justine asked as they climbed into bed.

"Nothing," he responded, and she did not pursue the matter, knowing he would tell her in his own good time.

The bedside lights were out and both were settling to sleep when his arm was pinched.

"The teacher denied such an instrument existed, didn't he, but the child took the Guardians to where it was kept and, sure enough, there it was!"

Vernon, still at that time exerting a degree of control, had slipped from the bed, made his way downstairs and so into the garden. The presence followed him.

"What do you want from me?" he demanded, "You used me to lure Clifford Raine to his death. You and the other one fought against us in the churchyard and almost killed Esme Owen. What more do you want? What purpose can you have. Hmm! Hmmm! Hmmm!"

He'd managed to plead without his usual elephant noises until the very end but then courage and his habitual pomposity crept in and the pleadings became demands.

"Well. Hmm! Hmm! Let's have it! Out with it! Even an excrescence such as yourself must have a purpose. Hmm! Hmm! This must stop! You hear me!"

The voice reverberated throughout the huge cranium, employing Vernon's echo chambers to full effect. Without a shout, his voice filled the garden., and so when the whisper came it seemed more dreadful than usual.

"It never stops," insisted Frank, *"not throughout all eternity."*

Justine found him, shaking with anger, frustration and terror.

"Vernon?" she said.

"The voice of concern, Vernon," whispered the presence.

"Go away! Go to whatever hellhole you inhabit!!

"Vernon?"

Her partner was unaware of her; she could see that was so. Justine tried to urge him towards the house but he was adamant, as firm as a rock.

"Come with me."

"Hmmm! Hmmm!"

"Vernon?"

It took a long time. How long they stood outside his study, Justine was unsure, but it was a long time and she feared for the children; but at last, her partner seemed to acknowledge her, seemed to know she was with him, and Justine eased him into their kitchen, away from the study.

The panic emerged then, it all came tumbling out – all she did not know: the voice, the presence in the house, no longer an annoyance but a threat, and she wanted to phone Frederick, her mind on exorcisms, but Vernon was firm against the idea.

"No, no. We will cope with this creature. He will not best me. The séance failed. The church failed if you must ..."

"But Vernon ..."

"No 'buts', Justine. This ... this *thing* defies all reason, all intelligence. It haunted my study silently and now it haunts me with its voice and our home with its contagion. The audacity of it! I will not have it! I will defy it! Hmmm!"

"Let's have a warm drink, Vernon. Let's be calm for the night."

And they were, that night and for several days. It was almost as though the creature was biding its time. The New Year passed without more disturbances and Vernon prepared for the coming term at school.

He was not lulled into a false sense of salvation: he still ventured cautiously about their home, wondering whether the ghost might whisper in his ear again: mealtimes were no longer the relaxed, social occasions they had once been; the bathroom held its threats, when he stepped into the shower; his study lost its energising influence and became a place of anxiety – the tap on the shoulder, the hissed incitement; at bedtime, he no longer turned to Justine as he had so often done in the past and he waited long into the night before he turned off the lamp on his side of the bed.

But Vernon pressed on, driven by his refusal to submit, fuelled by his anger, determined his lessons should challenge his pupils as they had always done; and Justine watched him in silence, waiting. Her woman's instincts told her that a storm approached; she was unsure of its nature – volcanic or cloudburst – but she waited and was ready when the phone rang on his second day back at work.

"Mrs Scuffil?"

"Sweet – my name is Justine Sweet. Vernon and I are not married."

Why did she always have to explain that too everyone who saw them together. Justine's voice showed its annoyance.

"I'm sorry, Justine. It's me – Norman Oldfield at the school."

Vernon's headteacher: the crisis was on them.

"I'm afraid Vernon has had some kind of a breakdown. Would you come and fetch him?"

"What happened?" she asked, having to know before she drove to the school.

"It was in class. You know what a good teacher he is. His children love him. It was history. He was sweeping them along with his enthusiasm for Saxon England …"

"What happened?" asked Justine for a second time, realising Norman Oldfield, a decent enough man but not one to grasp the nettle, was waffling, afraid of consequences.

"Vernon went berserk – in class. The children were terrified – there'll be repercussions – the parents will want to know …"

"What happened?" repeated Justine, her voice still quiet, her mind always unnaturally calm when events threatened her home and happiness.

"He began to lash out at something and scream. What he said made no sense. The children told me. We're trying to pacify them. 'Punished by confinement in a dark room at night, is that it?' He was screaming at someone, the children said, but they couldn't see who it was …"

"What else did he shout?" asked Justine, knowing Vernon would refuse to speak when she fetched him home, knowing he would sit for days in silence.

"He was yelling about a trough and children kneeling and being fed like animals. He grabbed a chair and charged at nothing. We were lucky no child was hurt. You must fetch him, Mrs ... Mrs Sweet."

"I'm on my way. Thank you, Mr Field."

"How long?" asked Vernon, sitting in the car on the short drive from his high school on Butcher's Lane to their home on Bridge Street.

"You're suspended indefinitely, Vernon. They call it 'garden leave'.

'Throughout all eternity' Vernon heard the voice whisper in his ear.

Book Four

Chapter 1

Maggie Henderson's Return

Lottie Henderson didn't know whether she was standing up or sitting down; that's what she said to herself, laughing at the common phrase – the cliché. Lottie always talked herself into a state of peace and calm. It was instinctive with her and had not come as a device to deal with life after her mother's death; but now she was withdrawing more and more into the safety of her own being.

The conversation with her father had never left her and she and her brother, Chad, had talked it over and over; both were terrified of this man they had never met, this Thomkins, who Chad believed, more firmly each time they talked, had killed their mother. He believed Thomkins was simply a wicked man.

Lottie wasn't so sure: there was talk at school that Mr Scuffil had gone mad in front of his class – he'd been yelling at somebody nobody else could see: there was talk in the village that Mr Dorling had died in strange circumstance – he had been killed by a poltergeist that wrecked his shop, "smashing everything up" as the gossip went. And there had been Myles's awful death. Edward had talked to her. He knew he shouldn't have done, her father said he shouldn't have done, but Edward needed to talk to someone, and Lottie was a good listener and he had been grateful.

But now it was all too much. She needed someone to hear her, someone outside the situation, someone like Mr Ryder who had listened to her on the memorial seat by the village green, but he didn't live in Thornham; he came and went. There was Jacqueline, of course, the vicar's wife, who had told her dad about her periods when they came so soon after her mother's death when Lottie hadn't liked to mention them to him. It would be the weekend soon, and she'd pop round to the vicarage. Jacqueline always seemed to be at home.

Lottie turned off her bedroom light: school tomorrow and she must sleep. The moon came in through the lattice window behind her bed. She always liked the moonlight. It was gentle and soothing; soon she would be asleep and she would wake refreshed and ready for another day. Her bedroom exhibited her life from the ice-blue teddy bear (now relegated to the top of the wardrobe, but there keeping an eye on her) through the souvenirs of family holidays carefully arranged on the main windowsill, the folders of sheet music on her small desk, the wall-case of classical and pop CDs and the bookcase containing her reading (from A A Milne to J K Rowling) to the poster of the boy band half-hidden on the door by her dressing gown,. All were shades of silvery grey in the dark, all containing their own memories and magic. Lottie turned over, snuggled her head beneath the duvet and breathed deeply: soon asleep, soon. Once off, Lottie slept deeply and well; unless it was her time of the month, she never woke during the night. Her father would look in on her. She knew that was so and didn't mind.

She wasn't sure what woke her or when. It certainly wasn't her father. He'd gone to bed long ago. Lottie was sure the house was still when she woke and it never was until all three of them were settled for the night; but she knew that she woke before she heard the voice; before the voice came the presence. Someone was in her room watching over her. Lottie thought at first she was dreaming; the figures of her thoughts raced through her mind as she tried to grasp and quieten them. She tossed over and turned. She sat up. The room was still lit by the moon and there seemed to be nobody within it but her sense of a presence was overwhelming. And then she heard the voice and recognised it as that of her mother, the mother who had always been loving but always distant, always more concerned with herself and what she was doing than with

Lottie and her brother. Lottie had known that at an early age but never acknowledged the fact to herself until now.

She heard her name called three times and answered twice.

"Mummy?" Come in, Mummy. Where are you?"

And Lottie realised the figure was sitting on her bed – not facing her, but on the bottom, leaning over and looking down at the floor. She was wearing the dress she had worn when she went off with the photographer: a Spanish gypsy style dress Lottie knew her mother thought made her look sexy.

When it heard Lottie's voice, the figure turned and looked at her; and then rose and approached around the foot of the bed. Her mother had been beautiful in life and death had done nothing to diminish her good looks; if anything, it had accentuated the haughtiness of her beauty. It was a haughtiness that demanded she be seen as a gift to the world, somebody to be worshipped. Looking down on her daughter, Maggie Henderson seemed more disdainful than ever.

Lottie, afraid but calm, watched the figure approach and wondered whether the look was more one of bemusement, the look of a woman in this world but not of it, one whose thoughts and feelings lay beyond. And then she saw the child in her mother's arms. It was a new-born child, wrapped in filthy clothing, little more than rags, whose body looked as though it was already smeared in the gutter of life.

"Lottie, would you take care of this child? Her mother is just dead."

Lottie, bewildered, hesitated to answer and her mother's tone became adamant.

"Promise me," she said, and, to her daughter's horror, placed the child in Lottie's arms, "Promise me! Promise me to take care of her."

Lottie felt the weight of the child and watched as her mother leaned over and folded the edge of the soft duvet around the dirty body.

"Promise me!"

"Yes, Mummy, I promise you."

Maggie Henderson turned away, not smiling but seeming to be relieved of a burden. She was going, leaving her daughter with the child. She didn't look back as she walked slowly towards the door where Lottie's dressing gown hung.

"Mummy, stay and speak with me. I am so wretched."

"Not now, child, not now," answered Maggie Henderson, as though speaking to a stranger

"Please! I've missed you so much."

But the figure of her mother was gone. Lottie wasn't sure whether or not the bedroom door opened and closed. She only knew that the figure was no longer with her and she could feel the weight of the baby in her arms.

Gerald Henderson woke with a start. He had never been a good sleeper – the nature of his work was against it – and he was not surprised to be wide awake staring in front of himself, wondering whether it was day or night. He was surprised to see his wife looking down at him, the expression on her face suggesting as always that she might have done better when choosing a husband. A queer sensation passed over him: it was his wife and yet it wasn't. After all, Maggie was dead; her grave was in the churchyard; he had come to it on that September night when he ran down the two young women.

Gerald rubbed his eyes and sat up. The figure hadn't moved. It was his wife and she was watching him closely. In some respects, she seemed more beautiful than ever, but gaunt. Her face, naturally tanned in life, was the colour of chalk and the eyes were brighter than he remembered; he had loved her once and gazed often into those eyes, brown and living, now colourless and dead. He recalled the dress. What a dance she'd led him finding it for some special occasion, an occasion he could not recall, only Maggie had been the star of the show, coming on to all and sundry.

Outside, it was a cold January night and there she stood in that gypsy dress. Gerald had never questioned his wife about her comings and goings. He'd never had too: Maggie was always ready to talk about herself. She was her favourite subject. But he had questions now and the first came unbidden.

"What on Earth have you come to me for?"

He realised as he spoke that he might equally have asked 'why in the name of Heaven', and the sadness of the implication overcame him; he felt the tears in his eyes before they came. She had, after all, been his wife. Who else was she to ask for help? And the need was in her eyes.

"Sit down," he said, "on the bed where you are."

It was an eerie feeling – his wife sitting by him on the bed as she had done so many times in life. Gerald almost expected her to reach out and touch him, to feel for the reassurance he knew in his heart she needed; but Maggie's hands dropped and remained in her lap, pale against the red dress even in the dark of the room.

"I was not to blame," she said, "All of them were old and inexperienced or young and eager to go even before they could be properly trained. Of the old ones, only two could read and neither could write. I had no one at night. If patients were very ill, I had to watch them myself. I heard the bell and knew I shouldn't answer, not after the doors were bolted, but I knew what I'd find. I'd found it so often. She was asleep on the stone steps, the child in her arms on the point of death. I took her in to be with the others, all crying out. What help could I be expected to give?"

Listening to his wife, Gerald realised the voice he heard wasn't hers; another was speaking through her – but who? The voice was coming from a dark side of life, a time of neglect and worse. Gerald had seen death come many times, had witnessed unbearable suffering, but the woman who had been his wife spoke of things remote from his world even as a doctor.

"Even when I was allowed sufficient help, it came in the form of drunkards, one so sodden, I was in constant fear of her doing bodily harm to the patients. If my back was turned, I found them black with bruises, especially the disabled and friendless ones.."

"And the young ones," asked Gerald, taken aback by the fact he had spoken, unaware of the origin of the question, even as he spoke.

"They would run. What else could they do? And even the kind ones could not cope. How would they – many were in their fifties and sixties and the long hours and physically hard work were too much. And many had endured a lifetime of hardship. They were already weakened."

Maggie looked up as she answered and their eyes met for the first time. They were his wife's eyes but the pain within them, the memories, belonged to another. The figure – he could longer think of it as Maggie, more an apparition – had not stirred as it spoke and was now slumped forward on itself.

"Let me help you," he said, "There's a chair …"

"Don't touch me!"

Now, it was Maggie's voice, authoritarian and demanding, the one he recognised; and yet, wheedling. He'd known her so, usually when she couldn't get her own way.

"Come along," he urged, "take the chair. We can talk. Thomkins. Tell me about Thomkins."

Gerald needed to know. Had Thomkins murdered his wife? If so, why? Who was Thomkins?

Maggie rose from the bed and staggered backwards; and Gerald was out from under the covers and he grasped her by the arm. There was no weight in her. His hand passed through solid flesh that seemed to bear no muscle. Maggie shrugged him off and shuffled backwards. The chair caught her fall and she sat looking up at her husband, each breath coming in short, slow inhalations.

"He knew the woman on the steps and abandoned her."

Guilt: everywhere there was guilt: guilt, whether you looked or listened. Gerald felt sorry for his wife, in a way he had never done so in life, except for those first few years, the years before the children came. But now at least he knew or could surmise the truth. Thomkins the photographer had been no more alive than Maggie was at this moment.

"Walk me out," she said, "My business here is done."

He did, unsteadily down the stairs and out through the front door that had once belonged to them as a family and so to the byroad that led from the home that had once been theirs and came to the high road running from Norbridge to Lowestoft. On the byroad, she drifted steadily away and Gerald watched her vanish into the cold, winter's night.

Back indoors, he looked in on his children. Lottie was sleeping with a frown deep between her eyes: Charles, peacefully, his dreams undisturbed by the events of the night.

Gerald did not have to ask himself what took him to Burghamton the following day. It didn't lay on his rounds; he simply knew that it was there Maggie's troubles had begun, so many years, so many generations, before. Looking back, it was easy to draw the right conclusions: as the saying has it – hindsight is always 20/20. Really looking back, it had not been so apparent.

Ambrose had been the first to die in unusual circumstances, but nobody had witnessed his death. Richard Revell had died next, but of exposure; hypothermia was the reason given on the boy's death certificate: only later, following Sam Whitham's revelations to Fred, did the bruising take on a significance. Suspicions yes, but none aroused in the right direction. Perhaps he, Gerald Henderson, the local doctor, should have paid more attention to Amelia Pritchard's death. He hadn't been sure what to write: 'old age' seemed the safest bet but there had been nothing wrong with Amelia Pritchard's heart. Even his recognition of Thomkins at Simon Pegg's psychic supper had only drawn him to wonder about Maggie's own demise. It wasn't until Fred brought them all together following the horrific killing of Clifford Raine that the vague – yes, that was the word 'vague' – suspicions of several people had begun to coagulate into a point of view, a belief in the unbelievable; and even then, the vigil at Vernon Scuffil's had begun as an investigation, nothing more. And yet the pattern was there all along, if only they had seen it, if only they had taken the trouble to look for it.

Gerald sat in his car for a while in the centre of this silent village – and it was silent: not a living soul moved anyway. He'd had the usual difficulty finding the place: signposted roads led him in any direction but the right one; but he had come there at last, almost lured to the place, wondering whether he might find a way out. A village that didn't want to be found but once it had you was reluctant to let go.

He walked across to Church Farm, adjacent to where the annual bonfire was held. There was no sign of the fire now. Rain followed by snow had washed the ashes clean away. Gerald looked beyond towards the old workhouse, the building that had been used at different times to rear pigs and then turkeys and was being converted into a row of terraced houses, mews, flats and apartments. The work was all but complete; Gerald could see the builder's men busy on the final, central section. Soon it would be landscaped.

He was now sure what had drawn him here to this deserted village with its grim past but was still unsure what he might do, apart from paying Fred a visit.

Chapter 2

Sleepless Night

Rollie was found the next morning. A passer-by, hearing the mournful howling of what sounded like a large dog or "even a wolf" coming from the churchyard, called 999. She didn't enter the churchyard but she could tell that the animal was in distress; however, when the police officers got out of their car she followed them at a distance.

The dog, a black Labrador, was sitting by the side of an open grave. The animal seemed to have dug its way down into the grave because there was a huge pile of crumbled earth at the foot. She didn't see any more because the officers told her to stand aside, out of the way; but they called an ambulance and when it came a man's body was lifted from the grave and taken away. The police officers – one a woman – then filled in the grave and "made it look nice".

Rollie had returned to his master's side as soon as the other man, Gabriel, left. He'd been puzzled that the man who smelled like his master had struck his master and buried him; but he didn't waste too much time thinking about the matter. It wasn't a pressing issue; more pertinent, at that moment, was digging Ryder out. It was easy work but when Rollie reached him and nuzzled his neck, the master didn't move and stroke him as he had always done. Rollie tried to turn him over and move him about a bit. Ryder liked that when they were playing but the leader of his pack was still and Rollie knew, instinctively, that they would never romp together again. He could think of nothing else to do except mourn his friend and leader and he set up a funereal howling until the police arrived.

They seemed kind. Others came, lifted Ryder from the grave gently and placed him on a stretcher. Rollie followed them to the ambulance and watched. Where the leader went, he must follow and he positioned himself to leap into the vehicle with Ryder. It wasn't to be. He felt the leash about his neck, heard the kindly words in his ear and struggled against his capture; but the ambulance was away and his master had gone. The police spoke to him gently but their possession of him was absolute and Rollie had no instinct to bite these people. He writhed and heard the word 'muzzle', one he'd heard at the vets despite Ryder's assurance that he didn't bite, but one of the officers said 'no' and his mouth was left free.

Rollie didn't complain again but lay quietly when the van came for him, accepting the treat the new people offered, pushed himself down on the soft bed and waited. Somehow, he would find the master or the master would find him; they'd never been apart for long. On the odd occasions he had strayed, the master's voice always arrived to call him home.

Lottie fell off to sleep the previous night, the pauper child in her arms and she had nuzzled it deeply against her breast, a maternal instinct coming to the fore. As the child lay there, warm and settled, Lottie went into a deep sleep. When she woke the next morning, the child had gone. There was nothing in her arms. Her nightdress bore the stains of the gutter and she could smell the baby on her but there was nothing

Her father had left early, leaving her and Chad a note. This was not unusual: Gerald Henderson was often called away before the medical centre opened. Lottie said nothing to her brother, determined to keep the horrible experience close until she returned from school that evening and could speak to her father; but Chad – even Chad! – sensed the terror within his sister and, as she placed his breakfast before him, asked the question:

"What's wrong?"

After the series of 'nothings' her brother seemed to expect and bear patiently, Lottie poured out her story.

"Where you awake at the time?"

"I think I dropped off but I wasn't dreaming, Chad. Look at my nightdress if you don't believe me."

"I believe you, Lottie. Had you been thinking about mum before you dropped off?"

"Yes - about Mum and all the other things that have happened."

"About Mum and that man, Thomkins?"

"Yes."

"Whose baby did you think it was?"

"I don't know. Mum said the baby's mother had just died."

"Mum was a nurse, wasn't she? Do you think she was responsible for a baby's death – or its mother's death?"

"I don't know, but the baby didn't seem to be of our time. It wasn't dressed like babies are today and mum worked in a hospital. Even if Mum had been responsible for a baby's death, the baby wouldn't have been dirty in the way this one was. The smell was awful. It was as though the child hadn't been washed since it was born."

"But it was Mum – Mum who came to you?"

"Yes."

They progressed no further; their talk went round in the proverbial circles until it was time to leave for school; but Chad did offer one piece of advice that Lottie had already decided upon.

"Don't just tell Dad, tonight. Go and talk to the vicar's wife, Jacqueline."

The lunchtime news was picked up not only at home on the television but also on i-phones at school, and so the discovery of a dead body at All Saints Church in Bungley and the digging up of a grave by a black Labrador was hot gossip long before school ended for the day.

The local newshounds, especially Stewart Burch of *Look Anglia*, were very active and even managed to secure a video of the dog, which Sam Whitham recognised immediately as Rollie.

"They all look the same," said his grandmother, Marjory Broome.

Sam knew differently: the expression in the eyes, the hang of the head, the way the dog turned its face up and to the side, told him that this was Mr Ryder's dog, Rollie.

"Take me to Meadow Farm, Nana – please! I must see him. And the man they found. It can't be Mr Ryder, can it?"

"I don't know, dear. The police haven't released his name yet. They always tell the relatives first "

Sam knew this was so but Mr Ryder didn't seem to have any relatives or, if he did, never spoke about them.

"Take me to Meadow Farm, please!"

"We'll have to ring first. They close in the evenings."

Meadow Farm was the local rescue centre for lost and abandoned dogs. It was situated only a short distance out of Thornham, along single-track lanes where Marjory had never driven. Ambrose always did the driving at those times if they went cross country to Bungley. And it was dark. She really couldn't go – not tonight.

Sam remembered the pub, the Swan, where the men had chided him but were friendly enough and where the landlord, Mr Douglas, had telephoned Mr Ryder, just as he promised.

It was a foul night. The boy slipped outside and made his way, lashed by the rain, along Bridge Street and so to the pub. He hesitated before going in through the awkward double doors but only for a second. When the men gathered round the bar saw him, the buzz of their conversation ceased and they looked sheepishly at each other: only one spoke, a young man.

"Here, Ned, that little boozer's back. I said he'd be propping up your bar every night of the week!"

"Steve!"

It was only the one word, spoken by an older man, and the one called 'Steve' went red in the face and looked down at his pint. The others exchanged glances and remained subdued. Sam didn't quite understand what all this was about but it made him feel uncomfortable, in the same way that adults going quiet when he walked into one of their conversations made him feel, as though they were talking about things he shouldn't hear.

"Hello, lad, what are you doing here on a night like this?" asked the landlord, as he entered behind the bar.

Sam told him.

"I don't rightly know they'd welcome you at Meadow Farm tonight, lad. The dogs 'll be settled down for the night. Tell you what – you come round in the morning and I'll run you over there."

Sam felt like arguing but didn't. He knew Mr Douglas was right: them arriving would set the dogs off but he didn't like the thought of Rollie being there alone. He wouldn't understand.

"You run along home now, lad, and I'll see you in the morning. It's Saturday. You won't be going to school."

The way Mr Douglas looked at him troubled Sam. The landlord obviously wanted to say more but couldn't bring himself to do so.

"Will you ring the police, then, and tell them that the dog, Rollie, is Mr Ryder's? I'm sure it is. I'd know Rollie anywhere."

"All right, Sam. I'll do that ... and I'll see you in the morning."

Sam wasn't the only one sure of the dog's identity. Lottie Henderson had gone straight to the vicarage (having phoned Jacqueline in advance and warned her dad as to what she was doing) and sat with the vicar's wife watching the early evening news. She saw Stewart Burch's video on *Look Anglia* and learned from the number of 'eyewitnesses' interviewed and eager to talk of how the dog had been found

"Sat by the grave he was, howling his eyes out!"

"He'd dug his way down. Now why would he want to do that, hey? What was he after? It ain't like a dog to go grave digging, is it?"

Stewart Burch had been obliged to agree.

"They took a body away – or so my friend said. Ambulance came and off they went."

"The rescue people came for the dog. Said how good he was."

Stewart Burch then went on to explain:

"We have been informed by Suffolk police that they have reason to believe the body found in the grave was none other than the dog's master. They have also indicated that a murder has been committed and they are pursuing several lines of enquiry."

The news team had also secured an interview with the Chief Constable of Suffolk and Stewart pressed him on several issues.

"This isn't the first murder to have occurred in strange circumstances in this region in recent weeks, is it?"

"No, Stewart, it isn't."

"Is there any indication of a link between this murder and the deaths of Jack Dorling, Myles Langstroth and Clifford Raine?"

"We have no reason to believe that Mr Langstroth's death was anything but a tragic suicide."

"But the other two deaths were certainly murders?"

"That would seem to be the case."

"Were these men known to each other?"

"Mr Langstroth and Mr Dorling certainly were but Mr Raine was not from Thornham."

"He was what people refer to as a ghost hunter, wasn't he?"

It was a gentle and courteous but insistent interrogation and Lottie listened intently. By the end of it, she was in tears. So much had come out she had not known.

"How can anyone fail to see what is happening?" she asked Jacqueline, as she poured forth her own experiences, especially those of the previous night.

Lottie wasn't known to cry. It wasn't a luxury she allowed herself before her father, since she believed he had enough to bear, and her mother had never been one to listen to the woes of others, childhood ones or otherwise; and so, it was a relief, at last, to let herself go while Jacqueline listened and said not a word.

By the time she'd finished, her eyes were red and sore and Jacqueline suggested she might like to stay the night.

"We have spare rooms now the children are gone. I'll phone your dad."

"He won't mind."

"No, of course he won't," replied Jacqueline, pleased that the girl was secure in the knowledge of her father's love.

"The vicar won't mind, will he?"

"No, he's gone to Norbridge station to pick up a friend."

"It's Mr Ryder. I don't – I mean didn't – really know him well but we met after Myles … died and … he listened like you've just listened and … he said … no, he didn't say anything but we both somehow knew we would meet again. Does that make any sense, Jacqueline?"

"Yes."

"But now he's dead, isn't he? And Sam. He was on his way to see Sam that day. Sam will be so upset …"

"I'll ask Fred to pop down to the mill when he gets back."

Jacqueline didn't think she'd ever come across a girl – almost a young woman – who was so caring, so thoughtful, of others, while so immersed in troubles of her own. Not even her own children had been quite that considerate.

It was only a short while after Lottie had spoken with her father on the phone, hearing him speak highly of Jacqueline's kindness, that Fred Mackenzie arrived home with the man Jacqueline described as 'a friend' and who the vicar introduced as Neil Ilkestone. Lottie was pleased and relieved that by this time her eyes had dried and her cheeks were clear of the stains because the man looked at her with eyes so searching that she knew immediately he was aware she was deeply troubled and had been tearful.

Lottie wasn't a teenager who judged old people by their age but even she was struck by the fact that Neil Ilkestone was, very definitely, old. It wasn't just the white hair and the short, rough, untrimmed beard: his body seemed to have shrunk within itself – a characteristic she'd noticed in old people, something her father explained by telling her that with age the muscles gradually grew weaker and smaller. He was, despite this fact, quite upright in the way he stood; there was no stoop in his legs or roundness in his shoulders. He seemed to hold his weight, as dancers do, by the muscles of his back rather than let his trunk slump forward onto his hips. He was lean and Lottie noticed during the meal they shared that evening that he ate little. Neil Ilkestone's face was lined, patterned rather than wrinkled, and always, always, the lines drew her attention to his eyes. Lottie thought she had never seen eyes so steeped in the sadness of life; there was wisdom in the old man and pity and a deep, deep sorrow – not a personal sorrow but one Lottie felt was reserved for all humanity.

He noticed her watching him and smiled, and it was a smile that bore no malice for her curiosity but an understanding of her fascination. He spoke gently to her, asking few questions and none that were impertinent but by the end of the meal he knew all about her, her interests, her family, her hopes for the future.

After the meal, while she and Jacqueline talked and watched a celebrity chef enjoying himself in the Mediterranean sunshine, while the rain beat down on the windowpanes of the vicarage, the old man disappeared with the vicar into the latter's study and they were still there when Jacqueline eventually showed Lottie to her bedroom, one belonging to her daughter who was now at university.

There were there well into the early hours of the morning.

It was a sleepless night for many in and around the village: Gerald worried about his daughter, despite knowing she was safe, trying to piece together some skein of sense in the events surrounding his friends and family; Lottie, tossing and turning with her memories of the previous night and the awful knowledge that Ryder was dead; Sam, staring with wide eyes at the wooden ceiling of his room in the mill, his thoughts focussed on a lost dog and a lost friend; Jacqueline, so wracked with fearful knowledge that she could only take refuge in simple solutions; Fred, when once he did get to bed, lying silent beside his wife, knowing what was to come; above the butcher's shop, the nightly conversation, the one conversation that now dominated their lives, continued between Reg and Myrtle Wilton; Vernon Scuffil, pacing about his home, trying to shed a voice that continued to whisper in his ear and Justine, following, endlessly attempting to sooth her husband; Edward Warburg had never slept since the day he found his friend hanging from the tie-bar of his bedroom, for him yet another night of unutterable sadness; Cynthia Revell, beside her drunken husband, mourning, unaided, the loss of her son; Amy Prentice, forever jerking out of sleep to see her ex-boyfriend's face in the dressing table mirror; Esme Owen, her soulmate gone, her psychic powers shredded; a dog, Rollie, awake, watchful and wondering, locked in a cage for the first time in his life.

A few slept: Mildred Ackroyd, still lamenting the loss of her friend but toughened by life's vicissitudes; Marjory Broome, for whom the day-to-day business of living had to go on; Juniper Wells, immersed in her anger, waiting for when the moment came to pounce.

In the churchyard of Holy Trinity, awake and alert, an old man who came out after his long talk with the vicar and after the rain stopped, was waiting to face an old enemy.

Chapter 3

Liberty and Light

The following morning, Fred Mackenzie regretted not having been able to sleep the night before: Neil Ilkestone, Deliverance Minister, had him up and on the move early. He wanted to speak with everyone who had been in contact with any 'guests', as the old man chose to describe the ghosts; he needed to hear their stories for himself.

Fred drove and Neil sat silently for most of the time; when he did speak, usually after one of the visits, sharing his thoughts propelled the vicar of Thornham Staithe into turmoil. Fred was an everyday priest, one who cared for the souls of his parishioners, one who concerned himself with their everyday worries; he was, to use the phrase of the moment, 'out of his comfort zone' and the other priest's words pushed him further in that direction.

"Our modern church has lost one of the key gifts and ministries that Jesus had and shared with His followers: the ministry of deliverance, dealing with evil."

This comment, an isolated one, had come soon after their visit to Edward Warburg, as they made their way back across the churchyard to Fred's house; the manner of Myles's death and the musician's conviction that suicide was not even a consideration had impressed the deliverance minister deeply. Once in the car, he shared his thoughts further.

"The deliverance ministry is rarely pleasant, and always involves dealing with hurt, sometimes very confused, people; but it was an essential part of the ministry of Jesus and He was upfront about it. We need to follow His example."

Fred said nothing. The old priest spoke as though he was in daily touch with the Son of God; there was nothing doubtful or fragile about Fred's own faith but he rarely thought of Jesus with anything but awe.

"It is, of course, not only a matter of deliverance from evil but also of bringing healing to the afflicted. There will be much work to do in the area of pastoral care, you understand, Frederick."

It wasn't a question and Fred merely nodded. He was amused by the old man's pronunciation of his name, emphasising as he did the second 'e' so that the name came across as Fred-e-rick.

"Our ministry draws its remit from the Lord's Prayer – 'deliver us from evil'. To be delivered is to be set free so that the person is no longer influenced or controlled by the present, the past or the demonic; that is real deliverance. You understand what I mean by 'freedom'?"

This time it was a question and Fred felt the old man watching him intently.

"Yes, you mean freedom to be in a true relationship with God as distinct from simply being free from restrictions, like debt?"

"Good. You and I, we shall make a team. And I shall need help; I cannot undertake this deliverance alone, experienced as I may be. We have to be able to speak and act with the love of Christ, and I sense that love in you. We need to face the demonic and rid the world of it when necessary. Evil will be challenged and not allowed to act. Jesus is quite clear on the issue: evil in all its forms is unacceptable. He challenged evil when He met it and He drew His authority from a living relationship with the Father. He was driven by compassion. We must never lose sight of that fact, Frederick. Dealing with evil in all its forms will always involve healing."

Neil Ilkestone had now, as far as Fred sensed, used the words 'evil' and 'demonic' up to a dozen times. They were words that none of those involved in the hauntings had used readily; even the term 'ghost' had been spoken almost apologetically. The old man, in the village less than twenty-four hours, had the bull by the horns. It was an unfortunate phrase, using as it did the word 'horns', Fred thought.

"It goes back to the first sin – that of Adam and Eve, when they decided to break their relationship with God; they were now the ones who would decide what was right and wrong, what was good and evil. There is something deeply rooted about sin that goes from generation to generation; but, of course, sin is not always a choice as in the Garden of Eden. Sometimes, it is a function of history. Whatever view is taken, the consequences of sin are deeply profound both for the individual and the community. Perhaps sin is passed down in our DNA – hey Frederick!"

The old man's comment, accompanied by a harsh laugh, shocked Fred. He was grasping at the truths the other priest spoke and trying to apply them to the people he knew; and they did not fit.

The deliverance minister's last comment came after their visit to Vernon Scuffil. Fred had drawn up on the staithe carpark and they walked the short distance to the house with the black doors, Neil having first examined the broken bridge from which Ambrose Broome fell to his death.

The history teacher, still plagued by the Presence, had both welcomed and resented their visit. He was not a believer himself but nobody else had been able to rid him of the whispering ghost and perhaps this old priest might. He was beside himself with fear and anger, and only Justine's calming influence carried forward the conversation. What had occurred in their garden clearly troubled Neil Ilkestone greatly.

The deliverance minister was silent as they drove on, after insisting that Esme Owen must be next on their list. There was disapproval in the silence, quiet but nonetheless present, and Fred began to wonder whether his decision to involve psychics and seances had been a wise one.

The old priest made only one comment on their way to the ghost hunter, one that picked up his previous thoughts, thoughts that seemed to have been provoked further by their visit to Vernon and Justine.

"The primary aim of the Devil is to cause sin because sin separates and compromises our relationships. Sin is, by definition, evil because it works against that which is life-giving. We see it in terms of what people do to each other, we see it in nature and we see it down through history. We shall, I have no doubt, be paying Mr Scuffil a further visit. He will be a mine of essential information in our hunt. That wife of his is a treasure. How often does a man find such peace and calm in his life's companion?"

He was gentle with Esme Owen, seeing distress in every line of her face and body. He listened quietly as she recalled for him what she had decided to do and why. When she finished explaining, he asked:

"You sensed the demonic in all of this?"

"Clifford and I were paranormal investigators. We had no wish to go down the path of spiritualism," she answered, avoiding his question.

"But you consider yourself psychic: you decided to hold the séance?"

His voice, despite the challenge in the question, was still gentle. Fred thought he had never seen anger so soothingly expressed.

"I thought we might help those lost souls willing to find the light."

"The power of the demonic is always subject to God. Choosing to engage in a séance is a deliberate act of sin that potentially exposes you to the demonic."

"You believe I did not help that woman, Bertha Long?"

"I believe that the hands of Christ are the safest place for demons to be."

"But you have no right to say that she was a demon! She was a lost soul, grounded to this Earth!"

"I have no such right, and did not do so, but you know as well as I that the line between the living and the dead is thin and in communicating with the dead you risk giving evil an entry into this world. Should that be *your* choice or is it best left in the hands of Christ?"

"What are you planning to do?" replied Esme, again dodging his question.

"At first, to listen: I have much to learn and a busy day ahead. From what you have said, from what others have told me and from what I learned by reading Mrs Mackenzie's diary, it seems to me that some of these hauntings are as you have said – these ghosts are the grounded spirits of troubled souls. Some may be genuinely lost, some afraid to move on, some the victims of injustice in this life ...", Neil Ilkestone replied, pausing deliberately: his manner and delivery had something of the theatrical about it but there was no doubting his deadly seriousness when he continued, "but some have been touched by the Devil."

"I want to be part of what you decide to do," said Esme, refusing to take up the challenge offered.

"And you shall be, but under grace. You must be honest and open in your relationship with God. His word must have its place in your heart. There must be no rebellion or you, too, will be vulnerable to the demonic."

"I understand."

And it seemed that the Welsh psychic did understand. Her face brightened and she led her guests to the front door when it was time to go, livelier than she had been for many weeks.

"Was I harsh with her, Frederick?" Neil asked, as he clambered into the car.

"Esme seemed to accept what you had to say."

"That's not what I asked."

"A trifle harsh, then – yes."

"I had to be – but with a touch of compassion, I hope."

The conversation raised questions for Fred but he decided to wait before raising them.

"I want us to return to the village, now, Frederick. I want to speak with Amelia Pritchard's companion and the young girl, the daughter of Jack Dorling, who you told me died so violently in his printshop. And then, the doctor, if we can find him free."

If Esme Owen had not wholeheartedly agreed with Neil Ilkestone, she had, at least, listened courteously; this was not the case with either Mildred Ackroyd or Juniper Wells when he asked for their help.

"A prayer walk!" questioned Mildred, "I've every respect for your cloth, vicar, but I've no time for such nonsense."

"It is an old custom and one practiced in many parishes such as yours. On rogation days, church members would walk the parish blessing the land and the crops. It is not a question of intoning set prayers – as you seem to suppose – but of walking prayerfully through a place and listening to what God wants to deal with there. It brings God's presence into the place, blessing places with God's peace and people with God's love."

"I'm sure it does but Amelia has gone and I do not see that what you suggest will bring her back."

"Walking prayerfully also addresses the memories that linger. No one knows better than you that the history of a community is passed down through the generations. There is the cognitive memory, which I need not explain to an educated woman such as yourself, but there is also emotional memory, when certain circumstances trigger those of a similar event perhaps long since; and then, of course, there is *body* memory, where the body reacts automatically to an event because memory is stored in the muscles. Do any of these memory types help to explain what might have happened to your friend?"

"Yes," replied Mildred, snappishly, looking at Neil Ilkestone as though he were the very devil himself. "I'll join your prayer walk."

Juniper Wells was even less gracious, although Neil afterwards dismissed her attitude as 'the young speaking their mind'. Sensing her hippie style, Neil had taken that line with Juniper, trusting his ability to draw her in.

"From what you have told me about the state of your father's printshop and your own belief that a poltergeist was responsible, I suspect you have no difficulty accepting that we have a demonic presence in the community?"

He ignored Juniper's frown and pressed on.

"I am convinced that communities have a corporate dynamic that is often sinful, in the sense that it works against relationships with God and with each other. The demonic may well be involved, feeding upon the sin of the place. This places the local church firmly into the area of spiritual warfare. For the church, the main weapons are worship and prayer. Worship in all its forms has an inbuilt dynamic: we are recognising the presence and nature of God ..."

"Excuse me, vicar, woah, woah. I have every respect for you, for everyone's different beliefs, but I don't myself go along with all this religious stuff. I'll come along on your prayer walk if it will help but I don't do this 'Our Father in heaven' stuff."

"If you accompany the prayer walk, there is no point in coming in a state of rebellion against God, Juniper. This will be a healing walk."

"If I catch whoever killed my dad – devil or not – I'll heal him."

Exhaustion showed in every inch of the Deliverance Minister's body as they left the printshop and walked back along the little pathway to the vicarage.

"Not home, yet, Frederick, please! The church! I need to find a moment's peace and quiet. Come with me. I know you have questions, also."

It was quiet in the church and the two priests sat together in one of the rear pews, abandoning rather than collecting their thoughts. They sat for a long time in communion with their god and through him with each other. Eventually, Neil spoke.

"We are privileged to worship here in this place that is so many centuries old. It is so easy, is it not, to fall in love with the place itself, bringing as it does such peace and stillness, and in doing so fall into the sin of idolatry. The Devil loves nothing more than idolatry because it deflects the worship from God. Any form of idolatry makes us vulnerable to demonic attack."

Fred sat quietly, knowing that the old priest beside him disapproved vehemently of his involvement in both the psychic supper and the séance, and yet was considerate enough to remain silent on the issue.

"You have difficulty with this talk of the Devil, do you not, Frederick?"

"I must confess that is so. Hell is not a place we talk much of these days. We usually focus on Heaven."

"Yes, I have read your letters to your parishioners. In one you point out that Matthew speaks of Heaven on Earth. If I remember rightly, you said *'In Matthew's gospel there is a suggestion that Heaven might be right here on Earth once the causes of sin and all evil-doers are thrown into the furnace of fire'*. Do I remember correctly?"

"Yes," replied Fred, taken aback, and chuffed, that the old man even read his newsletters let alone remembered what he'd said.

"Matthew has made an important point. We must ask how it applies to our work here in Thornham Staithe. Remember what I have said about the Devil and sin and try to rid your mind of this picture people have of the Devil. We are so bound up with artist's representations of the Devil or, worse still, the pantomime figure he has become.

"Do you not think he must be laughing at us, Frederick: once a figure of unimaginable terror and now a figure of fun? The modern world cannot accept the figure that sits at the witch's sabbath, the one who turns our Lord's cross on its head and appears through flame and fire, red in muscle and sporting a pair of goat's horns on his head; and so, we dress him up in a red costume and give him a pitchfork – oh, not forgetting the horns of the goat. Does it not occur to people that he wants us to see him in that guise? It is so much easier, then, to dismiss him as nonsense.

"But he is not nonsense, Frederick. He is here, there and everywhere, working always against our relationship with God. We shall only come to the Father through the Son, unless the Devil gets in the way!"

The old man's dark humour disturbed Fred but he said nothing, knowing more was to come. The old priest, so long on this Earth, was tired and wanting, after a life's work, to be with his Lord; but there was conflict to face and he could not afford to falter.

"Does it not strike you as ludicrous, Frederick, that in a world quite willing to accept zombies, vampires, fairies, aliens from other galaxies and all manner of other unbelievable monsters that such people – our people – find it difficult to believe in the existence of God? It seems to me that the further we go from the Truth the more falsehood becomes a reality."

"We left the Devil behind with the gospel of Love?"

"We failed to shed our nonsensical image of him, and yet his work is everywhere for all to see. Our capacity for evil has few limits – wars, greed, abuse: the Holocaust, apartheid in South Africa, the Rwandan genocide, the Syrian conflict, the war between the Serbs and Croatians, the Troubles in Ireland. Do you not see his hand in this? It is the Devil's desire to break the relationship of love between people and God and people and each other."

"These atrocities were founded in the evil of people, one to another."

"Frederick, the election of Adolf Hitler was welcomed by many in the churches. After Hitler's Reichstag speech in March 1933, it was only a few months before a truce was signed between the Vatican and Hitler. Rapidly, groups of pastors within the German Church became united and, eventually, a national bishop was appointed, approved by Hitler.

"None of these priests were evil in themselves, but none of this was centred in Christ. And what followed? The anger and hurt people felt due to the economic collapse of the 1920s led to the rise of Hitler and the subsequent tragedy that engulfed the world. You cannot fail to see the Devil's hand in this, can you? And if in this, then surely in the tragedies that now engulf your village."

Chapter 4

The Hidden Village

Ned Douglas was as good as his word: the next morning he was parked at the staithe and Sam came running eagerly from the mill. It was a cold, wet, January morning but the boy was immune to the weather. His face was alive with expectation brought about by the simple, boyish thought that he might now be able to do something to help his friend: he knew, had Ryder been able to speak with him, the engineer's first thoughts would be of Rollie, his beloved black Labrador.

The twisting, single track roads brought them to Meadow Farm Rescue Centre and the owner, Janet Davis. She was a short woman, scruffily dressed and covered in dog hair; benevolence shone from every line of her face, meeting fully in the smile she bestowed on Ned and Sam.

"You understand, don't you, I can't let you have Rollie. This is just to put your mind at rest. The police placed him here temporary like and I'm to keep my eye on him. I hear it's a funny business, his master being found like that. You'd wonder what the dog was a-doing. For that matter, you'd wonder what his master was a-doing poking about in a churchyard at that time of night ..."

Janet continued to talk as she took them into the kennelling area. As in all such centres, a sad sight met their eyes. In the far cage, looking hopefully through the bars, Sam saw a very old, very shaggy dog, its eyes holding the usual plea.

"... Martin. His owner passed on a month or so ago and we can't place him with no one. Folks don't really want an old dog. They cost too much to look after ..."

Across from Martin, a Saluki trembled continually. Sam couldn't decide whether from fright or as a response to the excited barking of the other dogs; whatever the reason, the dog look terrified. If any creature seemed to wish itself dead and out of this life, it was the Saluki.

"... poor old thing. Not that she's old. Owners bought her and then didn't want her. Need too much exercise, see. Hunting dogs, aren't they? If only people would take the trouble to find out about the dog before they bought one ... And here, here's another – the Staffy. Popular, weren't they? Couldn't live without a Staffy, so folks went out and bought one. Soon got tired of walking them. Lively dogs. Not one you can keep on a couch all day. Too much trouble ..."

The Staffordshire Bull Terrier was leaping at the bars and barking furiously, more in excitement than anger but setting off the other dogs and upsetting the nervous or lonely ones. Martin peered gloomily through the bars: he must have come to this moment, the moment he wondered whether these people were to give him a forever home, many times. The Saluki's trembling became almost a spasm; she lay prone, stretched out on the newspapers that covered the concrete floor.

And them Sam saw Rollie sitting quietly, tucked into the rear corner of his cage.

"... a good dog he is. Not a murmur from him. Just a nudge with his head when I fed him. Peaceful nature, Labradors. Did you know his owner, Ned? I'd say he was a kind man. You can always tell when an animal has been treated kindly. You can see it in their eyes, somehow. I don't think we'll have any difficulty finding a home for him ..."

Sam's heart sank. He knew his grandmother's view of dogs: 'messy things – and a lot of work'. He also remembered Mr Ryder's response: 'but great company. You're never alone with a dog'. Sam had always been alone. A dog like Rollie would make all the difference to his life and it would be a way of thanking his friend, the man who had shown an interest in getting the watermill working again.

"… You can say hello to him if you like. He seems to know you and like you …"

It was so obviously true; Rollie came across to the bars as soon as he saw the boy, his tail wagging, his ears erect, joy in his eyes. When Sam placed his hands through the bars to stroke him, Rollie nuzzled the boy's arm. and Sam's hands were soon deep in the thick fur of the Labrador's neck.

What happened next took Sam and Janet by surprise: Ned Douglas slid back the bolt of the door and let the dog out of the cage. It wasted no time and was soon outside the kennelling area, leaping around the boy, begging attention.

"…you can't do that. You'll be getting me into trouble with the police. He's got to stay here until …"

"Don't you worry yourself, Janet. You send John Sharpe to me and I'll settle matters with him."

Before either Sam or Janet Davis realised what was happening, Ned had opened the rear door of his car, nodded the dog in, indicated that Sam should shift himself and was driving off down the lane.

"… You can't do that …,"

was the last remark Sam remembered hearing from the 'Rescue Lady', as he later called her, but he did notice a smile on her face despite her protestations and Ned Douglas gave him a wink. They seemed to be on the way home, Rollie's head was in his lap and the landlord of the Swan was whistling merrily.

*

It was the following day, Sunday, when Neil Ilkestone suggested they should visit the village of Burghamton. The morning service, taken early that Sunday at All Saints, was over; and the previous day, late into the evening, they had listened to the stories of all those who had been haunted.

"It was important – it *is* important – to take time to listen, Frederick. We have their backgrounds, now; we have them in our heads. It is the people who are haunted, and not the place, as your wife has emphasised so many times. We will collect Mr Scuffil on the way …"

"You've asked him?"

"I have persuaded Mrs Sweet that having Sunday lunch in the evening will not hurt – just once. Always set the agenda, Frederick, where spiritual matters are concerned," suggested Neil with a smile that was almost wicked.

Fred smiled his agreement but his eyes showed otherwise and the deliverance minister was not one to let such a discrepancy pass unnoticed.

"You are troubled about our visit to Burghamton?"

"No, but it's a strange village. Perhaps I've known all along."

"Perhaps we close our eyes too often, Frederick, when it would be best we kept them open. Hmm! Events, tragic events, are coming together now, are they not? So many people, so different, and yet all linked by the same set of circumstances."

Fred was familiar with Burghamton, once a village, now a hamlet. On his arrival at Thornham Staithe, he had paid the place several visits. The people who lived there were his responsibility as a priest; but there was no doubt it was a strange place, a place out of time. This was not unusual in Norfolk; it was a running joke at diocesan conferences that many villages and hamlets in the country existed several centuries behind the rest of the country; he had even heard it suggested that dragons nested on the outskirts of such places as Wymondham.

The difficulty of finding the hamlet was notorious: single-track byroad after byroad led nowhere. When, at last, the first scattering of houses appeared as a hill was breasted for the umpteenth time Fred always heaved a sigh of relief.

Those houses that remained of the once-upon-a time village straggled along their own stretches of road, those still inhabited nestled up against those that were derelict. It was sad sight for the young priest and an unusual one because rural dwellings in Norfolk were usually snapped up as second homes by Londoners, but not in Burghamton. It was close to the main Lowestoft-Norbridge road but out of sight. Once reached, the noise and bustle of the outside world faded and a sense of unreality settled upon the visitor.

Fred had first come, alone, on a beautiful autumn day. The morning sun slanted through the branches of sycamore and beech trees, whose leaves lay scattered, dying and stricken with patches of fungi, and toadstools were pushing their way up through the wet grass. In the distance, Fred thought he heard the sound of a tractor. A farmer harvesting his potato crop, he'd thought – food for his harvest festival sermon. The narrow, winding roads brought him to the village pub, The Maypole, and he found himself entering cautiously for no other reason than he feared he might disturb the atmosphere within.

It was an old inn: the flagstone floor and the wooden settles had clearly been installed when it was built two centuries before and worn uneven by its customers. A few of them sat drinking and gave Fred a glance that was anything but welcoming: this was not unusual in country pubs, frequented largely by locals, but mingled with the looks had been nervousness, if not a touch of resentment. The roof of the room was low and hung lower by smoke; the passages to the toilet and the back garden, narrow and oppressive; the dark panelling of the walls closed in on the drinkers.

When he introduced himself, the landlord looked him over and nodded at the pumps instead of asking him what he might fancy. He was a big man and sweaty, giving the appearance of an old dog past its time. His hands as he pulled the pint Fred noticed were broad and white; the blue veins stood out prominently against the flesh. Handing over his money, the priest noticed they were also cold. When he spoke, since Fred gave him no option but to do so, it was in whispers.

"The church, sir, just along the road, though you won't find much there."

The drinkers looked across as the man spoke but their expressions were inscrutable, showing neither the embarrassment

the young priest had come to expect nor concern. Two of the men
– and the drinkers were all men – looked through him as though he
might not exist.

Pleased to down his pint as quickly as possible, Fred left the pub
and found himself meandering rather than walking with purpose.
He felt as he had done when on holiday soaking in the spirit of a
new place, feeling apart from the real world; only, where joy was
brought by such feelings on holiday, here in Burghamton he was
saddened.

The hedgerows had been layered rather than bushwhacked in
the modern fashion, once again suggesting a place with time on its
hands, and he knew it was the place as much as the people for
whom time was no longer an issue. His attention was drawn to the
figure of a man leaning on a gate by one of the fields. He thought
initially that it was scarecrow but when it moved Fred realised it
was a man dressed smartly in what used to be described as a suit of
the English colonial style; white and slightly creased, and very
unsuitable for a British autumn.

At the time, he thought nothing more of the man; even had he
done so, his attention was immediately claimed entirely by the
ancient church: everything about it was in a state of dilapidation:
the gate jammed as he tried to open it, the graves were covered with
rank grasses, the footpath weed-strewn, the roof had collapsed
into the nave, birds fluttered from the bent rafters, ferns sprang
from the walls of the Saxon tower. Fred sat on a broken memorial
seat in the churchyard for a long time, attempting to understand
why this desecration had been allowed to happen.

When he had come again in the summer, he remembered being
even more puzzled. He and Jacqueline had walked the famous
Burghamton Sculpture Trail, an event attended by hundreds of
people from across Norfolk and beyond. Nothing could have
contrasted more vividly with the downtrodden spirit of the village
on his visit that first autumn. Apart from the sculptures themselves
– all mapped, notated and given pride of place in gardens, on
roadsides and every green space available – the village had been
alive with stalls, games, music and dancing. Folk and jazz groups

had sung and played from gardens, Morris dancers adorned the field by the side of the village hall, a maypole had been erected outside the pub and children from local dance groups entertained the visitors. He had wondered why a hamlet with such a life-giving spirit had allowed its church to disintegrate.

Thinking back on it now, with the deliverance minister keen to visit, Fred recalled thinking that the hamlet was bewitched, a place living under a spell that from time to time showed itself in different lights, the solemn and the wild.

Sitting, disconsolate, in the churchyard, he'd heard the murmur of voices and the sound of feet rustling the fallen leaves on the lane but when he rose to acknowledge whoever might be approaching he found no one; he had only the sense that someone, perhaps several, had passed by and talked about him.

He had walked along the strangely named Threadneedle Street, nothing more than a lane in reality, back to what now constituted the centre of the hamlet; and this was where he'd come across the bakery. It was situated in a row of picturesque cottages whose gardens held the charm of the fading summer: skeins of ivy yet to flower ran along the tops of walls, the flowers of campanula were in violet bloom as were the geraniums and the magenta flowers of lychnis rose from the grey leaves of the plant, honeysuckle holding its scent back for the evening flopped gracefully around doorways.

Fred ran his hand along the wall of the bakery in a moment of hesitation and then walked into the shop. The warm aroma of fresh bread invaded his nostrils and from the rear of the bakery he could smell, rather than feel, the fading heat of the oven. He looked around and saw that the shop was also a grocery. Tins, bags and packets of produce lined the shelves, all basic ingredients for cooking and eating with no indication of luxury items, such as chocolates and sweets, as though what the villagers needed they made for themselves; a few loaves of bread were stacked in a wooden tray. Fred tapped on the wooden counter and a tall man appeared, bringing the warmth with him; but when Fred showed an interest in buying one of the fresh loaves, the man's answer bore none of the warmth of his trade.

"We only bake for the village … sir."

The pause before his 'sir' was noticeable, as though it were a long time since he'd used the term. He looked Fred up and down and disappeared; it was clear he had no intention of serving him at all. As Fred stood, perplexed, deciding whether to argue with the man, a woman entered. The baker immediately re-appeared and served her with some tinned fruit, a bag of flour and some coffee, all the while ignoring Fred, as did the woman who spared him not a glance.

He left the shop, bewildered. He'd come here as their priest hoping to strike a chord or two of friendship with these people. Nobody it seemed wanted to know him. Determined not to be thwarted, Fred spent the remainder of the morning wandering the lanes and byways among the scattered houses. At a general store, where the services of a handyman were advertised in a notice pinned to the wall, he came across an Aladdin's cave of useful, domestic items – nails, tap washers, mop heads, balls of string, garden tools, broom handles and the like – but with no urge on the part of the owner to make a sale.

When he passed villagers in the lanes, out and about, perhaps digging up vegetables for the midday meal or chopping wood to keep the fire in and the cold out, some nodded, some spoke, others walked by as though he were invisible to them; some disappeared into their homes, others seemed to vanish before his eyes, all talked or chatted among themselves absorbed in a life secret to them.

Fred realised as his morning drew to a close that these people lived in a world apart, as though the central purpose of their existence was elsewhere. A stranger was unwelcomed in Burghamton because he served no purpose in the life of the village; he might even be an intrusion. Fred wondered what that life entailed and why it was hidden for all but two events of the year; but the longer he stayed, the more he realised that he might, nevertheless, come within its grasp, come to be part of this silent acceptance of a reality that he felt the people themselves – his people – might not even comprehend, a slow, spectral drift into another domain.

Neil Ilkestone listened intently as Fred recalled his first visit to Burghamton. The old priest had experienced nothing to match what his younger friend detailed but, recalling a conversation he'd had with Robert Urquhart, the Bishop of Norbridge, he accepted that there was a fine line – perhaps 'veil' would have been a better word – between the living and the dead. He smiled but said nothing.

Neil appeared to be gathering his bearings. Watching him, Fred and Vernon realised he was an old man, rather tired and worried, which was unnerving: he was their leader and they assumed he knew what he was doing and why they had come. He continued to ponder, meandering his way along hedge-lined tracks to narrow lanes. In truth, he was irritated. He felt himself to be under the spell of the place; the village was charming but it was a charm that unsettled him.

Although there was no one about, Neil knew that they were being observed. If only the silence would give way to a murmur of voices there would, at least, be someone they could challenge with a question or two; but the village was challenging them. The village was waiting for something to happen. He led the way back to the main road. Why was he dithering? He knew the reason for their visit: they had come to familiarise themselves with the place.

"We have yet to look at the old workhouse, Mr Scuffil. I think it warrants a visit and you are the expert, I believe. *Practical Results of the Workhouse System as adopted in the Parish of Burghamton 1833-34* – hm! A seminal work?"

Vernon was pleasantly surprised and even more pleased that the old priest was familiar with his intended masterpiece: obviously, a man of the right academic calibre.

"Hmmm!" trumpeted Vernon, a sound Fred noticed that contrasted distinctly with Neil's quieter hm!

"The New Poor Law required parishes to provide their own workhouses to cater for those too ill, too old or too young to work. A charitable notion, of course, but one that hung like a shadow over ordinary people who fell on hard times. Unfeeling, mean, bleak – are these not the words that come to mind when we see photographs of rooms full of identically dressed elderly men and women with no spark of life in their eyes? Their choice was *to be starved to death slowly in the workhouse or opt for a quick one out of it* – hm?"

"If you care to pay too much regard to Dickens, that might be the so," replied Vernon, "but something had to be done. The system was abused by able-bodied shirkers and idlers. Many parishes had their workhouses long before the Poor Law was reviewed in 1834. There was one not far from here – Shipmeadow, near Bungley in Suffolk – where they lived the life of Riley at the parish's expense. A woman called Elizabeth Stannard *arrived home drunk and obstreperous after her usual Sunday outing loaded with three quarters of a pint of rum, two pounds of pork, half a pound of sausages, six eggs, apples, bread, half a pound of cheese, three packets of sweetmeats, £1 9 shillings in silver and £5 10 shillings in gold.* Not exactly starvation rations, I'd say. Hmmm! Hmmm!"

It clearly gave Vernon great delight to reel off his knowledge of the workhouse system and to dash to pieces the public misconception shared by the deliverance minister. Out and about, away from his home, the history teacher for one morning was able to shuffle off the whispering Presence that had driven him to a nervous breakdown. He smiled, the first in a long time, and sallied forth.

"Here in Burghamton, the inmates fared even better. *Two local beer-houses were especially opened on Sundays to cater for the male paupers, while the females had boxes in the neighbouring cottages,*" said Vernon, sweeping his arm along those on the road, "*containing dresses which they exchanged for their workhouse garb and thus attired in more attractive style, flaunted about the neighbourhood with young men turning the nearby woods into what was described as 'the Groves of Isis, goddess of love'.*

"There were 450 paupers here; the aged, the infirm, the able-bodied men, women and children shared common yards and dayrooms. The manufacture of sacking was their main employment but little work was done except in the gardens: the paupers would arrive at the weekly market in Thornham laden with baskets of fruit and vegetables for sale.

"They received a greater weekly ration of meat than the average labourer could afford and the *paupers would feast their friends within the workhouse walls on Sundays and high days on butchers' meat, pies, sweetmeats and spiritous liquors*. All on the house.

"Understandably, they didn't take too kindly to the new regime. *The paupers, wild and disorderly, rushed out and assaulted the vicar and the local landowner, who was a guardian, when they visited*."

Vernon smiled again – a long, deep, satisfied smile that seemed to embrace his large, commodious head. The resonance of his trumpeting, a sound not heard for weeks by Justine and the children, reverberated around the village. There was triumph in the sound, as though he had come and settled a score.

"Let us go then, you and I, and acquaint ourselves with the old place," he concluded, with a smile, and led the way along the lane that flanked the village hall to the long stretch of land well to the fore of what had once been the parish workhouse on which the bonfire was always erected.

"It has taken years to get permission to transform this into housing. Problems have always arisen but they seem to be moving on nicely and many of the old buildings are now re-designed, re-furbished and people are living here while the work goes on. I haven't been here for years but it's Sunday, there aren't any workmen about and I think we'll be free to look around.

"This was already established, as I've said, and so it's different to those workhouses built after 1834 to the Poor Law Commissioner's design. It's also larger than most rural workhouses."

Vernon was in his element. He brushed aside the security man with a bellowing trumpet sound and a wide wave of his arm. He marched his way past the builder's machines, deposits of sand, piles of rubble, stacks of breeze blocks and bricks, yards of cable and piping until they reached the entrance hall.

To their left, along a dark passage, were the porter's rooms, the surgery, the male and female receiving rooms and the bathroom where newcomers were washed and de-loused. This took them to the women's yard (now landscaped and transformed into a pleasant garden and play area) off which the paupers cloth store, the able-bodied women's ward, the old women's ward, the girl's school and the girl's dining hall, washroom and privy had all been converted to modern housing, where families were now living.

Crossing another landscaped area, once the girl's yard, they came to more housing, once the vagrants' wards and a coalhouse, and so to the infirmaries, men's and women's, which linked to the central block containing the men's dining hall, the chapel, the laundry yards, washhouse, kitchen and master's office.

Another passage took them to the workshops, adjacent to the boy's yard and so to the able-bodied men's ward, the old men's ward, the boy's ward and school, and their separate dining halls with adjacent yards and washrooms. In this area, too, was the pump room. These were in the process of being converted to housing.

Finally, as they re-approached the entrance hall, Vernon indicated the board room, the cleric's office, the pantry and two smaller rooms labelled as reformatory cells.

"Mr Scuffil, I cannot thank you enough for this little tour of the old workhouse. It complements nicely our visit to the hamlet and Frederick's experiences. I feel I could find my way around both in the dark – as, indeed, I may be obliged to do," Neil added with a grim laugh, "I have yet to lay my plans and hope the need to call upon you again will not arise. If it should, I trust I can rely on you?"

"Hmmm!! Trust? I don't see why not, do you! I may even persuade Justine to move here. No Whisperers, hmmm!. The place must have something to say for it! Hmmm!"

*

It was on the evening of that same day, the third day, that James Ryder rose from the dead; while his corpse lay frozen in the morgue, his ghost (or, as Esme Owen would explain it, his grounded spirit) found itself wandering along Bridge Street on its way to the staithe where, instinctively, he knew Rollie was living. James was uncertain how he came to be in the old market town but the sight of one of Barbara Wilton's missing posters stirred memories not only of the young girl but also of the manner of his own death.

Chapter 5

The Iniquity of the Fathers

"While I fast, Frederick, I must leave much of the early planning to you," said Neil Ilkestone the following morning, "Prayer and fasting draw us into the presence of God, opening us up to His loving care, enabling us to face our sin and weaknesses. My relationship with Him has to be clear. I need to know my vulnerabilities, face my weaknesses, clear my decks as they say in the Navy. Now, listen very attentively and I will outline what must be done. There is more devilry abroad and we must face our enemy as soon as possible. I would prefer the Lord's Day, but I think we need to act before then. St Anthony of Egypt's feast day is celebrated by our Catholic and Orthodox brothers and sisters on January 17; I don't think they will mind us leaning on his mighty arm."

It took the deliverance minister much less time to explain what Fred needed to do than it took the vicar to complete his tasks. Once Neil Ilkestone had finished speaking, he retired to the room Jacqueline had allocated for him and was not seen again for three days; once a day, in the evening, a light broth was placed on a tray outside his room with a fresh flagon of water, and he left the room quietly only when nature called. Fred, on the other hand, barely felt his feet touch the ground and arrived home, exhausted, at odd times during the day.

Jacqueline had not stopped worrying about her husband as he walked, sometimes ran, about the village or took their car to reach those people Neil wanted involved, people who lived on the outskirts of Thornham Staithe. He remained intensely agitated the whole time, refusing to be drawn into conversation about what the deliverance minister intended, emphasising only that everyone, including her, must co-operate without question.

"This is no time for debate, Jacqueline. Everyone, including you, must pitch in and help or all is wasted," he said on one occasion, and she knew he was deadly serious because he never usually called her anything but 'Jacqui'.

His efforts were brought to fruition before her eyes when she walked from their home across the churchyard from the gate in the wall and saw up to fifty or sixty people gathering, person by person, singly, in couple or in groups in and around the churchyard; the pathways were full and some people were obliged to step off and perch themselves gingerly on the grass, carefully, out of respect for the graves of those buried beneath. She recognised their regular churchgoers and they were matched by those people she had come to know since the haunting of Thornham Staithe began. Neil was among them, standing unsteadily by her husband, clearly ready to make some kind of speech; and her eyes sort out Lottie with her father and brother. Jaqueline wasn't a woman noted for any darkness in her sense of humour but she smiled wryly to herself knowing that Fred would be wondering why attendance wasn't like this every Sunday.

As it was, unexpectedly, Neil said very little, only:

"Frederick has told you all what must be done, and how and when. Please heed him for the sake of the very souls of those departed. We shall be in the hands of God tonight. Those of you who came to Communion this afternoon, whether to partake of the holy bread and wine or simply to be blessed are in God's keeping. May the Lord go with you on your prayer walk."

The crowd then dispersed, calmly and purposefully, Jacqueline noted. Her role was to join the service in Holy Trinity. She was pleased that Lottie and her brother, Charles, were quick to join her and puzzled that Gerald Henderson moved away with the prayer walkers; she welcomed Bradley Hall into her little group. Jacqueline recognised most of the newcomers immediately as she stood aside to let them enter ahead of her through the south door: Catriona Pegg with her children, who usually attended All Saints; Emma Gooch with her grandson, Brian; Belfast Billie with Carmen Quay, together under the same religious roof for the first time. Cynthia Revell gave a nervous smile as she entered and Jacqueline, knowing instantly who she was, gripped her hand and indicated that the dead boy's mother might sit comfortably with her: it was never easy for non-churchgoers, she knew.

Her husband opened the service with a traditional reading from the Evening Prayer; given the circumstances of this very special service, his choice did not surprise Jacqueline. Fred was a modern priest but a pragmatic one: many of his regulars were elderly and had a liking for the traditional service from the Book of Common Prayer. It was his custom, therefore, to hold Evening Prayer for those, a dwindling congregation, who still remembered the days when churches were full.

"When the wicked man turneth away from his wickedness that he hath committed, and doeth that which is lawful and right, he shall save his soul alive."

Neil himself led the prayer walkers, lantern-lit, from the churchyard, by the village green and so along Edmund's Lane and to the church of St John, where Father Crouch and his small congregation waited. The priest acknowledged the deliverance minister with an incline of his head and settled his group into the procession. Fred, during the mission he carried out for the deliverance minister, had insisted upon involving Father Crouch; the churches in Thornham worked closely together for the community. The Catholic priest had made a comment about "gathering the faithful"'

The tight party, smaller in number than those at the church service, crossed the Norbridge-Lowestoft road and took farm tracks and bye lanes to Burghamton, the very route taken by Richard Revell and Sam Whitham in November. Sam was with the walkers together with Rollie and his grandmother who had said he could "mind the dog until the police found a proper home for it" and made some remark about Ned Douglas "having a way with him". Edward Warburg walked with Mildred Ackroyd, sharing memories of lost friends; Juniper Wells talked with Esme Owen and Justine Sweet and her children, while Vernon walked ahead with Neil and Gerald; Simon Pegg and PC Sharpe rear-guarded the party.

Neil stressed the importance of them sticking together; it was a small group, carefully selected, one likely to be vulnerable; he'd have preferred Justine and her children to be with the church group but Justine was not to be persuaded.

One of Fred's missions over the three days of Neil's fast had been to consult Robert Urquhart, Bishop of Norbridge, over the nature and format of the service.

"More *Songs of Praise* than a religious service, Fred?"

The bishop's response had left Fred unenlightened and so he decided to press on with what he thought best; it was necessary, Neil had told him, to send a blast of holy power into the darkness of the night.

Fred actually enjoyed the BBC's *Songs of Praise* and had noted eagerly the country's choice of their favourite hymns six years before. After his opening challenge, he announced his first choice; there were to be many hymns in this special service. And that night's congregation knew the words and they rang out:

> *"Oh Lord, my God*
> *When I, in awesome wonder*
> *Consider all the worlds Thy hands have made*
> *I see the stars, I hear the rolling thunder*
> *Thy power throughout the universe displayed"*

Fred, no mean singer himself, took up his stand below the choir stalls and addressed his people from the steps of the nave.

"Dearly beloved brethren, the Scripture moveth us in sundry places to acknowledge and confess our manifold sins and wickedness ... '

And so began the general confession.

Neil paused his little group when they reached the place where Richard Revell had been found: the mere, the door still half-open set in the flint wall standing alone, the horse chestnut tree under which the boy had hidden, the ploughed field now showing winter wheat and the blackthorn hedge the boy had clutched; these objects meant nothing to the prayer walkers: they could only imagine where the boy lay freezing on the farm track. Knock-knock! Who's there?

Esme Owen stepped forward, her eyes scanning the place, her attention drawn to the door. She moved slowly from the group and walked steadily and easily towards the wall.

"There have been presences here," she said, "and ... and I can feel them even now."

"That's far enough, Esme," called Neil, "You may expose us all to whatever spirits may come through. We are here to listen to what God wants us to do."

"Your way is of your choosing, Neil. It is not my way and it is not the only way. Let us settle. Be quiet and listen. Let me ... be aware. I have a sense of foreboding."

The two priests exchanged glances, both convinced psychic powers were either gifts claimed by frauds or fools in the hands of the Devil. Neil moved towards Esme, intending to break the mood that had overcome the young woman, but felt Vernon's hand grip his shoulder.

"Leave her alone. Your faith doesn't have all the answers. Hmm! Indeed, one might say it has more questions. Hmm! Hmm!"

The elephant noises were quieter than usual, blasted as they were into the deliverance minister's ear. Neil looked askance; Father Crouch shook his shoulders.

"He was attacked there by the door. He went through the door time and again. Glass was smashed, window frames were torn out, a knife was taken, a girl was abused, there was terror and kicking and beatings ... but not here ... and there was a name ... Quire ... he, too, was a victim ... a knife was taken from him," Esme staggered out her apprehensions and then fell against the blackthorn hedge, exhausted.

Gerald went to her, lifted her from the ground and carried her back to the group. She looked up into his face and smiled.

"Did any of it make any sense?" she asked.

"Almighty God, the Father of our Lord Jesus Christ, who desireth not the death of a sinner, but rather that he may turn from his wickedness ...

During the Absolution, Fred became aware of the disturbance; it was centred around his wife. Jacqueline, absorbed in the service, watching her husband intently suddenly felt Lottie pushed forward. In the next instant, the girl was dragged across Jacqueline's legs and yanked from the pew. She part-stumbled, part-fell along the nave, propelled and shoved by a man in a tweed jacket.

"Thomkins – no!"

The cry came from the back of the church. Jaqueline rose from her seat and turned. Still wearing the gypsy dress, Maggie Henderson, her right arm outstretched, pleading with her persecutor, ran along the nave after her daughter.

"You cannot blame the sins of our mothers and fathers on us," she cried.

"I the Lord thy God am a jealous God, visiting the iniquity of the fathers upon the children of the third and fourth generation of them that hate me – Exodus 20: 5," screamed Thomkins.

"William Quire was the victim of one of the gangs, the rowdies, who terrorised the workhouses. They were vandals, thieves, thugs, pure and simple – hmmm! An honest man was pleased to have his possessions removed before he entered the workhouse because if they weren't taken into care, they'd be stolen from him," replied Vernon, in answer to Esme's question, "Quire seems to have lived on with his grievances. A pound to a penny, young Revell was the descendent of one of these gang members. Quire has taken his revenge on the Revells – grandfather, father, son. Hmmm! Hmmm!"

"Touched by evil," said Father Crouch quietly to Neil Ilkestone.

"We must cleanse this place," replied the deliverance minister.

Sam Whitham was about to speak. Events were now making sense: Revell had passed him on the track shortly after he saw the strange man, the one with the crushed top hat and the ill-fitting clothes. He was about to speak when Esme said:

"It began elsewhere. Not all the sounds originated here."

"We know, my dear, but we must cleanse this place before passing on. You have been of great help."

He spoke gently, not resenting her admonishment of him or his faith, realising her experience had been unnerving: being psychic was not necessarily good news.

The blessing took only moments. Neil and Father Crouch spoke not a word but clasped their hands together in silent prayer. Vernon, watching them, heard himself intoning the old song 'Bless this house O Lord we pray ...' and smiled, ruefully, at Justine who stood close by him and Esme with her two children.

Afterwards, they moved on and it was not long before Sam recognised the place on the track where he had seen the man he now knew as Quire: the cold, wet ground edged by rank, yellowing grasses, the overhanging silver birches, the silence of the woods on either side and that strange figure from another time. They all listened as he spoke and Rollie growled as though he had been with the boy that night.

Back in Thornham, Amy Prentice watched the face of Richard Revell grinning at her from the mirror of her dressing table. Night after night he came with never a break. Of late, when his face disappeared, she had turned to find him sitting on the bed behind her, still grinning. She would feel him run his fingers down her back, knowing he would eventually clutch her buttocks and try to touch her up, as he used to do when they were walking down the street together. She hadn't minded it then: it had made her feel grown-up – a real woman – and, after all, she had the coolest guy in the school: all the other girls envied her. But she didn't like it now he was dead. It terrified her to think what he might do – something they'd never done. They'd not gone the whole way, and ghosts couldn't, could they?

Lottie was thrown on the steps at the very feet of Fred, bruised and shaken. Her brother, Charlie, struggling past Jacqueline and the others in their pew, ran to his sister and threw himself into her arms. Quite what he hoped to achieve, Lottie was unsure (perhaps to shield her from further blows, she thought) but she cradled him there as a mother once cradled her dying baby on the steps of the workhouse; the image was not lost on Maggie who fell to her knees weeping.

Fred reached down and knelt beside Lottie. Thomkins towered over the three of them and Fred looked up into the ghost's eyes.

"The Lord God pardons all who truly repent and absolves them from their sins. Your guilt hangs upon you, the guilt you have carried since you abandoned your wife and child. Repent now that you may rest pure and holy."

The creature raised its head and gave a long, harsh cry, stretching its neck back so far it seemed the sinews would crack.

"Even now, you acknowledge Jesus as your risen Lord?"

It was a question and Fred knew what the spirit's answer must be. Jesus knew who needed healing, who needed compassion, who needed casting out. It was knowledge rooted in His relationship with the Father. Fred had never felt further from his God than at that moment.

"Never!"

The cry came from the tortured throat and Thomkins brought his right hand down onto Lottie's neck and jerked her upwards by her hair.

It was Edward who first realised that their little group, the prayer walkers, were not alone. Every so often, Neil would call a halt and ask for God's guidance.

"We are here, Lord, to listen to what you want us to accomplish in your name. We are here to bring your presence to this place. We bless this place with your peace; we bless these people with your love."

Mildred Ackroyd, remembering Neil's comments on the three types of memory, closed her eyes. She had loved Amelia in the way that two women, friends for many years, love one another, and she, too, held her hands together in the way she'd been taught to do at school so many years before.

Juniper Wells, averse as she was to the religious life, did likewise. She and her father had not always seen eye to eye but she loved him and missed him more than she'd thought possible.

Edward cried, and unashamedly; he and Myles had not merely been friends, they had been lovers; and their life as musicians had woven deep within each of them a spiritual understanding of the inner meaning of this life, here and now. Together, they had transcended the reality of the day to day. His eyes had been closed, out of habit, out of respect, and when he opened them Myles stood beside him. There was a smile on the dead man's face but also a warning; much as he desired to do so, Edward did not reach out and touch his friend but his face lit up with a joy he could not have expressed even in music. Myles replied with a smile of his own but a sadder one, one unfulfilled.

Edward looked across as Neil Ilkestone and the priest smiled back but seemed unaware of what had transpired. Wanting to share his joy and yet unsure of how things stood, Edward looked about him, at the others in the group. Their faces lit only by lanterns in the darkness, the prayer walkers re-assembled and walked on; no greetings were exchanged, no acknowledgements that Myles was present in the company; and then Edward looked at Mildred who had walked with him all the way and her face bore the same expression of elation and Edward knew her eyes, also, were on her friend. Behind him in the straggled line he saw the same expression on the face of Esme Owen and Juniper Wells, who walked together, and on the face of Marjory Broome, who now walked with her grandson, Sam Whitham and the dog, Rollie. Dead friends and loved ones had returned, and Edward couldn't but wonder what it was they must now face together.

What might have happened at that moment, Fred was never to know and the knowledge of his own impotence as a priest was to haunt his dreams for years to come.

A fresh voice called from the west porch and all eyes turned. James Ryder stood in the open doorway, both hands cupped, outstretched, in front of his chest. His large hands held firmly together, he made his way along the nave steadily, his workman's boots taking the necessary steps in firm strides. He walked by the distressed figure of Maggie Henderson with no glance in her direction; his eyes were fixed firmly on his hands and what he held within them.

Thomkins turned and looked at Ryder, who approached steadily, his hands seemingly in a begging gesture; when he neared his fellow ghost, Ryder tossed his hands upwards and into the other's face. Thomkins choked and spluttered; his eyes blurred. He seemed perplexed, released his hold on Lottie and pulled at his face, which sagged and, seemingly, fell in on itself.

Fred alone in the church realised what had happened, what Ryder had done. The one-time engineer, entering through the porch and seeing Lottie slung on the steps, had dipped his hands into the stoup, the small niche containing a recessed basin, where holy water was blessed every Sunday. Intended for worshippers who liked to dip their fingers in it and make the sign of the cross on their foreheads to remind them of their baptism as they entered the church, the holy water had now saved the girl. Fred reached over and blessed Thomkins's face with two strokes of his hand. It was an instinctive act on his part, nothing more, as it had been on Ryder's.

Thomkins screamed and clawed at his eyes; Ryder took his opponents right arm, the one that had grasped Lottie by the hair, tossed him round his shoulders in a fireman's lift and hurried from the church.

The prayer walkers brought their journey to an end by joining Crooke's Road – another strangely named byway in Burghamton – from the track that led down from the farms and came at last to the village hall and the long stretch of land behind that fronted what had once been the parish workhouse. Behind them was the row of cottages that included the bakery, where Fred had attempted to buy a loaf of bread.

Neil halted his little party as they stood in the road. It was as he turned to speak that he became aware the prayer walkers had been swelled by the dead. For a moment, the priest faltered – after all, he had met none of these people in life – and seemed about to remonstrate when Father Crouch touched his arm and whispered in his ear: the Catholic priest knew the village and had broken bread, as the saying goes, with many of them.

"Here is the parting of our ways," said Neil, after the temporary hiatus in his plans, "Soon I will go into the old workhouse accompanied only by Gerald and Vernon, both of whom have been kind enough to offer their companionship. Father Crouch will remain with you in this hour of need, as your spiritual comforter.

"Back in Thornham, your priest – by that I mean the priest of Holy Trinity," he added hurriedly with a look of apology to Father Crouch and his congregation, "Frederick Mackenzie is leading a special service – more an Evening Song than an Evening Prayer," he interjected (humour was not one of Neil's distinctive qualities), "and now it is time for you to join in their singing the Lord's praises.

"I want your prayer walk to become a prayer chain. I want you to join hands along this road, forming a barrier of acclamation between the village and the workhouse. The church is under sustained spiritual attack. The key to the kingdom is worship; only in this way can we meet with the living God and bring His presence to this accursed place. Sing as your fellow worshippers are now singing, sing your hearts out, sing your praises to the Lord."

It was a strange prayer chain that arranged itself along that strangely named road, the living with the dead, holding hands. As Neil, following his prayers, moved away towards the workhouse with Gerald and Vernon, they were followed by Esme and Juniper with the ghosts of Clifford Raine and Jack Dorling. The voices of the singers followed them into the darkness:

"Make me a channel of your peace
Where there is hatred let me bring your love
Where here is injury, your pardon Lord
And where there is doubt true faith in you."

"No! No, no!" called Lottie, as the congregation rose as one to hurry from Holy Trinity, despite Fred's call for calm.

She stood, now, holding her brother by the hand, a slight and dominant figure below the steps of the choir stalls. She caught her mother's eye and looked across at Jaqueline, who she thought might know what she was about.

"Reverend Ilkestone has asked us to sing our hearts out tonight. He needs our help and our support or he is alone to face his enemy. Fred?"

Lottie looked up into the vicar's eyes as she spoke and Fred, deciding the Absolution might wait, announced the next hymn.

"Abide with me."

The organist struck the first chord, the congregation sat and then stood, some eyes on the nave, some still behind them on the open door of the west porch, some on the figure of Maggie creeping to the rear of the church, some on Lottie, who began to sing:

"Abide with me, fast falls the eventide
The darkness deepens, Lord with me abide
When other helpers fail and comforts flee
Help of the helpless, oh abide with me"

At the butcher's shop that evening, Barbara Wilton returned. Myrtle knew she would: she'd felt it in her bones all day but had said nothing to Reg. He was a good man, he'd listened over and over again to her anguish, night after night, day in and day out, but Myrtle knew her husband had had enough: there's just so much a man can take and then he closes off. That was one reason they'd refused to go on the prayer walk, even though the Rev Mackenzie had tried to persuade them in that nice way of his.

They were in their sitting room when the man came. It was the one she'd seen in the shop, the one who had walked her down the stairs that night, out and into the neighbour's garden where she thought she found Reg sitting on that seat. Only it wasn't Reg: he came down later and found her there. The man was still wearing that suit, the one of heavy cloth that looked as though it had survived many summers and winters. He still had the scarf round his neck and the fingerless gloves on his hands., and he still wore that narrow-brimmed trilby. But it was the eyes that got you – green and evil.

They heard him knock on the door and Reg answered. He walked in as bold as you like and stood in their sitting room watching them. Barbara wasn't with him. Myrtle thought Reg was going to turf him out but it was obvious you couldn't do any such thing; the man was a ghost. Reg didn't believe in ghosts. He'd always said 'I'll give them bloody ghosts if I catch one of them, I can tell you': only, he didn't. Reg stood as pale as a sheet. It was the man who spoke:

"Your business goes back a long way, doesn't it, Reg Wilton – 1836 it says above the door. You're proud of that, aren't you – a business built on the misery of others? Your forebear was one of the guardians, wasn't he? And he supplied the meat to the workhouse, didn't he? Old meat, wasn't it – the stuff left over you couldn't sell? Coarse. The children were left so hungry, they'd steal bread and be whipped for it. Remember the seven course meals you served to committee members. Starving girls waiting on you all. Watching you eat soups, chickens, sweets – all on the rates, more for the coffers of the Wiltons …"

"I'd nothing to do with anything like that. I've built my business as an honest tradesman …"

"Built on the misery of others."

"I've never done anyone down in my life."

The man didn't answer. He looked at Myrtle and Lucy, both cowering on the family sofa in tears and walked out. Myrtle knew where he was going and followed. They found Barbara on the bench seat in the neighbour's garden, looking like a queen in her pantomime costume. Reg remembered the woman who had come for his daughter just before Christmas.

"Mum, dad – it was an accident. The lady let me ride her bike. The hill was steep and it had no brakes. I couldn't stop. I hit the tractor and I was thrown over the hedge …"

Myrtle, her eyes running freely, walked towards her daughter who was also crying in desperation. Barbara looked so cold, so frail, as white as the dead; if only she could hug her warm, things would be all right. She was thinking all the while that there were no steep hills in Norfolk. What was the girl talking about?

The man stepped between them, took Barbara's hand and led her from the garden. The last her family saw of her was Barbara looking back at them over her shoulder.

"... and that the rest of our life hereafter may be pure, and holy; so that at last we may come to his eternal joy; through Jesus Christ our Lord. Amen"

Fred concluded the Absolution. Looking down he saw, kneeling by the steps of the nave, the woman who had haunted the conscience of his calling, Elizabeth Beeston, dubbed a common prostitute by a priest who pilloried sinners. She had given birth to four children by different fathers and met with rejection and sneers. Grounded by her hate ever since, she had now come to seek her chance of redemption.

Fred leaned down and she took his outstretched hand; the contempt for his calling had gone.

Chapter 6

The Fall of the House

In the entrance lobby, Neil halted. He was unsure what to expect. All he knew was that this was the place where the grievances were grounded, where for almost two centuries, the dead or the relatives of the dead had festered, brewing their anger into violence and murder. The task before his friends and himself was to free them to God's judgement and mercy. He also had no doubt that their rage – righteous, no doubt, in every respect – had been further incensed by the Devil: Satan knew how to sever the relationship between God and His people.

He'd wanted to come with Gerald and Vernon only: the latter because of his knowledge of the building, the former because of his calm nature and because injury was possible. He wasn't afraid; experience told him that fear was a hindrance; besides Neil had no doubt his God was with him. He was fearful only for Esme, whose insistence on coming had swayed his better judgement, and for Juniper, who brooked no denial. A wild card, indeed. And now, with them, he turned to see the ghosts of Clifford Raine and Jack Dorling. Neil felt particularly sorry for Jack; Clifford, at least, knew where he was and why, while Jack was bemused, a dead man clinging desperately to his beloved daughter. Neil had never married – he was wedded to the Church – but he shared a father's feelings.

They would come to him – he knew that was so – and he would pray and do his best to lead them to the Father through the Son. His was the ministry of the cross and the defeat of evil. Jesus dealt with the demonic simply and directly, and Neil knew that he moved with the same authority and power. Bless, cleanse, release: how often had those three words come to his mind in moments of crisis.

"We will now make our way to the men's dining hall and the chapel. Vernon will be kind enough to lead the way. I must stress how important it is that we stay together. It may well be that the forces we are up against will attempt to divide us," he said, adding, "I am certain they will attempt to divide us!"

Vernon led the way along a passage, no doubt dark and musty in its own day and worse with the passing of decades. It was narrow, giving barely room for two abreast. Neil brought up the rear, his eyes forever watchful of who might be following them; the two ghosts kept level with their loved ones: solid figures, yet ethereal, caught between this world and the next.

The dining hall, which doubled as a chapel, was on the first floor. It had ceased to be a consecrated place long ago, long before the old workhouse has come to be used to rear pigs and, later, turkeys; but Neil knew that its once special role would draw the demonic: nothing delighted evil more than the sullying of good.

Neil visualised the row upon row of men who would have eaten here, perhaps more than two hundred at a time, sitting in rows of twelve abreast, all dining under the rule of enforced silence. On the beams that held the roof, stretching back as far as his eyes could see in the light of the lanterns, Neil read the biblical texts 'GOD IS GOOD', 'GOD IS HOLY', 'GOD IS JUST', 'GOD IS LOVE', each gracing its own beam. All true, but how would the poor and destitute have read those truths? Not for the first time at such moments, Neil felt his heart sink, not in doubt but in supplication.

At that moment, his moment of temporary weakness, the terrors began; the Devil always knew when to strike. The words of his first prayer came to Neil's lips and were drowned in the noise of suffering. Two women crowded in upon Gerald Henderson. Neil had not expected the doctor to be attacked and the sight of the paupers pulling at Gerald appalled him. The women were drunk and gleeful, out for mischief though they could barely stand, no doubt prostitutes who Vernon had told him were always a problem in the workhouse.

Beyond them and their struggles with the doctor, a strange shape was forming, undefined and not quite human, more a shadow than a substance, it stood apart from the women and yet was clearly influencing their every wanton grope at Gerald, who fell to the floor with the women on top of him.

Neil moved towards them and the women retreated, their eyes fearful of the priest, their knowledge of his power embedded deeply by the daily sessions of prayer they had experienced in life at a time when the Church's authority was never in doubt. They kneeled; he blessed them, cleansed them and released them with a prayer into God's safe keeping, and they were gone.

It had been a test, nothing more; the ploy of someone or something testing the strength of its enemy

A feeling of intense heat permeated the stale air of the chapel, drawing at his nostrils and throat; the already fetid air was so stale that breathing became nigh impossible; the air drawn into their lungs was like that experienced in deserts. Neil turned to Gerald who had struggled from the floor, but the doctor smiled and waved the priest aside, indicating that they had other matters to concern them.

Neil looked again at the strange form hovering in the darkness beyond; tempted to shine his lantern at whatever this was becoming, Neil resisted. He'd seen what he thought to be a pair of red eyes peering down at his little group and had no wish to spread fear among them. And then the girl walked out from the shadows. In arms clutched across her chest, she carried loaves of bread, and Neil knew this was the child who had led Ambrose Broome across the broken bridge and to his death. Her eyes, red with crying and dark with fear, shot left and right. Her face was ravaged by hunger and everyone in the party realised here was theft and theft would not go unpunished.

The loaves were snatched from her and placed upon her head and so she was made to walk backwards and forwards across the darkness of the room keeping them balanced. A man loomed over her, a man Neil supposed was Broome's ancestor, miller and guardian, munching a chicken's leg and watching the girl's torment. Every time she passed, the girl would beg at the table and a bone containing some scrap of meat was dropped at her feet. Bend to retrieve it and the loaves would fall; she knew that was so. Time and again this happened. Much to the amusement of the man.

When at last her punishment was deemed sufficient, the girl was handed his plate to lick. 'Make us doubt the worthiness of our purpose – that is what he does'; the thought came to Neil as he looked again into the darkness. He felt weighed down as though an immense and overwhelming power was now his master. The knowledge of his own inadequacy overcame him. He was opposed by a will stronger than his own; and if he, a priest of God felt this, how much more fearful was it for his friends.

The ghost of Clifford Raine stumbled forward into the blackness that now confronted the group. He was striving to reach something none of them could see; and then a birch rod appeared in his hand, only to be snatched away by the little girl, Susan Farmer, who had called to see her 'grandmama', two weeks before Christmas, at what was now Vernon's house. And then, Clifford's arm fell to his side and he dropped to the ground. The darkness around him suddenly severed and he was isolated on the wooden floor of the chapel; and the young women came, hell bent on revenge, tearing the birch rod from each other's hands, beating and beating the figure until the wheals on his back turned yellow and green.

Esme, despite knowing this was mere illusion, rushed forward into the melee of anger and reprisal. As she did, the light around Clifford began to wane. It died to a flickering that only added to the eeriness of the old chapel and so the darkness, when it came, was sudden and left them blinded. Neil heard Esme scream, a cry followed by the rush and clatter of many feet; when the light came up again, she was gone, she and her beloved Clifford.

Neil knelt and spoke the verse from Paul's letter to the Christians of Rome:

"... avenge not yourselves, but rather give place unto wrath: for it is written, Vengeance is mine; I will repay, saith the Lord"

From the shape in the darkness beyond came a groan that melted into a laugh. Neil recognised it as an expression of desperation, but dread was overcoming his friends, each knowing that the horrors so far were but nothing. Gerald Henderson seemed calm, as far as Neil could judge in the light of their lanterns, but Vernon, already bedevilled for so long by the whispering presence, was experiencing a terror that clutched at his every sense; the historian was at cracking point when he screamed:

"I don't fear you – hmmm! Damn you. Come into the light! Let's see your damned face!"

He twitched and fell, writhing on the ground. Neil saw him raise his right hand and point into the darkness, and then the hand seemed to freeze and Vernon's body was rooted to the floor. Gerald gave Neil a glance. Should he move to help? Neil shook his head. They watched as Vernon struggled, seeing that his head would not turn; and then he rocked backwards and forwards, and sobs shook his body and a cry, awful to hear, broke from his mouth. The muscles of the historian's jaw pulled at the mouth, wider and wider, and his sobs resounded across the room, agonised sobs, sobs of the deepest despair.

In the darkness, nothing moved. All eyes, all thoughts were on the man writhing on the floor, a man struggling, Neil thought, to retain his very soul. And then he was up, so suddenly that it seemed something had snapped within him.

"Come here," he screamed, "I'll awe you. I have the rod – the one approved by the guardians. You friendless bastards! Who are you calling to for help – hey? Come here and I'll tie your jaws with my handkerchief. No one will hear your screams then – will they! They'll find your bodies in the mortuary, covered with bruises and gashes. Mispronounce the name of the Lord's mother's husband would you? Jo-seph! That's how you say it. Scratch the workhouse table would you? I'll flog the lot of you, one by one!"

There had been no elephantine trumpeting, and both Neil and Gerald realised that it was his ancestor, the workhouse schoolteacher, who was ranting. Vernon was no longer with them. The man who had risen from the floor leaving his glasses smashed was someone else entirely, someone quite different to the history teacher admired by his pupils.

Light! If only they had light! Neil regretted coming in the dark but it had been necessary: the church service, the prayer walk – both so essential to the blessing and cleansing – needed people, people who worked during the day. He looked about him. There were plenty of windows, all blackened by age and dirt. Neil rushed at one and struck it with his lantern; pane after tiny pane shattered to the floor. After a while, he saw the moon but it cast no light. St Anthony's feast day may have given them his mighty arm but it had also provided a new moon! Neil smiled. At such times what else could one do?

He looked back into the chapel. The shape in the darkness had gone. The Deliverance Minister could see only shadows. Casting round at his friends, he saw, too, that Vernon was no longer with them. He and Gerald were left with Juniper and the ghost of her father, both bewildered. Faintly, through the broken windows, he heard the sounds of hymn singing from the prayer chain:

"Great is they faithfulness, O God my Father
There is no shadow of turning with Thee
Thou changest not, Thy compassions they fail not
As Thou hast been Thou forever will be ... "

'No shadow of turning with Thee' – no, none. Neil turned to daughter and father and waved them to their knees. As they knelt together – the priest, the atheist and the ghost who had never experienced strong feelings, one way or the other – there came the sound of a drum being beaten, beaten inside their heads as much as in the room around. The whole chapel vibrated with the sound and, at the far end, spears of light rose from the floor. They jerked about the room, leaping into the air from place to place as they advanced on the group in prayer; and beyond them and between them, where the shadow shape had loomed, stood the man called Kent.

"Have you asked yourself, Jack, the question I raised in your printshop – whether your line should survive?"

Here was the one the parish council had met first that night in the White Horse, when he'd quizzed them about the meeting place of the Vestry – the overseers of the poor. He advanced between the shafts of light, holding out his hands in welcome to Juniper. She rose, despite Neil gesturing she should remain on her knees, and advanced towards the dead man. In every line of her body, in every movement of her legs, her father saw his daughter's independent spirit, and he wondered what she had in mind. Neil, also watching her, could only remember the red eyes that had peered from the formless shape, the shape he now believed had taken form in that of Kent.

The chapel was lit by the shafts of light, a dark, dancing light that menaced. The prayer on his lips waited. He had no idea what the girl had in mind but the determination in her very movements made him fearful; too many had failed to own their sins, and Neil doubted whether Juniper Wells was aware she possessed any weaknesses. It was not the way of the world and yet knowing one's frailties was a pre-requisite for success in deliverance.

The two were within a hand's length of each other, the dead man holding his steady, cupped to receive those of the girl. Eye for eye they matched each other, unblinking, both confident of their own success. As he watched, Neil found it difficult to discern which of them was the ghost and which the person, so substantial did they seem, so fixed, so certain of themselves. Shadows cast by the shafts of light flitted here and there across the walls and windows and Neil's old eyes were tasked to see clearly, one moment, as they were, in darkness and the next lit brightly. Neil looked up and realised the light was the light of stars on this moonless night: stars, occasionally obscured by moving clouds, shining through the torn and broken roof.

Suddenly, the light of the stars became the red of blood. Juniper's hands held a crucifix – not merely a cross but one bearing the body of Christ crucified – and the blood was dripping from it. She was handing it to the dead man and Kent was laughing.

"What power has the Cross in the hands of one such as you?" he asked, "'I don't do this 'Our Father in heaven' stuff'. Do you remember?"

She did, but too late; the devil had his hands upon her and the crucifix was dashed to the ground, spilling its blood, staining the floorboards. Neil rose, but the ghost of Jack Dorling was faster than the priest; the printer rushed between Kent and his daughter, grasped the dead man in his arms and cast them both into one of the rays of starlight. They shuddered for a while as the light consumed the air around them and then closed upon their corpses. Neil dropped to the floor, pulling Juniper with him.

"Blessed are the dead that die in the Lord ... May it please Thee to deliver our brother Jack out of ... the bitter pains of eternal death ...Our Father, which art in heaven ... Pray, Juniper, pray!"

Quite how he selected the precise phrases he needed from *The Order for the Burial of the Dead*, Neil was unsure, but they came readily to his mind, brought forth by his concern for Jack Dorling, wrapping Kent in his arms as the light consumed their spirits. And Juniper joined him in saying the Lord's Prayer, remembered from her schooldays, unspoken for years.

"Now go! Both of you," cried Neil to Juniper and Gerald, "Find Esme, find Vernon and get them out of here. Vernon – the boy's schoolroom, try there, down and to your left across the men's yard. Esme will be with Clifford. Go back to the porter's lodge. Call them! Find them!"

It was a mess; Neil knew it to be a mess. He should have brought Gerald to the village that morning; the doctor had only been given a brief description of the layout of the workhouse and Juniper knew even less. But the need was now near: he had to get them away.

They were gone, and to his right Neil saw a sudden movement. He wasn't sure which of them it was but knew the ghost that approached him was one touched by evil. Something about the face, a livid face, bleached white like a piece of driftwood expressed the kind of viciousness that delights in cruelty and he assumed it to be Crozier, the man who hanged Myles Langstroth. At least they were coming for him, and not the prayer walkers. There would be more, others touched by evil.

301

Behind Crozier another shape appeared. 'He wore a long riding coat that covered his body from head to calf and had a wide-brimmed hat'; the description given by James Ryder of the man who had, eventually, killed the engineer. Gabriel! The ghost's face was an ill-nourished face with dark shadows underlining the bright eyes. Like Ryder before him, Neil noticed that the lids never seemed to move. He was weighing up the priest as he done the engineer.

Behind both men, the shape in the darkness had re-appeared following the spiritual death of Kent. Neil watched for the eyes, those red eyes, eyes delighting in the corruption of others. The beams of light still sprung from the floor, spasmodically as though to catch the unwary walker or one running to escape. The air smelled of burning metal. From somewhere else in the building came the sounds of shouting and crying; a voice was pleading urgently.

Neil knew what God wanted of him: bless, cleanse, release. He must choose his moment.

The shape in the darkness shook itself and from its shadow emerged two men; both walked to Neil's left, as the others had stood to his right. One was 'dressed smartly in a suit of the English colonial style, white and slightly creased'. Frank had been described to him so many times, he thought he knew the ghost. The other was dressed in a 'crushed top hat and an ill-fitting coat'. Quire – the ghost who kicked Richard Revell to death.

The stances were threatening and meant to be, and Neil smiled: his old enemy was underrating him: the devil thought he could be made to fear.

The four men did not move – it was as though they were waiting orders – but he was touched, nonetheless, touched by fingers that stroked, fingers that probed, fingers that teased, fingers seeking a sensitive spot. They clutched his shoulders, ran down his chest and stroked his throat. The eyes in the shape became clearer and roved over him; in them was recognition. For the first time since the horrors began, Neil was aware of his enemy's will, a force for evil, working against his own.

The smell of the burning metal now made the air unbreathable. For a second time he heard the beating of the drum, the chapel shook as before and out of the darkness the shape moved forward behind the four men. As it did, Neil heard a voice 'I know what needs healing; I know what needs casting out', and Neil knew who spoke to him. His moment had come.

"When the wicked man turneth away from his wickedness that he hath committed, and doeth that which is lawful and right, he shall save his soul alive."

The words of Ezekiel, spoken already that night by the vicar of Holy Trinity, sprang unbidden from the lips of the Deliverance Minister.

"Rend your heart ... and turn unto the Lord your God: for he is gracious and merciful, slow to anger, and of great kindness, and repenteth him of the evil ..."

Joel's words, too: a challenge, a chance for release.

Quire, Crozier and Gabriel advanced on the priest. Now, it was their hands that gripped him, held him fast and bore him towards and through the shape in the darkness, dodging the starlight, to the smashed windows of the old workhouse chapel. It was clear what they intended: they held him as soldiers of old held battering rams, ready to smash an entrance into the enemy's fortress. As they lifted him high, Neil heard Frank's voice:

"This man has done no harm!"

The shadow moved upon Frank and enclosed him. The three who held the deliverance minister heard the scream and paused. It was then that the first stone fell as a creaking was heard from the roof.

"Wherefore, let us beseech him to grant us true repentance ... that the rest of our life hereafter may be pure and holy ..."

Once more the words came, the words of the Absolution, as they always did when Neil needed them as he now needed them. Frank grappled with the shadow, a struggle for his very afterlife. Another stone or tile fell from the roof and the shadow sank to the floor. Frank staggered forward, the arrogance gone, his eyes on the priest, pleading for the mercy he had never shown Vernon Scuffil.

"Almighty God ... who desireth not the death of a sinner, but that he may rather turn from his wickedness ..."

The three who had grasped Neil dropped him to the floor, turning their eyes to Frank's struggles, and the priest knelt in prayer.

"... and hath given power ... to His ministers, to declare and pronounce ..."

Frank reached one of the shafts with his right hand so that the light shone on it. Neil was now desperate. He had blessed this accursed place; his God was in the process of cleansing it; he was to offer this wretched man release.

"He pardoneth and absolveth all them that truly repent, and unfeignedly believe His holy gospel ..."

The roof and the walls that held it were now falling tile by tile, brick by brick; the beams displaying the Biblical texts groaned and creaked, twisting inwards, offering their certainties for the last time. Neil crawled across the floor towards the stricken man, eager to reach out through the beam of light and drag him into it. As he did, he felt the others, driven he did not doubt by the evil of the shadow, fall upon him, determined to prevent the absolution.

"Wherefore, let us beseech him to grant us true repentance ..."

And the walls caved in and the roof was upon them, stone by stone, beam by beam, as elsewhere in the building newly plastered walls, newly rendered brickwork collapsed, wiring was torn from sockets and drains subsided.

Families woke in terror. Mothers and fathers grabbed children from their beds and urged, pulled and thrust them into the open air, into the newly landscaped gardens and play areas. There they stood, watching their homes and possessions turned to rubble.

The noise given off by the old building in its death throes was abominable. Dust filled the air, blotting out the stars, and those watching were choked and blinded as it filled their lungs and eyes. The debris of wood, brick (old and new mingling together), plasterboard and breeze block scattered far and wide; chimneys crumbled in upon the ruin.

The prayer walkers gazed, some in horror, some in wonder, as before their very eyes the old workhouse – and the new rows of terraced houses, mews, flats and apartments built within it – at last acknowledged an old evil.

Chapter 7

The Healing

Morning arrived, bright and clear, the kind of winter's day loved by all, one that stirred memories of Christmas or, at least, Christmas cards.

The fire officers and the other emergency services worked through the night, looking for bodies and homing the now homeless residents of the premises that had once been the Burghamton workhouse.

Surprisingly, it was considered, only one body was found: the residents had all escaped unscathed: only the body of Neil Ilkestone was drawn from the rubble, broken in many places but still breathing. How he had survived puzzled both the fire officers and the ambulance workers. 'It was though he'd been under several other bodies,' said one of the paramedics, "but there was no one else there'.

Neil was taken quickly to the Norfolk and Norbridge Hospital, where Fred visited him early the following morning. The old priest was conscious and the pain he must have been experiencing did not seem to bother him.

"Frederick the healing must begin. You understand? And it must begin now – today. Bless, cleanse, release! Hm! Esme, Juniper, Vernon and Gerald – they are safe, I understand?"

"Yes, although Vernon has had a nervous breakdown."

"We experienced it with him, but the good Justine will care for her husband. And Esme has now seen her beloved Clifford along what she calls the pathway of light and we call God's love."

"Before the collapse of the workhouse, others emerged – Susan Farmer and the child who must have been the one who led Ambrose Broome to his death. Both, I believe, led rather than touched, by evil."

"I agree, and both now in the arms of the Lord, absolved of their torments – I use that word instead of 'sin' – by our good friend of the other persuasion, Father Crouch?"

"Yes, and also Ambrose himself, Amelia Pritchard and Myles Langstroth who formed part of the prayer chain, I hear. What of the others?"

"Well, Frederick, as the popular saying goes 'the Devil looks after his own'. Only the one called Frank showed any remorse – indeed, I owe him my life."

The deliverance minister was silent for a long time, regaining a little strength, calming his thoughts, wondering if he could have done more. Eventually, it was Fred who broke the silence.

"The young girl, Barbara Wilton, has passed over. She burst into the church last night followed by the man her mother described. They were not a churchgoing family but she must have remembered us from her time as a Brownie. I sent her peacefully on. The man hesitated in the porch. I went after him but …," Fred shrugged; there was only so much a priest could do, "but Maggie Henderson was at the service and has found peace at last. Such a restless spirit!"

"It has been a good night's work, Frederick, but there is still much to do. The man, Lansmore and his woman, Ruby Land, and James Ryder and Thomkins – what of them? And the boy, Richard Revell. If his spirit is restless, he must be helped – released. Keep Esme in your love, Frederick: she has no one now. And Frederick, take care."

"You take care, Neil. When they *release* you from here, you're coming to us to convalesce. No arguments."

The old priest smiled at Fred's reference to 'release' and they parted.

Back in the Thornham, Fred first visited Cynthia Revell. He wasn't expected, although he'd called on several occasions since her son's death, but said she'd been about to call him and was excited to see him. Amy Prentice had, at last, broken the silence imposed by her fears and told Cynthia of Richard's nightly visits – the mirror and the bed.

It was rough absolution, one Fred felt guilty about for years but only slightly. Richard Revell, the one-time school bully, found himself running his fingers not along Amy's fanny but the priest's cassock. Suddenly, he was kneeling at the feet of the man he would normally have considered it cool to despise, the man's hand on his neck, the man's mouth intoning a prayer about wickedness and himself repeating after the priest something about having 'erred and strayed from thy ways like lost sheep'. At the end of it all, he felt better for it; and much to Amy's relief was never seen or heard of afterwards.

On the evening of the same day, January 18th, he visited Reg and Myrtle Wilton with their daughter, Lucy. He had called earlier but the butcher and his wife were busy in the shop and so they asked him to come back in the evening.

The Wilton's had always been a close family, following religiously the father's motto 'First look after yourself, and then you're better placed to look after others'; but suffering had changed that attitude. The loss of Barbara and the awareness that the sins of the fathers had their way of percolating down several generations made them more sensitive to the suffering of others and more aware of their need to contribute.

"We cannot dispense with grief," Fred had suggested on his several visits, "There is value in grief and sorrow; it strengthens us, it helps us grow as people, it helps us develop a compassion for others."

And now, he could tell them that their daughter was at rest.

*

Simon Pegg, returning from the prayer-walk and re-joining his wife, Catriona, and their children, Bruce and July, was troubled.

His Burns' Night, only a week away, had been planned since before Christmas: Ian Cumforth, the piper, was ready and eager with wind in the bag; an old actor living in the village – one Simon had performed with several years before in a local production of *Scapino*, when Simon played one of the young lovers and the old actor, his father – had honed his Aberdonian accent for the big night; Simon's mother, Christabel, and his wife had refined their comedy routine bouncing Norfolk colloquialisms against the Scottish as they did every year to the amusement of those at the supper; Simon's children now contributed, providing the Selkirk grace and a reading; an elderly lady from the village, Molly Truelove, was waiting, breathless, to give a *Farewell to Clarinda*.

Besides this conglomeration of eagerness, Simon's chef, Dafyd Phillips, had his menu prepared: leek and potato soup or smoked salmon followed by venison stew, haddock fishcakes or the great haggis itself and rounded off with Granny Jean's clootie dumpling or rhubarb and raspberry parfait. This was not a meal to be missed; and, as Catriona, who always had her feet firmly on the ground, said:

"Butchers don't stop butchering, bakers don't stop baking, shopkeepers don't stop selling because there are a few ghosts in town!"

This wasn't as heartless as it might have sounded. Catriona was the one with the business acumen, whereas Simon provided the artistic flair.

He was a sensitive soul and sat brooding on his problem when he opened the White Horse the following morning. He knew his wife was right: people needed taking out of themselves: it had been a terrible time: there was only so much misery anyone could absorb. But: there was always a but! Would it be respectful to the dead? Was a night of unbridled merriment appropriate only a week after the tragic events at Burghamton and all that had preceded the fall of the workhouse?

His quandary was resolved when Edward Warburg walked into the bar and ordered a pint. He had come to check that the piano was correctly tuned.

"You wish to go ahead, Edward?"

"My dear boy, how can we not proceed as intended. Wait a year and Bradley's voice may have broken. Over the next week, they need a focus for their thoughts and their creativity – especially Lottie, who has suffered so intensely. Besides, would Myles forgive me if I failed to present Britten's wonderful song. He was very fond of Benjamin, you know. And the children – they are dying to perform."

"You're sure?"

"Dear boy, would I not be sure of what Myles intended? We loved one another for many years, you know."

"Of course. The piano is tuned."

"I'm sure but ... um ...," replied Edward, not liking to appear to doubt Simon but not wishing to take chances where music was concerned, "We shall need to practice here a few times when the hostelry is quiet – the acoustics, you know, will be different to those in our studio, and Lottie has such a fine ear and Bradley will need to hear his voice as it soars. Now!"

Edward raised the lid of the iron-strung grand and struck a chord and scale or two before playing *I Love a Lassie*, Harry Lauder's tribute to his wife. He left with a smile on his face and an even broader one on Simon's, commenting as he reached the door:

"He'll be there, you know."

And he was, visible to Edward and, perhaps, others who had known him; when Bradley took centre stage, beside Lottie at the piano, the smile on Myles's face was broadest of all.

The two youngsters were clapped vociferously by, among others, Lottie's father and brother, Fred and Jacqueline, Carmen and Billie, Justine's family with Vernon sitting very quietly in the corner his back against the wall and Juniper, Esme and Mildred each of whom were seen to smile often at someone who stood by their side; and each, on their way home, was seen to be talking to another walking with them.

Maybe, plans for a way forward were discussed that night – who knows? Certainly, Esme was to continue her and Clifford's work as ghost hunters; Mildred redoubled her efforts with the help of Edward to raise the quality of opera at Saxstead; J DORLING AND SON - PRINTERS continued their work at Thornham, only the 'J' was now a woman and the 'SON' was hers.

*

Despite all of Fred's efforts, Lansmore and his woman, Ruby Land, were never found and brought to account, but they never troubled anyone ever again. Neil, who spent three months recovering at Thornham before returning to his mobile home on the south coast, considered that with the fall of the workhouse an evil, which had battened on the grievances of others, was now denied a place in the parish.

He also observed that the people of Burghamton came to life in a way they never had, trading with other villages and towns across Norfolk: bakers, farmers, market gardeners, home producers and craftspeople of all kinds.

Ryder's flight from Holy Trinity with Thomkins across his shoulders was not the last the village heard of the ghost who had murdered Maggie Henderson and threatened the same fate for her daughter, Lottie, however.

It was claimed that he haunted the banks of the Thorn, particularly the spot where Maggie Henderson was found drowned. Summer cruisers, hearing the village stories, would recall how the doors of their boats rattled at night, as though someone was attempting to enter, and when they opened the curtains to check who might be there they saw a 'green and ghastly face, the face of a madman staring in at them'. Youths, eager to protect their girlfriends, would take them to the mooring place, repeat the stories and welcome their girls, screaming, into their protective arms.

Townships need their ghost stories, naturally, but Fred Mackenzie smiled, feeling the truth may lie elsewhere. A few days after the night of the fall, salted bones were found burned on one of the brick barbecues at the picnic sight that lay across the water meadows, a short distance from Thornham. Later, when he was assisting with the reclamation of the old church at Burghamton, Fred discovered that one of the graves, whose headstone had long since eroded but on which the name Thomkins could just be discerned, had been cleared of grass and dug out.

James Ryder was never seen again but careful observers would have noticed that Sam Whitham was often alone sitting on the staithe, apparently in conversation with someone, and that the black Labrador, Rollie, would sit by his side looking up as a dog looks into the face of its loved master.

Several villagers did comment, however, that it was wonderful what the boy knew about engineering and how forceful he was in approaching local firms with the skills needed to repair the mill wheel to working order and the bridge across the Thorn to its former glory.

www.ingramcontent.com/pod-product-compliance
Lightning Source LLC
Chambersburg PA
CBHW022028260626
47156CB00017B/456